THE LAST
VOICE YOU HEAR

MAIN

HAYNER PUBLIC LIBRARY DISTRICT
ALTON, ILLINOIS

OVERDUES .10 PER DAY MAXIMUM FINE
COST OF BOOKS. LOST OR DAMAGED
BOOKS ADDITIONAL $5.00 SERVICE CHARGE.

FORTHCOMING BY RICHARD B. SCHWARTZ

After the Fall
Into the Dark

ALSO BY RICHARD B. SCHWARTZ

Frozen Stare

A JACK GRANT MYSTERY

THE LAST VOICE YOU HEAR

RICHARD B. SCHWARTZ

Midnight Ink
WOODBURY, MINNESOTA

The Last Voice You Hear © 2006 by Richard B. Schwartz. All rights reserved. No part of this book may be used or reproduced in any manner whatsoever, including Internet usage, without written permission from Midnight Ink except in the case of brief quotations embodied in critical articles and reviews.

First Edition
First Printing, 2006

Book design by Donna Burch
Cover design by Gavin Dayton Duffy
Cover image © 2006 by Brand X
Editing by Connie Hill

Cover model(s) used for illustrative purposes only and may not endorse or represent the books' subject.

Midnight Ink, an imprint of Llewellyn Publications

Library of Congress Cataloging-in-Publication Data
Schwartz, Richard B.
 The last voice you hear : a Jack Grant mystery / Richard B. Schwartz
   p. cm.
  ISBN-13: 978-0-7387-0830-0
  ISBN-10: 0-7387-0830-5
   1. Private investigators—Pasadena (Calif.)—Fiction. 2. Revenge—Fiction. 3. Pasadena (Calif.)—Fiction. I. Title.

PS3569.C56735L37   2006
813'.54—dc22   2006041983

Any Internet references contained in this work are current at publication time, but the publisher cannot guarantee that a specific location will continue to be maintained. Please refer to the publisher's website for links to authors' websites and other sources.
 This is a work of fiction. Names, characters, places, and incidents are either the product of the author's imagination or are used fictitiously, and any resemblance to actual persons, living or dead, business establishments, events, or locales is entirely coincidental.

Midnight Ink
A Division of Llewellyn Publications
2143 Wooddale Drive, Dept. 0-7387-0830-5
Woodbury, MN 55125-2989, U.S.A.
www.midnightinkbooks.com

Printed in the United States of America

for Judith Alexis

Lesson One was: The world is seamless. Everything is related to everything else. Old boys clinked glasses at the Harvard Club and, on the other side of the world, villages exploded. Lesson Two was: History is crime, and never underestimate the thrill of the game. They do it for money, sure, but the money's a way of keeping score. They also do it for the sheer pleasure of proving that they can get away with murder. Lesson Three was: Think small, it's the little mobile groupuscules who write the plots, make things happen.

—Harry Kramer

PART ONE

A Death in the Underground

ONE

LONDON. SEPTEMBER 26, 1992. 8:37 A.M. A light mist and drizzle with heavy clouds trapping the steam and damp. The tube crowded, with the Bakerloo shut down between Edgware Road and Regent's Park and threats of a dawn strike on the Northern Line. Piccadilly east holding to its schedule but Piccadilly west slow, with the trains bunching out of King's Cross and Russell Square.

Green Park jammed, with commuters hurrying from the tunnels and converging on the single escalator, hitting the platform a handful of steps beneath ground level, working their way through the incoming crowd, then breaking into the streets of Mayfair like so many floods seeking their channels and straits.

The buskers frustrated, waiting for the tourists with time to listen and to dig for the odd 10p piece. The commuters' eyes on their watches, their hands occupied with briefcases, purses, and umbrellas. Kevin McGinn in the tunnel playing Haydn on a silver flute over the sound of arriving and departing trains, his brother Michael at the base of the escalator, his open violin case at chest level between the opposing handrails. Playing Mozart. Forgetting himself for the moment, playing over the sounds of feet, gears, and tracks, the tap of umbrella tips and the polite but insistent *excuse me's* as impatient men in dark suits and coats hurry up the left side of the escalator. Playing Mozart as if no one could hear but him, enclosed in a white booth, the notes hanging in the air like tiny clouds of gold. Then returning, with the clink of 2p pieces in his case. Nodding in the directions of a child's hands and attacking again with his bow, playing again for himself and perhaps his brother. The crowd turning away. Hearing Michael only faintly. Now playing over the sound of a woman's screams.

The victim standing near the top of the escalator, shifting from left foot to right in his agony and grabbing at the rail as his blood runs down his legs and over his polished brown shoes into the black treads of the moving escalator, then onto the open-toed pumps of Mrs. Eleanor Rumson of Sudbury Hill. Her favorite shoes, actually. The yellows with the small white bows across the insteps. Summery; matching the soft-brimmed hat and cotton frock that were their usual mates. Now covered with droplets of blood, which are falling like the outside rain as the man gasps and churns and loses his grip, Eleanor's cry cutting through the echoing sounds of the hollowed, angular tunnel of tile, steel, plastic, rubber, glass, and grease.

Eleanor moving to the left as he fell, those behind her doing the same, and pinning those anxious to pass against the left rail. The body tumbling now. Red streaks along the moving steps like random wipes of a vandal's hand, the cries increasing with each bounce and bloody flip.

Michael McGinn below, freezing at C#, no chance now to return to the dominant, the jarring sound hanging in the air with Eleanor's last scream. Reaching for the case but not in time, as the man's body was tossed, his loose, right elbow thrusting into Michael's chest like a blunt spear and throwing him to the ground as coins skittered over the tile and blood spattered into the rust-toned velvet lining of the instrument case. Michael clutching his violin safely against his chest all the while, but neglecting the bow, whose pointed ivory handle had found its way into the man's left cheek. A pity that, but the least of the man's problems now.

Eleanor suddenly off of the escalator, standing at the top, shaking and clutching her gloved palms to her cheeks. Michael below, bracing himself with his right hand, cradling his violin like a threatened child, shoving his feet over the moist grit, sliding away in horror across the dirt- and blood-streaked tile.

The victim convulsing now, the last moments of life spilling between his legs. Forming breath bulbs of blood, not words, his chest rippling in vague spasms, shattered limbs pointing randomly, a collapsed and abandoned string doll.

Then dying without further pain or ceremony, his lips open, imploring, and then freezing blankly like the vague mouth of an unfinished bust.

Gerald Helmond of Ravenscourt Park staring, aghast. Grabbing for his handkerchief to catch whatever remnants of his breakfast his belly could not hold down.

Hillary Denham of Hatton Cross, holding the pink cheek of her daughter Caroline and attempting to avert her eyes. Caroline straining against her mother's hand, fascinated by the blood and by the screams. Her brother Henry not there. Tales to tell tonight over dinner.

Laurence Eusman, curate of St. Swithin's, Woodstock, Oxfordshire, uttering pieties, his imagination fixed upon the symmetry of the dark pools forming between the victim's thighs and the fact that his shin bones lay in exact parallel with one another. Only possible with a terrible fracture. The tile floor and wool slacks accommodating the legs, wherever they wished to turn.

Deirdre Porter of British Rail, happy it hadn't happened in her station on her shift, looking into the victim's brown eyes, staring blankly into her own. Thinking how sad it must be to die so stupidly. Toppling down an escalator. And so early in the morning, even for a sot. Then seeing the blood, running over thighs and knees and shoes and knowing that it was not an accident. Choking then and gulping at the damp, thin air.

Christopher Lytton of Church Street, Greenwich, proud in his school uniform, but clutching his mother's hand and asking about the horrid smell, wondering why she would not answer him. Asking again and then being pulled away.

Geoffrey Harmsworth of Albemarle Street and Cecily Harmsworth, his thoughts running to these times and how perfectly awful things had now become, hers running to the poor dead man's hands. Small and gentle hands, really, though now so cut and crushed.

Both making way for the tall Pakistani in his dark uniform, the Underground badge affixed to the center of his cap. With him a ticket seller and the operator of a magazine kiosk, pressed into service, trying to preserve order and evidence. The Pakistani reprimanding Mrs. Emma Carrington of Kennington Lane, Lambeth, for poking at the victim's feet with the tip of her umbrella. Mrs. Carrington responding promptly that someone must establish the fact of death and how sad it was that so little is appreciated in these unpleasant times.

The magazine seller looking up in the direction of his stand, wondering how many thieves were taking advantage of his absence. Troubled enough by their reading without buying, but what hope now?

The Pakistani instructing Mrs. Carrington to move along now; she replying with a succession of forced sighs designed to speak volumes and affix blame.

The ticket seller and kiosk operator fully aware now of the failure of the victim's bladder and bowels. Turning away from the deep eyes of the Pakistani and forming a broken circle around the body, facing outward. Guards. Not nurses or dustmen.

The arrival of another train and another wave of onlookers. The Pakistani telling them to *move along*. Michael McGinn trying to clean his sleeves and pants with newspaper and any clean waste he could find. Kevin offering the use of a wipe cloth from his instrument case.

The smells from the body of the victim now spreading in a widening circle, moving the curious to the periphery. The escalator still moving in its unending round, thinning the blood on its steps and spreading it through the grease and gearwork below the surface. The heedless stepping in what remained and carrying it into the streets of Mayfair and the London beyond.

Outside, approaching Berkeley Square now, a dark figure, moving briskly and carrying a black vinyl case. Hurrying out of the station, then along Berkeley Street, past the Holiday Inn, Mayfair, past the Stratstone Daimler/Jaguar showroom to the west and the darkened, gold-trimmed windows of the Mayfair bar; past Hay Hill and several dozen blurring hats, suits, cases, and umbrellas and into the Square proper. Holding the bag close all the while, keeping it from those who might collide with it, protecting its contents—the ticket, the bottles, and the single plastic glove resting quietly in its slip case. Covered with broad streaks of fresh blood.

Moving into the park at the center of the Square, finding a seat behind the largest of the towering, sycamore-like planes, and opening the black case to reveal the two bottles, one filled with clear liquid. Taking out the bloody glove in its plastic bag, carefully rolling the bag and its contents, trusting gravity and a steady hand to keep the red ooze on the inside. Then inserting it carefully into the empty bottle.

Opening the other bottle now and pouring out the liquid over the plastic trapped against the walls of its partner. Watching the glove and bag quickly dissolve, the now-pink acid forming large bubbles like those of plonk champagne.

Capping both, returning them quickly to the black case, and proceeding across the Square, west on Mount Street, past the Connaught on Carlos Place and north to Grosvenor Square. Standing at the southeast corner now, looking toward the U.S. Embassy. Pausing silently. Then opening the case and dropping the two bottles, one by one, into the sewer below. Hearing each of them shatter and feeling the mist and drizzle, watching the stream along the gutter that would carry the remnants of the evidence away forever.

Raising a hand toward an oncoming taxi. A red one this time. Mulling over the long odds of that happening in a city filled with black cabs and a rare blue or green. Climbing in, placing the vinyl case on the seat, and instructing the driver to drive quickly.

The Green Park underground station now in chaos. Traffic stopped east and west on Piccadilly. Police and emergency vehicles blocked. Pedestrians firing questions at one another and at anyone in uniform. Underground officials trying to reach their employees by phone. Their employees still huddling around the body, protecting it from the eyes and hands and umbrella points of passersby. Trains arriving on schedule, the waves of people swelling every seven minutes. The escalator turned off now. Curses and complaints everywhere as arriving passengers pull themselves up the fixed steps of the stopped *down* escalator, brushing against the endless line making their way past them.

The temperature and humidity intolerable. Mrs. Myrtle Cardwell of Wapping attempting to climb the stair. Her green coat and scarf hugging her neck, a ripple of perspiration stain circling the heavy collar. Veins appearing on her forehead as she raises and pulls thirteen and a half stone one high step at a time. Her face flushed, those near her watching, anticipating imminent strokes and heart attacks. She pausing and trying to catch her breath. The others turning to the Pakistani now, soliciting his help, warning that the woman cannot make the climb. He holding his temper. Suggesting there are other concerns at the moment. Raising his voice to the level of outraged politeness. Suggesting she return to the platform and proceed to the next station. Being told a dozen reasons why that was impossible. The crowd gridlocked on the single stair. Finally raising his head and turning it away, fixing his expression and refusing to speak again.

Myrtle sitting now, wiping her forehead with her scarf, resigned to the fact that she will not move without the escalator's help and resolved not to be bothered by that fact. The crowd turning on her now as they attempt to get past her broad hips, spreading across the narrow stair. Calling her names under their breath as she says *yes, yes, move along, yes, yes.*

The red taxi turning at Park Lane and passing Grosvenor Gate, turning again at Hyde Park Corner, passing the Wellington Arch and the former police station there. The driver commenting on the great, bloody line of traffic heading east on Piccadilly, then apologizing for his language and wondering aloud about the source of the tailback. His passenger silent, looking straight ahead, with thoughts elsewhere.

Into Knightsbridge now and talking on his radio. Turning to his passenger. *A man was killed in Green Park tube stop. Still there, I'm told*. No response. A fixed expression, thoughts elsewhere, the look of heavy responsibility. The driver giving up, concentrating on the road and easing the accelerator pedal down. Passing Harrods, the Brompton Oratory, the Victoria & Albert, the Natural History Museum, and the rows of white tourist hotels of Cromwell Road. Past the bustle on Gloucester Road, the students smoking cigarettes, the remnants of the empire carrying filled, plastic shopping bags. Yellow, from the Duty Free. White, with Rothman's ads. The taxi moving much faster now. Driving gratefully against the morning traffic. West through the city edge. Into Chiswick and past Hogarth's house. West past the breweries and the soap factories. West through the red-bricked neighborhoods with yellowed lace at the windows. West past the hard pubs of hard neighborhoods. West into the countryside with bright green grass in black earth under lead-gray skies, and beyond.

TWO

CLAIRE HARDING REACHED FOR the office electric kettle, shook the bottom, listening for sediment, and then poured. The tea bag puckered as the steam came up to meet her hand and wrist. When her tea was ready she added a day-old slice of lemon, which fell to the bottom of her cup, twitched, turned, and gave up its single pip, its scent barely perceptible. The morning was not going well. Traffic was at a standstill from the moment she left her second-floor flat in the Barbican to begin her drive to the Yard. The files on her desk had multiplied overnight and the fluorescent light over her desk was flickering in its death-throes. The stack of message slips on her desk spike looked like the limbs of a wilted paper tree, and her appearance schedule for Central Criminal Court was already devouring the months of October, November, and December. A Detective Police Constable named Willis brought her six more files and three more message slips as the red phone rang.

"Harding."

"McCarren here." Kenneth McCarren. The Deputy Commissioner of the London Metropolitan Police.

"Yes, sir."

"Pop round to Savile Row, will you? A chap's been killed in the Underground. Green Park. Quite bloody, I'm told. Give the lads a hand, will you?"

"Certainly, sir."

"And Harding..."

"Yes sir?"

"You will keep me informed, won't you?"

"Of course, sir."

McCarren rang off. Harding took a deep drink of her tea, walked back to the sink to dump the remainder, returned to her desk, and put on her beige raincoat. She picked up her purse, slid the strap over her shoulder, and walked over to Willis' desk. "I'll be at Savile Row station."

"Right," he said.

Mayfair and the adjoining west end were finally beginning to clear. From Victoria Street Harding drove north, circling the park, then headed up St. James Street to Piccadilly, left on Old Bond Street to Burlington Gardens, then on to Old Burlington Street, to Clifford Street, and finally to the police station in Savile Row. Seemingly out of place there, with uniformed officers coming and going, passing the haberdasheries and tailors' shops, looking for thieves, rapists, and murderers: fine clothes, fine streets, fine crimes.

"Detective Inspector Haaaeding," a voice said, stretching the *a* into an endless diphthong, just as McCarren had. British affectation.

"Hello, Gered," she said, turning toward a middle-aged uniformed sergeant, with gleaming bald head, thick moustache, and florid, puffed cheeks.

"So nice of you to come by," he said, putting down his cigarette. "The lads will be happy to see you."

"Always my pleasure," she said. "Who was first on the scene?"

"Henley," he answered. "Got quite a story to tell you."

"Where can I speak with him?"

"Room 2; you remember it—just down the hall."

"Summon him, please."

(The politeness forced) "Yes, mum."

Harding walked down the hallway to the second interrogation room. She put her coat and purse on a folding chair and took out a pen and notepad. A young man appeared at the door. He was young and eager, with soft helmet in hand, light brown hair, blue eyes, and a slight scar between his eye and left ear.

"Police Constable Henley, mum."

"Come in, Henley, sit down."

He slid out the chair on the opposite side of the table, scooted to the front of it, and held his hands together in his lap.

"How old are you, Henley?" Harding asked.

"Nineteen, mum."

"Then you must have just completed your training."

"Yes, mum, nine weeks ago."

"This is your first assignment then."

"Yes, mum."

"I'm sure you'll do very well."

He didn't answer, but he let slip an appreciative smile and scooted farther forward in his chair.

"Henley, I want you to think about what you saw today and I want you to tell me everything. Every detail. Every one, mind you. Leave nothing out."

"Yes, mum."

"Go ahead."

"It started about 8:40, mum. I was having my tea and a bit of toast. I had been on patrol throughout the evening and I was writing up my report."

"On patrol in the immediate area?"

"Hanover Square, Oxford Circus. Right. Just nearby."

"So you were going off duty and you had something to eat just before leaving."

"Yes, mum. At about 8:42 the call came in."

"From where?"

"Green Park Underground Station."

"From one of the authorities there?"

"No, mum. A citizen."

"Name?"

"She wouldn't say, mum."

"Very well. What *did* she say?"

"She said that a man was dead and that someone should come at once."

"Did she say that the man was *dead* or did she say that he was murdered?"

"*Dead*, mum."

"What else did she say?"

"That's all. She said there was a great lot of blood."

"Did she say anything else, anything at all?"

"No."

"Did she have an accent? Anything identifiable?"

"No, mum."

"Very well. Then what did you do?"

"I ran to the station."

"You took no one with you?"

"No, mum. There was no one free. I told the desk sergeant to call in anyone who might be available. Then I left."

"And what did you find when you got to the underground station?"

"The body was at the bottom of the moving stairway. The floor was covered with blood. The victim's leg was broken; it was pointing . . . in the wrong direction."

"He fell down the escalator?"

"Yes, mum."

"Go ahead."

"There isn't much more to tell. He had dark hair, brown eyes. He was well dressed, though his clothes were soiled when I got there. He looked tall. Hard to tell with the broken leg and all. I'd say about six feet and another inch or two."

"White?"

"Yes."

"English?"

"How can you tell that, mum?"

"What color were his socks?"

"Dark, I think. Like his pants."

"What sort of umbrella was he carrying?"

"He didn't have an umbrella, mum. Unless it was stolen."

"What sort of hat was he wearing?"

"No hat, mum."

"Did you check for identification?"

"They wouldn't let me, mum. The medical officer arrived with a Detective Sergeant and they took the body away for examination."

"What was causing all of the bleeding, Henley?"

"I couldn't tell, mum. It was coming from between his legs."

"Between his legs? You mean from his groin?"

"Yes, mum, from that general area."

"But he was fully clothed."

"Oh yes."

"And he fell from the top of the escalator or nearly so."

"Oh yes, mum, there was blood everywhere. He fell from a distance, what with broken bones and marks such as he had."

"So the wound was inflicted on the escalator itself."

"It appears so, mum."

"What about witnesses, Henley?"

"It was very crowded, mum, what with people hurrying along, late for work and appointments. There was a woman behind him on the escalator. A Mrs. Rumson."

"You spoke with her?"

"Oh yes, mum. She's here at the station now. I thought you might want to speak to her yourself. Sergeant Gered said that you'd been put on the case and that you were about to pop round, so I asked Mrs. Rumson to stay a bit. She's having some biscuits and tea."

"Very good, Henley. That's very helpful. We'll also need to talk to the doctor and the Detective Sergeant. By the way, which one is on the case?"

"Detective Sergeant Clarence."

"Charles Clarence?"

"Yes, mum. He hasn't returned as yet."

"And neither he nor the doctor has called?"

"No, mum."

"You'll tell me the moment that they do, won't you?"

"Certainly, mum."

"Thank you. Do you have anything to add, Henley?"

"Only one thing, mum."

"And what is that?"

He straightened up, cleared his throat, and said, "If the man *was* murdered, mum, and it looks as if he was, whoever did it was very, very expert."

"Why do you say that, Henley?"

"Because the man was killed in a crowd of hundreds of people and no one saw it happen."

"Or no one will say."

"Yes, mum."

"Thank you again, Henley. Ask Mrs. Rumson to come in, won't you? Off you go, now."

He stood up, curled his lower lip at the corners, and backed out the door, as Harding smiled at him.

Mrs. Rumson appeared in the doorway, clutching her purse impatiently and looking over her left shoulder disapprovingly at Police Constable Henley. She stared at Harding as if some mistake had been made.

"Who are you?" she asked.

"I am Detective Inspector Harding."

"A woman?"

"Yes, Mrs. Rumson, by all accounts I am a woman."

"They told me I'd be speaking to a proper detective."

"I try so hard to be proper, Mrs. Rumson. Won't you sit down?"

"Wait . . . wait," she said. "You're the one that caught the sex fiend in White City, the filthy thing, the one on the telly. You're the one who caught him and thrashed him with your torch. Gave him a right proper beating too."

"Yes, Mrs. Rumson. I apprehended the serial rapist."

"And what did you do with him?"

"As you said, he resisted arrest, threatened me, and I disabled him with my torch."

"After that, I mean."

"Mr. Glennis was convicted and sent to Wormwood Scrubs."

"For how long?"

"Quite some time, Mrs. Rumson. You needn't worry about Mr. Glennis."

"They should have put the shears to him; that's what I think."

"That thought crossed many minds, Mrs. Rumson. He was a most disagreeable man."

"He might think twice the next time. How many times did you hit 'im?"

"Thrice, I believe," Harding said.

Mrs. Rumson smiled.

"Now," Harding said, "Would you be so kind as to tell me what you observed in the Green Park station this morning?"

"*Observed*? I observed a man bleeding all over my coat and yellow shoes is what I observed. I observed a man nearly knocking me down and dragging me the length of the moving stairs. I observed blood, Inspector Harding. A flood of it. Here, see for yourself."

She lifted her right foot and raised the front of her coat. The shoe and coat were both soaked with blood.

"You were directly behind him."

(Proudly) "I was."

"Do you have any idea how the wound was inflicted, or who might have inflicted it?"

Silence.

"Mrs. Rumson?"

"No."

"You saw nothing?"

"I saw blood all over my yellow shoes. I saw a man about to fall and knock me down the moving stairway. I saw a man terrify a great lot of innocent people trying to go about their business . . ."

"But you did not see anyone actually inflict the wound?"

(Belligerent this time) "No."

"Where was the wound, Mrs. Rumson?"

"I'm . . . I'm not certain. It all happened very quickly."

"In his back? In his leg?"

"I didn't see anything on his back. It must have been lower."

"Tell me, Mrs. Rumson, were there people hurrying up the escalator on the left side?"

"Yes, yes," she said, relieved at the thought of a possible explanation. "One of them must have done it. You know—the usual lot. Men in a hurry, not willing to wait. Running up the moving stairs with their 'Excuse me's.' Afraid they'll be late for something."

"You saw such men?"

(Willing to please now) "Oh yes. I certainly did."

"You're quite sure."

"Yes."

"Do you remember anything particular about any of them?"

"No."

"But you did see such men."

"I told you that I did. They were the usual lot—well dressed, hurrying to their offices."

"With umbrellas?"

"Some of them, I suppose."

"An umbrella could be used as a weapon, Mrs. Rumson. Did you see anyone pointing an umbrella or jabbing with it?"

(Pausing) "No."

"How many men would you say you saw running up the escalator?"

"I have no idea. Five, ten. Enough of them."

"Running together or separately?"

"How would I know that?"

"Were they running in groups?"

"Each one was on a different step."

"Was there a break between them as they hurried by?"

"I have no idea."

"But you did see them."

"I told you that I did."

"Is there anything else that you would like to tell me?"

"Yes. Who is going to pay for my coat and shoes?"

"Speak with Sergeant Gered. I'm sure he'll be anxious to help."

"The bald one with the red cheeks?"

"Yes."

"I didn't like the way he looked at me when I came in."

"He's really quite harmless."

(Apprehensively) "May I leave now?"

"Certainly, Mrs. Rumson, and thank you very much for your help. I trust I can call again if I need to talk to you."

"And what do you intend to do now, Inspector Harding?"

"I am going to Green Park Station, Mrs. Rumson. You'll forgive me, but I always like to have a look for myself."

THREE

Harding checked with Henley and then followed his route to Green Park station. The escalator was back in service. The blood samples had been collected and photographs taken. The victim's soiled body was on the anatomist's table and the foetid air had begun to clear. She took the *down* escalator and stood on the platform between the moving stairs, her hand on the wooden partition between the parallel handrails, at the precise point where Michael McGinn had reached for lost notes that would now never be heard.

She leaned to the left and looked toward the top, imagining a falling, bloodied body toppling toward her. She imagined the darting faces and the shock; the blood, the limbs shattering silently amid the noise of the crowd and the gearwork, the muffled cries of the victim, his face reduced to a horrid pantomime of gaping mouth and anguished eyes. She imagined the smells of death and incontinence, of fear and sweat, of soot flecks and smoke hovering in damp air, of the collected detritus dragged in on the soles of dirty boots and deposited in the station amid grit and oil. She imagined the footsteps, the men running up the stairs and hurrying past the victim. She imagined the blank stares of horror and realization. She thought of the Eleanor Rumsons, beginning their Wednesday mornings in a bath of stranger's blood. Most of all, she thought of the murderer.

Riding up the stairs now she realized how it might have happened. Henley's words: "Whoever did it was very, very expert." True enough. At the very least, a master of planning or the beneficiary of immeasurable luck.

On either side of the escalator was a parallel, diagonal line of framed posters, all designed to seize the eye: at the Strand: *Me and My Girl*, the Lambeth Walk Musical, with Tommy Noone, now in its ninth season—a young man in an ermine robe with a crown tilted over his eyes; Yo-Yo Ma, cradling his cello in front of the Royal Albert Hall—three dates in October; Austin Reed, 103 Regent Street—a man in a silk suit, standing on a cliff in Torquay with the wind tossing his Italian tie and a pair of women in cocktail frocks reaching for his face and torso; the Imperial War Museum, Lambeth Road—the T. E. Lawrence Exhibit, closing October 11—Lawrence in his white robes, superimposed on a map of the Underground, standing near the Elephant & Castle station, his hand pointing toward the museum, Bedlam in its nineteenth-century incarnation; the Museum of Mankind, 6 Burlington Gardens—two men of identical height with identical faces, one in a tiny loincloth carrying a sharpened wooden spear, the other in a vested wool suit with smart leather wingtips, carrying an attaché case; *Phantom* at Her Majesty's, Haymarket—*now accepting orders until May*; Foyle's Bookshop, Charing Cross Road—"Quite Simply the Largest"; Harvey Nichols, Knightsbridge—a troop of Sloane Rangers with slim legs and braceleted arms, feverishly crowding through a single swinging door; Hamley's, Regent Street, "Christmas is but three months away"—stuffed animals and wooden soldiers staring into the observer's face and pointing accusingly.

No one could take their eyes from them.

No one could look straight ahead at the mass of damp and anxious humanity when such an alternative was calling out from either side.

Least of all Eleanor Rumson, her eyes exploring the male body in the clingy loincloth or the blue-eyed idol with wind-blown hair and adoring, clutchy females, balancing his manly frame on a broad rock atop a Devonshire tor.

The blood was already running before anyone was aware of its source or cause.

And all of it depended on the planning. Striking at the precise moment. Checking the timing and the pacing. Running through the rehearsals. Measuring the crowds. Planning. Checking the stop-watch. Planning. Figuring the escape routes. Planning. Then doing it. Swiftly. Surely. Very, very expertly.

Harding stood on the platform, watching the averted glances of those on the escalator, their eyes locked on the billboards. She listened to the footsteps of those running up the left side, heard their "Excuse me's" and saw the indifference of those they passed. She played it over and over in her imagination. The movement of the stairway. The boredom of the people. Morning life on a damp day, then suddenly the screams and the blood and the horror. The images freezing in her brain, like segments of a reel of film that had jumped its sprockets, the single frames tilted and bent and wedged, burning into the memory forever as the operator struggled hopelessly to free them from the heat of the lamp. And always most vividly: a man with blood running down his legs, his life draining into rubber ridges and gearwork, falling into oblivion.

She found a public phone in Berkeley Street and called Savile Row. She got Gered.

"Clarence is back," he said.

"Are the doctors finished?"

"Yes, quite."

"I'll be right there. Ask Clarence to wait."

"He won't be leaving," Gered said. "I asked him if he wanted some tea and biscuits—the ones the Rumson woman left. He said he couldn't possibly. What do you think he did?"

"Pinched your whiskey?"

"How did you know that?"

"It's my job to know those things," she said.

"Come on."

"I've never known Clarence to be unable to eat. He must have been sickened by what he learned."

"He's sick all right. He looks like a man who's drunk curdled milk."

"I'll be right there."

FOUR

Clarence was sitting in an interrogation room when Harding arrived, a cigarette in his left hand, a coffee cup in his right. The smell of whiskey hung about his hair and face. He grasped at the table top with the fingertips of his left hand, steadying himself.

"Good morning," Harding said.

"Good morning, mum," Clarence answered. He took a drink of the laced coffee, squinted, and swallowed.

"How much of that is coffee, Clarence?" Harding asked.

"Very little, mum," he answered.

"Shall we start?"

"Yes, certainly," he answered, finishing the coffee and whiskey and taking a long drag from his cigarette. "Sorry about this," he said, wiping what was left across the bottom of a copper ashtray.

"That's quite all right," she said. "Do we have a name?"

"Oh, yes," Clarence said. "We have that. The victim was one Michael Crimmins. Actually, Representative Michael Crimmins, Democrat of the state of California."

"From the American Congress?"

"Yes, quite."

"Have you contacted them?"

"Oh yes. Both Washington and Grosvenor Square."

"You say California?"

"Yes, mum."

"And have you contacted them?"

"Yes. Representative Crimmins was from Los Angeles. We called their Chief of Police and Mayor."

"We'll be up to our elbows in yanks."

"Yes, mum."

"And how did Representative Crimmins die, Clarence?"

He reached for his cigarettes, glancing at her.

"Go ahead," she said.

He shook a cigarette loose from the cardboard package and lit it with a wooden match, taking in the sulphur with the first puff.

"Wait, I'm game to guess," she said. "Hollow point bullets fired from a small pistol with a silencer. Two or three quick rounds, each atop the other, tearing up everything in their path."

He took a long puff. "No, mum."

"Well?"

"He was stabbed, mum. No, not stabbed. Impaled."

"Impaled?"

"Yes."

"With what?"

"With this, mum." He opened a brown folder and handed her a color photograph.

Across a white linen towel were laid the weapon and a wooden ruler. The steel weapon measured eleven inches in length. It looked like a miniature sword with no hilt and a bare tang in place of a grip. It was covered with blackened blood, smeared waste, and fragments of tissue. The lengths of each of the blades were barbed. Pointed dorsal fins with razor edges.

"Rather nasty, I'd say."

"Yes, mum."

"And where was Representative Crimmins struck, in the groin was it?"

"Behind, mum."

"Then he *was* impaled."

"Yes. Through his bowels and into his stomach."

"And his wallet and cards and papers were all intact. Nothing was stolen. You were able to identify him immediately."

"Yes, mum."

"Murder pure and simple. And with a flair."

"Yes, mum."

"The barbs on the blades face the tang. It must have been quite messy to remove the weapon."

"Yes, mum. That is their purpose. Even if the victim *could* reach the handle and tried to remove the weapon, all he would do was tear himself further. He could wait and die, with all that pain, or suffer more and die sooner."

"Very efficient."

Clarence nodded.

"How much of the tang was protruding from the victim's body?"

"An inch or two, mum."

"So the end of the weapon was concealed by his trousers. All that anyone in the Underground could see was the blood."

"Yes, mum."

"It must have been quite a thrust, wouldn't you say?"

"Yes, mum," he said, his face falling and lower lip quivering.

"Someone with strength. Someone very practiced."

"Yes. There was very little time. No room for error. None at all."

"Quite a rude way to die, wouldn't you say, Clarence?"

"Yes, mum."

"Almost like a rape, wouldn't you say? Straight up the arse. No nonsense."

"Yes." He reached again for the pack of cigarettes, forgetting the glowing stub he still held.

Harding thanked him and stood up. "Please tell Gered I'll be back later, won't you. And call the medical people. Tell them I'll pop round in an hour to see the body and ask a question or two."

"But mum, they'll be looking for you—the yanks from the embassy."

"Of course they will," she answered.

"What should Gered tell them?"

"Tell them that when I return I'll speak with them straightaway."

"And what if they ask where you've gone?"

"Tell them that I'm attempting to find the individual who murdered their congressman. Offer them tea."

"They won't take tea, mum. They'll be too upset for that."

"Yes, I know," she said, slipping on her coat.

Harding saw the black Daimler pull in in front of the station. She watched the tall American in blue pinstripes, with red pocket square and regimental moustache. State department affectation. He was brandishing his umbrella and leather folder, glancing politely at his aide, who was holding the limousine door. He approached the station with the posture of a liberal conqueror, prepared to smile benevolently and then dictate terms.

"The last thing I need," Harding said to herself, as she walked out the side exit. Taking Sackville Street to Piccadilly, she waited as the traffic cleared, crossed to the south side, and walked into Richoux.

"Good day, Inspector," a young woman said. She was cradling a stack of green menus.

"Hello, Charlotte."

"A table in the back?"

"Yes, thank you."

Harding slipped off her coat, put her notepad and the photograph of the murder weapon on the cushioned seat beside her, and removed the napkin from the table.

A waitress in a black dress with white apron approached. "Tea, ma'am?"

"Yes," Harding said. "I'd like scones with currants, strawberry jam, and clotted cream. And a pot of the Darjeeling. Is it too early for sandwiches?"

"No, ma'am. What would you like?"

"Ham, smoked salmon, and some with the soft cheese and sprouts."

"We also have scones with sultanas, ma'am."

"Really?"

"Yes, would you prefer those?"

"Hmmm . . . no, let's stay with the currants this time. Perhaps tomorrow."

"Pastry, ma'am?"

"Are there any tarts?"

"Raspberry and also the mixed. The raspberry are quite nice."

"Raspberry will be fine. Thank you so much."

"You're welcome, ma'am."

———

The tea was steaming when it arrived. Harding sliced open the first scone, covered half of it with a thick layer of cream, and dotted the center with a teaspoon of strawberry jam. She took a sip of the tea, looked at the picture of the murder weapon, adjusted her napkin, and took a third of the scone in a single bite. "How fascinating," she said to herself.

The remainder of the cream was nearly as thick as butter. She spread a thinner layer of it on the second half of the scone and covered it with a full teaspoon of jam. She looked at the picture again and studied the blood that had run from the murder weapon. It was thick and nearly black. Then she added a bit more jam and tasted her creation. Very nice, she thought. Much nicer than having a nasty steel sword shoved into oneself. And in a London tube stop at that, she thought, taking a drink of her tea. Not at all decorous and not at all pleasant. Of course, he may have deserved it. They so often do.

FIVE

The traffic began to break along the Coastal Highway as the sunset tinted the skies above Newport Beach with thin-streaked banks of orange and pink clouds. The timed lights in the marina came on and their glow rippled in the water as the waves washed over the bows of the sailboats and the motor yachts moored there. Nothing under 45 feet, marina rules. Except for the sounds of the traffic and the gulls, the only sounds in the marina were the wash of the water and the periodic ring of a distant, nautical bell.

LAPD Lieutenant Frank White handed his car keys to a young attendant in a snug, black, uniform suit with short, honey-blond hair. His name tag read *Kerry*. He handed Frank a numbered, preprinted card and drove off to the adjoining ramp, a few hundred feet north of the circular driveway.

Frank and his friend and sometime working partner Jack Grant walked into the John Dominis restaurant, a Newport Beach mainstay. Its counterpart was in a slightly gritty, industrial section of the Honolulu harbor; Jack had eaten there often during a tour at Schofield. The two of them waited for the maitre d' as they felt the eyes of the restaurant's patrons—estimating Frank's size, wondering about his occupation and the occupation of his tall, white friend. The sides of the restaurant were walls of now-pink, now-white glass with views of the marina and the bay beyond. Cut into the floor were two deep, open stone tanks filled with fish and lobsters, swimming and scuttling in pale-green, indirect light. At the end of the narrow bridge separating the tanks was a display case filled with magnums and jeroboams of first-growth California cabernets and chardonnays. On a table to the right was a mound of shaved ice with a display of the fresh fish available that evening.

"Check out the Onaga," Jack said. "It's fabulous."

"That's the ugly one, isn't it?" Frank asked.

"Yes. Deep-sea snapper. The Ono and Uku are nice too."

Frank pointed at one of the lobsters. "Look at him," he said. "He's already trying to escape. The last time we were here two or three of them poked each other to death trying to get away from you."

"What do you mean?" Jack asked.

"It was *your* birthday and I was buying. I thought for awhile that you were going to dive into the tank in your street clothes and eat some of the fish as sushi. As it was, you played a hard number on several of them. I remember that the few who survived swam under the rim of the tank, lurking there and praying that you wouldn't see them."

"I don't remember it quite that way."

"The memory is the first thing to go, Jack."

"I almost forgot that it's *your* birthday tonight."

"And your treat," Frank said.

"I vaguely remember saying something to that effect."

"So do I," Frank said. "Come on, let's sit down. I'm hungry."

The maitre d' approached. "Good evening, gentlemen. How are you this evening?"

"Fine, Paul," Frank said. "Anything available by the window?"

"I saved something in the far corner."

"Thanks," Frank said.

It was a table for four, with two sets of tableware removed. "He knows how you like to eat all their bread," Jack said. "There's enough room here for a small plate for me and your normal four baskets."

Frank just smiled. "How's the Dover sole tonight, Paul?"

"Exquisite, lieutenant."

"And I'm sure you'll find a wine worthy of it, won't you?" Smiling again.

"I still have some of the Montrachet that we stocked for Orson Welles."

"Oh yes, the Montrachet. Wonderful. And *worth* the price."

"Every penny."

"How many bottles do you have left?" Frank asked.

A half-dozen pelicans were jockeying for position in the harbor master's dinghy, poking and flapping and displaying. "Why can't they get along?" Frank asked. "No matter where they happen to be, they somehow have to turn it into a battlefield. Look at the big one there on the right. He's not happy just watching the sunset and letting his dinner digest. He's got to push the rest of them around a little so they won't forget that he's still in charge."

"He's looking for the ultimate seat," Jack answered. "He's tried the back of the boat twice and he's tried the front twice; now he wants to move everybody out of the middle and check that out."

"They all hang together but the only thing they seem to enjoy is beating up on one another," Frank said. "That and food. I feel like I'm still at work."

The waiter approached. "Gentlemen—what can I get you?"

"I'm ready to order dinner," Frank said. "I'll have the spinach pasta with the lobster and shrimp. And the salad with the beefsteak tomatoes, mozzarella, and Maui onions."

"I'll have the same," Jack said.

"And to drink, gentlemen?"

"Beer for me," Frank said. "I think maybe a Pacifico."

"Certainly, sir."

"Letting me off easy, huh?" Jack said. "Pacifico for me too."

The waiter nodded and left.

"This is the first time this week I've been able to eat dinner sitting down," Frank said.

"I know what you mean. This is the first time this week I've been able to eat dinner outside of my car."

"Are you still working on those construction site rip-offs?"

"Yes. I hate tough times like this. The fees are good, but the things you see are unbelievable. People are stealing anything and everything—loose shingles, plastic plumbing pipe, doorknobs, mismatched sheets of formica, *anything*. The insurance companies are screaming, but the police are too busy with car-jackings and crack-turf battles. That's why Cliff put me back on the building-trade watch. Lately I've been spending most of my time in the east San Gabriel Valley. They'll be calling me the man from the Puente Hills. Thursday was the high point. Two sad cases from Nogales drove into a new development in Diamond Bar with a block-long flatbed hooked to the back of an old Chevy truck. After scoping out the pickings they started to load up a stack of the contractor's masonite: the large sheets—the ones the builders use for siding. I spotted them, put in a call to our brothers in blue, and tried to make a citizen's arrest. I was trying to keep them from escaping, but as soon as they heard me they jumped into their truck and took off. I didn't shoot at them. Nobody should get hurt over a load of masonite. I got in my car and a few minutes later I caught up with them. They were on the 210, heading toward San Dimas, when the driver suddenly hit a pothole the size of Orange County. His brother was on the back, holding onto the piece of heavy-cotton belt they had strapped around the masonite. They had never really had the chance to lash it down properly, since I had been running after them back on the site and making a lot of threatening noises, but it did its job as long as they were driving on smooth road at a reasonable speed.

"That all ended when the driver hit the pothole. Suddenly the masonite started to slide around. His brother braced himself and tried to steady the pile, but then the belt gave way. I was a car-length behind, taking all of this in and listening to Dr. Laura on the talk radio station, counselling a woman from Oxnard on her needs and options as a modern woman. The guy in the back was cursing and jumping up and down and since he couldn't get the full pile of masonite to obey him, he tried to rearrange it one sheet at a time. Big mistake. He lifted a four-by-eight sheet while he was standing up on the back of the truck. I started yelling, 'Don't do that, don't do that,' but he couldn't hear me because I had my windows up, what with trying to listen to Dr. Laura and all. Anyway, he was standing there for a fraction of a second, clutching the sheet of masonite, until he and the board were suddenly turned into a makeshift sailboat. By now the driver was doing seventy-five, trying to get away from me, while his brother and the masonite were wind-surfing over the side and off the back of the truck. As soon as he lifted the sheet, I said to myself, 'Brace yourself, he's coming through the windshield,' so I hit the brake and swerved behind this woman in the center lane who was choking the life out of the steering wheel on her '72 Volvo, probably thinking about the coronary she was about to have. Suddenly, for no apparent reason, she began honking her horn. I guess she figured that Mother Nature would obey her horn and the man and his masonite sail would blow in some other direction. I'm thinking, 'This woman is seriously deluded,' but it must have worked, because they didn't hit any of us. The force carried the wind surfer into the burn on the east side of the highway. The sheet of masonite flew off into a patch of dried manzanita and the guy started rolling down the hill in the general direction of Diamond Bar."

"Why didn't he just let go of the damned thing to begin with?" Frank asked.

"Pride, I guess. I think he was also surprised when the wind came up, so he decided to hold on to something solid—even if it happened to be flying off the back of the truck. You know, some of those guys spend most of their waking hours on the bed of a pickup truck, tooling down the freeway. He forgot that if you want to keep getting by with that you can't stand up and attach your hands to a broad, flat object."

"So what happened?"

"The CHIPS got the driver. I pulled over to check on his brother. He had broken both of his arms and one of his legs and skinned the hell out of himself in the gravel, but the masonite must have protected him somehow. I think he was floating there for a second or two before he actually hit the ground. When I got to him he just kept moaning 'Sonovabeech, sonovabeech, sonovabeech,' over and over. I asked him if he was all right and he said, 'Focking sonovabeech, focking sonovabeech.'"

The waiter brought the beer. "The salads will be up in a second," he said.

"That sounds like fun compared to what I've been doing," Frank said.

"I thought you were working the downtown parking ramps, chasing muggers."

"That's right, we were."

"You told me they were hiding between the cars and hitting the parkers when they came to get in their Mercedes and BMWs."

"Right. That's what they were doing. It turned out to be a group of four. We caught up with a pair of them in a public ramp by the Civic Center. One of them had tripped over this old man—a homeless guy who was sleeping under a minivan. His legs were projecting out on the side and the mugger tripped over him when he walked by. He turned and kicked the hell out of him and the homeless guy started screaming in pain. The punk told him to shut the hell up and when he didn't he took out his 9mm and blasted him with it."

"Jesus," Jack said.

"Right. By then one of the attendants had heard the noise and called the station. We blocked all of the exits and hunted the two of them, row by row, car by car. One of my patrolmen took a round in the head. A guy named Jimmy Rivers. He'll live, but he lost an eye trying to take them down. We finally trapped the two dirtbags in a corner. They fired on us. We dropped one of them and arrested the other. We talked to him about his future prospects and he quickly rolled over on the other three members of the club."

"What did you say to him to persuade him to do that?"

"Don't ask."

"And I'll bet the homeless guy died."

"Yes."

"And the mugger will walk."

"Not the one who did the shooting—the other one."

"That's reassuring."

"A little," Frank said.

"What are you working now?"

"I was working a homicide case in Hawthorne for a little more than a week, but the prime suspect floated up on Redondo Beach last Tuesday, all blue and puffy. Somebody got to him before we could.

Today I was putting together a group to try to catch the slasher who's been causing all of the trouble in Hancock Park."

"The Wilshire bandit?"

"Yes. That's what they've been calling him, but the situation is actually a lot worse than it sounds. Originally he was just weaving through the crowds on the sidewalks—cutting straps, stealing purses—and then taking off like a crazed son-of-a-bitch, but now we think he must be on PCP or something, because lately he's been slashing indiscriminately. He's got a set of razor blades stuck in one of those toy baseball bats they sell downtown, and he's been swinging it wildly, like a batter trying to hit a high outside pitch or a kid with a blindfold trying to bring down a birthday-party pinata. He put a couple of women in the hospital with deep cuts on their arms and shoulders and he took one sixty-year-old woman's right ear off before he started going to work on her hands and fingers. They were able to reattach the fingers, but they couldn't do anything about the ear."

"Jesus."

The waiter brought the salads.

"These are great," Jack said. "The onions are always so sweet."

"Perfect; ice cold," Frank said.

The waiter brought a second round of Pacificos without asking if they wanted them. Frank nodded in appreciation and the waiter said, "Paul informed me of the depth of your thirst, gentlemen."

"Right," Frank said, smiling and taking a drink. "When you care enough to drink the very best," he said.

"I have reason to believe that they can bring us a few more, should we need them," Jack said.

"If not, there's always that cache of Montrachet."

The waiter approached the table with a worried look and no food. "What now?" Jack said. "Don't tell me the lobsters all escaped." The waiter didn't smile.

"I saw three in the tank you could still dive for," Frank answered.

"Lieutenant, I'm sorry, but there's a call for you. The caller says it's very important. I can bring a phone here or you can take it in the back where it's a little more quiet."

"Thanks, I'll follow you," Frank said.

———

It was fifteen minutes before he returned.

"I caught the waiter on the way back and asked him to hold the dinners a couple more minutes and bring us two more beers," Frank said.

"Is it that bad?" Jack asked.

"That depends on your point of view. I have to leave tomorrow for London."

"For *London*?"

"Yes. It seems that your favorite congressman and mine, the Honorable Michael Crimmins, has just been murdered."

"That *is* good news," Jack said. "I should propose a toast. How did the son of a bitch buy it?"

"Are you ready? Somebody followed him through the London subway system, ran past him on an escalator, and paused just long enough to unceremoniously shove a miniature, steel sword straight up his ass."

"They did *what*?"

"You heard it right the first time."

"I *like* it. Any suspects?"

"None."

"How long had he been over there?"

"Two days."

"That's not usually enough time to develop mortal enemies, but with an asshole like Crimmins you can never tell."

"Loram thinks he could have been followed there." Carl Loram was Frank's captain.

"Then the murderer could already be back here," Jack said.

"Exactly. He wants me to fly over and find out whatever I can. The press will squeeze this for all it's worth and the spin doctors will be casting around, looking for ways to turn this into political capital. Loram wants somebody there who will report directly to him."

"Somebody he trusts."

"Right," Frank said.

"Somebody who will tell him the truth."

"Yes."

"Somebody who will handle the locals with the utmost professionalism and respect."

"Right."

"Somebody who will represent the country, the city, and the LAPD in an exemplary fashion."

"Correct."

"Somebody who will be able to deal with all of the fucking Washington suits and talking heads without losing his temper."

"I'm not so sure about that part."

"Damn, I wish I could go with you," Jack said. "We could drink some British beer, take a walk along the river on the embankment, check out the spiked, purple hair around Piccadilly Circus, and put a wooden stake in that son-of-a-bitch's heart to make sure he doesn't come back to bother us again . . ."

"You should."

"I can't. I've got three and a half weeks of solid work on these construction-site thefts. I had to bring in Dave Hagan and Carl Enders to help and I can't walk out on them."

Frank took a long drink of his Pacifico.

"A miniature sword, huh?" Jack said.

"Yes. Tempered steel. Very ornate, apparently."

"That's very interesting."

"It's certainly different," Frank said.

"You know what I think?"

"What?" Frank asked.

"I think you're tracking a crusader."

SIX

Frank caught the 11:30 United flight to Dulles, where he connected with the British Air 8:05 flight to Heathrow. The American carriers flying to London had been fully booked and the LAPD accountants were still wringing their hands in anticipation of the red tape they'd be wrapped in by the city auditors. The ticket price was the same, but the auditors weren't in the business of saving money. They were in the business of avoiding investigative reporters with poisoned pens and overactive curiosity glands.

The philosophy of British Air has always been to pacify their cramped, coach passengers by making them as drunk as they can as quickly as they can. They start with drinks before dinner, add wine with, and cordials after. When Frank asked for doubles they handed them over without a blink. The TV dinner tasted the same as always, even with the stylish gray menu with the picture of a pink cyclamen plant and the swooshed British Air logo, but the Gordon's gin, passable red burgundy, and endless miniatures of Drambuie made it all bearable. When the flight attendant offered coffee, Frank told her he'd prefer to switch from Drambuie to Kahlúa. She brought him three.

His seatmates on the 747 were mostly British; the duty-free cigarettes and bright-colored socks were instant giveaways. The in-flight movie had something to do with Dade County, dope, explosions, automatic weapons, and CIA operatives gone bad. Clu Gulager and Michael J. Parks starred, with Kathy Ireland along for the beach shots and car chases. Frank passed.

Instead he pulled out a paperback mystery novel he had picked up in the Dulles bookshop. It was called *Go Directly to Hell*, a story about a world-champion Monopoly player who finds out, long after the fact, that she has been cheated by three of her former competitors she thought were her friends. Logically enough, she loses a set of houses and apartment buildings she has spent the better part of her life acquiring, using them as real-world collateral during a weekend marathon game with table stakes. She takes her revenge by killing each of the plotters in turn in ways that relate to their preferred Monopoly pieces. The first is nudged in front of a high-speed train, the second is shredded by a boat propeller, and the third is found in his garden, with four broken limbs and a crushed skull, sprawled across his wheelbarrow like an out-of-service scarecrow. There are muddy footprints found in the garden, on the dock by the boat's slip, and along the railroad siding—the footprints of the murderess and of her Scottish terrier Mitzi—the pup being her favorite pet as well as a real-life replica of her personal Monopoly token.

The detective, Randolph Hindley, is totally befuddled by the clues, which are deciphered by his wife, Emma—a woman with ample, alabaster breasts and more-than-ample insight, with a taste for Amontillado and a penchant for forgetting to wear her undergarments. Emma leaves her husband in his den, worrying over his reports; she strikes out on her own, and promptly finds the murderess in her apartment: a set of quirky rooms decorated with Monopoly boards; Monopoly money; cardboard cards; and houses, apartments, and tokens of all ages, shapes, and sizes. In the final scene the murderess is seated at a large game table, with a chocolate Monopoly board (a Nieman's Christmas special from the 1970s), and all of the money, cards, houses, and apartments in precisely the same position they were in when she lost her real estate to the three cheats. In the other chairs are large photographs of her opponents—in death—with their pieces before them, laying on their sides in defeat. The table is covered with napkins and half-filled cups and glasses—all just as it was during the tournament finale—with the murderess shifting her glance from victim to victim, smiling serenely as Mitzi rests on her lap, digesting the hunk of Park Place which she has just devoured.

I guess that could happen, Frank thought.

"And did you enjoy that?" a woman's voice asked.

Frank turned to his right. The woman was sitting across the aisle. She was no more than five feet tall, eighty or ninety pounds at most, and at least seventy years old. She was wearing a brown sweater and dark plaid skirt with white tennis shoes and a burgundy wool scarf. "I love her books," she said. "That one's not as exciting as the rest, but it's quite good, don't you think?"

"I enjoyed it," Frank said. "I didn't know that the author was a woman."

"R. P. Henning? Of course. Regina Patricia."

"That's interesting," Frank said. "With all that blood and violence..."

"Is that your first Henning?"

"Yes. I saw the title, I read the first page, and I decided to invest the $4.99."

"Try *The Dungeon Floor*. You'll find it a bit more exhilarating. It's about a shy solicitor in Yorkshire who lives in a stately, Jacobean home with a modern torture chamber. 'State of the art' you yanks would say. 'Cutting edge'—ha ha. When the population of the local village declines by half, the authorities become suspicious." She laughed and scooted around in her seat, leaning closer. "All good fun. Lots of spice and rowdiness—women in their knickers tied up with ropes, detectives chased through long hallways by starved Weimaraners and Mastiffs, honey-covered vicars nibbled to death by furry African insects, virginal village girls licked and sniffed by tropical reptiles—the whole lot."

Frank tried to make conversation. "Does the detective's wife solve those crimes too?"

"Of course. Emma always solves them. In *The Dungeon Floor* she is trapped by the murderer, who wants to tear away her blouse and have a feel. Randy bugger. She tells him she'll have none of that and then promptly gives him a kick where it will do the most good. He gasps, slips, and then falls backward into one of his favorite acid pits. Emma *will* have her touch of irony . . . by the time her husband arrives all that is left of the sex-fiend solicitor is his skeleton and a bit of grease on top of the bubble pool. Emma apologizes for fizzing away the evidence; Randolph pats her on the shoulder, gives her bum a squeeze, and says, 'Quite all right, dear. We'll match up the teeth. Well done as usual.' You see, it's really a love story after all."

"It doesn't exactly sound like a love story," Frank said.

"Oh but it is," the woman answered, smiling, and then pausing. "I shouldn't be bothering you like this . . . my name is Helen Gimston."

"How do you do. I'm Frank White."

"And do you play American football, Mr. White?"

"No, Mrs. Gimston, why would you think that?"

"Because you're a black man, you're large, and you appear to be so fit."

Frank suppressed a smile. "I'm forty years old, Mrs. Gimston."

"And does that matter?"

"It matters a great deal," Frank said. "If I were to play football now, I wouldn't have any more chance of surviving than one of Emma's adversaries."

"What *do* you do, Mr. White?"

"I'm a police lieutenant."

"Oh my. You're a true expert then."

"Not on the kinds of crimes in these novels, Mrs. Gimston."

"But of course you are. There really are only two kinds of crime, lieutenant: crimes of calculation and crimes of passion."

"Do you really think you can separate them?"

"But of course. Do you disagree?"

"Well, take the woman in the novel—the one who played Monopoly. She committed murders—calculated murders—and *her* motive was revenge. Revenge is a strong passion."

"But were those really *crimes*, lieutenant?"

"She murdered them, Mrs. Gimston. Murder is a crime."

"I suppose *you* have to think so," she said, smiling politely.

The flight attendant passed between them. "Young lady," Mrs. Gimston called.

"Yes, madam?" the woman said.

"Could you be so kind as to bring me two more whiskeys?"

"Certainly, madam. With ice?"

"No, don't bother with that," she said.

The flight attendant walked away and Mrs. Gimston turned back to Frank. "I always fly the flag," she said. "Best cure for a thirst. Try *The Dungeon Floor*, lieutenant. I *know* you'll like it. If you can't find it, try

Planting the Vicar or *The Telltale Molars*. Then there's always my personal favorite: *A Scalpel in Four-Four Time*."

"Tell me something, Mrs. Gimston."

"Yes?" she said.

"Have you ever read of anyone being murdered by being impaled on a miniature, barbed sword?"

"Impaled? On a barbed sword? You mean straight up the bum?"

"Yes."

"Why no. That sounds fascinating. A rude way to die, wouldn't you say? Being turned into a lolly?"

"I hadn't thought of it in quite those terms."

"Quite humorous in its way, I would say."

"But not for the victim," Frank said.

"No, not for the victim, but the victim never really has a choice, does he? He's not the clever one."

"No. His job is simply to die."

"Well there you have it," she said.

———

Frank leaned back with a fourth Kahlúa. Most of the rough edges were gone after number three; the fourth was a bonus. He looked at the dark windows on either side of the plane, thinking about what lay beyond as Regina Patricia Henning might describe it: cloudless emptiness surrounding a thin-skinned projectile hurtling through the atmosphere at 37,000 feet and eight miles a minute in subzero temperatures. Below: the North Atlantic in its chill vastness, dotted only by scattered icebergs. Inside: the assembled comforts of civilization; inches away: a quick and nasty death. He wondered if she had dispatched any victims by sucking them through airplane windows and hurling them into frozen oceans. On second thought: not R. P.

She'd mince them in Rolls Royce aircraft engines or strap them to the business side of the landing apparatus. Scuff the poor sons of bitches to death when the plane touched down.

He checked his watch and thought of Jack, stuck somewhere on a freeway, his leg cramping. Seven operations so far. The last may have actually done him some good. Chinese grenades were supposed to split in two and miss everything. One caught Jack and took the rest of his Army career along with the bone and tendon.

He thought of Carl Loram, Captain of Detectives, fending off the feds, the press, the pols, and the local feeders on congressional pork whose support had put the carving knife in Michael Crimmins' willing hand.

He thought about his wife, Marie. Ex-wife now, though he still didn't think of her in that way. Doing the six o'clock news for Channel 7, returning his calls when she could, seeing him occasionally. He thought of her in black sheath dresses with long gloves and diamond earrings. Or fresh from her bath, in white satin sheets and candlelight. It had been a long time since he had seen her like that.

She would just be wrapping her broadcast, getting ready for dinner with someone who would be staring into her brown eyes rather than into the blackness of the night sky or the red and blue abstract mosaic fashioned from a section of nylon carpet that someone had glued to the bulkhead directly in his line of sight.

Worst of all, the 747 was not only taking him away from her and his friends; it was taking him to meetings with people he didn't know, to rooms that smelled of death, to a slotted table holding the mutilated body of a politician about whose passing he didn't really care.

Michael Crimmins was little more than a dried flyspeck on Frank White's desk blotter. Newly elected to the House of Representatives, his campaign platform had turned on the single promise to "Look Homeward," a cant phrase that wrapped the hopes of public-trough largesse in the robes of responsive, representative government. His predecessor, an economist named Mary Elisabeth Connors, had been a judicious participant in now-forgotten activities that once held out the distant possibility of actual benefit to the citizens of the state and the nation. Crimmins' agenda was far more specific, far more pragmatic, and far more successful. He carried his district with a seventeen-point spread and celebrated his election at a black-tie feel-up funded by PAC-men and trade association executives.

Now suddenly he was dead and Frank White found himself in the unenviable position of having to investigate his murder rather than toast its accomplishment.

"One for the forces of righteousness," Jack had said, over dessert. "The world will be a nicer place without him and the public tit will be a good bit less sore without his fat mouth to suck at it."

"That's pretty strong, Jack," Frank said.

"Not really. Michael Crimmins was essentially a worthless piece of shit in a twelve-hundred-dollar suit."

"What makes you say that?"

"How many reasons do you need?" Jack answered.

"I'll settle for one good one."

"OK. One good one. I saw him at a rally last year. Valley Mutual held the paper on the building where the event was being staged and they asked me to check on the security. I was outside the green room after he finished addressing the crowd. One of his secretaries congratulated him on his speech and instead of saying thank you he put his arms around her and kissed her on the mouth. Hard. She tried to break away and he tightened his grip, sliding his hands up and down her back and buttocks and laughing all the while. When she finally broke away she was in tears. She tried to slap him, but she missed. When she did he stood there and laughed at her again. I tried to say something to her, but she just walked away. How much could she do? She was worried about her job and by then he was yelling at her to go check on his fucking limo. How's that?"

"Good enough," Frank said. "What makes assholes like him think they can get away with that kind of shit?"

"They think they're born to it," Jack said. "They're the men who make the laws that the rest of us are supposed to obey. They're above all that, of course. They give the orders; they don't take them. They're our guardians, lieutenant. They tell us what we must do and in return for this favor we're supposed to let them empty our wallets and work their way through our wives and mothers and daughters."

"You were never really fond of Washington, were you, Jack?"

"Washington's OK. There's really nothing wrong with it that a tactical strike or two couldn't cure."

"Come on, Jack. You're exaggerating now."

"Yes, but not by much. This Crimmins dick—you check him out; I'll tell you what you're going to find."

"What's that?"

"More and more reasons to wish you had been there on that escalator, so you could have shoved that short sword a little harder and a little deeper . . . then given it a sharp twist and a good pull."

"You're really serious."

"You're damned right."

"Did you know the secretary personally?"

"No. But neither did he. He called her Marsha. She told him her name was Martha. When she came back and told him his limo was ready, he called her Marsha again. Then he told her she had a nice, firm ass and that he'd like a sample of it. I walked over and told him to watch his goddamned mouth or I'd break his nose. He told me to shut the fuck up and mind my own business. I told him I'd be happy to, but that I expected him to apologize to the young lady first. He expressed a certain reluctance to do that, so I turned him around, grabbed his fat, sweaty neck, shoved his face against the wall, pulled back his legs, and let him support his weight against the bricks with the tip of his nose, while he thought about my request. Ten seconds later, he apologized. Ten minutes after that I got a cell-phone call from Valley, telling me to ease up or I could lose my job."

Flying over Ireland and the west of England, Frank looked down at the green land and gray skies. A nice place to die, he thought.

The seat belt sign came on and with it the comforting voice of the English pilot, wishing everyone a good morning and announcing the final guesstimate on their arrival time. Frank sat up, checked his seat belt, and tightened his tie. The sun still hadn't broken through the clouds as they flew into a light drizzle. The Heathrow tower diverted them briefly and as they headed east the city came into view. Frank could see the Thames snaking around the Isle of Dogs in the distance. He started to count the bridges and look for landmarks across the skyline, but the 747 banked abruptly and headed toward the network of crowded runways encircled by cement strips of highway carrying the early rush hour traffic.

SEVEN

Bland gray carpeting with repeating, rust-red accents covered the jetways and ramps of the international terminal. The bright yellow, international-logo signs marking the toilets and customs counters were flat and brash but, after the dull carpet, a pleasant relief. The customs line was long but it moved swiftly; the official—a man named Harris—asked Frank the purpose of his trip to the United Kingdom. When Frank told him, the official asked if he was carrying a firearm and he said no. The suitcases came up promptly and there were ample luggage carts to accommodate everyone, even though the international flights were all converging on Heathrow within the same thirty-minute window.

Frank checked his watch; he was only ten minutes behind schedule. He passed through the customs declaration gauntlet—no one really there—and was finally in the terminal proper. The tired American tourists and return-trip Brits were suddenly encircled by rows of people freshened by a full night's sleep, holding up cards with handwritten names and looking for familiar faces.

Frank stopped and turned, reading the signs and cards, but saw nothing with his name on it. Suddenly a woman appeared at his side and said, "Lieutenant White?"

"Yes?"

"Claire Harding. Welcome to London."

"How did you know who I was?" he asked.

"Trained eye," she said, smiling.

———

"I expect you would like some coffee," Harding said, maneuvering her dark blue sedan through the Heathrow roundabouts.

"That would be very nice," Frank said.

———

Twenty minutes later they were in Chiswick. "There's a little hotel here, with a small tearoom," Harding said. "It's quiet and we'll be able to chat."

"Won't they be expecting us at the station?" Frank asked.

"Perhaps, but I can never get my work done there."

———

The Stanhope Hotel was a sixteen-room conversion with heavy lobby furniture and a small tearoom overlooking a walled garden with scattered pink and yellow roses. "What would you like?" Harding asked. "Coffee? Tea?"

"Coffee is fine."

"It's too strong here, you know," she said.

"That's all right. I'm used to it that way."

"They cut it with the hot milk. Otherwise it would take the top of your head off." She signaled the waitress. Five minutes later the coffee arrived with a steaming carafe of milk of equal size. The waitress poured the coffee and milk simultaneously.

Frank tasted it and said, "It's very good."

"Do you have some of those nice biscuits today, Mrs. Watley?" Harding asked.

"Yes, certainly," the waitress answered, hurrying back to the kitchen and returning with a tray of cookies and butter crackers.

"Thank you so much," Harding said.

The waitress left as Frank was finishing his first cup of coffee. "May I?" Harding asked, picking up the two carafes.

"Thanks very much," Frank said. "I suppose you've been buried in official calls and visits from the embassy staff."

"Oh yes, quite," Harding answered. "They were upon us instantly. They never seem to understand that our job is to find the criminal rather than just to sit and talk with them."

"Sitting and talking is what they consider a job."

"Yes," she said, "isn't it?"

"Has anyone arrived yet from Washington?"

"Oh yes, someone from your Justice Department named McGann. A very unpleasant fellow, if you don't mind my saying so. He strutted into Savile Row station, expecting us all to collapse at his feet in reverence. I said to him, 'Mr. McGann, we are quite anxious to find the murderer of your congressman. We are doing what we can and we could do ever so much more if you would only permit us to be about our work.'"

"And he promptly asked to speak with your superior."

"Exactly. You must know his kind."

"I do," Frank said.

"Well, fortunately the Deputy Commissioner was available to speak with him. That made him very happy indeed. Of course, it didn't take us any closer to discovering the identity of the murderer, but that didn't seem to matter greatly to him."

"All he wants to do is be able to report back to Washington that he's in contact with a senior official. That can then be reported in the press and the voters will be pacified."

"Indeed. I thanked the Deputy Commissioner, wished him well with Mr. McGann, and told him I'd be off to check the evidence once again."

"How about the embassy people?"

"Oh, I dodged them straightaway. They're always first on the scene, but they disappear quickly when the people from Washington arrive."

"They have to carry their luggage," Frank said. "It sounds as if you've been through this sort of thing before."

"Oh yes, we get the odd tourist from time to time who has some trouble and of course there are always the visits from the Vice President and the congressmen and senators on—what do you call them—junkets?"

"Yes."

"A murder is rare, of course, but there are accidents and natural deaths all the time. We try to be helpful. By the way, what are you here to do, lieutenant?"

"I'm here to find out what I can and keep my captain informed. If the murderer is found here—well and good. If not, I'll continue to work on the case back in Los Angeles."

"I'm afraid he won't be found here, lieutenant."

"Why do you say that? And please call me Frank."

"Claire."

They each smiled. "Would you like some more coffee?" Frank asked, picking up the carafes somewhat awkwardly and attempting to pour from each at an even rate.

"Thank you," she said. "The reason he won't be found here is that he's left the country."

"You're sure of that?"

"Quite sure. Congressman Crimmins was in London for a meeting with a business delegation from southern California, what you yanks would call a photo opportunity. Your computer people were talking to our computer people, attempting to strike some sort of deal. A rather large deal, I gather. The congressman had nothing whatsoever to do with it. The meeting had been arranged by the chief of the American delegation and the congressman was simply popping over from Washington to be seen in their midst. Helping out the home economy, you see, taking whatever credit he could for its improvement."

"Then he wasn't involved in the deal itself."

"No, not at all. The talks would have proceeded with or without him. If anything, he was something of a bother. We have not released this to the press, of course, but we have been informed that he was not even invited to the meeting."

"So the meeting will be held anyway."

"The meeting was held the day before he died. Their work was finished long before he stepped onto the moving stairs in Green Park Station. There really is no discoverable connection between his death and that business meeting. Congressman Crimmins stopped by for a luncheon and reception, spoke a word or two, had his picture taken, and promptly left. Something may surface later, of course, but there's nothing at all at this time. Nothing."

"Where was he going when he died?"

"To breakfast, with an old college chum. He had actually arranged to meet with him just across the street, at the Ritz Hotel. The next day he was scheduled to return to the states."

"And there is no evidence to suggest that he was killed for some mundane reason—robbery, for instance."

"Absolutely nothing was taken, at least so far as we've been able to determine. There was nothing apparent taken from his person and nothing taken from his hotel room. Of course, we can't fully exclude the possibility of something exotic, but Congressman Crimmins was not a particularly exotic man. In my considered opinion, this was a murder pure and simple. The person who did it was extremely expert. His mission was to take the congressman's life and he did just that. Every step was planned in detail and executed to perfection."

"And there was not a great deal of time for the planning. The murderer was ingenious as well as careful."

"Precisely."

"But the murderer would have had to have known his victim's schedule."

"No problem there. As I said, Mr. Crimmins spoke briefly at the business luncheon. He mentioned that he was seeing his friend today. The friend is quite well-known in London; I'm sure Crimmins mentioned him in order to impress the businessmen. Anyone at the luncheon or anyone with a contact at the luncheon would have known of their arrangement, though they would not have known the specific details."

"Who is the friend?"

"A man named Dunphy. In import-export. Quite clean as far as we can see. Also quite prominent in the business community."

"Does Dunphy have any idea who might have done this?"

"None whatsoever. He was on his way to meet Crimmins when it happened. In fact, Crimmins was a few minutes early; Dunphy was stuck in the traffic on Piccadilly which resulted from Crimmins' murder."

"So he couldn't have done it himself."

"Oh no. And he has at least two reliable witnesses to testify to that fact."

"Did you talk to Dunphy personally?"

"Oh yes."

"What was his relationship to Crimmins?"

"There was no relationship at all, really. They attended university together some years before. Dunphy said they had seen one another once or twice over the years. They were just 'touching base' since Crimmins was in London."

"Keeping their options open for the future, in case one needed the other."

"So it seemed to me," she said. "Dunphy seemed sincerely disturbed by the news of Crimmins' death, but there was nothing in his behavior to suggest that he could have been connected with it."

"You had him followed, then."

"Certainly. That's quite routine. He simply went about his usual business of making large amounts of money. Mr. McGann has also had him investigated in Washington."

"I'll bet he has."

"Yes. Well, for what it is worth I believe that Mr. Crimmins' murder was a crime of passion."

"But a very calculated crime of passion."

"Yes. That's what makes it so very interesting. Have a look at this . . ."

She handed him the photograph of the murder weapon. He looked at it and put down the cookie in his other hand.

"Isn't that fascinating?" she said, picking up a butter cracker and biting into it hungrily.

"It looks very nasty."

"Oh it is," she said. "One would not wish to be impaled upon it."

"When can I see it?"

"Whenever you wish," she said, "but wouldn't you like to check in to your hotel first and have a shower?"

"I would," Frank said, "but . . ."

"Don't bother over the time," Harding said. "The murderer is gone. Back to Washington, I'd say, or possibly Los Angeles [pronouncing it *Los Angeleez*]; I'm certain of it. His mission has been accomplished. His quarry has been taken. Mr. Crimmins is no more."

"Unless there are others on his list."

"Possibly, but I very much doubt it," she said. "My advice is simple. I think you should learn as much as you can here and then get right back on his trail. Not that we want to send you packing. Quite the contrary. There are a number of things *I* should like to learn from you. I wonder, for example, if we might do that tonight, over dinner."

"I'll do it if you let me pay. I'm already heavily indebted to you . . ."

"Nonsense. I'll take you to your hotel. You can check in and have a shower and nap and then do some work. Here, I have a surprise for you."

She handed him a folder. He began to open it.

"The Crimmins file," she said, "the sum total of facts on the case. After you're rested you can study it. I'll pop round to the Yard and to Savile Row today and see if anything new has turned up. Later I'll swing round and pick you up for dinner. We can talk tonight and then start in tomorrow. There's someone I want to see and I think you should come along."

"Who is that?"

"An expert on swords. His name is Jaffee."

"Has he identified the murder weapon?"

"No, I haven't spoken with him yet. We'll do that tomorrow. First thing."

Frank finished his coffee. "This was really very nice of you," he said, reaching for his wallet.

"Hold your money, lieutenant," she said, smiling. "They don't charge me here. What kind of food would you like this evening?"

"Anything. Whatever you would like."

"Fine," she said.

"Could I ask you a question?"

"Certainly."

"Why have you gone to all of this trouble for me?"

"I spoke with your Captain Loram," she said. "Last night. I'm afraid I woke him up. He's not a very cheery fellow."

"No, but he's very good at what he does."

"That's what he said of you. You see, lieutenant, I have little interest in talking to men such as McGann or the twits from the embassy. I'm interested in one thing only: the solving of crimes. So, I believe, are you. You, I should say, are my counterpart. I am very protective of my time, lieutenant; I believe that working with you would not be a waste of it."

"One other question."

"What?" she said.

"Why don't they charge you here?"

"Would you really like to know?"

"Yes."

"Mrs. Watley's employer is a gentleman named Cranley. Charles Cranley. He and his wife own the Stanhope. Last January he was robbed and his wife was assaulted. Savagely assaulted, I might say. The Deputy Commissioner asked me to look into the case."

"And you arrested the criminal?"

"No," she said, "he resisted arrest. I was forced to *stop* him."

"You killed him?"

"Yes, I did."

"How, if I might ask? You don't carry a gun, do you?"

"As a matter of fact I have several guns; we all do, but I didn't shoot him. I struck him across the bridge of his nose with a steel rod. I thought that might catch his attention and he might come along quietly, but I was mistaken. He came at me in a mad rage. I stood aside, swung again, and shattered his right arm. He kept coming and I was forced to break his left leg. Finally I had to strike him across the chest. A blow directly to the heart. In point of fact, the actual origin of the term *coup de grace*—did you know that?"

"No, I didn't."

"Neither did he, I should say. It was very unfortunate that it happened that way."

"There was nothing else you could do, not if he kept resisting."

"I didn't mean killing him. That was quite the thing to do. Filthy bastard. He deserved every blow. I meant it was unfortunate that I had to kill him in a *French* manner."

EIGHT

McGann was fuming when Harding arrived at Savile Row Station. "We're in the midst of a murder case here and I can't reach you when I need to. I refuse to tolerate this lack of cooperation. What have you learned?"

"Good morning to you as well, Mr. McGann," she said. "Please talk to Sergeant Gered, won't you. I've asked him to provide you with all the information that we have."

"We want the killer caught, Inspector Harding. *Now*. Not tomorrow. Not next week. *Now*."

"As do we, Mr. McGann. I assure you we're doing all that we can."

"We have put the full resources of the United States Government at your disposal, Inspector, something that we do not do lightly. When we provide that level of cooperation we expect results. Promptly."

"And we are ever so grateful, Mr. McGann, but please check with Sergeant Gered, won't you?"

McGann shook his head and hurried out to Gered's desk. His chair was empty. "Where is Sergeant Gered?" he said to a constable named Lewis.

"He should be back straightaway, sir," Lewis said. McGann cursed under his breath and marched back down the hallway to the spot where he had spoken to Harding. When he got there she was gone. He stopped a young woman coming out of one of the interrogation rooms. "Have you seen Detective Inspector Harding?" he asked.

"No sir, but I'm sure she'll be back straightaway."

"God *damn* it," he said, as the young woman walked into the kitchenette and slowly poured herself a steaming cup of tea.

"Would you care for some tea, sir?" she asked. "I have both Darjeeling and English Breakfast."

"No, I would not," he said.

"The Darjeeling is quite good," she said.

"I'm sure it is," McGann said, pacing angrily. "I don't want tea; I want information."

"Then I'd suggest you speak to Sergeant Gered," she said.

The line at the Holiday Inn, Mayfair was short. Probably driven off by the prices, Frank thought. The room was pleasant enough and he liked the heated towel bar next to the bathtub. He took a hot shower, stepped onto the cool white-tile floor, wrapped up in the thick, heated towel, and walked back into the bedroom. He closed the double drapes, darkening the room, set his travel alarm to London time, allowed himself four hours to sleep, and fell across the bed.

Harding arrived at the Yard to find a message from the Deputy Commissioner. She took off her coat and called him. "Detective Inspector Harding for the Deputy Commissioner."

"One moment," his secretary said.

"McCarren here."

"You called, sir?"

"Yes. Did the chap from Los Angeles get in?"

"Yes, sir. He's at his hotel now. We discussed the case for approximately one hour; we're meeting tonight to talk further."

"What do you think, Harding?"

"The yanks are fluttering around the station, thinking we're not doing all that we might."

"Yes, especially that McGann fellow. We gave him a good stroking here, but he can't seem to get enough." McCarren raised his cup and took a sip of his coffee.

"I think we're dealing with someone very shrewd," Harding said. "If we run about in all directions looking for the odd clue we'll simply waste our time and allow him to get even farther ahead of us. If he does decide to kill again our best chance at stopping him is to attempt to think things through just as he does. We must get inside his clever little head. I don't think we'll catch him in a stupid mistake."

"Yes, quite. The yanks are anxious, of course, but they always are. Calling for whistles and bloodhounds."

"Yes. My own feeling is that our killer is already gone. We must do what we can, of course, and will. If he is indeed the yanks' problem, we'll do our bit and pitch in. Hands across the water and all that rubbish."

McCarren looked at the whiskey-flavored chocolate biscuit beside his saucer. He turned it over, inspecting it further. Then he nibbled at it. "I'll keep McGann busy with his sources in Washington," he said. "He may even come up with something. One never knows. You talk to the fellow from California and get back to me. He may have something from his end that could help."

"Yes, sir."

"I'm told he is quite good. Determined sort. Rather quiet but also rather firm. Black, isn't he?"

"Yes, he is. Looks a bit like the large fellow on the Birmingham football team. Rogers."

"Good lord, is he that big?"

"An inch taller perhaps, and just as broad."

"By the way, thank you for the photograph of the murder weapon and the copy of the doctor's report. The killer rather skewered him, wouldn't you say?"

"Yes, sir. A very unpleasant way to die, but the barbed sword *was* a lovely touch. The chap does have an imaginative streak."

"Helps hold our interest, wouldn't you say?"

"Yes, sir."

"Well, let's get on with it. Thanks ever so much."

"Good-bye, sir."

―――――

Frank awoke and called room service for a pot of coffee. "Regular or coffee Hag, sir?"

"What is coffee Hag?" he asked.

"Without the caffeine, sir." Accenting the word *caffeine* on the first syllable made it sound more stylish.

"Regular is fine."

"Very good, sir."

―――――

Frank finished the first cup of coffee and tried one of the wheat biscuits that accompanied it. It tasted like pressed sawdust with a coating of sand and ground glass. He drank a full glass of water to wash it down and then poured a fresh cup of coffee. His London map was spread across the table. He used a small plastic ruler to calculate distances. Starting at the Green Park station he traced a series of concentric circles with quarter mile, half mile, and mile diameters.

He was walking through the protocols; he already knew the conclusion: in little more than a matter of minutes the killer could be in Green Park, St. James's Park, or Hyde Park. He could be in the center of the dense pedestrian traffic on Oxford Street or hiding in any one of a dozen lanes, streets, rows, mewses, or alleys in Mayfair. The morning throngs covering the sidewalks in Piccadilly stretched out before him and those in Victoria Station were only a few minutes away.

The city was ringed with tube stops and railway stations. Driving against the morning traffic, Heathrow was little more than twenty-five minutes beyond Mayfair. Boats departed every few minutes from Westminster Pier to Greenwich or Hampton Court. There were taxis everywhere and hundreds of restaurants, hotels, coffee shops, sandwich bars, and tea rooms; there were endless churches, museums, parks, squares, flea markets, and brass rubbing centres. There were tourist centres, bookshops, sex stores, and partially occupied office buildings.

Frank poured a third cup of coffee and asked himself the obvious question: if he had just committed a violent murder in the midst of a crowd in the Green Park tube stop, where would he run?

The answer that followed was equally obvious: assuming he was not caught instantly, he would go any place he damned well pleased. Needles and haystacks were child's play; London was hard.

He picked up a second wheat biscuit, broke it in half and looked at the inside. He felt some of the crumbs that had fallen on the table, examining them with the tip of his index finger and wondering aloud, "How hungry would I have to be to eat another one of these?"

Green Park station was crowded; the busy Londoners there did not appreciate a Los Angeles policeman standing in their way, estimating distances and attempting to imagine the scene with the mind and eyes of a murderer. The killer had counted on all of that hurry and impatience. He knew that he was clever enough to impale Crimmins, then run through the large crowd in the station without attracting the slightest attention. But why do it there? Even if he was that skilled, why take the risk? He could have waited until Crimmins crossed the street and entered the Ritz. He could have killed him in an elevator or a cloak room, in a telephone booth or in a toilet stall. He could have taken him earlier, in his hotel room. Why in the tube stop? Why in public?

The answer was inescapable. He wanted an audience. Not to identify him and certainly not to catch him, but to observe the effects of the pointed and barbed weapon that he drove into Crimmins' entrails, to hear the screams, to see the blood flow and then pool and spread, to know that a violent murder had taken place. It was important that they saw and knew.

Frank checked his watch and saw that he could allow himself a few minutes for shopping. He walked down Piccadilly, looking for a shop that might have something he could buy for Marie. He crossed Old Bond Street and turned left into the Burlington Arcade. He looked at crystal and cashmere, silk and silver, wishing he could forget the limit on his VISA card. Moving from window to window, he stopped at a silversmiths named Poole's. In their window was a blue velvet panel covered with antique silver pins. He considered a tiny butterfly poised above a flower, then a curved hunter's horn. He looked at a kingfisher and a long-stemmed, sterling-silver rose. Finally he settled on a pin with a Scottish terrier in profile. Marie's family had had a Scottie when she was a child; she might like it. He handed the clerk his credit card without asking the price. She turned over the tiny card attached; it read £45.

She praised his choice, told him that the pin was of high quality, and wrapped it in lined gift paper with a gray ribbon. She took one of Poole's silver seals and attached it to the top of the box. The seal read:

Poole's of London
Purveyors of Fine Silver
Est. 1832.

Marie would like that.

He crossed Piccadilly, dodging the double-decker buses in their reserved lane, and went into Fortnum & Mason's to look for something for Jack. He thought about buying something for a gag present: a jar of jellied North Sea eels or potted larks' tongues, but they were too expensive to joke about. He looked around a little longer but couldn't settle on anything. He bought a two-pound tin of shortbreads for his aunt and uncle and some marmalade for Marie, looked at his watch, and realized he would have to hurry to get back to his hotel in time to meet Claire Harding.

NINE

Harding arrived at 6:00 sharp. "This is early for dinner in London, so we can go anywhere we'd like without having to worry about reservations. What would you like to eat?"

"Something I can't get in Los Angeles."

"Indigestion, perhaps?" she said, smiling. "England's really not that bad for food. You simply have to know where to go. I have a place that I think you'll like."

She drove through the West End, swinging south of Leicester Square and passing Covent Garden. The pedestrian traffic was already dense. She turned left on Drury Lane, heading north toward Great Queen Street. Frank noticed a crowd around the backstage door at Drury Lane theatre. Harding dodged a couple slinking out of a pub, shifted gears, and accelerated. Turning onto Great Queen Street, she immediately found a parking place near Freemasons Hall. "Here we are," she said.

"How did you do that?"

"Do what?"

"Find a parking place that easily."

"Oh, it's not as difficult as it appears." She nodded toward a row of buildings. "There's our restaurant."

Wedged between an Indian and a French restaurant on the north side of the street was a small place called Goldsmith's. "No relation to Oliver Goldsmith," she said. "It's English, not Irish."

The glass in the front window was beveled and the name of the restaurant was carved in the dark oak door. There were freshly cut wildflowers on the mint-and-matches table.

"This looks very nice," Frank said.

"Their specialty is Scottish beef." Harding pronounced it *spec-i-al-i-ty*.

She approached the maitre d'. "Some place in the back, Harry, if it's no trouble," she said.

"Certainly, Inspector," the maitre d' said.

"They know you in all of these places, don't they?" Frank said.

"Only the good ones."

"I have a friend in Los Angeles named Grant," Frank said. "He and I have a restaurant circuit that we travel—places where we've stopped fights or holdups, calmed down angry drunks, or persuaded walkouts to return and pay their checks."

"And your meals are always free."

"Yes, but with the understanding that we'll go on duty the minute they have a problem they want us to handle. We're like floating house detectives."

"Fair enough."

The waiter came to take drink orders. "How about some musty old whiskey?" Harding asked.

"That sounds good," Frank said.

"The Macallan forty-five-year-old," she said. "Doubles for each of us, in large glasses."

"This is wonderful," Frank said, sipping it slowly.

"Would you like another?" Harding asked. "You can have it for dessert also, if you like."

"I may," Frank said.

The waiter returned to take dinner orders. "Shall I?" she asked.

"Yes," he said.

"We'll start with the smoked salmon, then have the sirloin. Medium rare? [Frank nodded yes.] Do go easy on the vegetables, won't you?"

"Yes, madam," the waiter said.

"How is the trifle tonight?"

"Very nice, madam."

"We'll have that. You will use the good sherry, won't you?"

"Yes, madam."

"Then some coffee, some stilton and biscuits, and the old Cockburn's."

"And for claret, madam?"

"Do you have some Palmer?"

"Yes, madam, and it's exceptional."

"Fine. We'll do the Palmer. Open it now, will you?"

"Certainly."

———

"This is very, very nice," Frank said.

"Yes, it is, isn't it? They'll never get the vegetables right, but then, who really cares about them?" She ate a large piece of beef and washed it down with the red wine, then cut another piece, that one larger than the first.

"So, are we on for Jaffee in the morning?"

"Yes, at 9:30. His shop opens at 10:00 and he's agreed to meet with us first."

"And he's an expert on swords?" Frank asked.

"*The* expert on swords," she answered. "I haven't yet met him. The Deputy Commissioner tells me he is quite fascinating. They used him on a case some six or seven years ago."

"A murder case?"

"No, a theft. A rather serious theft, I might say. They burgled the Duke of Argyle's estate at Inverary, then attempted to sell the goods in London."

Frank finished his glass of wine and the steward poured a second.

"It's quite lovely, isn't it?" Harding said. "A little young yet, but I rather like it that way."

"It's wonderful."

"The English love wine, you know. The French do the work and in return the English offer them their appreciation."

Frank smiled.

"Shall we talk about your late congressman?" Harding asked.

"There's not a great deal to tell," Frank said. "He was recently elected for a first term. Prior to that he worked in Washington as a lobbyist for various trade associations. He had spent a short time in government after he graduated from college and he was able to capitalize on that experience for years."

"Why the sudden career change?"

"Probably to boost his career as a lobbyist. Michael Crimmins has never been known for his dedication to public service. One or two terms in congress and his minimum retainer would jump several orders of magnitude. He could make new contacts, work his way through the newest list of Washington influentials, and collect a new set of i.o.u.'s."

"Also make himself attractive to much richer clients."

"Exactly. It's not really a career change, more of a career boost. His old contacts are thinning out. He's returning to the well. For him, the well is any place where he can upgrade and polish his image. That's why he was in London—to get his picture taken. In the short run he wanted to warm the hearts of the voters from his district, but Crimmins would be thinking ahead also—trying to raise his profile in the ranks of the influence peddlers."

"An exercise in self-promotion."

"Yes, and little more as far as I can see."

"Who would want to kill such a man?"

"The taxpayers, if they understood how the system really worked," Frank said.

"He appears to have been quite innocuous," Harding said. "Corrupt in conventional ways, of course, but not the sort to attract the attentions of a professional assassin."

"No, just the odd television journalist or investigative reporter." Frank thought to himself that he was starting to speak British English. He checked and made sure he still had his fork in his right hand.

"That's what I thought," she said, "so who would want to kill him?"

"An unhappy client? Someone who couldn't forget a broken promise or a lie? Try some basic scenarios: Crimmins promises a man a government job in return for a serious favor; the man delivers on his end and when he shows up for work Crimmins suddenly develops selective amnesia. Or how about this: Crimmins takes some under-the-table support in return for a vote. When the bill in question comes up before the House, Crimmins suddenly comes down with a twenty-four-hour virus. The money man gets cheated and he can't appeal to anyone official, since the contribution was illegal to begin with. You want me to go on?"

"Why not?"

"OK. Crimmins agrees to support a bill in return for some small consideration, but he already knows that several of his colleagues intend to attach a rider to the bill which will poison it. Crimmins casts his aye vote, but the president vetoes the bill and it dies faster than a two-dollar goldfish—as they all knew it would. They had no real interest in passing a law; their purpose was to force the president to say no to something and sacrifice a portion of his political capital. Crimmins and his congressional cloakroom friends indulge in some self-congratulation and then go get a subsidized haircut and a subsidized lunch. They bounce a check or two at their private bank, send out some self-serving mail on franked envelopes, order their staffs to do their next day's work for them, and quickly forget the fact that everybody else is being shorted: the constituents back home, the local and federal taxpayers, the political left and right, the young and the old, the black and the white, the rich and the poor . . . the whole damned country—the north, the south, the east, and the west. In good times people have a way of overlooking the cracks in the system. In tough times it's different; people get angry. Maybe this time somebody did something about it."

"Plunging a piece of steel into his entrails would be a rather extreme solution, but it *would* have the advantage of being a final one."

"Yes, but the problem is that the average person—no matter how angry or outraged—would lack the skill and the wherewithal to kill him in that manner. The problem is that it doesn't look like a contract killing either."

"No, it does seem rather a risky method for an amateur to attempt."

"That's right. Of course, the mob always likes to send a clear message, but if they want to see you dead they generally just shove an ice pick in your heart or fire a bullet into your ear."

"Perhaps they decided to make an exception for your congressman."

"Always a possibility."

"What about his personal life—anything there?"

"Crimmins was divorced six or seven years ago. Standard California settlement: fifty-fifty. No kids. I don't know of any other involvements. His *mother* likes him. He used her in two of his campaign commercials."

"You're joking."

"No, I'm not."

"What on earth are you yanks doing with the traditions we handed on to you?" Harding asked, smiling.

"Don't ask."

She held the smile but only briefly. "I'm certain of two things," she said. "First, we need to know a great deal more before we can hope to find Mr. Crimmins' killer." She cut another slice of sirloin and took a sip of the claret.

"And what's the second thing?" Frank asked.

"That I must ring up my wine merchant and have him send round a case of this Palmer."

———

"What do you think of the trifle?" she asked.

"Subtler than what we get in the states. Not as sloppy and sweet. The good sherry helps too."

"Yes, quite. We'll have some cheese and biscuits and then the port. I'm certain you'll enjoy it. Food is my one indulgence. I love to share it with someone who appreciates it."

———

Halfway through the stilton and biscuits Frank looked at his watch. "What do you expect from Jaffee?" he asked.

"The weapon is the only piece of physical evidence that links us to the killer," Harding said. "It's the only thing we have that can help us sketch out a profile of him. We may be able to find him before he kills a second time."

"You think that he might kill again?"

"Oh, I know that he will."

TEN

"*That is an act* of hate," Charles White said.

"What do you mean?" Jack asked Frank's uncle. "Every murder but a contract killing has some hate involved in it."

They were sitting on the wooden deck that Charles had just built off of his kitchen. Jack was opening the first bottle in the second six-pack of Tecate; Charles was cutting large slices from a wheel of Sonoma Jack pepper cheese.

"Some people kill in a moment of passion and some kill because they think they're on some kind of mission, but this was a matter of hate, Jack. When I was in Korea they talked about hate. They did in Vietnam too, but it's not the same thing. Defending your own land is different from seeing a man punished and shamed. Now, you look at old Bull Connor—that was a man who could hate. You knock a man down with a high-pressure hose, flip him over and wash him down the street, turn dogs on him to rip his clothes . . . now that is hate. You want to take something away besides his life, maybe his manhood, maybe his humanity itself. That's your real goal. And *that* is hate.

"Now you take the late Congressman Crimmins. Somebody wanted him dead, but whoever wanted him dead wanted something else too. If you give me an edged weapon—I don't care what it is, a letter opener, a knife, a sharpened spoon handle—I can take a man's life very quickly and very efficiently. And I can do it with a minimum of pain for the victim."

"Here, Charles," Jack said, handing him another Tecate.

"Thanks," he said, cutting some more of the Jack cheese. "Now, as I was saying, I can kill a man very efficiently with an edged instrument, but there wouldn't be any hate involved. Now, you add hate and you get something like what the congressman took. That was a specially made weapon, one-of-a-kind. It was designed to hurt that man, not just kill him. It was designed to take more away than just his life."

"I think it was designed to attract attention too," Jack said. "Why go to that much trouble? Why take such a risk by killing Crimmins in such a public place? Whoever killed him wanted to make sure that the killing didn't go unnoticed. He wanted headlines."

"I don't know about that," Charles said. "You could attract a lot more attention if you wanted to. Hang him from the bottom of one of those London bridges. Drive up and drop off his body in front of Buckingham Palace. If you felt like you had to cut him, you could slice open his neck and prop him up in the archbishop's chair in Westminster Abbey. *That* would catch the tourists' attention. In that town you'd have a lot of choices, Jack. Hell, you could tie his body to the front of one of those tour boats down on the river. Or lash him to the back of one of those lions at Trafalgar Square. Let him greet the tour buses when they pulled up in the morning. If you wanted to do something for nature you could fill his ears and mouth and clothes full of birdseed and feed him to the pigeons at the same time. Choices, Jack. Plenty of choices in *that* town. On any given day there are 200,000 people in L.A. who don't live here. How many are there in London? If you wanted to kill somebody in such a way as to attract the maximum amount of attention, you could do a hell of a job there."

"That's true, Charles, you could. But the killer didn't. Maybe having him eaten by pigeons would have been a little over-the-top. What do you think?"

"Depends on the hate, Jack. That could be a merciful way to go. It all depends on the hate. I was driving by the schoolyard the other day, just down the street, off of Hill. There was this kid there, wearing a thousand dollars worth of clothes, walking around the edge of the playground. I slowed down and pulled over, parked, and got out of the car. 'Could I help you, young man?' I asked. 'What the fuck do you want, old man?' he said, strutting around, flashing his palms at me and showing off his jewelry and shoes. 'You appear to be lost,' I said. 'You couldn't have any business around a schoolyard full of children. I thought I could give you some directions.' He looked at me and there was some top-of-the-line hate in his eyes. He clenched his teeth and said, 'If you think you be dissin' me, I'll cut out your heart and piss on it, motherfucker.' And, you know, they like to stretch out the *motherfucker*—add another syllable or two and hit it with an extra accent toward the end—give it a kind of ripple effect. *Mo-th-er-fuck-k-her*."

Jack smiled and shook his head. "And what happened to this poor young gentleman, Charles?"

"Well, he got out this ivory-handled gravity knife and flicked it open. He pointed it at my eyes and threatened me again. He called me a few names, including some I hadn't heard in awhile, and he told me I had five seconds to get the fuck out of his sight or he'd start cutting on me."

"And I bet you didn't leave. You probably just stood there, dissed him a little more, and then took away his knife."

"I did for a fact."

"And probably broke his wrist in the process."

"The wrist did go. That is true."

"And a few fingers."

"Only three."

"And then you hit him."

"Only once—in the stomach. I wanted to take away his breath so he couldn't use any more of that foul language around the children."

"And then *he* left."

"No, then he coughed. And then he bent over in pain. And then he threw up his breakfast all over those pretty white shoes. *Then* he left. But you see my point, don't you? He said he'd cut out my *heart*. He wanted more than just my life. That was hate, Jack."

"But you've got to have more than just hate," Jack said. "You've got to be able to deliver. Whoever took out Crimmins had more than hate. He had skill. He was very accomplished at what he was trying to do."

"Not bad at all, I'd say," Charles responded. He picked up one of the Tecate bottles by the neck, put the base against his body, then thrust it out at arm's length and jerked it straight up. "He had to move quickly and precisely. That weapon would be a lot heavier than an empty bottle of beer. He would need strength in his wrist and fingers. And there were no second chances. No mulligans, Jack. One shot is all he got."

"He made good use of it—assuming you're happy to see the congressman gone."

"I hate to see anyone die like that," Charles said, "but then I didn't hate him. If I had I might have given that little sword an extra shove."

ELEVEN

FRANK PUT DOWN HIS cracker. "That is very good, by the way. The stilton is smooth, almost creamy; the kind we get back home is usually dry and crumbly. Now, what did you mean when you said you knew that Crimmins' murderer would kill again?"

"I've been holding out on you," she said.

He stared at her without responding.

"Actually, I just found out today. They finally finished all of the tests on the murder weapon and cleaned it up. They found it right on the end of the tang—on the tip. It was quite small. Here . . ."

She opened her purse and handed Frank a photograph. "It's been enlarged, so it's a bit grainy."

"It looks like lettering," Frank said.

"The laboratory staff looked at it under the microscope. There's no doubt about the letters. They spell out the word *One*," Harding answered.

"Number one in a series?"

"Oh, I think so," she said. "I'll be interested to hear what Jaffee has to say, of course, but I'm certain this is a unique weapon. I've never seen or read of anything like it. Whatever that *One* is, it is definitely not a model number. There's something else too. Notice that he didn't just draw the arabic numeral, 1. That could have been misread or misinterpreted. He spelled it out to make sure we would understand his intention."

"What would you call that—an act of bravado?"

"Perhaps," she said. "It all depends upon his intention, wouldn't you say? If he wanted us to know that the death of the congressman was only the first step in his plans, I would say that labeling the weapon was a very effective touch."

"Generally the competent murderers attempt to escape attention, not attract it. The nuts like it, of course, but they usually admit to the crimes as well—whether they actually committed them or not."

"Perhaps we have a competent murderer who is also a bit off," Harding said.

"That would be a dangerous combination."

"Yes, but a terribly interesting one, wouldn't you say?"

"There's nothing related to this case that I would consider dull," Frank said, "except possibly the late congressman."

"He may be a symbol only; the real target might be the system itself. Perhaps he intends to kill all of your congressmen."

"How big a number would fit on the tip of the sword handle?" Frank asked.

"It's large enough to cover the whole lot," Harding said.

The waiter brought the port. Harding tasted hers and nodded approvingly. "You'll like this very much."

Frank tasted his, smiled, and put the glass down. "Is there anything else that you haven't told me?"

"No, no," she said. "I hope you didn't think that was an act of *bravado* on my part. I really didn't know about the lettering until this afternoon and I did want you to enjoy your meal first."

"I'm really not surprised," Frank said. "Considering the trouble he went to for Crimmins' death, it would almost be a pity if he had stopped there."

"Exactly my thought," Harding said. "Not that I like to see blood spilled, but if people are going to kill *anyway*, I consider it thoughtful that they do it in an interesting way. After all, so much of our work *is* drudgery and routine. It helps hold the attention."

"Excuse me for a second," Frank said.

―――――

He returned in ten minutes. His port glass had been refilled. "I let the people in L.A. know that there may be more killings in the future."

"How very thoughtful. And did you talk to your friend Mr. Grant?"

"As a matter of fact I was able to reach him too; why do you ask?"

"You told me that Mr. Grant is your dining companion; I thought you might have told him about our dinner. Food is my passion, remember?"

"I told him about it and he told me to get back to work. He was with my Uncle Charles; Charles told me to get back to work too."

"They sound like a dour pair."

"They're terrible, both of them," Frank said, smiling.

"You're not serious."

"No, not really. Jack and Charles are actually very nice, considering."

"What do you mean, *considering*?"

"Jack was a career military officer; he was wounded in Vietnam and retired after twenty years of service. He works as a private investigator now, doing insurance work mostly. From time to time he and I are able to work together. He always holds up his end. My uncle was a career soldier also. He was never wounded seriously. I can't say the same for those who fought against him."

"Was your uncle a commando?"

"We don't use the term, but yes, he was—that and more. Charles was the most highly decorated enlisted man in Korea. He was also in Vietnam . . . for three tours. He was nominated for the Medal of Honor three times. "

"But he never *got* the Medal of Honor?"

"He only got one."

"*Only?*"

"He deserved three. Two of the nominations were initiated by the soldiers in his platoon. The one that he actually received was initiated by his brigade commander, whose life Charles had saved."

"What actually happened?"

"The commander, his staff, and the remains of a chopped-up company were pinned down by sniper fire on the edge of a village which the RVN's had claimed was friendly. They were cut off from the rest of their unit and the enemy had each of their possible escape routes covered by mortar and automatic weapons fire. Charles neutralized the enemy forces and enabled them to rejoin their unit."

"How did he do that?"

"He garrotted each of the snipers and marked the location of the other forces with a smoke canister. He escaped just moments before the tactical air strikes came in. The kills had to be silent and the air strikes had to be timed to the second."

"Or he would have been killed as well."

"Yes."

"What does your uncle do now?"

"Charles? Mostly he reads and exercises. He helps my aunt around the house. From time to time he gets involved in cases with Jack or me. Sometimes with the two of us together."

"No hobbies? In England he would have a hobby."

"He does have a hobby."

"What kind?"

"He likes to guard playgrounds."

TWELVE

Harding picked up Frank at 9:00. When he got in the police sedan he noticed the long package resting on the back seat. They arrived at Stanley Jaffee's shop on the west side of Chancery Lane at 9:25. Harding parked in front, picked up the package and carefully locked the car. Jaffee was on the second floor, above a silversmith and a wine merchant. There was a doorbell below a modest brass sign: S. Jaffee: Antique Weaponry. Harding pushed it. After a few seconds the door opened; they were greeted by a thin young man in gray slacks and a mismatched, wrinkled, blue shirt. His belt was several sizes too large and its tip hung down the front of his pants.

"Detective Inspector Harding?" he said to Frank, suspiciously.

"That's me," Claire said.

"Oh yes, quite," the boy said. "Mr. Jaffee is having his breakfast. Would you care to join him?"

"Yes, thank you," Claire said.

He led them up the stairs. "Just through there," he said, pointing to a door at the end of a short hallway. Harding knocked and a high-pitched voice answered, "Come in."

Stanley Jaffee was a stout man with straw-colored hair, red cheeks, and thick, puffy fingers that curled toward the center of his palms. He was wearing a bow tie and a white shirt with a pocket full of pens and miniature rulers; he was seated at the end of a long oak table that adjoined his desk. He gestured at Frank and Claire with his curved fingers. "Sit down, sit down," he said. "Can I offer you some breakfast? There are still some kippers and bacon, a fried egg or two and some grilled tomatoes. I'm afraid I've just finished off the sausages."

"I would like coffee," Claire said, "if it's no trouble."

"And for me," Frank said.

Jaffee yelled, "Gerald." The young man with the wrinkled shirt appeared at the door. His stringy hair was hanging over his right eye. He brushed it back with his right hand but most of it fell over his eye again and when it did he left it there.

"Would you be so good as to get us some coffee?"

"Two more?"

"Yes."

Gerald turned to leave and Jaffee said, "There's a good lad."

A minute later the introductions were completed and Gerald returned with a china pot and two additional cups and saucers. He carried them in his hands, without using a tray. "Would you like milk or sugar?" he asked. They both said no and he left, closing the door behind him.

Frank was scanning the room. Two of the paneled walls were covered with makeshift bookshelves. The contents appeared to be in total disarray. Many of the books were stacked on their sides and a noticeable number were shelved upside down. There were protruding notes, clippings, pictures, and other loose materials that were ready to fall from the shelves at any moment. On the opposite walls were swords and foils, resting uneasily on wooden pegs. As Gerald entered and left the room, Frank noticed that the swords moved slightly. Beneath each of them was a yellowed identification card. Some time in the past each card had been carefully lettered in black ink. At the end of the table was an iron safe and on top of it were two walnut display chests with glass tops. The first contained a highly ornamented cavalry sword, the second a pair of pistols with ivory handles and inlaid gold.

"So you've come for free advice, is that it?" Jaffee asked.

"Yes," Claire said. "You're very kind to see us."

"Nonsense, I'm happy to do so. McCarren tells me you have an interesting case."

Harding raised the package from her lap and placed it on the table.

"Ah," Jaffee said, "you've brought it. Let's have a look." He picked up his breakfast dish and put it on his desk, then reached out eagerly toward her with his curled fingers.

It was wrapped in brown paper and secured with two pieces of heavy twine. Jaffee took it carefully, set it down in front of him, and reached in his pocket. He took out a small knife with a mother-of-pearl handle, slipped the blade under the twine and cut it instantly. He cut the twine at the other end, carefully closed the knife, and returned it to his pocket. Then he unfolded the brown paper like a mother pulling back the corners of a blanket from the face of her child.

He spread the paper flat and examined the weapon. For a second he looked at Claire and Frank but remained silent. Then he lifted the weapon to the light, turning it slowly in his hands. He got up from his chair and walked around behind his desk, going through the side drawers there. His frustration increasing, he called out, "Gerald."

The boy appeared at the door. "Yes, Mr. Jaffee?"

"Where *is* my magnifying glass? I can't find it anywhere."

Gerald walked over to the desk, moved some loose sheets of paper, and said, "Here, sir."

"Thank you, Gerald," Jaffee said, as the boy walked toward the door. "You are really quite indispensable, you know."

"Yes sir, thank you sir," Gerald said. The words were formulaic.

"Now," Jaffee said, "let's have a closer look."

He studied the weapon for at least ten minutes, hurrying back and forth between the reference books on his desk and those on a distant shelf. He jotted down notes and did some crude drawings. Then he returned to the weapon and went over it a second time, and a third, with the magnifying glass. Frank wondered why Jaffee would keep important reference books on a shelf at the opposite end of the room, but after witnessing the search for the magnifying glass he didn't ask.

Finally Jaffee broke the silence. "This is quite remarkable. *Quite* [stretching out every syllable] *re-mark-a-ble*. Inspector Harding and Lieutenant White, I must tell you that I am not a person who is easily given to hyperbole. I see interesting things every day; rare objects pass through my hands like so many cabbages at a greengrocer's stall. Many of the pieces that I see are accounted priceless and a good many of them actually are, but what you have brought me today is something quite special indeed. What do you know about swords?"

"Very little, Mr. Jaffee," Claire said.

"Here, have a look." he sketched quickly on the back of an envelope. "The classic sword consists of two basic structures: the hilt and the blade. The hilt usually consists of a guard—sometimes a highly ornamented one, a grip, and a pommel. The Spaniards do love their guards, as do the Italians. The blade, of course, consists of a point and an edge, sometimes several edges. The sword is designed to inflict damage either through cutting or thrusting. Many, of course, are capable of doing both.

"This particular weapon, which was used to dispatch the American congressman, consists of an extremely interesting blade portion and a simple tang. Its use would require some strength and skill, since the leverage usually afforded by a grip and pommel is not available."

He paused, picked up his magnifying glass again, and reexamined the weapon. As he did he shook his head from side to side. "Fascinating," he said, "simply fascinating . . ." He opened several of the reference books and stacked them one on top of the other. "The basic structure of the instrument is that of the stiletto with quadrangular blade. Each edge has been sharpened for maximum effect. I've always liked the stiletto, what with all its associations and lore. Vengeance and all that. A very personal weapon. I remember as a child reading of such things . . . swarthy figures with capes, aching to settle scores . . ."

"You were speaking about the blade, Mr. Jaffee," Claire said.

"Yes, sorry. Look here. You see these barbs?"

"Yes," she said.

"Quite effective. Here . . ." He opened one of the reference books and showed them a line drawing. "In the South Pacific, sword blades have been fitted with actual sharks' teeth. The Australians have used flints and the Mexicans obsidian. Here, just a moment . . ."

He walked the length of the table, spun the combination dial to four numbers, and opened the door of his safe. "Have a look at this." He pulled out a blue velvet case, opened it, and held up the sword that it enclosed. "This is Mexican from the fifteenth century. The sword itself is actually wood, but it has been fitted with subsidiary blades of black obsidian."

He put the sword back in its case, returned it to the safe, locked it, and spun the dial. "Here, look at this," he said, picking up a book. "This is old Burton. See the weapon there, on the left. That is a dagger-sword from Unyoro, on the northern shores of the Nyanza Lake—we would say Lake Victoria. The blade is four-sided, quite effective for both cutting *and* thrusting. And look here . . ."

He held up the magnifying glass. "You see those slots along the sides of the blades?"

They both nodded yes.

"Italian. The holes and grooves were designed to contain poison. You see, the sort of people who use edged weapons have always liked to have what you yanks would call back-up systems."

Frank smiled politely.

"But these are different. What appear to be standard holes and grooves are actually small channels cut into the four blades; my guess is that they were designed to enable the blood to flow more easily. Certainly they would accomplish that purpose."

"How would you actually describe that weapon?" Claire asked.

"Good question," Jaffee said. "It appears at first to be quite eclectic, but it's not simply a succession of references to earlier styles. The person who made that weapon—and whoever that person was, he was quite expert—took the features of a number of earlier weapons and combined them for his own quite precise purposes."

"Which were?" Claire asked.

"To penetrate the body of his victim as deeply and as violently as possible, to make the removal of the weapon both difficult and, shall we say, counterproductive, and to increase and facilitate the flow of the victim's blood. This is a very efficient instrument of death, Inspector. Also a very *basic* weapon. Edged weapons always are. The personal touch, you see. Not the anonymity of a bullet hurtling through space. The adversaries peer into one another's eyes, then one dies at the other one's hands."

"You said that the basic structure is that of the stiletto with quadrangular blade?" Frank asked.

"Yes," Jaffee said, "and that's quite symbolic as well, but the symbolism has largely been lost, what with the possibilities now afforded by modern medicine."

"What do you mean?" Frank asked.

"Such a weapon was said to be capable of inflicting a wound that would not heal."

———

"By the way," Claire asked, "did you notice the lettering on the tip of the tang?"

"Yes, isn't that interesting?" Jaffee answered. "I wonder if he'll use a different weapon the next time. He'll have to work hard to outdo this effort, of course. Did you notice the balance?" He lifted it above the table, using his palm as the fulcrum, his curled fingers nearly caressing the edges of the blades. "And the weight? The weight is simply sublime."

"You understand that I must return it promptly," Claire said.

"Certainly, certainly, but just a few photographs first? I'll not publish them, of course."

"I don't see any harm," she said, "particularly when you've been so very helpful."

"Gerald," he called. "Bring all of the cameras and lights."

THIRTEEN

GERALD SNAPPED THE PHOTOGRAPHS as Jaffee directed him. "There . . . one more from that angle . . . now let me turn it . . . yes . . . and from above . . . come in close now . . . get the whole thing, Gerald . . . now just the point . . . close on the grooved slots . . . yes . . . and the lettering on the end of the tang . . . do you see it? . . . more light . . . yes . . ."

———

"Thank you so very much," Jaffee said to Claire later, after they had finished.

"Thank *you*," she said. "We are in *your* debt."

"Could I ask you to do one more thing?" Frank asked.

"What is it?"

"I would like to summarize what you have told us and I would like you to tell me whether or not my summary is accurate."

"Certainly. Proceed."

Frank read from his notebook. "What we have in this weapon is a homemade, tempered steel sword, approximately two-thirds normal size. It includes the characteristics of several different types of swords, both ancient and modern, and those characteristics were all designed to enable whoever used it to inflict the precise kind of mortal wound suffered by Michael Crimmins. The sharpened point would allow for quick penetration. The barbs on the sword's four edges would increase the damage done and add to the blood flow as well as magnify the results of the wound if someone were to attempt to remove the weapon from the dying man's body. The grooved slots would enable the blood to flow more easily, so that death would follow quickly, assuming a vital organ was not pierced by the initial thrust, again frustrating any possible attempts to save the victim. Symbolically at least, the wound was intended to be one that would not heal. Finally, whoever used the weapon may well have chosen it in order to personalize the action. The killer was doing more than simply taking a life; he was expressing some deep emotion—hatred perhaps, or a desire for revenge. However, given the lettering on the weapon, it is also likely that the killer will kill again, perhaps in a similar manner. Would you say that that is an accurate summary of what you have told us, Mr. Jaffee?"

"I would say that your summary is closer to the facts than my own comments, lieutenant. The length might be an inch or two less than two-thirds normal size, but what is normal size with an eclectic weapon? You are a very astute man, lieutenant. Do you know armament well?"

"No, Mr. Jaffee, not really, but I know murderers."

"That was useful, don't you think?" Claire said, as she closed the door of her sedan.

"Yes, very."

"You're starting to sound British," she said.

"It's hard to keep from doing it," Frank said.

Claire smiled. "How about some breakfast? I'm starved."

"I could drink some more coffee," Frank said.

She turned onto Fleet Street, passed St. Clement Danes and the line of taxis waiting for the solicitors and barristers of Chancery Lane, and turned into the Aldwych semicircle. When she reached the west side she stopped and parked. "Let's try the Waldorf," she said. "They do a nice breakfast and they're right here."

―――――

"Are you sure you won't have something besides coffee?" she asked.

"No thanks," Frank said. "Coffee's fine."

The waiter was standing behind her, smiling formally. "I'll start with the fresh orange juice," she said. "Then bring me . . . let's see . . . fried eggs and sausage, a brioche with butter and marmalade, and coffee."

"White, madam?"

"Yes."

"And for you, sir?"

"Coffee with milk, yes."

"Anything else, madam?"

"Not just yet," she said.

―――――

"You're leaving for Los Angeles, aren't you?"

"Eventually, of course," Frank said.

"No, I mean today, or tomorrow at the latest."

"Why do you say that?"

"Because you keep looking at the clock on the far wall."

"It's a very handsome clock."

"Not that handsome. Anyway, I think you *should* go. There's nothing left for you to learn here. I have a copy of the Crimmins file for you back at the Yard. I'll let you know as soon as anything else breaks here, but I think it's over."

"No one else in the trade delegation was touched," Frank said. "They've all gone home. If one of them killed Crimmins I won't find him here. If Crimmins' death had no connection with their meeting—which seems most likely—then I have to look for something new, something in Crimmins' present or past life. That means L.A. or Washington."

"Why do you think he was killed *here*? I agree with what you say, but I just don't see the London connection."

"I don't either," Frank answered, "but I don't think I'm going to find it here. Maybe you will."

"I'll try," she answered. "You can be sure of that. How about one last cup of coffee?"

"That sounds good," Frank said, as she signaled the waiter. "Let me just make a phone call in the meantime."

The traffic was completely stalled at Trafalgar Square and slow the length of Whitehall. "You're not going to make a plane today," Claire said.

"I go out tomorrow," Frank said, as she approached Parliament Square and signaled for a right turn.

"I'll just be a minute," she said, when they arrived at her office. "I've got your copy of the file locked in my drawer." She opened the door to her office. McGann was sitting on the top of her desk.

"Well, at last," he said.

"Hello, Mr. McGann, I see that my staff have already asked you to make yourself comfortable."

"They told me you were meeting with a weapons expert. Why was I not informed?"

"You'll receive a full report," she said.

"Who is this?" he asked, staring hard at Frank.

Frank stepped forward and extended his hand. "Frank White, Lieutenant, LAPD: robbery/homicide."

"What are you doing here?" he asked, not taking Frank's hand.

"Congressman Crimmins was a Los Angeles resident. I'm here to investigate his murder for the City."

"This is a federal matter, White. You're out of here. Go back to La-La Land."

"Did you actually say *La-La Land*?"

"Don't get smart. If you or your boss have any questions, send them to the Justice Department, in writing. Now, if you don't mind, I've got business with *Ms*. Harding and you just became a tourist."

Frank didn't move. He looked down at McGann, sitting on the desk.

"Didn't you hear me?" McGann asked.

"What did you say your name was?"

"The name is McGann."

"How about the first name?"

"Chet."

"You mean Chester?"

"Look, White, don't give me any crap to impress the lady."

"Oh, I assure you, Mr. McGann, I'm not impressed at all," Claire said.

Frank leaned forward and whispered several sentences in McGann's ear. McGann's face dropped. Then Frank turned to Claire. "Could I see you outside?" he asked.

"Of course," she said.

They walked out in the hallway beyond her office. "Could you send the file over to my hotel?" he asked. "I don't think McGann has to know that you made a copy for me."

"Certainly," she said, "as soon as I get rid of him. Just one question..."

"Yes?"

"What did you whisper to him just now?"

"I wouldn't repeat it in front of a lady," Frank said.

"Repeat it in front of a fellow professional."

"Are you sure you want to hear it?"

"Of course."

Frank paused for a second. "You realize that this is police talk."

"Yes, of course, what did you say?"

"You really want to know?"

"I won't let you leave until you tell me."

"All right. I told him if he gave me or the LAPD any more of this Washington crap I'd hoist him in the air by his throat and hold him there until he danced like Howdy Doody. He was a marionette on a puppet show."

"I figured so," she said.

"I also mentioned that if he gave *you* any more trouble I would personally hunt him down and pound on his face and body until he was covered with more blood and shit than his friend the congressman. Or at least words to that effect."

"*Jolly good*," she said, kissing Frank on the cheek. "You'll have that report within the hour."

"Thanks for everything," Frank said.

"Stay in touch," Claire answered. "I mean that."

FOURTEEN

CROSSING BERKELEY STREET TO the Mayfair Hotel Bar, Frank thought about the killer escaping through these same streets just a few days earlier. He turned for a second at the corner of Stratton Street, trying to hear silent footsteps and trying to catch the scent of a dead man's blood. An hour before he had received the Crimmins file, read it, and faxed copies of the most important documents back to his captain. It was 6:30 A.M. in Los Angeles, but Loram was there to receive them on his private machine.

The Mayfair Bar was dark walnut and frosted glass, with Victorian sporting prints, polished wooden tables, and white china ashtrays. Frank ordered a pint of bitter, finished it quickly, and ordered a second. It was smooth and cellar-temperature cool, just like the first. The waiter also refilled his white, plastic tray with Brazil nuts, filberts, and cashews. Frank took a deep drink of the second pint and thought about where they now stood in the matter of the death of the peoples' servant, Michael Crimmins.

Half way into the third pint it struck him that there had been a similar case in the early eighties. The first victim's name had been Demmler. His body was found high in the San Gabriels on a cold Monday morning in early February. The coroner's report stated that he had died of exposure and, indeed, he had, but the man responsible for William Demmler's death had broken both his knees and his hands with a thirty-two inch Adirondack baseball bat made of fine-grained white ash. Demmler had been left on the side of a 4,000-foot mountain with his broken hands and knees, the clothes on his back, and two, simple choices: to lay down and die or to attempt to crawl through ten miles of snow, rock, and icy underbrush to the spur of a one-lane dirt road.

The bat was ten yards from his body when he was found. He had tried to crawl on his knees and elbows and had given up quickly. There were other footprints found in the area, but they were from new, untraceable Kmart boots. There was no other physical evidence.

For a year nothing else was learned. Then, suddenly, a second body was found, this time in the Mojave. The man's name was Brownley. Again, the victim's hands and knees were broken and again there was a thirty-two-inch Adirondack baseball bat left at the murder scene. It appeared that the victim had tried to fashion some kind of flag, using the bat and a blood-stained section of his T-shirt to signal pilots or dune buggy drivers. Part of another man's footprints had escaped the blowing sands; the shoe that made it was new, an Adidas knockoff from Kmart.

Once Brownley's body was found the killer was arrested in a week and a half. The story made the front page of the *Times* for three days. It was the kind that made you wonder why God would soil his creation by making human beings a part of it.

Thirteen years earlier the two victims had been manager and coach of a Little League team in Clarkson, Oklahoma. To discipline their players when they made mistakes, Demmler and Brownley had developed a simple punishment. They made the players who had let the team down stand alone in center field, while the manager, coach and other players yelled and cursed at them. Those who refused to participate were forced to join the players in the field and be ridiculed with them. The lesson was simple: if you failed you would be punished. If you failed a second time the punishment would be increased. If you failed a third time no member of the staff and none of the other players could speak to you and you were forced to resign from the team.

One of the smallest members of the team was named Timmy Eldridge. One day, in the sixth and final inning of a key game, Timmy Eldridge, playing second base, cut off a strong throw from right field to home plate and gave up the winning run. After the crowd cleared and the parents drove home, Demmler and Brownley began raving at him. They made him take off all of his clothes and stand alone, exposing his eleven-year-old child's body in center field until he cried uncontrollably. Then they and the team members yelled and swore at him for a full forty minutes. By the time they were finished he was choking on his tears, begging them to stop. His parents had never known what had happened, since he was too ashamed to tell them and the rest of the team was too frightened to reveal the disciplinary system of their manager and coach.

By the time he was twenty-five Tim Eldridge had decided to do something about the nightmares and recriminations that he had suffered for nearly a decade and a half. He located Demmler, purchased a bat just like the one he had used years earlier, and drove his former manager to an open classroom in the San Gabriel Mountains, where he proceeded to give him some elementary instruction on how it felt to be alone and to cry out in pain when no one else was willing or able to help you.

Demmler and Brownley had had no contact for over eleven years, so that finding Brownley took him a great deal of time, but Tim Eldridge finally found him and when he did he taught him the very same lesson he had taught Demmler. He taught him slowly and methodically; then he calmly walked across nine miles of desert, drove home, and left Brownley's screams and his own nightmares behind him.

Once the connection was found between Demmler and Brownley the case was easily solved. With both of them dead most of their former players—now adults—were ready to talk about life on the Clarkson Little League team. Without that connection the case would never have been closed. The fact that the other players had alibis for the time of at least one of the two murders and the fact that all of them vividly remembered what had happened to Timmy Eldridge made the investigation and arrest that much easier.

It was a violent case and a hard way to die, no matter how well deserved by each of the victims. "An angry man will do that sort of thing," Charles White had said. "Not a crazy man, but an angry man. Add hate and it's that much worse." Two homicide officers had been relieved in the course of the investigation and one lieutenant had been forced to retire. Public pressure escalated day by day but there was no fresh evidence to be found until the second body was discovered. Then the two lines suddenly crossed and the hunt for Tim Eldridge was on. Until then there was nothing—nothing to report, nothing to investigate, nothing to do but wait patiently and helplessly for a second victim.

Michael Crimmins' age and experience were different from William Demmler's and Daniel Brownley's: blue-collar drifters who thought they were men because they humiliated little boys. Crimmins would have made more contacts in a single year of his life than they would have made in ten, so many that they could never be quickly and completely traced. Unless something obvious presented itself, Frank knew that all that he and the LAPD could realistically do would be to listen patiently to the swelling cries of the public and the media, knowing that there was nothing more to be accomplished until another body was found.

He put down his pint glass and hurried out to the telephone in the hotel lobby. He punched in the country code for the U.S., the area code, the seven-digit number, and his international credit card number. He waited for the ring before he put his credit card away. You could never trust British phones. Loram was at his desk. "What have you got for me?" he asked.

"Nothing new here. I was calling to make sure that I could put my whole team on the Crimmins case when I get back."

"Why are you calling me to ask that now?"

"Because I just realized that if we don't find something fast we may not find anything at all."

"Relax, Frank. I've got as many people working on it as I can spare."

"Any possibilities?"

"Not yet; remember—we didn't have the file until a few minutes ago."

"Who do you have on it?"

"Frank?"

"Yes?"

"What's the problem?"

"Remember Demmler and Brownley?"

"The Little League murders?"

"Yes."

"What about them?"

"We couldn't do anything for a year; we couldn't find anything until Eldridge found Brownley."

"So?"

"I don't want to wait a year."

"Maybe you won't have to."

"What do you mean?"

"Maybe we'll turn something quickly."

"And if we don't?"

"Then maybe we'll find a second victim with a sharpened piece of steel shoved up his ass."

"I want to get there before that happens."

"It took Eldridge a year to find number two, Frank."

"We're not dealing with Timmy Eldridge now, Captain."

FIFTEEN

HEATHROW WAS CROWDED. THERE was never enough space for the torrent of people who washed through its doors and gates within any given twenty-four-hour period, so British Air tried its best to break them into small groups for herding. Security had been increased in recent years and the trip from the sidewalk to the gate took Frank through seven or eight separate stations, most with lines. By the time he made it to the Duty Free area, he was ready for some refreshment. He quietly took his place among the frazzled and now exhausted tourists, the restless babies—saving their lungs and vocal cords for the higher altitudes—and the turbaned remnants of the empire, wearing Western coats over Eastern robes and clutching two or three plastic bags in each available hand.

He checked the cafeteria. He wanted something plain and simple—a piece of cheese on a roll—but he couldn't find it. As he kept looking he saw the sign on the center pillar behind the counter. It said: *Operated by the Marriott Corporation.* Heathrow Airport. London. England. The United Kingdom. Marriott. Marriott Resorts, Marriott Hotels, Residence Inns by Marriott, Courtyard by Marriott,

Marriott Suites, Marriott's Hot Shoppes, Marriott's Roy Rogers, Marriott's Big Boy, Marriott's Child Care Centers, Marriott's Retirement Homes, Marriott's in-flight meals, Marriott's meals on the ground in the terminal—in London . . . in London, England. Frank looked at the layered rows of generic meat and gravy and the blobs of congealed vegetables, the cream of something soup and the cubes of lime jello, the lumps of cottage cheese stained by the juice from canned maraschino cherries, and the crinkled, aluminum-foil packets of preservative-rich salad dressings. He looked and he thought: somewhere in the hottest corner of hell there must be a place where the fallen angels float on a puddle of molten rock, where the soot falls through the darkness into their mouths and ears and eyes, where the soles of their feet twist with pain as they wrinkle into contorted shapes like dead leaves, and a line of foul-smelling, smiling demons stand before them, hurling burning coals at their naked bodies, watching as the coals roll over their foreheads and lips, down their throats and chests and bellies, sliding into their groins, and coming to rest with an unspeakable pain, atop their shriveled, smoldering scrotums, all beneath an 8 x 10 red and white sign with the modest corporate logo and the words: *Charcoal by Marriott.*

Frank looked at the food floating in the trays above the cafeteria steam tables and thought about the food they were probably now loading on the 747—hundreds of trays of chicken, beef, unidentifiable fish, and, God help us, pasty, chewy, dried, and wrinkled lasagna. He walked over to the bar, commandeered a cup of peanuts, picked up a handful, and ordered a double scotch.

"Ice?" the bartender asked.

"Yes, thanks," Frank answered, forgetting that the bartender might spoon cracked slivers from a watery ice bucket and dilute the scotch.

"I'm sorry, forget it," he said, as the bartender probed for something solid with his teaspoon.

"Are you sure?"

"Yes, thanks very much," Frank said.

"How about some more nuts?"

"Sure," Frank said.

He filled the cup to the top and put the large plastic jar behind it. "There," he said, "just help yourself."

Frank smiled appreciatively and took a drink of the scotch. It was smooth and peaty. "Very good," he said.

"That's not a beverage, you know," the bartender said. "Not something you drink just for a sudden thirst. It's twelve-year-old single malt Scotch whiskey. That's *medicine*."

"I'm not sure what's wrong with me, but I feel better already," Frank said.

Five minutes later he ordered a refill. "I knew you'd like that," the bartender said.

It was almost as good as the stuff from Goldsmith's, which, until the second sip of the scotch, had seemed as if it was now a thousand miles away.

A kindly flight attendant named Deirdre noticed Frank's long legs and promptly moved him to a bulkhead seat. He slipped the miniature pillow on his seat between his cheek and the window and closed his eyes. Twenty minutes into the flight they brought out the beverage cart. He had forgotten the things that they managed to do well.

"What can I get you?" the flight attendant asked. Her name was Clarissa. British women always seemed to have old-fashioned names.

"Scotch," he said. "The oldest you have."

She smiled. "I have just the thing," she said. "It was loaded . . . let's see . . . last week. *Early* last week."

"You're an angel," he said.

"Take two," she said. "One is never enough. And here . . ." She gave him three packs of peanuts. "I've already seen what we're serving you for dinner."

He dug out the airline magazine. It was October now. The movies had all changed since he flew over. The feature was a remake of the Lou Gehrig story, starring Tom Cruise. He shook his head and put the magazine back in the seat pocket.

Clarissa stopped off on her way back up the aisle and passed him two more bottles of Dewar's and three more packs of peanuts.

"Miss, could I have another drink as well?" his seatmate asked. She was an elderly woman working feverishly on a piece of needlepoint.

"Certainly, Madam. What was it you were drinking?"

"Gin," she said. "Gordon's, if you have it."

Clarissa smiled and handed her two bottles. The woman dumped one in her glass and slipped the other under her needlepoint. Frank looked at the design. It was a black Scottish terrier sitting in front of a white frame doghouse with the name *Robbie* across the roof. Frank poured both of his bottles of scotch into his glass, toasted the Scottie, and took a deep drink.

After a short nap Frank noticed that the woman was reading a book printed in large-type. She seemed serene, as if she were reading Ecclesiastes or *Goodbye, Mr. Chips*. He leaned over slightly and tilted his head so that he could see the words:

The curtains parted, revealing his slender fingertips as he slid them along the right curtain's smooth, soft edge. He clutched the dark velvet in his hand, pulled it aside, and stared at her directly with his black eyes.

She stepped back, still drawn to him, but fearful.

"What I offer, my darling, is life everlasting. A life with me, and with the others, free of the constraints of the world of day."

Her lips trembled as she felt his eyes exploring her face and body. She stood silent as he stepped toward her and his hand passed over her breast and nipple, cradling it like the smallest sparrow. She leaned toward him, yielding to his touch, and tilted her head to the side, offering the blue vein that crossed her blushing throat to his lips and tongue and teeth.

His breath was sweet as his lips parted, but as she felt his teeth puncturing her flesh and his tongue greedily tasting her warm and flowing blood she felt a heat rising up from inside of him, taking all that she offered, and more.

The gentle touch of his fingers at her breast was gone now. The endless hunger that drove his lips and tongue was in his hands and arms and fingertips, pulling her, twisting her, trapping her in his embrace, squeezing the breath and blood from her trembling body, possessing her, feeding on her.

Her vision blurred as her eyes filled with tears of fear and terror. She tried to search his black eyes for answers, for meaning, but they were closed, as he fed himself at her throat, tracing the errant crimson streams with the tip of his tongue as they flowed over her swelling right breast.

Finally, when he was finished, he stood back, still holding her by the waist, and slowly catching his breath. She opened her eyes and saw a face bathed in blood, with clots and smears covering his lips and teeth and nose and cheeks, running over his chin and onto the collar of his silken shirt, staining its pearl buttons, and trailing off into its folds like so many rivers, streams, and crimson brooks.

"You will do very nicely, my darling," he said, rolling her bare nipple between his thumb and forefinger, pinching, teasing, and toying, as she fainted with weakness and incipient horror.

The woman turned the page slowly and carefully, like an aged scholar examining a fragile manuscript or a poor child handling her only book. There was the slightest smile on her lips as her eyes traveled over the next page. She reached for her plastic glass of gin, sipped at it slowly, and returned to her story.

The international terminal at LAX was crowded but everything moved quietly and efficiently. Frank cleared Customs and walked into the public terminal area. Jack was standing on the edge of the crowd, holding up a cardboard sign with the words *Defender of the Realm* in blue magic marker.

"How was the flight?" he asked. "I hope they didn't disappoint you and let you get comfortable."

"The seat was OK," Frank said. "They put me in front of the bulkhead next to an old lady doing needlepoint and drinking straight gin."

"What was she reading, S & M romances or vampire books?"

"Vampire books," Frank said.

"Yeah, they always do," Jack said. "How about some dinner?"

"Sure. I passed on the airplane glop."

"What'd you do—peanuts and scotch?"

"Yes."

"It always works for me, too," Jack said.

"My car's right on the bottom level," Jack said. "What time is it on your body clock, last Wednesday night or something?"

"Yes, something like that," Frank answered.

"You can nap while I drive."

"I'm OK," Frank said.

"I know. I just don't want you to see where I'm taking you."

Frank smiled, dropped his luggage in the trunk, slid into the front seat of Jack's Celica, and closed his eyes. Forty minutes later he opened them and saw a row of warehouses and industrial buildings lining an open boulevard. "Where are we?"

"Glendale. I'm going to Topline."

Topline is a wine and liquor store in a rented garage just off of San Fernando Road, with the best wine selection for the price within 2,500 square miles. Jack was gone for about ten minutes. He returned with two brown paper bags.

"Couldn't you make up your mind?" Frank asked.

"So much candy. So little time."

Jack drove east on the 134, noticed the lights to the north around the Rose Bowl and those to the south on the rebuilt Arroyo Seco bridge, and clicked on his right turn signal. He took the Colorado exit and drove into Old Town Pasadena. He parked behind the old Braemar Building on Raymond and he and Frank walked into a dark restaurant called Perry's. Perry was actually a person named Mary Elizabeth, but Perry's had a better ring to it for a place that specialized in steaks, lobsters, and deep-dish peach pie.

"Hi, Beth," Jack said.

"Hi, Jack," she answered. "Home from the war, huh Frank?"

"Hi, Beth," Frank said.

It was too early for the fashionable crowd. The restaurant was practically deserted. Jack gestured toward a booth in the far corner. Beth nodded OK and handed them a corkscrew and two wine glasses as they passed.

"This will bring you back to life," Jack said, pouring half a glass of dark red wine into Frank's glass as the waitress approached.

"Hi, Karen," Jack said.

"Jack . . . Frank . . ." she answered. "What can I get you?"

"A big filet, medium rare, a tail on the side, Caesar with some shaved parmesan, a baked potato, and some hot rolls," Jack said.

"You want the lobster on a separate plate?"

"Please."

"Frank?"

"I'll have the same. What's the soup, Karen?"

"Cream of leek or French onion."

"Give me whatever looks best," Frank said.

"Good to see you guys again," she said.

"You too, Karen," Jack answered. She left and he turned to Frank. "How's that wine?" he asked.

"That's not wine, it's medicine," Frank said.

"You're damned right," Jack answered.

"So what have you got?" Jack asked, as he tasted the last piece of his steak and poured the third glass of wine from the second bottle.

"What have I got? A hell of a glass of wine and a ticking clock."

"Waiting for the second victim?"

"Yes."

"Maybe it'll be awhile. Maybe you'll turn something first."

"Maybe," Frank said. "Then again, he may have already finished with number two and be working on number three."

PART TWO

Revenge Land

SIXTEEN

Los Angeles. October 8. 11:58 a.m. Lead-gray skies with yellow streaks and blotches arching across the basin, the air still, even on the coast, the morning mist not yet cooked off. Traffic hellish. William Devens driving north on La Cienega, his eyes darting from his watch to the temperature gauge on his white Town Car. Pulling so hard on his shirt sleeve that he almost loses a gold-knot cufflink. Olympic Boulevard gridlocked. A van on fire in the center lane heading east, rubberneckers slowing as they head west, trying to avoid the smoke but still catch a look. Worrying now about the crease in his slacks. Running his fingers nervously over his knees. Looking at the cuff buttons on his blue Oxxford suit. A cool $1,795. The salesman said the buttons were made of horn. Wilshire gridlocked. Century City spilloff. Under his breath: "God *damn* it." A rap on the steering wheel with his right fist. Then a second.

Already ten minutes late for his showing in Holmby Hills, a mid-seven-figure Spanish revival. His buyers skittish and impatient; they won't wait for him and they won't be interested in his excuses. The wife wants Bel Air or the Palisades. He promising to meet only as a personal favor. She looking for any excuse to pull the plug on the pink palace.

"Just look at it. That's all. Just look at it. There is nothing of this quality on the market in this price range. Just look at it. Please, trust me on this. If you don't like it I'll be more than happy to show you something else, but you should at least see it."

Devens' own listing. He takes the whole commission.

Looking at his tie knot in the rear-vision mirror, then checking his watch again. "Son of a bitch!" Hitting the horn in anger. Nobody moving any faster or paying any more attention.

The car phone rings. He hits the speaker button.

"Hello," he says. Cheery, upbeat. Just *maybe* they're willing to wait for him. Thinking seven percent of 5.35 mil.

Quick and cold: "Hi, Billy. Did you hear about Mikey?" Then silence. A machine voice. Like a robot in a tunnel. Electronically filtered.

"Who is this?" Guarded, edgy.

"I asked first."

"Yes, I heard about it."

"*It*? Don't you mean *him*?"

"Who is this?"

"A friend of a friend, Billy."

"What do you want?"

"Oh, I want a lot of things, Billy."

Devens clicking off the phone. "Asshole." Hitting the horn again and checking his watch.

Five minutes later, up to 15 mph and grateful. The car phone rings again. He reaches for it, stops, says "Fuck it," then realizes he can't afford to take the chance on losing the showing. He hits the button.

"Hello." His normal voice.

"You know what C-4 is, Billy?"

"Yes."

"What is it, Billy?"

"It's a plastic explosive."

"Guess what. There's a quarter-pound of it just beneath your accelerator pedal. Don't bother trying to feel around for it. It's on the other side of the firewall. And Billy . . . if you even try to get out of the car I'll set it off. You can't outrun it, Billy. By the way, you should lose that yellow tie. Much too eighties."

Beads forming above his upper lip.

"That's right. I can see you, Billy. I've been following you ever since you dragged yourself out to your driveway this morning. Bad night, Billy?"

"What do you want?"

"I want to talk, Billy. Now about that C-4 . . . there's enough of it there to blow your balls through your belly and into the trunk of your Lincoln. That's a long car, Billy, but they won't have any trouble making the trip. Probably take most of the rest of you with them too. Now you leave that telephone on and you talk to me. If you try to signal a cop or try anything else funny it will be 'Good-bye to Billy and good-bye to Billy's balls.'"

"Please tell me. What do you want?"

"Turn left on Sunset."

Driving through the flats of Beverly Hills, coming up on the corner of the Los Angeles Country Club.

Eight minutes later: just above UCLA; snaking through Westwood.

"Get on the 405, Billy. Head north."

Ten minutes later, approaching the ramp.

"It's jammed."

"So it is. Did I ask for a traffic report, Billy?"

Trying to catch a glimpse in one of his mirrors as he pulls onto the ramp. Too many cars and vans. Too many tinted windshields and sunglasses.

"Stay on the right side, Billy."

Leaning his head back, trying to look relaxed, but his eyes frantically searching the rear-view mirror.

"Just look straight ahead, Billy."

"OK." Trying to sound cooperative.

"What do you think, Billy? You think this could all be a scam? A bad joke. Run you around town, maybe make you piss in your pants a little?"

"I don't know."

"Would you like some proof, Billy? Lean over and reach under the passenger seat. Right in the front, Billy. You can't miss it."

"Jesus."

"What is it, Billy?"

"It's a steel box."

"Just about the same size as a container for kitchen matches, right?"

"Yes."

"Tell me how many catches there are on it, Billy."

"No, you tell me." Burning the little courage he has left.

"There are four, Billy. And a cute little red line running around the center."

"Jesus."

"You know what that means, don't you?"

"Yes."

"Tell me."

"It means you were able to get past the security system on the car."

"Very good. *That's* what it means. Put the box on your lap, Billy."

"Why?"

"Just put it there and drive."

His forehead soaked now and his tie tightening around his throat. His hand running over the top of the box. Pressing down slightly. Feeling the spring tension on the lid.

Through the pass and into the Valley now. Thicker smog. Darker skies.

"Keep heading north on the 405, Billy."

Feeling the box again. His left hand an inch from the power window switch. What if the C-4's in the box?

"Do you like that box, Billy? There's a surprise in it and it's just for you."

"Did you kill Crimmins?" Choking on the words.

"Maybe. Why? Do you miss him, Billy?"

No answer. Thinking about the window again. And the box. Trying to keep his head clear. Rehearsing.

"Push up your rear-view mirror, Billy. You don't need it now . . . good . . . now the outside mirrors—turn them away from the car . . . OK. Get off on Nordhoff. Head west."

Eight blocks from the freeway now. "Turn into the mini-mall on the right, Billy. Park in the back corner, facing the wall."

No way out.

"All right, Billy. It's time for your surprise. Hold the box in front of you and slowly open it up. The latches are numbered. Make sure you start with number four."

"Look, can't we talk about this?"

"If we talk you won't get your surprise, Billy."

"Please. I'm begging you."

"Would you rather I detonate the C-4?"

"No." His voice quivering now. Forcing the sounds through his lips.

"I didn't think so. Open the latches. Remember—start with number four. I want to hear each click."

Four.

Three.

Two.

His hands trembling, feeling the pressure beneath his fingertips. Turning the box away from his face. Holding his breath but unable to stop his heart from pounding against his chest wall.

One.

Slowly releasing the pressure of his fingertips. The top thrown open like a trap, smashing his index finger. Devens gasping, his body jolting as if a bolt of electricity had struck the base of his spine. A sudden click inside the box. A wire figure snapping upright, holding a miniature sword in one hand and a tiny envelope in the other.

Devens convulsing now with anger and relief.

"Open it, Billy."

Taking the envelope from the hand of the wire figure. Opening it and removing a card the size of a postage stamp. Three words lettered in red ink: ONLY THE BEGINNING.

"What the hell is this?"

"It's only the beginning, Billy. Can't you read?"

"I don't think this is very goddamned funny."

"But it's only the beginning, Billy. You have to be more patient. Wait until you see what I have planned for you later."

"Look. We've got to talk. We've got to straighten this out. You can't do this to me."

"But I just did, Billy."

"Tell me what you want."

"I've already told you, Billy. I want a lot of things."

"Like what? Tell me. You can't keep doing shit like this. We've got to talk. Please. Just talk to me."

"I've been talking to you for the last forty minutes."
"That's not what I mean."
"What *do* you mean?"
"I mean . . . we've got to work this out."
"We certainly do."
"OK. Then where do we start?"
"I've already started, Billy."

SEVENTEEN

Without wasting too much time on preliminary pleasantries, Frank asked the expected question: "Who do you think would want to kill your ex-husband, Mrs. Brander?"

They were sitting on a bluff just above the Pacific in Rancho Palos Verdes. As the sky cleared Mrs. Brander had suggested they move to the patio—a red-tiled expanse beyond the dining room with six groupings of white, padded wicker chairs and steel tables with umbrellas. A tall, thin woman in her late forties, she was sitting primly in a white linen suit with yellow accents, holding a Mont Blanc pen in her right hand, bracing it with her thumb and twisting it counterclockwise. Frank was sitting in the sun, sipping his iced tea, and trying not to be distracted by the pair of gulls that kept flying above them. At Mrs. Brander's insistence he removed his coat. The holstered magnum and back sling didn't seem to bother her.

"Who would want to kill Michael?" she answered. "A large number of people."

"Why do you say that?"

"Because I was married to him, Lieutenant."

"Is there anyone in particular who comes to mind?"

"None that I'd care to mention. It's a very long list and I'd want to be fair in giving equal time to everyone."

"You divorced about six years ago, didn't you?"

"Seven, actually."

"Grounds?"

"Irreconcilable differences."

"I don't want to pry, Mrs. Brander, but . . ."

"Don't worry about it, Lieutenant. My mother's grandfather was Charles Stone. Charles Stone founded Tempco Industries. Are you familiar with that company?"

"I'm afraid I'm not."

"It's an interesting story. After the first commercial applications of solar energy in southern California, the gas company started to become nervous. All those swimming pools . . . all that free power to heat them. They decided to give away free hot water heaters to anyone who would be willing to use their natural gas. They contracted with Tempco to make the heaters. That was all the start that my great grandfather needed. He took the profits from the hot water heaters and bought land. He bought a great deal of land, Lieutenant. Land was very inexpensive then—like the natural gas. He purchased most of what is now the western quadrant of the San Fernando Valley. The family fortune fluctuates with our investments, of course, but it's currently in the high nine figures. When Michael found out about my share he fell in love at once."

"He used you to advance his career then."

"I'm afraid so. I only wish I had known earlier. You see, Michael was a good actor, a far better actor than a husband."

"But you split everything you acquired in the course of your marriage."

"Yes, we did. That's California law."

"Then why was he still working? Why wasn't he in Aspen or Cannes or Nice?"

"He had to work, Lieutenant."

"Excuse me, but you just said you split everything you acquired in the years of your marriage."

"We did, but the instant I suspected what Michael Crimmins was about I sheltered my portion of the income. You see, I have very good lawyers and accountants, Lieutenant."

"He must have been surprised."

"He was aghast. It was one of the happier days of my life. Would you care for more iced tea?"

"No, thank you."

"Lemon? Mint?"

"No, really."

"Let's have something to eat."

"Mrs. Brander, I really should ask another question or two and leave."

"Nonsense." She picked up the cordless phone on the table. "Alice, please bring us something to eat, won't you? What? . . . Yes, that will be fine. Thanks so much."

The cook brought a salad with strips of marinated beef, black olives, and artichoke hearts. "You have to eat anyway, Lieutenant. This will save you time. By the way, I think you'll find this refreshing."

"Thank you," Frank said, taking a cloth napkin and silverware from the black lacquer tray.

"So what you're saying, Mrs. Brander, is that your former husband might have had a motive for killing *you*, but that you took your own revenge on him years ago."

"Yes, exactly. And I would never have killed him, Lieutenant. You see, I would have missed all of the joy of seeing him squirm and flounder."

"He was finally successful."

"Yes, but not for long," she said, lifting her wine glass in a small toast and taking a long sip.

"Do you have any idea who he might have been involved with?"

"You mean women?"

"Yes."

"No. There were women, of course, but Michael was always more interested in himself and in his position. It was never the sex. It was how the women made him look and feel. They were ornaments, Lieutenant, things to be seen with."

"*Things?*"

"Yes, things. Like stylish apparel, Italian automobiles, or photo-op stills on a den wall. Do you know Washington, Lieutenant?"

"Not well."

"They hang their lives on their den walls there."

"The last pictures they took of him wouldn't do much for the set."

"I can imagine. Do you have any of them?"

"Yes, but . . ."

"Could I see them?"

"I don't think . . ."

"Don't worry, Lieutenant. I promise you I won't be shocked."

Frank took three of the pictures from his inside coat pocket and handed them to her.

"Yes, yes," she said. "And is this *exactly* how they found him, sprawled on the floor in all this dirt and blood?"

"Yes, it is," Frank answered.

"Thank you so much, Lieutenant," she said, handing him back the pictures. "You've made me very happy."

Frank held his fork in the air and stared at Lorraine Brander directly. "It's fair to say then that you hated your former husband, hated him deeply, in fact."

"Hated? No, I'd say *loathed*, or perhaps *despised*. *Hated* is too soft. No woman enjoys being treated like a fool, Lieutenant, especially one in my position. Headlines . . . whispers . . . amused smiles on the faces of those you once considered friends . . . questions from the members of your family, pointed fingers."

"Then you must know what my next question will be, Mrs. Brander."

"Of course. You want to know how I felt when Michael finally achieved some success. Did my loathing run so deep that I might have hired someone to murder him?"

"Yes . . ."

"Well, I'll tell you the truth. I might have done it. I truly might have." She was musing out loud, running possibilities through her mind. Then her tone changed. "But I would have done it quite differently. This was too . . . *symbolic*. I would have wanted his death to be more direct, more—shall we say—*elemental*."

"What do you mean?"

"I think the real murders are best committed with one's own hands, don't you, Lieutenant? I wouldn't have been able to overpower Michael by myself, of course, but with a piece of pipe or a small bat I could have done very well indeed. That would have been my way—to strike him again and again. All across his face and body. And to do it slowly, of course. I'd want to see the blood run and hear the bones shatter. And the moans, of course, and the begging. Excuse my manners, Lieutenant. Would you like some more salad?"

"No, thank you."

"Here I am, running on and on."

"I appreciate the time you've spent with me, Mrs. Brander. You've helped me a great deal."

"Really? How?"

"You've satisfied me that Michael Crimmins was a man who could engender a great deal of hate."

"I told you, Lieutenant. The suspect list will be a very long one. By the way..."

"Yes?"

"Will my name be on that list, Lieutenant?"

"At least for the moment it will have to be, Mrs. Brander. You must understand—that would be standard procedure."

"That's quite all right, Lieutenant. I prefer to be on the list."

"Really? Why?"

"It helps me to imagine what it might have been like to actually have had the pleasure of killing him."

EIGHTEEN

"It's a dummy," Carl Flagler said. "I mean, it looked at first as if it could have been an explosive device. There were these insulated wires attached to the miniature antenna (see—this is it here), and the box was bolted down securely to the firewall, but when I opened it up there was no explosive inside and no detonator. It looked like whoever installed it was pretty professional, but once I was able to remove the box and check it out I could see that somebody was just jerking you around. Of course, they could have put the real thing in there. And that would have been nasty as all hell. Believe me, it would have blown you right through the back seat of the car. The steel's pretty thick under here on a Lincoln, but a box this size filled with C-4 would have made one hell of an explosion. The firewall would have been like a fragmentation grenade, breaking into pieces and cutting the shit out of everything in its way. You were actually very lucky, Mr. Devens. Better you should be fucked with by a practical joker than by a real bomber."

"God *damn* it," Devens said. "That son . . . of . . . a . . . bitch!"

"You'd be surprised how often it happens. People want to scare the shit out of other people—you know, to get their attention so they can get something from them. They see all this crap in the movies and they decide to go into business for themselves. They go down to the local hardware or auto parts store and buy some flares. Then they take the spikes out of the ends, tape an old alarm clock to them, and attach them to a car or an office desk or something. Then they make threats or try to extort money. Happens all the time. People call me since I deal with construction demolitions. They ask me to check the bombs and see whether or not they're real. I make a pretty good living at it. You'd be surprised. We're gonna open up an office in the Valley . . . soon as we can get our lease straightened out."

"That cocksucker."

"Oh, I know how you feel," Flagler said, wiping off his hands with a piece of orange cloth. "You feel helpless. You don't know whether they're serious or not. You don't know what the damn thing is. A lot of times people don't even know who the person is who's fucking with their head. It's mean as hell, but you know what?"

"What?"

"It works like a son of a bitch. You know why?"

"Why?"

"Because people are afraid of things they don't understand. Switches . . . fuses . . . timers . . . solenoids. They see a big lump of something soft and they don't know whether it's plastic explosive or modeling clay. It's not like a gun or a razor or anything they're familiar with. They see it and they don't even want to touch it. It's like a poisonous snake or spider. They wouldn't know where to grab it if they wanted to. Like I say, it's damned effective. I saw a guy actually shit in a four-hundred-dollar pair of silk pants over a fake bomb made out of silly putty. That stuff is fun, you know. The guy who put together the phony bomb typed up a message and then put the silly putty over the message, so that when the mark looked at it he could read all this shit that the guy was threatening him with. He never figured out what that gray stuff was."

"How much do I owe you, Flagler?"

"Two hundred and fifty dollars."

"What? You were only here for twenty minutes."

"Twenty-seven, actually. I had an hour's driving time; and remember—you pay for a portion of an hour at the same rate as for the full hour."

"But you were coming from Brentwood. That's only ten minutes away."

"That's right, Mr. Devens, but we charge driving time on the basis of distance to and from the office. You see, we're like plumbers. Only we save lives sometimes instead of just keeping your toilets flushing."

"Jesus," Devens said, walking toward the house. "Turn off the goddamn meter. I'll write you a check."

"I prefer cash, Mr. Devens."

"Yeah? Well, I don't have two hundred and fifty bucks in cash. I'm gonna write a goddamn check. Don't worry; it won't bounce." Devens reached for the door handle.

"Right. I hate to charge for returned checks, but I'm a businessman and I have to do it. With cash you never have the problem." By that point Flagler realized he was talking to himself.

———

"Here's the check," Devens said.

Flagler examined it and then slid it under his clipboard clamp, above the work-order sheet. "Thank you very much, Mr. Devens. Be sure to call us again if you need us."

Devens just shook his head and cursed under his breath. He walked past his Town Car on the way back into the house and thought about what had happened to him. "That son-of-a-bitch!" he said. "This is *not* going to happen a second time. That is for *goddamn* sure."

He walked into the kitchen, got an old-fashioned glass from the cupboard and some ice from the refrigerator, and went into his den. The liquor cabinet was bolted to the far wall, above a sink with a goose-neck faucet and small, black formica counter. Devens reached for the cabinet's antique-gold handle, thinking about four fingers of Johnny Walker black. When he turned the handle he felt a fiery jolt hit his right arm. The shock was strong enough to knock him to the floor. His body was on fire as he lay there clutching his arm, trembling and shaking in a spreading pool of warm urine.

———

After three or four minutes his head started to clear and he got back up on his feet. His arm and back were sore and the fingers of his right hand were burned. The liquor cabinet door was half open. The bourbon and scotch had been removed and replaced with a set of wires that filled a quarter of the cabinet space. Three words had been lettered on the back of the cabinet in white chalk: *Round Two, Billy.*

"No," he said, "no, this is *not* happening to me. This is some kind of goddamn nightmare. First some asshole follows me around, telling me there's a bomb in my car, puts some stupid fucking box under the passenger seat with a goddamn message inside, then he wires up my liquor cabinet and tries to fucking electrocute me. What in the *hell* is going on?"

The phone rang.

Devens walked over to the bookshelf behind the TV and automatically reached for the receiver with his right hand. "God damn it," he said, as the pain shot through his fingertips and up his arm. Then he took it in his left hand.

"Hello," he said.

"Hello, Billy." The robotic voice.

"What the hell are you trying to do to me?"

"Interesting, isn't it? How you can wire something now so that it signals you when it's been tripped off. How are your fingers, Billy? Did you piss in your pants?"

"What the hell do you want from me?"

"What's the matter, Billy? Aren't you enjoying this?"

"Hell no. Look, we've got to talk."

"I'm talking, Billy."

"That's not what I mean. We've got to sit down and work this out. I don't know what you want but we've got to be able to come up with some kind of deal."

"A deal, Billy? But you don't understand; I'm enjoying this. I don't want it to end. I want to see it last and last."

"Look, we've *got* to talk."

The phone went dead.

"Sonofabitch. Chicken-shit sonofabitch."

Suddenly it rang again. Devens grabbed it immediately.

"Hello?"

"Watch your language, you cowardly bastard," the voice said.

The phone went dead again and Devens unscrewed the earpiece on the phone. The miniature transmitter fell on top of the television set. Devens threw it on the floor and crushed it with his foot, stomping on it again and again, grinding its components into the beige carpeting.

NINETEEN

Frank left Lorraine Brander's house, caught the 110 north, and then the 405 south, crossing Long Beach, and heading toward Costa Mesa, where Michael Crimmins' parents now lived. He tuned in one of the Orange County talk-radio stations to help pass the time on the San Diego freeway.

"Once again, this is WCOB, talk radio in Fountain Valley. I'm Roger Clymer and we're talking today about revenge. Carole from Huntington Beach, you're on WCOB."

"Hi Roger. I love your show. I listen every afternoon."

"Thanks, Carole. Talk to me about revenge."

"I've got a story, Roger. It's about my ex-husband."

"OK."

"He did something really terrible to me."

"What did he do, Carole?"

"Well . . . I caught him in *my* bed with my sister."

"With your sister?"

"Yes."

"What did you do, Carole?"

"It was pretty bad, Roger."

"Come on, Carole. In *your* bed with your *sister*! That's pretty bad too."

"That's what I thought, Roger. They didn't know that I had seen them. But I did, because the door was open a little ways. They didn't expect me home from work, but I had to come home and take our dog to the vet. I could never count on my husband to do those kinds of things. He always said he was too busy. Now I know what he was busy with. Anyway, he forgot about me coming home . . ."

"What did you do, Carole?"

"What I did was go down to the kitchen . . ."

"What did you do, Carole, get a butcher knife?" Apprehensive chuckles.

"No, Roger, I got out the utensil I use to make mashed potatoes with. It's kind of a round thing with these bars running through it on the end. It's made out of metal. What I did was turn on one of the burners on the stove (it's a gas stove) and I heated that thing up until it turned bright orange and red."

"Oh-oh."

"Yes. Then I hurried back upstairs, ran into our bedroom, and burned each of them right on the butt. It was easy with my sister. She was on top then, but when she screamed and my husband saw me he threw her off and tried to get away from me. He burned his hand grabbing at the metal thing but then I got him pretty good, maybe a little too far down his leg, but most of it was on his butt."

"So you branded them, Carole."

"That's right, Roger. That's what I did."

"So then they had to explain to everybody what happened. I wonder what they told the doctor in the emergency room."

"I don't know. I didn't think about it at the time, but now they'll have to explain those marks for the rest of their lives. Unless they get some kind of plastic surgery. I don't think they can do that, though, because I really got 'em good."

"Did either of them call the police or threaten to?"

"No. They're trying to hush it up. I threw my husband out of the house and my mother's mad at me, but I don't care."

"It sounds as if you really got your revenge, Carole."

"Yes, I think so, Roger."

"Thanks for calling. Charles in Garden Grove. You're on WCOB."

"Hi, Roger."

"Hi, Charles. Did you just hear Carole?"

"Yes, Roger. That is *revenge*."

"It sure is. Talk to us, Charles."

"Well, Roger, I've got this boss who just never lets up on me. You can't do anything to suit him."

"Where do you work, Charles?"

"In this drycleaning place. I drive one of the trucks."

"You make deliveries."

"That's right."

"Well, what does he do to you, Charles?"

"Well, he's always checking my logs. He's always questioning how much gas I buy for the van. He tells me there are too many complaints that I'm late with the deliveries. He tells me I should only hold the clothes by the hangers. Once I had about fifteen suits and dresses to carry and I bent some of them over my left arm. He called me a bunch of names, said I was stupid, told me they'd have to redo everything if I wasn't more careful. Told me I wasn't half the driver the former guy was. Somebody named Larry. It was always Larry this, and Larry that . . ."

"What did you do, Charles?"

"Well, last week he was really on me, ordering me around, and it was just about noon and it was real hot out. I went over to the machine to get myself a Pepsi and he told me I should get back in the van and get to work, that I had already goofed off too much."

"So what happened, Charles?"

"I couldn't take it anymore, so I backed the van around and drove right over his foot. He started yelling and stumbling around. Then he fell down and started holding onto his foot and screaming. I rolled down the window and said, 'OK, you (I called him a name, Roger), at least you've got something to say now instead of bad things about me."

"What did he do, Charles?"

"He fired me. Then he called the police and had me arrested."

"Did you have to go to jail, Charles?"

"Nah. I told them it was an accident and I told him that if he continued to press charges I'd file all kinds of complaints against him. He just dropped it."

"But you'll probably still lose your job."

"Yeah, but I'm not walkin' funny."

The traffic began to slow. Frank checked his watch and then feathered the brake, trying to keep moving.

"I think we have time for one more call before we break for a commercial. Mary Beth in Santa Ana: welcome to WCOB."

"Hi Roger, how are you?"

"I'm fine, Mary Beth. How are you?"

"Just fi-i-ine." Drawing out the vowel as far as it would stretch.

"Do you have a story for us?"

"I surely do."

"Well don't be shy."

"Nobody ever accused me of being shy, Roger."

"OK. Go for it."

"All right. This is about this crook and my grandma. My family is all from Ohio originally and after my grandpa died my grandma moved out here to be near us. She's seventy-seven."

"Yes?"

"Anyway, she had all of her life savings in this duplex which she bought. She and my grandpa had some savings and she got a cash payment on his pension. She needed her own place and she figured she could live on the rent from the other unit, you see."

"Right."

"Well, this contractor—at least he said he was a contractor—told her that her building didn't meet code and that there were a lot of repairs that had to be made or the city would shut her down and not allow her to rent."

"Was it true, Mary Beth?"

"No. He was a liar. He was just trying to get some business. My grandma believed him and went ahead and started havin' him do all these expensive things, none of which were needed and none of which he really did right anyway. He just kept talkin' and she just kept believin'."

"How much did he cheat her out of, Mary Beth?"

"When he was all done . . . forty-seven thousand dollars."

"How did she pay that?"

"She couldn't. She had to take out a mortgage, but then the place was torn up for so long that the renters moved out. After the crook was finally finished, grandma couldn't find a renter who would pay enough for her to cover the mortgage and still have enough money left to live on. So she had to sell the building and move in with us. She lost just about everything."

"That's disgusting, Mary Beth. What did you do?"

"Well, first I went to the police. They said they couldn't do anything because the crook had all this signed paperwork and my grandma had authorized him to do whatever he thought he needed to do."

"So they were no help."

"None at all. So then my husband and I hired this lawyer. He charged us four hundred dollars to look at all the paperwork. Then he made a couple of phone calls and finally told us that if we wanted to fight it we'd have to give him ten thousand dollars up front, but that he didn't think our chances were all that good."

"Great. So what did you do then, Mary Beth?"

"Well, I told my husband we were going to have to take this into our own hands. He started to get nervous, so I went on over to the crook's office myself."

"What happened?"

"I told him I wanted my grandma's forty-seven thousand dollars back and that if he didn't give it to me right then and there he'd be damned sorry."

"What did he say?"

"He told me it was already spent. He also said that the money was part of the company assets, that I'd have to sue the company, not him, and that it wouldn't do me any good because the company was ready to go bankrupt."

"Wonderful." Sighing sympathetically.

"You know what I think, Roger . . . I think that's just a way of protecting himself. He lets those companies go broke and then starts up new ones."

"Of course, Mary Beth, that's exactly what he does. But what could you do?"

"Well, I could keep him from lyin' and cheatin' like that again."

"How?"

"I kept him from talkin'."

"How could you do that?"

"That wasn't hard. I knocked him down with this marble paperweight I have and then I got out my sewing scissors, which I brought with me, and cut off the end of his damned lyin' tongue."

"You did what?"

"I cut off his tongue, Roger."

"My lord. What did he do?"

"He didn't do anything. I told him if he did I'd cut somethin' else next time."

"That's incredible."

"I think he thought so too. He wasn't used to anybody standin' up to his lies. He thought everybody'd just take it. Well, I didn't. And now he knows."

"Yes, I'm sure he does."

"If you don't mind, I just want to say somethin' to all your listeners, Roger—if some guy tries to cheat you like that, don't sit still for it. The police can only do so much and the lawyers just charge both sides money and get rich themselves. You have to be ready to stand up for yourself. I did and I'm glad I did."

"How do you feel about him losing part of his tongue, Mary Beth?"

"Real good, Roger. Real good."

"O-o-o-K. Let's break for these messages."

———

The traffic started to break up and Frank was able to accelerate. When he got up to fifty-five he turned off the radio. He thought about the crook who lost his tongue. Then he thought about Michael Crimmins. Michael wasn't cheating anyone now either.

TWENTY

Jack finished his lunch, paid his check, and walked over to the bank of phones in the Westin Bonaventure lobby. He needed to call Frank. Instead he got Jerry Dailey, Frank's med tech.

"Hiya, Jack. Frank's running around Orange County, trying to find the Congressman's parents and see if they've got any bright ideas."

"When do you expect him back, Jerry?"

"Hard to say. He's got other stops to make too. He saw the ex-wife this morning. I think there's a cousin in Whittier. We're pulling out the stops on this one, Jack; we're all really stretched."

"I know, Jerry That's why I called. I told Frank I'd try to help if I could. Just sniff around a little, nothing public."

"Good, Jack."

"When he comes in, tell him I've got a quickie in the Arco Building. Then I'll try to catch Mary Beth Connors' campaign guy and see if he's got anything on Crimmins."

"Good idea, Jack. If you turn anything juicy let me know right away and I'll let Frank know. Otherwise, you guys will probably be seeing one another soon anyway."

"Right."

Mary Elisabeth Connors was the incumbent congresswoman who Michael Crimmins defeated in the last election. Connors' campaign chief was a suit named Goodman, who managed to land safely after the loss. He was working as the director of something called the Pacific Institute for Commerce and Cooperation (PICC). Goodman changed the name from the Pacific *Rim* Institute when one of his staff assistants pointed out that the organization's original acronym would not win friends and influence people. Goodman's actual job was to advise the Japanese auto industry on possible American sites for their domestic operations and scout out those investment opportunities which would involve the least amount of negative political fallout. He was trying to help some old friends, as well as doing his best to line his own pockets during the interim between Connors' defeat and the next major political campaign.

Jack had called ahead and asked to see him, and though Goodman was not anxious to give away anything free he had enough contempt left for Michael Crimmins and his political associates that he agreed to do whatever he could to help.

"Harry Goodman," he said, taking Jack's hand. He was in his San Francisco mode, wearing silk suspenders with a pattern of bridges and cable cars and an angled Victorian mansion just above each gold clamp. "I'm a little short for time, but I'd be happy to help in any way. Coffee?"

"Thanks," Jack said.

Goodman picked up the phone. "Two coffees please, Linda. Thank you." He was still groomed for the cameras, his horn-rims leveled and his gold Cross pens at the ready.

"As I told you, Mr. Goodman, I'm working with the LAPD on the Crimmins case. Informally, of course. They're looking for possible suspects and I thought that one of the people who would know the most about a dead congressman was the person who ran the opposition's political campaign."

"Very astute," Goodman said. It wasn't, but Jack remembered how the suits always spread praise around when it was free—a way of creating markers they could call in later.

The secretary came in with the coffee. She brought it on a walnut tray with fresh cream and a bowl of sugar with a tiny silver spoon. "Can I get you anything else, Mr. Goodman?"

"No, thank you, Linda," he said.

"Mr. Grant, can I get you anything?"

"No thanks," Jack said.

"If Miller calls from Commerce, put him through," Goodman said. "Otherwise hold the calls."

"Yes, Mr. Goodman," Linda said, as she closed the door.

"Sorry about that," Goodman said, "but I need to talk to a man about a trade agreement."

"I understand," Jack said. "I appreciate your seeing me."

"OK," Goodman said, "Michael Crimmins . . . the *late* Michael Crimmins. The public isn't missing much. Your basic congressional type. Before that, your basic lobbyist. Just a second . . ."

Goodman opened his desk drawer and took out a file. "I knew you were coming, so I dug this out." He opened the file. It wasn't very thick.

"We ran the usual checks on him. Episcopalian. Practiced whenever the cameras were rolling. Lived in Hancock Park. Nice address, but a small place for that area. Good for the constituents, make them think you were only in it for the opportunity to serve. Married to Lorraine Brander. That's her maiden name. She took it back after they split. That was . . . let me see . . . about seven years ago. Lorraine was an heiress. Her grandfather started Tempco Industries. Good old Charlie Stone. Rich as Midas and a hell of a lot smarter. His daughter married Louis Brander. He was a judge."

"Why did Crimmins and his wife split?"

"Crimmins was in it for the money from the beginning, at least as far as we could tell. He was running around on her too, so Lorraine dropped him like a bad habit. Smart lady. Just like her grandfather. Anyway, no big deal. He wasn't running for president or anything and adultery isn't a capital crime in the state of California. We brought it up during the campaign, but we didn't make a big deal out of it."

"Were you able to identify any of the women he was involved with?"

"A couple, but they're all married now and don't want to be bothered. I don't really think any of them could have killed him."

"Why do you say that?"

"Because none of it ran deep. These were just quickies and one-nighters. Crimmins wasn't into sex; he was into money and power. No, *power* isn't really the right word. He didn't want to really *direct* anything. He just wanted to order other people around. You know—make himself feel like King Shit."

"Anything in his work as a lobbyist that gave off a bad odor?"

"Some, but nothing out of the ordinary. We're not talking about Trappist monks here. The principal part of his job was to *deliver*. He delivered well. His electors and constituents weren't all that concerned about how he did it."

"Personal habits?"

"Too smart to gamble. He liked good scotch, but who doesn't? We could never link him with anything that had to do with drugs."

"How about in the past? Anything still rattling around in the closet?"

"Not that we noticed. He started out as a college intern, spent a year at Defense, and then went private. There was a lot of money for defense in those days; he did well without really exerting himself very much."

"Which administration, Nixon's?"

"Johnson's."

"I didn't think he was that old."

"He was young when he started."

"What did he do at Defense?"

"Scut work. The job was all title. He was special assistant to the deputy assistant to the undersecretary for something or other to do with procurement. He wrote memos and drank coffee, dressed up for cocktail parties and impressed college girls and secretaries."

"I see. Let me ask you something, Mr. Goodman."

"Go ahead."

"If you were in the LAPD, where would you look to find a suspect?"

"I don't know. It's hard for me to imagine Michael Crimmins doing anything by himself. There's no there there. He was a talking head with a good Rolodex. It was all contacts and relationships. This guy wasn't a godfather or a general; on a good day he was a middleman. He wouldn't do anything interesting or important alone, nothing, at least, that would get him killed in that way. I got the British papers when the story broke. They were a little more detailed than the *Times*. That sword up the ass—anyone who would do that was carrying something heavy. Michael Crimmins wasn't the prince of darkness. He was a dweeb, an insider. He'd bend the truth and kiss the right asses. He'd do what it took to keep himself in cashmere coats and Armani ties, but this guy wasn't Jack the Ripper or Dracula. You have to have a soul first. If we were in Washington I could open up that window there, throw out my coffee, and splatter a hundred guys like Michael Crimmins."

"Whoever put the sword to him must have felt strongly about it."

"No question," Goodman said. "All I'm telling you is that for me it doesn't fit. I know these kind of guys. Trust me, I do."

"So what are you saying, that he was killed by mistake?"

"No. I'm just saying that whatever he did, he didn't do alone."

"Thanks for your help," Jack said, getting up to leave and taking his hand.

"I know what you're thinking," Goodman said.

"What's that?"

"That I know these guys because I'm one of them."

"I wasn't thinking that," Jack said.

"Think about it this way. People come to me because I know *things*; people came to Michael Crimmins because he knew *people*. There's a big difference. Look, I'm no Galahad. I consult. That means people pay me big money knowing they can fire me at will. I've got to come across or they never call again. I'm a hired gun, some would say a whore, but I'm no different than a lawyer or a stockbroker. Crimmins . . . people like him . . . they're parasites. They feed on the system without contributing anything to it. And they get by with it for years."

"His time just elapsed."

"I know. It kind of renews your faith, if you know what I mean."

"I know exactly what you mean," Jack said. "Thanks again."

The wind was brisk when Jack left the Arco Building. He buttoned his jacket and started to walk back to the garage where he had parked his car. He checked his watch and then picked up his pace; downtown rates were like New York's. A quick walk would save him four dollars. As he walked he thought about what Goodman had just said and he remembered Frank's telling him the opinion of the Scotland Yard inspector. Michael Crimmins was not going to be the only one to die. The only question was how soon the next person would go down.

TWENTY-ONE

"Thank you for seeing me, Mr. Crimmins. I know this is a very hard time for you."

"You're welcome, Lieutenant," Harold Crimmins said. "Anything I can do to help you catch my son's murderer..."

He was wearing a brown plaid shirt over wrinkled gray slacks, held in place by functional, not decorative, suspenders. His gray-brown hair was tousled and unwashed.

"I gather you've spoken with the federal authorities."

"Yes. They were here last night. Actually they were here nearly all night. Michael's mother finally couldn't stand it any longer. She's staying with a neighbor now. She's very tired, Lieutenant. I can't tell you what this has done to her."

As he spoke, Harold Crimmins began to rub and twist the tips of his fingers, nervously turning them around and inward, almost as if he were winding himself up, tightening himself, so that he wouldn't collapse in pieces.

"I know it's hard for you to keep going over the same ground, but I'd appreciate it if you would take me through it too."

"There's not that much, Lieutenant." Again he was twisting his fingertips, squeezing and turning them until they became reddish-purple. "Our Michael was a wonderful son and a wonderful leader. Our loss is the country's loss. There's no telling what that boy might have accomplished if this hadn't happened. The whole thing is just terrible; it's a tragedy, Lieutenant White. I can't imagine why anyone could have possibly done that to him. I still can't believe it."

"He didn't speak to you about any threats?"

"Never. He had critics. What person in a position such as that doesn't? But threats . . . no. Why would anyone threaten Michael? He tried to help people. He tried to help his country. Who would want to prevent him from doing that?"

"Do you know whether or not there were any anticipated or pending lawsuits against him?"

"I think there was one, Lieutenant, something to do with some rental property he owned. Somebody wanted an easement or a right of way or something, but they didn't want to pay for it. It wasn't anything serious. He mentioned it to me over a year ago. He was trying to make the point that everybody in the country is so quick to sue now. That's all. He never mentioned it again."

"Do you know whether or not your son was seeing anybody steadily?"

"You mean a young lady?"

"Yes."

"No, Michael was too busy with his political responsibilities. He had some friends he dated from time to time, but there was nothing steady or serious. Michael was divorced several years ago. I think he was taking that part of his personal life very slowly; he didn't want to be hurt that way a second time."

"I understand. Mr. Crimmins, did your son happen to say anything to you about his trip to London? For example, did anyone communicate with him regarding the trip in any way that might be considered out of the ordinary? An odd invitation, for example . . . a warning . . . a change in the arrangements or the itinerary . . . anything at all that might be worth mentioning."

"I didn't even know he was going, Lieutenant. I think it was a spur of the moment kind of thing. He found out that the trade delegation was going to be there and he just decided to go over. I'm sure that what he wanted to do was be there to encourage them. It was important. He wanted to do his part to help out. That's the way he was, Lieutenant. There were no long-term plans that I know of. If somebody was following him—somebody who wanted to hurt him—they must have gone over there with him. I can't imagine why any British person would want to kill him. It must have been somebody from over here."

"I agree. There's no reason to believe that the murderer was a foreign national. But why do you think whoever killed him would have killed him there? Anyone who was following him closely should have known that he would be coming right back. Why go to all that trouble? If it *was* an American, why take the risk of committing a crime in an unfamiliar setting?"

"I really don't know, Lieutenant. That's what Mr. McGann and his people were trying to figure out. They asked me again and again, but I just didn't know." He twisted his fingers and chewed at his lip. "I wish I could do more."

"Did your son ever have anything to do with swords, Mr. Crimmins? Did he fence in college or collect weapons of any sort?"

"No. He played sandlot baseball when he was a boy, but he never fenced. He collected trading cards and records, that kind of thing, but he never collected any weapons. I've never had them in the house. His mother feels strongly about it."

"Did *he* own any weapons?"

"I think he might have had an old shotgun somewhere, but that was all. Sometimes people wanted to take him hunting. You know how that is when you're in that kind of work."

"Yes, I do. Mr. Crimmins, do you know whether or not he had any arguments or disagreements with anyone lately? It doesn't have to have been anything major."

"No. Everyone who knew my son liked him. Some may have disagreed with him, but he was the sort of person who tried to see the good in everyone. In return, I think they all saw the good in him. Not everybody loved him as much as his mother and I did, but I can't imagine anyone wanting to kill him."

"You really admired your son, didn't you, Mr. Crimmins?"

"He was a wonderful young man, Lieutenant."

"How would you characterize his marriage?"

"I wouldn't really be able to say. His wife had her own friends. We didn't see them very much. I think she was spoiled, Lieutenant. You know, of course, that she is very wealthy."

"Yes, I understand that she is."

"I don't think that they were a good match. Michael loved her very much. He told me that. He told his mother too. I don't think he ever understood her ways. Rich people have different ways. They worry about different things."

"Yes. Why did they divorce, do you know?"

"I think she was a person who could never really share. Do you know what I mean, Lieutenant? To stay married to the same person for a long time means that you have to learn to share."

"Yes."

"She had always gotten her way and it was difficult for her to share her life and her things with another person. Not that Michael would have ever made unreasonable demands on her. I just think she was—how would I say it?—a small person, Lieutenant. Do you know what I mean?"

"Yes, I do know what you mean. Who would you say were your son's closest friends, Mr. Crimmins?"

"He had so many . . . let me see. *We* were very close, of course. His staff was devoted to him. I know he was close to all of them. I suppose his attorney, Richard Campbell."

"In Los Angeles, Mr. Crimmins?"

"Yes."

"Is there anything else that you can tell me, anything at all that you think might help?"

"No, not really. All I can say is that Michael was such a fine young man. Whoever did this to him must have been a very sick person."

"How often did you see your son, Mr. Crimmins?"

"All the time, Lieutenant. Whenever he was here. Whenever we could." His bloodshot eyes began to run with moisture.

"Once a week?"

"Oh no, he was very busy, Lieutenant," he said proudly. "Once every other month or so—when he was in town, of course. He spent a great deal of time in Washington, Lieutenant. He had to; that was his job. He saw us whenever he could. I know he did."

"I want to thank you for talking to me, Mr. Crimmins. I really appreciate it. We'll do all that we can to find the person who killed your son. If you can think of anything else that you haven't mentioned, please call me."

Frank took out his card and made some jottings on it. "The second number is my private line."

"Thank you, Lieutenant," Harold Crimmins said, reading the card carefully and slipping it into his shirt pocket. "I'd have to talk to Mr. McGann. He said that any new information has to come to him first.

But if I think of anything I'll call him, and if he has no objection, I'll call you too."

"I'd appreciate it," Frank said, taking him by the hand, then walking back to his car, trying not to shake his head.

TWENTY-TWO

"What are you going to have?" Frank asked.

"Veal, probably," Jack answered. "The last time we came to Donato's I had veal and it was good."

"Gentlemen?" the waiter said.

"We try to be," Frank answered. "Sorry . . . it's been a long day. Bring me a bottle of Peroni or Moretti. I want to look at the menu some more."

"Sir?" he said, turning to Jack.

"Bring one for me, too."

―――――

"Why doesn't he have a pigtail?" Frank asked, watching the waiter walk back to the bar. "I thought they all had to have pigtails now."

"Not if their name is Guido or Dominic," Jack said. "What did you learn from Crimmins' parents, anything?"

"No. I was only able to talk to the father. The mother was with a neighbor. She had to rest up after the feds finished with her."

"Assholes."

"Yes. I talked to the father for about an hour. He thought his son was Jesus Christ on a bad day. I don't think they spent much time together and now that his son's dead the father's trying to think about him as he might have been."

"That's not surprising."

"No. The one thing the feds are fixating on is the fact that Crimmins was killed in England rather than over here. Nobody really understands that."

"The difference in penal laws?"

"Maybe, but English prisons are a hell of a far cry from the Ritz-Carlton. They don't really like you to go around killing people."

"Maybe it's a time thing," Jack said. "Maybe he only kills during a full moon or in months with r's in them."

"Yes. Or maybe it's like a sex thing," Frank said. "He was all worked up to kill Crimmins on a certain day and he couldn't stop himself once he was getting close."

"Yes, Frank, except that this guy looks like a world-class planner. I don't see him suddenly letting himself be taken over by his emotions. This is a guy who makes charts and outlines, a guy with graphs and diagrams and computers, not the kind whose head starts to come apart because of chemical imbalances."

"He could be a genius and a nut at the same time," Frank said.

"That's always possible."

"What did you learn?"

"I didn't really *learn* all that much," Jack said. "I talked to this guy named Goodman—the pol who ran the Connors campaign."

"Crimmins' opposition."

"Right. I was hoping to see what kind of dirt they might have dug in the course of the campaign."

"What did he say?"

"He said that Crimmins was nothing more than a suit with a good Rolodex, a junior-league power junkie who spent most of his time keeping his political network intact—the sort who would place a bet every now and then, throw back a scotch, or maybe bed down with a starry-eyed secretary, but not the sort who would ever really get seriously entangled. He was the kind who would sit up every night staring at an organizational chart and wondering how he could move his token closer to the center and then move it farther toward the top."

"A government wonk."

"Exactly. Goodman said he couldn't imagine Crimmins doing anything alone that would ever be important enough to make somebody mad enough to kill him. He was a middleman, never out in front on anything—in his life or in his work: never more than a short step away from the pasty faces, riding on image and bluff, placing calls and kissing asses, poring over the *Post* and the *Times* every day, wondering how he could get invited to the right events with the right people and get himself seated as close as possible to the center of the photographers' line of sight."

"You've been stationed in Washington, Jack. Those people can turn nasty."

"Sure they can, but usually on their terms and in their ways. I can imagine him really pissing off somebody who's on the same wavelength as his, but most outsiders would have a hard time even figuring out the game. It's like a Victorian novel, Frank. They kill you with these little slights and odd glances. They change the color of your stationery or say something about your pocket square not quite matching the pattern in your tie—ruthless shit like that. People who have played for real stakes wouldn't even know they were under attack."

"But somebody in their world would."

"That's right," Jack said, "but I have trouble imagining somebody in that world running up a moving escalator and ramming a steel sword into somebody's ass. Somebody from Crimmins' world would attack with different weapons."

"You're probably right," Frank said, as the waiter returned with their beer.

"Are you ready to order?" he asked, dropping the *gentlemen* just to be on the safe side.

"Go ahead, Frank," Jack said.

"OK. I'll have the gnocchi with Italian sausage and a small antipasto—hold the anchovies."

"It doesn't come with anchovies, sir."

"That's good," Frank said.

"Sir?"

"I'll have the veal chop with some fettucine on the side."

"Marinara sauce?"

"That's fine," Jack said. "And the sliced tomatoes with mozzarella—easy on the oil."

"I'll put it on the side. Would you like some wine with your dinner?"

"Frank?" Jack asked.

"Something simple," Frank said.

"The Antinori riserva is a nice wine and a good value," the waiter said.

"That sounds good to me," Jack said. "Frank?"

He nodded OK. The waiter squeezed out a thin smile and walked away.

"So what do you think?" Frank asked. "Crimmins *did* get himself killed, so whether he acted alone or acted with somebody else, he did do something that made somebody very unhappy. If he didn't act alone, then we can probably expect number two in the not too distant future."

"So it seems to me," Jack said, taking a long drink of his Peroni.

"And what do we do in the meantime besides wait?"

"We could have a second beer," Jack said.

TWENTY-THREE

"Hi, Billy, having a nice evening?" The voice.

"What do you want?"

"Oh, you know how I am. Always thinking. Always thinking about *you* especially. I've got another one of my little surprises..."

"Jesus. What is it? Just tell me, straight out."

"Be patient, Billy. First, let me congratulate you on the Caller-ID phone you got. Top-of-the-line, Billy. Cutting edge. State-of-*the*-art. I didn't think the clerk was as nice to you as she could have been, but what can you expect these days? How do you like it by now?"

"You were there?"

"I'm with you all the time, Billy. You should know that by now. By the way, I'm using a stolen cellular right now myself, so don't worry about trying to figure out who I am or where I am. I've got to be state-of-the-art too, you know. I thought it would be a good idea to tell you that up front—sort of clear the air, keep us focused, if you know what I mean."

"What do you want?" His voice was becoming tired now and the tones of pain were noticeable.

"Come on. Where's that old Billy? Maybe my surprise will pick you up a little. I want you to roll out your refrigerator and look at the ice-maker connection."

"Just a second."

He was back in about thirty seconds, his voice thick with anger and frustration.

"There's one of those poison stickers attached to it."

"You're going to have to learn to be more precise, Billy. That's a 'Mr. Yuck' sticker. Do you know what that means?"

"You've put poison in my ice-maker line."

"Go to the head of the class, Billy. Actually, just enough poison so that the water picks up a little at a time. All of your ice cubes contain poison, Billy. *All* of them. You see, when I stopped by to install my surprise in the line, I dumped the old tray. I wanted you to get a fresh start, Billy. That's the bad news. The good news is that while the poison has been building up in your system there's probably not enough there to kill you yet—just enough to make you sick. You *have* been using those ice cubes, haven't you? You wouldn't want that Johnny Walker black to be warm and lonely, would you?"

Devens looked at the sweaty glass sitting on his countertop. "Look," he said, "this has gone too goddamned far. Talk to me. What do you want from me, money?"

"Billy, I thought you'd never ask. All these conversations, all these surprises . . ."

"How much?"

"How much do you have?"

"I haven't been doing too badly," he said. "When the housing market started to turn around I still had a lot of listings. I never stopped working, even when the industry was in the toilet. I know we can work something out."

"Brave Billy."

"How much?"

"Well, let me see . . . I'm thinking of a number with a lot of zeros behind it, Billy."

"How much?" There was more strength in his voice now.

"Three million five."

"Holy Christ. I couldn't raise that much money if I liquidated everything I had and sold the whole business."

"Billy . . ." Admonishing him now. "I've been working hard too and I *know* you can raise that kind of money. Think of it this way—you could clean out your present operation, get rid of all of my little phone calls and surprises, and start fresh. It would be a whole new life for you."

"I can't raise that kind of money without a lot of time."

"We've got all the time you need, Billy. In the meantime, I've got a nice long list of fresh surprises. Why don't you get yourself a drink and we'll talk about the next one. By the way, if I were you, I'd skip the ice this time. Of course, that's up to you."

"We've got to talk. I know we can work this out."

"You mean *negotiate*? I'm afraid I don't do that very well, Billy."

"Let's just talk."

"I'll call you back in a couple minutes."

"Wait . . ." he said, grabbing and poking at the phone, but the line was already dead.

———

For the next five minutes he sat at his kitchen table, nervously running his left hand through his hair. He was perspiring heavily and there was a taste in his mouth like oxidized metal. Maybe the poison. If there *was* any goddamned poison. He got up, opened the door of his freezer, and dumped the ice tray into the sink. Then he twisted the tiny brass spigot in the ice-maker line and rolled the refrigerator back into place. He looked at his drink and poured it over the ice in the sink. Then he turned the hot water knob and grabbed the faucet, directing the stream at the pile of congealed cubes—making holes and tunnels, round, shrinking edges, ice cobwebs. Doing something at least, trying to take control.

Suddenly the phone rang.

"Hello," he said anxiously.

It was a squeaky woman's voice. "Good evening, Mr. Devens. I'm calling from your Neighborhood Association. Would you be willing to take a turn this Saturday driving the noon watch?"

"No, I-I-'m busy this Saturday."

"Billy, Billy, I surprised you again." The robot's voice now. "That was one of my voice filters just now. Neat, huh? State-of-the-art, Bill. I bet you *would* like to drive that neighborhood watch, looking out for yours truly, huh?"

"Can we talk?"

"You sound like Joan Rivers, Billy."

"Can we?"

"Yes, I think it's probably time that we did."

"When?"

"How about tomorrow, Billy?"

"That soon?"

"What's wrong with tomorrow? You weren't planning any surprises of your own, were you?"

"No, of course not. Where?"

"I thought maybe some place that was nice and public. When was the last time you were at Disneyland, Billy?"

"A long time ago."

"Good. Then you'll be able to combine our little business with some pleasure. First rule, Billy: come alone. Understood?"

"Yes."

"It's an important rule, Billy. You know what happened to Mikey."

"I understand."

"I'm still not sure I can trust you, Billy."

"You can trust me."

"Well, let's do this. I'll follow you awhile and then when I'm ready I'll approach you. If I need to contact you before we sit down and talk, I will, so stay alert, Billy. If you're standing next to a phone and it rings, pick it up. If strangers approach you, don't brush them off. Answer their questions; listen to what they have to say. I'll be communicating with you in creative ways—you know me, Billy. Understood?"

"OK."

"Have you got something to write on, Billy?"

"Just a second."

He took a pad from the shelf above the utensil drawer.

"OK, I'm ready."

"I want you to start by riding on . . . let's see . . . six rides. When I'm convinced that you're alone I'll make contact with you and tell you what to do next."

"OK, which rides?"

"I'll try to pick some that you'll enjoy, Billy. Why don't you start with Pirates of the Caribbean, then go on to the Jungle Cruise. Then ride the Thunder Mountain Railroad, and then Splash Mountain. That's a new one, Billy. I know you'll enjoy it. By the way, I kind of like this mountain motif, don't you?"

"Which ones then?" he asked, writing hurriedly.

"Then the Submarines, Billy, and finally the Matterhorn. Another mountain, eh? And Billy . . . ?"

"What?"

"Just walk at a leisurely pace. Don't look around. Don't try to figure out where I am or which one is me. Just enjoy yourself. Now, read the list back to me."

"Pirates of the Caribbean, the Jungle Cruise, the Thunder Mountain Railroad, Splash Mountain, the Submarines, and the Matterhorn."

"Actually, it's the *Big* Thunder Mountain Railroad. I like to be precise about these things. I'm sure you appreciate that. When you've finished with all of those rides, go to the Tomorrowland Terrace. That's the big refreshment stand with the stage that comes out of the ground. It's right in between the Submarines and Star Tours. Look for it on the map they give you. Sit as close to the stage area as you can, facing in that direction. That will be east. If I approach you there and start talking, don't turn around until I tell you that you can."

"OK. The Tomorrowland Terrace."

"Right. Very good. Start at 11:35 sharp. And don't worry if the lines are long. Just go with it, Billy. If you get nervous, I don't want you worrying about the clock. I want you to be thinking about something else."

"What's that?"

"Three and a half million dollars and a realistic timetable for the payment."

"I will."

"And you'll be alone."

"Yes."

"And you'll follow all of my instructions."

"Yes."

"To the letter."

"Yes."

"Then I'll see you in the Magic Kingdom."

The phone went dead.

"You son-of-a-bitch. You're goddamned right you'll see me in the fucking Magic Kingdom. This time it'll be different. I'll be ready for you. You won't have any goddamned car to drive away in and you won't be able to pull any of your funny shit with all of those damned people around us. And this time I won't be alone and helpless. Three and a half mil. Ha. You're not gonna get dick, you stupid fuck. You're gonna get a razor across your throat or a knife up your ass. I'm not gonna sit back and take your shit anymore."

―――――

Rummaging through his cupboard now. Talking to himself. Where is it? Not here. Shit. Throwing boxes out on the middle of his bedroom floor. Shit. Not this one. Not this one either. God*damn*it. Wait, what have we here? Opening up an old Florsheim box and lifting it out— wrapped in oily cloths inside a thick, terry cloth hand towel. Soaked through now, but still smelling fresh. Ready for action. A snub-nosed .38 special. Blue steel. Pretty as a picture, even if it wasn't state-of-the-art anymore. But who gives a shit—it would make that bastard just as dead.

OK, two more stops. No, three. Find the boots. There they are. Nice and chewed-up. They'll look fine with the jeans. Nice and natural. Nothing suspicious. With all the fucking blue collars at Disneyland they'll fit right in. Back to the dresser. Top drawer. Feeling around for it. Got it! A gravity knife. Snapping it open now for practice. Cutting and slicing the air. I'll see the blood run down your shirt, you smartass son of a bitch. And you won't keep calling me fucking *Billy*. Trying to get to me. Knowing how I feel about that. Chipping away at me. Trying to control me. Not this time, cocksucker.

One more stop now. Where is it? In the towel closet. No. In the bathroom. An old gift. An antique. Grandpa's. Where? Checking drawers, feeling around in the back. Where? Behind the Ramses with the reservoir tips. Behind the pills. Yes. There. With an ivory handle and some abalone inlays. Opening the straight razor. No rust. Angling it against his arm. Cutting a few hairs. Slick. Smooth. Sharp as all hell. Maybe I'll get some time for a little payback. Take that bastard off to some quiet corner. Start with the nose. Nosey motherfucker. Not anymore. Then the ears. You like to listen, fuck? Try it this way. Then head south. Slowly. Maybe switch to the gravity knife. Not as sharp. Cut deeper and slower. Let the son-of-a-bitch know that the fucking game is over now. You like surprises? I'll give you surprises, you son-of-a-bitch. You want to fuck up my life? You want to torment my ass? We'll see if you can take it as well as you can fucking dish it out.

 The pistol inside the jacket. The knife in one boot and the razor in the other. And that's just for fucking starters. If you think I'm coming in there alone, you're out of your goddamned mind. The odds just changed, fuck. This time we're going by my rules.

TWENTY-FOUR

"Can I bring you dessert?" the waiter asked.

"Jack?"

"No thanks."

"None for me either," Frank said, "but I'll take some black coffee."

"Bring me some too," Jack said.

"No cream or sugar for you either, sir?"

"No," Jack said.

The waiter left. Jack slid his chair back and put his napkin on the table. "Give me a couple of minutes," he said. "I want to call my electronic secretary."

———

He returned six minutes later.

"Anything momentous?" Frank asked.

"No, mostly the usual stuff. Some guy trying to offer me a free VISA card, another pressing me to join the newest and most exclusive men's club in the San Gabriel Valley."

"So exclusive that they're making random telephone calls."

"That's right. I had another call just like that no more than two or three weeks ago. This guy kept telling me that he and the other members were offering me the chance of a lifetime, that I was *precisely* the sort of person they were seeking for their club. It had some cutesy name—something that sounded religious but really wasn't: the St. Mark's Club, I think, or maybe the St. Andrew's."

"*They* were in a pretty exclusive club," Frank said.

"Right, but you won't be seeing either of them at this place. Anyway, the guy also told me that membership fees would be raised *very* soon and that the special enrollment period would then be closed *forever*. He sounded very urgent, which impressed me, since I figured he had probably made seven or eight hundred of those same calls since he strapped on his headset that day."

"And after all of his persuading *you* didn't join."

"No, you know what a prick I am, Frank. I said to him, 'You mean they'll stop letting in the kind of people who make important decisions over the phone at dinnertime and instead start to get *really* selective.' He said, 'Not at all, sir; this is a *very* exclusive organization.' I asked him how much it cost to join and he said not to worry, that we could talk about that later and if there was any problem I could always pay on the installment plan."

"Sounds pretty damned exclusive to me," Frank said. "I've probably arrested half of their current membership. The poor bastards are in Lompoc or Vacaville now and they can't keep up with their dues."

"That's what I thought. So I took a deep breath and passed up the chance of a lifetime."

"Anything else on your answering machine?"

"There were two wrong numbers that were semi-interesting. The first was some guy trying to buy live bait. He wanted to know if I had any leeches or catalpa worms. The second was a guy who thought he was calling a dating service. He said he wanted to meet somebody tall and dark."

"That's not a wrong number; that's you, Jack," Frank said. "I think you should open up your horizons—go out with him once or twice, see if there's any chemistry there."

"I think I'll give him *your* number," Jack said. "Your social life is in worse shape than mine."

"You got that right," Frank said. "Anything else?"

"If you can believe it, one *bona fide* job offer. Some guy who wanted to hire a bodyguard. Actually he wanted to hire two of them."

"Are you going to call him?"

"No, the job's tomorrow and I've already got something on. Besides, I never liked that kind of work. You have to stick a plastic tube in your ear, get a bad haircut and an undertaker's suit, and keep saying 'Ten-four' into your lapel or armpit."

"I wonder why he called you."

"He was just turning his fingers loose in the yellow pages."

"How much do you think he was willing to pay?"

"Probably a lot, from the sound of his voice. Why? Are you thinking about moonlighting?"

"No, not just yet. Was it anybody whose name I'd recognize?"

"All he left was a 213 telephone number and a first name. He said if I was interested I should call *Bill*."

TWENTY-FIVE

The doorbell rang just as Devens was getting out of the shower. He hurried down the steps with a maroon and gold towel clutched around his waist; his head and back were still wet. When he got to the front hall he looked at the mahogany wall clock: 7:00 AM. Sonofabitch. He wasn't due to meet the rent-a-cops for another half hour and he had specifically told them to stay the fuck away from his house, no matter what happened. He looked through the peephole and saw a Mexican in a DHL uniform. He was holding a clipboard and a thin package and he was cleaning out his right ear with the tip of his ballpoint. Great. Next it'd be the goddamned Avon lady and the Jehovah's Witnesses.

"You got something for me?" Devens said.

"Yes, sir. Sign there, please. On line 29, right next to the X."

There was no return address on the package. "Do you have any idea who sent this?" Devens asked.

"Not if it isn't on the package," the man said.

"What about the item number there? Don't people have to give you some kind of an address or phone number when they send something? What happens if something gets screwed up and you need to reach them?"

"I don't know what they do when that happens. I just started two days ago," the man said. "I could ask."

"Do you know your station number?" Devens asked.

"Sure."

"Write it on the package, will you?"

"Sure. No problem." He got out his wallet and pulled out a card. Devens could see the DHL logo on it. Looking at the card, the man wrote the number across the bottom of the package, just under Devens' address.

"Let me see the number on line 29 again," Devens said. "I want to make sure it's the same as on the package."

"Sure." The man turned the clipboard around, slid the rubber band out of the way, and held the board up, just above the package.

"OK," Devens said, "I got it."

He closed the door and slowly pulled the slip tab on the padded mailer. He spread it open and looked inside. There was nothing there but a single, unmarked, audio cassette. He looked at the clock again: 7:08. Shit. Twenty-two minutes left and his head was still wet. What the hell. It wouldn't take that long to get dressed. He hurried into the den and popped the cassette into the tape player.

There was ten seconds of hiss before the voice came on. The *Mission Impossible* government automaton: "Good morning, Mr. Devens. Your mission—should you choose to accept it—is to proceed to Disneyland and follow your previous instructions to the letter. If you fail to do as you are told, the secretary will disavow any knowledge of your actions . . . and of their consequences. This tape will self-destruct in three seconds."

"That smartass sonofabitch," Devens said, as he hit the eject button. "Fucking jokes. Always the fucking jokes."

Nothing happened. He hit it again.

"Goddamnit." Again.

The first wisp of smoke seeped from the deck.

"That *asshole*. No!"

More smoke began to come out now as the heat increased. Then the arcing started and the sparks.

"God*damn*it."

The plastic was melting on the front of the deck and the smoke was increasing. There were more sparks.

Devens reached behind the credenza to pull the plug from the outlet, but there wasn't enough space between the credenza and the wall for him to reach it. He scuffed his wrist in the attempt, tearing loose a long, thin patch of skin. He hurried to the end of the credenza and, forgetting himself for a moment, pulled back on the corner with both of his hands. The pain shot through his burned fingers.

"That *cocksucker*!"

He got down on the floor and pushed the credenza with his feet, but it had settled too far into the nap of the carpet to slide easily. As he pushed harder it started to rock rather than slide. The whole stereo setup started to wobble.

"Oh no, oh no," Devens said. He pulled back his feet and the system fell back against the wall, gouging the paneling. Screaming now in anger, Devens shoved the credenza again with both feet and the entire setup began to fall forward.

"Oh no, why in the *fuck* now?"

The tape deck was still smoking as it fell to the floor in the middle of the components of the stereo system. Devens pulled the cord from the outlet, got up, and hurried into the kitchen. He took a plastic pitcher out of the refrigerator, threw the juice it contained into the sink, splashing part of it against the kitchen window, and filled the pitcher with water. Then he hurried back into the den and poured the water on the smoking tape deck and scorched rug.

He stepped over the broken and melted equipment, his nose and lungs filled with electrical-fire smoke.

"That sonofabitch. Trying to fuck with my head, trying to screw up my timing and break my concentration. He's gonna find out it isn't that goddamn easy."

The phone rang and Devens turned to look at the clock on his desk: 7:29.

"Is this Bill?" the voice said.

"Yes."

"This is Lou. We spoke last night."

"Right."

"Dan is here with me and we're ready to go to work."

"So am I," Devens said. "I'll be there in about twenty minutes."

He hurried up the stairs and pulled the towel away from his waist. His back and head were still wet, this time with sweat. He toweled himself off and got dressed, slipping the razor into one boot, the gravity knife into the other. Then he checked the .38. It was loaded. He shoved it into his belt and put on his jacket.

"No more of your bullshit now, fuckhead," he said. "It's my turn for fun and games."

He had a minute and a half to spare when he got downstairs. He picked up the padded mailer and called the DHL number.

The voice at the other end was sleepy. "DHL . . ."

"Hello, I just received a wonderful gift in a DHL package, but there was no return address on the package and no card."

"Have you got the number?" the voice asked. Devens could hear him take a sip of coffee.

"Yes, I have it right here. It's L197321."

"Just a second, read it again."

Devens read it again, slowly, checking his watch when he was finished.

"OK," the voice said. "What I'll do is check with my supervisor; he has the computer in his office. We'll see if we can find out who sent you the gift. If the person wanted to be anonymous we won't be able to tell you his name. They have to make a point of telling us if they don't want anyone to know who they are. That doesn't happen very often; most of the time they just forget to put in a card or write down the return address."

"I understand."

"And what is your name, sir?"

"William Devens."

"How do you spell that?"

"D-e-v-e-n-s."

"And how about a phone number?"

"Is this going to take awhile?"

"Well, it shouldn't take too long. My supervisor is out at the moment, but we'll get to it as soon as we can."

Devens gave him his mobile number.

"We'll get back to you on this just as soon as possible."

"Thanks," Devens said, "I'd appreciate it. And I'd appreciate it if you could do it sooner rather than later."

"I understand," the man said, as he took another sip of his coffee.

"Asshole," Devens said, as he put down the receiver. "They'll have their fucking sweet rolls and their morning nap before they get around to doing anything for me."

He reached behind him for the fourth time to check for the revolver. He liked the feel of it there; he liked running his fingernail through the edges of the grip and bringing that scent of oil on his fingertip up to his face. He thought about pulling it out, about smoking the son-of-a-bitch who was riding him so hard. This time I'll have my chance, he thought to himself.

TWENTY-SIX

Devens pulled his Town Car into the Dunkin' Donuts lot on Santa Monica. He went inside, bought a large black coffee in a Styrofoam cup, and walked over to a table in the corner. Two men were seated at the next table. He talked to them without turning his head.

"I'm Bill," he said.

"Hi," the man closest to him said. He was tall and thick and he was wearing new jeans and a worn leather jacket. "I'm Lou Carmichael. This is Dan Mallin." The other man was smoking a cigarette and eating a bear claw. He didn't speak.

"What it is," Devens said, "is some asshole is following me around, threatening me on the phone, putting fake bombs in my car—that kind of shit. He's trying to shake me down, says he'll meet me at Disneyland to talk about it."

"Where at Disneyland?" Carmichael asked.

"That's pretty complicated," Devens said. "He wants me to walk around the park for an hour or two and ride a couple of rides. Then he wants to meet me at this refreshment stand. I think he wants to make sure that no one else is with me."

"He won't know," Carmichael said.

"He *can't*," Devens said. "The guy is an asshole but he's not stupid. If he thinks anything is wrong he might try to kill me."

"Nobody's going to kill you, Mr. Devens, not in Disneyland," Carmichael said. "They always act tough; they think it'll make you reach for your wallet. These pricks are all mouth."

"He's killed once," Devens said.

Carmichael put down his coffee. "He *has*? Where?"

"I can't tell you that, but he has. Look—don't fuck around with this guy. He's playing for keeps."

"Don't worry," Carmichael said. "Did you bring the retainers?"

"Yes. I've got two envelopes in my pocket. Each one has a list of the things I'm supposed to do and each one has five hundred dollars in it. If something happens to one of you I want to be sure that the other is still on me."

"What do you think's going to happen to us?" Carmichael said.

"How the hell should I know? Maybe he'll approach me early and change the whole goddamned plan. Maybe some old lady will fall over with a stroke and one of you will get cut off by the crowd. It's fucking Disneyland; anything could happen there. All I know is you're gonna have to spread out. You can't just climb up my goddamned back or he'll catch on right away. And remember—whatever happens, I want at least one of you on me all the time. Understand?"

"Don't worry. We'll both be on you the whole time. How about the rest of our fee?"

"I've got it, don't worry," Devens said. "Let's just get the job done first. Then we'll talk about the other money."

"Fair enough," Carmichael said.

"Doesn't he talk?" Devens asked, nodding briefly toward Mallin.

"No, not very often," Carmichael said. "What time are you supposed to arrive at the park?"

"At 11:35."

"Hell, we've got hours to spare. It won't take any more than an hour and a quarter to get there."

"Look, I want you to make sure you'll be there and ready when I arrive. I don't want you caught in traffic or pulled over on the shoulder by some goddamned cop. I want you in the park, not back on the fucking freeway."

"You like to worry a lot, don't you?" Carmichael asked.

"It's *my* ass," Devens said.

"Well, stop worrying," Carmichael said. "It only makes it harder if you look as if he's got you running scared. We'll drive down to Anaheim now, get some coffee and a sandwich. We'll be there when you get there. And Mr. Devens . . ."

"What?"

"Whatever you do, don't look around for us. Not even for a second. Believe me—he won't see us, but he *will* see you, and if you're looking around all the time he'll catch on quick. Don't worry; we'll be there. You just go about your business. Do exactly what he told you and forget all about us. When he gets close to you we'll have him by the shorts before he knows what's happening."

"Just be careful," Devens said. He took the envelopes from inside his jacket and put them behind him on his seat. Then he got up, threw what was left of his coffee in the trash bin, and went back to his Town Car.

"Why do we always get the nervous ones?" Carmichael said. "They always fuck up and make things harder." Mallin shook his head once and took another bite of his bear claw.

Devens pulled out of the lot and headed east on Santa Monica. Then he turned right on Bundy, snaking his way south toward the freeway. He didn't see the dark sedan two blocks behind him.

"Poor, stupid Devens," the voice said. "Two thick-shouldered PI's in a donut restaurant. You aren't any smarter now than you were then. I guess I'll have to be the one who teaches you..."

———

By the time he reached Anaheim, Devens' back was raw and sore from rubbing against the steel revolver wedged inside the back of his belt. He thought about putting it in the glove compartment of the Town Car, but figured it was good practice and good discipline to try to get used to the pain and annoyance. He turned off the Santa Ana at Harbor Boulevard, checked his watch, saw that it was 10:30, and drove across the eastbound traffic and into the parking lot of the local International House of Pancakes. He checked his watch again and turned off the ignition. For a moment or two he thought about driving into the park and doing a walk-through before 11:35, but he remembered Carmichael's advice and decided to follow the asshole on the phone's instructions to the letter.

Waiting there in his car, he checked his boots four times. Twice he took out the gravity knife and snapped it open. He liked the feel of it in his hand. He thought about plunging it into a back or belly, then turning it, probing and slicing whatever he could reach.

He took out his list of instructions and read them over a second and third time. There was no reason why he couldn't stop in the park, take out the list, and check to see where he was supposed to go next, but he wanted to look professional and self-assured. Checking would be a sign of weakness. He knew where he was going and he knew what he had to do. He wouldn't give the asshole any edge.

The air was clear and though the breeze off the coast was cool, the morning sun was already too warm for a closed car. He opened the window on the driver's side and cracked the passenger window for cross ventilation. The yellow smog that had blanketed the freeway from Downey to Buena Park must have been blowing inland or cooking off, because he could see the tops of the fan palms all along the boulevard, and the low-hanging clouds to the north and east were wisps of pure white against a madonna-blue backdrop of Orange County sky.

Another look at his watch: 10:50. He scooted forward in his seat, relieving the pressure of the revolver against his spine. He opened the glove compartment and took out a map, checking the local roads and freeway interchanges. What if he did make a clean kill? How would he escape? Where would he go? Where could he wait? Where could he hide?

Forget the kill, he thought. All he had to do was cut the bastard up, let the fucker know that he wasn't going to take any more of his shit. Let him know that the goddamned games were over.

Maybe just one good poke. Puncture a lung or a kidney. Maybe cut the Achilles tendon—cripple the bastard for life. That would be good. He wouldn't even have to kill him, wouldn't even have to pull his gun. Get the two strongarms to hold the son-of-a-bitch. Take him into some quiet corner and make a believer out of him. They could hold him while Devens busted him up. Let the little prick know that Devens could hire muscle whenever he needed to. Break him up, cut him, and throw him on the ground. Kick him a couple of times. Let the bastard know how lucky he was to be crawling away alive.

Checking his watch again now: 11:05. Close enough, he thought, I'm going in.

The kid at the gate's name was Ronald. He took Devens' parking money and gave him a numbered outline of the lot to mark, so that he wouldn't forget where he had parked his car. Two hundred yards into the lot Devens fell in line behind a row of cars. There were a lot of vans and 4x4s, old sedans filled with Mexicans, Grand Marquis and Taurus rentals. Disneyland employees in yellow shirts with their names embossed over the pocket directed him into a row within walking distance of the main entrance mall. Just above him was a picture of Goofy on a metal sign, indicating the general area of the lot in which his car was located. Goofy. Jesus.

Devens checked his boots, got out of the car, and started walking toward the mall. He looked at the lines in front of the ticket windows. It was 11:19. He walked directly to the window with the shortest line. In front of him was a Mexican with a blue T-shirt, a camcorder, a wife wearing shorts and a straw hat, and three kids. Two of them were crying and the third was asleep. They bought their tickets and moved on. Devens looked at his watch: 11:24. The only people left in front of him were a boy and girl on a date. She was wearing skin-tight white jeans and a bare-midriff pink cotton blouse. He was wearing his work shoes, more-or-less clean jeans, and a Save the Bales T-shirt. When he saw the price of admission he fumbled around in his wallet until he could locate a credit card. He looked at it closely and then handed it to the woman in the ticket booth. She swiped it through the card reader, waited, and then shook her head and said something to him. He said something under his breath and started fumbling in his wallet again.

Jesus, Devens thought. He's reached his goddamned limit on that one and he's going to try another one. He checked his watch again: 11:28. Shit.

The guy pulled out some wrinkled bills, placed them on the counter of the ticket window and started to count. The ticket seller said something to him; he counted the bills again, and then turned to his girl friend. She rooted around in her purse and handed him a couple of bills. Finally they got their tickets and walked toward the turnstiles.

Assholes, Devens thought, as he walked up to the window. "One adult," he said, handing the woman a fifty-dollar bill.

"Would you like any Disney dollars with your change?" she asked.

"No," he answered.

"Would you like a one, two, or three-day passport?"

"Just give me the ticket," he said.

"Certainly." She handed him the ticket and a souvenir guide to the park. "Enjoy your day in the Magic Kingdom," she said.

"Don't worry, I will," he answered, as he turned and started walking toward the row of turnstiles. He looked at his watch as he approached the flower sculpture of Mickey Mouse in the garden beneath the Town Square railroad stop: 11:35. "Fucking perfect," he said aloud as he checked the location of the first ride in his souvenir guide.

———

He couldn't hear the voice behind him. "Good morning, Billy. Right on time. Very good."

Devens walked around the garden, past the stroller rental station, and into the Town Square. The happiest place in the world, he thought. Not for you, asshole.

A minute and a half later he was walking down the sidewalk on the west side of Main Street, past the penny arcade and the Carnation Ice Cream Parlor and Restaurant. Carmichael came out of the Disney Clothiers, Ltd. on the east side of the street, crossed quickly, and fell in line behind Devens. As they approached the Central Plaza, Mallin was standing outside of Carefree Corner, smoking a cigarette. He flicked it into the street, fell in behind Carmichael, and the three of them walked into Adventureland, spaced at intervals of fifteen to twenty yards.

———

A few yards behind them walked a figure in dark clothes, murmuring quietly, "Billy. Muscle number one . . . and, yes, Muscle number two. So the little gang is all here. Hail, hail."

TWENTY-SEVEN

Pirates was practically deserted. There was no line outside of the building and only one of the cattle chutes inside was in use. There were even empty boats emerging from the lower level, floating toward the loading dock to take on the next riders.

The dark figure stopped at the turnstile receptacle to discard a food wrapper and size up the situation. Carmichael was right behind Devens, but Mallin was outside, moving toward the ride's exit point by the Blue Bayou restaurant. Mr. Inside and Mr. Outside, boxing in their enemy. They had as much imagination as the stuffed mechanical gull in the pirate's hat, endlessly greeting the entering riders with the same squawk and twitch.

Carmichael rode two seats behind Devens. He kept his hand inside his jacket, resting on the handle of his weapon, protecting Devens' back and flanks. As the boat left the dock they each sat up straight, forty-year-old kids on a Disneyland ride—alone, there to have the time of their lives on a Tuesday afternoon. Who needs bourbon or basketball or a willing woman when you can sit back, relax, and take a nine-minute cruise in the dark through recycled water?

Who would ever give up the chance to look at the mechanical movements of clockwork figures and wait for the opportunity to listen to three-year-olds scream? And then the capper—watching the grandmothers from Nebraska and Kansas get splashed in the face with a few drops of tepid water, as they came out of their seats smiling and giggling, ready to tell their war stories to the people back home. Where else would a forty-something modern man possibly want to be than there? It made perfect sense. Devens and his bodyguard could fool anybody—anybody, that is, without a functioning central nervous system.

When the ride was over Devens stopped at one of the French Quarter souvenir shops and picked up a plastic pirate's cutlass. He was following his instructions—acting like he was in no hurry, just enjoying his day in the Magic Kingdom. He waited for another second or two, put down the cutlass, and started walking slowly toward the Jungle Cruise ride.

The crowds were heavy on the sidewalks though there were short waits for the rides. Devens had to turn sideways to work his way between a large family of eager Japanese tourists. They were each wearing Mickey Mouse T-shirts and red plastic leis. As Devens was dodging knees and elbows, the Disneyland train was slowing to its stop at the station behind New Orleans Square; he turned his head when its whistle blew. A kid at the top of the Swiss Family Robinson Treehouse dropped something that hit the ground behind him. At the sound of the impact Devens jerked his head noticeably. Then he recovered and kept his eyes focused straight ahead. Carmichael was five steps behind him, Mallin ten steps ahead. When they got to the Jungle Cruise Mallin peeled off and started checking the rubber snakes and Bwana hats at the souvenir stand opposite the ride. Devens walked through the gate and into the maze of chutes leading to the ride. Carmichael let two couples get between himself and Devens and then followed after him. He didn't look at Mallin, who was busy inhaling deeply on a cigarette, leaning against the fence next to the boat dock. Carmichael was going along for the ride again, while his partner was guarding the exit gate. At least the two of them were consistent.

Devens and Carmichael both boarded a boat called the Nairobi Nell, Devens at twelve o'clock, Carmichael at nine. Their captain was named Rick and he took them through his whole Jungle Cruise shtick: "Wave good-bye to the people on shore (waving and smiling). You won't be seeing them again. Ha. Ha."

"Look at that plastic rhino. You don't see one of those every day . . . I do."

"Now we're going to ride behind the falls. Think of it. You just witnessed . . . the back side of water!"

"That's Trader Sam there with the shrunken heads. He wants to trade one of his heads for yours. Ha ha."

"Well, folks, it's time for the *really* dangerous part of your trip now—the ride back home on the Santa Ana freeway."

Carmichael's expression never changed; Devens forced an occasional smile. He tried to look as if he was enjoying himself, even though he was wedged against a fat woman in black lace toreador pants who was sweating heavily and laughing uncontrollably. Every time she laughed, her husband put his hand on her left knee, squeezing her into a state of temporary calm. He himself was laughing with his mouth closed, his expression a moving smirk. He was wearing an old yellow polo shirt with a penguin over the left breast and a baseball hat with the logo of the Columbus Cougars. She was stretching her toreador pants at the seams and fiddling with the cotton ball trim at the base of her blouse.

When the ride was over they tried to engage Captain Rick in a conversation about his maritime career at Disneyland. He smiled politely, said he had enjoyed having them along, and told them to be careful getting out of the boat. They were still smiling and waving at him when they walked through the exit gate past Mallin. Devens was talking about them under his breath as he headed toward Frontierland. Goddamned out-of-town rubes, pissing away their money on a kids' ride. Carmichael followed close behind; the crowd was increasing and he didn't want to break contact with Devens. Mallin stayed back an extra ten yards. As he walked past the shooting gallery he covered his right ear. He kept his eyes on Devens and Carmichael, trying to make his way through the crowd.

———

The Thunder Mountain railroad ride was crowded. The line started just beyond the height-line gate and twisted through the rough-sawn wooden chutes, past the displays of rusting train parts and imitation dynamite kegs. It was an even forty-seven minutes before Devens emerged at the exit gate.

As he came out, Carmichael and Mallin fell in line behind him. The dark figure estimated the time it would take Devens to reach the Splash Mountain ride and stepped in behind Mallin.

———

Slowly unzipping the fanny pack at the waistband. Taking out the plastic gloves and easing them on. Folding the hands to tighten the gloves around the base of the fingers. Then taking out the tiny canister, positioning it in the right hand, aiming at the back of Mallin's head and neck and releasing a quick heavy spray. Then passing beside him quickly and melting into the crowd. Mallin's hand sliding reflexively over the back of his head and neck, sniffing now, wondering if it was birdshit or worse. Catching the full force in his nose and eyes and pulling it into his lungs.

Half mace, half CS. The pepper filling his eyes, nose, and lungs, blinding him with pain. Spitting and coughing first, then rubbing his nose and eyes with his hand and sleeve. Making it worse. The vomiting agent taking a little longer but now having its effect. First the retching, then the dry heaves. Rubbery-legged now. Falling to the ground. A crowd forming around him until the smell of the remains of his breakfast began to fill the air.

Park officials arriving quickly. Telling him to stay calm and try to remain comfortable. Mallin telling them he had to leave, had things to do, had things to do *now*, but standing up, disoriented, and sliding in his own vomit back down to the sidewalk.

The officials fearing litigation and headlines, forcing him to stay put, making him wait for the arrival of one of the park doctors. Mallin raving and insisting. His eyes still filled with peppery tears, his clothes covered in vomit.

Carmichael back in New Orleans Square now. Not suspecting. Not hearing anything except the general din of twenty-seven thousand people at play. Especially not hearing the footsteps of the person behind him. Staying in step. Inches away. Suddenly something wet on his head and neck. God*damn*it. Just what he needed now. Birdshit. Putting his hand in it instinctively. Then checking the smell. But nothing visible on his hand or fingertips. What the hell? His eyes glazing over with pain as if someone were grinding salt and acid into his face and eyes.

Rubbing his eyes fiercely now, trying vainly to focus. Seeing a gray blur spinning at his feet. Falling down with dizziness and nausea. Turning on his side, his stomach heaving uncontrollably. Coughing and spitting the remains of his dinner and breakfast on the ground.

His head throbbing, as if the hour were being struck against his temple with a ball-peen hammer.

The crowd flaring out at the smell of the vomit and closing in again a few yards beyond him. An insulated oval, moving toward the next ride, the next restaurant, the next concession stand. Flowing around and beyond him like the sea washing past something dead on the beach.

Then the park officials. The second case in five minutes. A single word rocketing across their consciousness: *liability*. Keeping Carmichael down, despite his protestations. Keeping him comfortable and quiet. Cold washcloths on his forehead. Moist towels swabbing the puke from his left arm and pants legs. Carmichael crying out in anger. Something about a job. Something about time being of the essence. But not being able to see, not being able to orient himself, not being able to keep his stomach from pumping sour bubbles into his throat and mouth and not being able to persuade his feet and legs to cooperate with his hands and brain.

Devens hearing nothing but the cries of infants and the screams of adults—careening down tracks, through tunnels, over plastic mountains, and into waiting puddles of water. The spray slicing through the air as the observers looked on with admiration. Splash Mountain. One of the newer attractions in the park. Station four. Then the fucking submarines and the Matterhorn ride. What the hell. Maybe this thing would be fun. The people in the logs coming down the mountain all laughing and whooping.

Wondering about Carmichael and Mallin. Why worry? They told him not to even think about them, so he wouldn't. They were there. He knew that, because he'd paid for them and because they were good. So let them do their jobs and let him enjoy the fucking ride.

Standing in line now. Shorter than he had anticipated. A little good news for a change. Reaching behind him with the tip of his finger. Feeling the .38 beneath his jacket. Still there. Good.

The line moving quickly now. Walking along briskly, in and out of the sun, through the chutes. In control now. A little more bullshit, then they move in on this asshole. In the meantime, why not enjoy himself?

Lining up to board the hollowed logs for the ride. Only six in a log. The wait for the ride must be a bitch when the line's long. The person behind him: short, nervous. Sweet. Asking him if he'd mind sharing a seat. Sure, why not. Any problem with the back of the log? No. In the front, he figured, you catch all of the water. In the back you feel the ride. Harmless woman. Scared shitless probably. Cute too. Get wedged in with her. Feel her tits up against your back. Let her wrap her legs around you. Why *not* enjoy it? She asked.

She dressed in black. Probably to make herself look thinner. Christ, she looked good enough. No reason to hide what she had. What she had looked pretty good. Something almost familiar in the eyes.

Getting into the log. Comfortable. She brushing up against him for a second.

"Sorry."

"That's all right."

Off and running now. Fast ride. Sharp, abrupt turns. Quick starts and stops. *Song of the South* motif. He didn't know that. Br'er Fox, Br'er Bear, and Br'er Rabbit. Cocky little son-of-a-bitch. Making fun of everybody. Born and bred in the fucking briar patch. When do we get *there*? Suddenly realizing it was at the bottom of the five-story drop. Plastic mountains; real speed.

Turning the corner, about to make the climb before the big drop. Pretty good ride, actually. Her legs clutching his sides. Soft but firm.

Nice. Thinking about the drop. Thinking about her grabbing him, rubbing up against him. His dick responding a little to that thought. How about that?

Unzipping the fanny pack now. Pulling out the roll of tape and resting it against his back, the center of it clinging to his jacket. No way he could be aware of it, not with the jerks and the noise and his knees wedged against the side of the log, bracing. Then taking out the prod. A quick hit at the base of his spine. His body jerking with massive spasms of pain and confusion. Suddenly the tape over his head and around his mouth, tight.

His hands jerking up in anger and surprise, but she grabbing his wrists and forcing his hands back to the seat, bending her arms and flexing her own wrists. The angle perfect. The steel shafts shooting from the brackets beneath her sleeves, through his hands, pinning him, impaling him. The blood starting to ooze around the base of the shafts: flagstaffs mounted on bloody islands. Then another jolt with the prod. Watching the body jerk, the hands staying firmly in place. No free tit rubs on this ride, just the feel of sharpened steel being driven through his hands as his body convulsed and his head filled with silent screams of anguish.

TWENTY-EIGHT

THE MOMENT THE LOG pulled into line at the back at the starting platform the shrieks of surprise and horror began. The four people in front of Devens were nonplussed, feeling the eyes of the crowd on them, their own eyes darting in shock and wonder. Their knees wedged in place, they were unable to turn and see what was waiting, silently, behind them. As the lead couple were finally able to extricate themselves from the log, they turned immediately, anxious to see for themselves the object of the crowd's attention. When they did they fell back in appalled silence. The other couple bolted out, stepping over each other, trying desperately to flee from whatever had so frightened the others.

"Oh, Jesus," one of the men said. "Jesus, Jesus . . ."

Devens' hands were pinned to the seat, the puncture wounds red and black, with fresh rivulets of blood running down to the creases at his wrists and forward, over the backs of his fingers. His face was an agony mask. His lips were pressed and distorted by a broad strip of clear plastic tape, which had frozen his mouth forever in a breathless, gulping scream.

"Oh, Jesus, Jesus . . ." the man said again, his companion moving behind him, trying to shield herself from the evil. One of the starters tried to turn the waiting crowd away, protecting them from the scene, but they only pressed closer, trying to catch a look at whatever it was that was suddenly more interesting and exciting than a forty-mile-an hour ride at a forty-seven-degree angle down a five-story plastic mountain.

"He's dead," somebody yelled. "Jesus Christ, how in the hell could that ever happen?"

"Who?" "Where?" The voices from the crowd billowed in intensity.

The supervisor of the starters, a thin man named Jeff with tight blond curls, closed the gate at the starting platform and told the crowd that the ride was closed until further notice. That led to a second wave of shouted questions and an onslaught of people pushing and elbowing, trying to see what it was that had happened.

Jeff directed one of his assistants, a young woman named Caryn, to call park security, but as she walked toward the telephone she was assaulted with shouts and questions.

"What the hell is going on? Is somebody dead or something?" one man yelled.

"Let's get out of here," his companion said.

"We can't get out of here," he answered. "The crowd's not moving. Besides, I want to know what in the hell is going on."

―――――

Caryn was screaming into the telephone, her right hand cupped over her right ear. Jeff was holding back the crowd, guarding the gate. Two other starters, Tim and Dinah, were trying to clear the platform.

"Wait a minute," Dinah said. "We've got to keep the people here who were in the log with him. The security people will want to talk to them."

"I'll tell them," Tim said. He approached the two couples and asked them to stay on the platform until they could be questioned by the security staff.

"You think we had something to do with that?" one of them asked. "Hell, you can't even turn around in one of those damned things. How could we have done anything to him when he was in the back of the log?"

"No one's accusing you of anything," Tim said, "but the security people will want to talk to you because you were the ones who were closest to him when it happened."

"I didn't see or hear a damned thing," the man shot back.

"That's fine, sir," Tim said. "Please, just wait here a few minutes."

The man shifted his weight from one foot to the other, impatient, put-upon. His date was standing motionless, staring at William Devens' lifeless eyes. The other couple were embracing one another, comforting each other, even though their eyes were riveted to the sight before them.

A uniformed security officer was there in three minutes. His nameplate read *Hadley*. He walked directly to the log containing Devens' body and placed his fingertips against the artery at the base of Devens' throat. Then he looked at his watch, made a note in a small book, and stood back from the body, running his eyes over the wounds and the dead man's face. After fifteen or twenty seconds he turned to the group of park employees and said, "Which one of you is Jeff?"

"I am," the tall man said.

"Curtis Hadley," the officer said, extending his hand. "Jeff, I want you to call extension 414. That is the private line of the park superintendent. Tell him that we have a murder victim on the Splash Mountain ride and that we need to contact the Anaheim police immediately."

"Do you want me to call the police first?"

"No. The superintendent will want to meet with them as soon as they arrive and he should be informed as to what has happened. Tell him all that you know. You go do that and I'll take over for you here."

"Yes, sir."

"You don't have to call me sir, son, just get on the phone."

"OK."

———

Hadley approached the two couples standing in the shade a few feet from the log.

"My name is Curtis Hadley," he said. "I'm with park security. Were each of you in the log with the victim?"

The embracing couple nodded yes. The second woman did as well, but her date—a short man with black hair and dark eyes—unloaded on Hadley. "How long are you going to keep us here?" he asked. "We didn't have a damned thing to do with this. Why are we being treated as if we did?"

"What's your name, son?" Hadley answered.

"Daryll Henderson. Now how long are you going to keep us?"

"Well, Daryll, you and these other three people have just been present for what appears to have been an act of violent, premeditated murder. I don't know how long you're going to be needed here, but if I were you I wouldn't plan on taking any more rides for a while."

"What does that mean?"

"What it means, son, is that the Anaheim police are going to be here in a matter of minutes. They're going to want to talk to you. I would advise you to cooperate with them."

"We haven't done a damn thing," Daryll said. "None of us have. Jodie and I were in the middle of the log and *we* sure as hell didn't do anything. The other couple was in front of us and they never moved during the whole ride. We could see them. They didn't do a thing."

"No one is saying that you did, son. Do me a favor, will you. Look at that man in the back of that plastic log. Tell me what you see."

"I don't know . . . a guy with his hands nailed to the seat and a piece of tape over his mouth. He's dead."

"Would you say that whoever did that was pretty slick or pretty sloppy?"

"Pretty *damn* slick," Daryll said. "We didn't hear anything and we didn't see anything. The ride ended. The log came to a stop and suddenly everybody was screaming and pointing."

"Well, think of it this way, Daryll: if whoever did this was slick enough to do what they did to that man, they probably are slick enough to also know that you were in the log with him. They don't know precisely whether you saw or heard *anything*, but for the moment they have decided to allow you to remain alive. If they were able to do what they did to the victim on a *rollercoaster* ride, what do you think they would be able to do to four potential witnesses walking unprotected through an amusement park?"

Hadley let that sink in.

"I guess we should stay and talk to the police," Daryll said.

"I think that'd be a real good idea, son."

Hadley directed them to a bench where they could make themselves comfortable and checked with Dinah on the rest of the crowd. A few minutes later Jeff returned. He was excited about something.

"Did you reach the superintendent?" Hadley asked.

"I did. I told him everything. He had one of his assistants call the Anaheim police; they should be here in a few minutes. I just remembered something, something important."

"What's that, Jeff?"

"It's *really* important," he said.

"Well, spit it out, son."

"We've got a *picture* of them in the log."

TWENTY-NINE

"You mean the concession pictures?"

"Yes. Each log with its set of riders is photographed as it makes its way down the mountain. When you come off the ride you see the most recent pictures displayed on a board. A lot of people buy them."

"I've seen that. What do you charge for them, son, six or seven dollars?"

"We charge $6.95 for one, but they're cheaper if you buy more."

"I knew there was a heart of gold beating somewhere in this park."

"Well, you have to remember, a lot of them are never bought. That's why we have to charge more."

Hadley put his hand against Jeff's cheek. "I know, son," he said.

"I'll get the copy of their picture now, so it's available when the police arrive."

"Good idea."

The golf cart mini-siren could be heard in the distance. Hadley saw the spinning, blue light and watched the crowds part as the cart came closer. A fresh crowd formed near the chutes at the entrance to the ride to see who it was that was arriving. Tim and Dinah asked them to step back. Both the Anaheim policeman and the park driver were in plain clothes. The crowd kept asking their questions.

"Calder, Anaheim PD," the thin man said, reaching for Hadley's hand. His hair was sand-colored and he was tall, at least 6'3", Hadley thought. His beige cotton suit was a size too large; it hung on him and rippled in the wind, concealing the weapon he carried beneath it. He wore a large ruby ring on his right hand. Hadley thought it was Masonic at first, but when he offered his hand to him he saw that it was a high school or college ring with a gold school emblem attached to the top of the stone.

"Curtis Hadley."

"What have we got, Curtis?"

"I'd say we have a premeditated murder."

"The superintendent said something about the victim's hands being pinned to the seat . . ."

"He's right back here; I'll show you."

By now the crowd had been cleared from the crime scene and there was some semblance of order restored. Except for the two couples sitting off to the side on a bench in the shade, there was no one near Devens' body.

"His mouth was taped, as you can see," Hadley said, "and two pins were driven through his hands. They're almost like steel arrows, except that they have some sort of barbs on the sides. I didn't want to get that close and disturb anything, but I could see the tops of them protruding from the victim's hands."

"Did you or anyone else touch anything, Curtis, anything at all?"

"I touched his throat to make sure he was dead. Otherwise I didn't touch anything."

"And no one else has been near him."

"Just the people riding in the log with him and they didn't touch anything."

"That's good. The lab techs will be here in a few minutes and they'll go over everything. What do you think was the cause of death?"

"That's a damned good question. There's nothing visible except for the steel pins through his hands. He could have been injected with something, I guess. His neck doesn't appear to be broken and there's no sign of blood except around the hands and fingers. At first I thought his heart might have given out or something, but then I figured, no, whoever did this was a planner and a calculator. They wouldn't leave anything to chance. If they wanted this old boy dead they would have made damned sure that they made him so."

"The tape doesn't cover his nose."

"No," Hadley said, "but with the tape in place they could have pinched his nose and killed him easily enough. That would have been a hell of a way to go—with your hands nailed down beside you and your lungs gulping for air. The only problem is the time. Whoever killed him didn't have the luxury of sitting there, holding on to his nose, and waiting patiently for him to die. Whatever happened had to have happened fast."

Jeff was standing at the entrance to the ride, waving to Hadley.

"Come on over here, son," Hadley said. "This is . . . I didn't catch your rank."

"Lieutenant."

"This is Lieutenant Calder, son. He's from the Anaheim Police. Lieutenant, this young man's name is Jeff. He was in charge of the ride when the murder occurred."

"What have you got for us?" Calder asked.

"The picture of the victim and the other people in his log."

"The picture?"

"Yes, sir. We take a picture of each log as it comes off the mountain. Then we offer them for sale to the people when they exit the ride—sort of a memento or souvenir."

"Let's have a look."

Calder looked at the picture and then looked at the two couples sitting on the bench. He reached in his pocket and took out a worn, black leather case with a fold-out magnifying glass inside. He opened it up and studied the picture. "Take a look, Curtis," he said, handing him the photograph and the magnifying glass.

"Damn," Hadley said. "There's only five of them in the log. Whoever killed him did it before they came down the mountain and went into the briar patch. Look at him there. He's got the same expression he has now, except that his head is tilted a little differently."

"That could be from the force of the fall," Calder said.

"Right."

"That log looks pretty snug."

"It is," Jeff interjected.

Both Hadley and Calder looked at him.

"You'd have to be in the log to do that to him," Jeff said. "Whoever did it got out before the ride down the mountain."

"Got out? In the middle of a roller coaster ride?" Calder said.

"Had to have," Jeff said. "There's not enough room in one of those logs to slide down and hide yourself. Everybody's wedged in too tight."

"Do you ever send the logs through without a full load of people?" Calder asked.

"Sometimes, if people are riding alone and there are no other single riders who want to get in with them. We don't make people ride together. It gets too . . . personal."

"Is there any chance that somebody might remember this fella and whether or not he rode alone?"

"I doubt it, but I could ask," Jeff said. "If he was riding alone, who could have done this to him?"

"Somebody who jumped in somewhere along the way," Calder said, "and then jumped out again."

"I don't know how that could have happened," Jeff said.

"Neither do I, Jeff," Calder said, "but look at that man sitting there with the steel pins through his hands and the tape over his mouth. He didn't get in the log that way—you would have remembered it. And he didn't do that to himself now, did he?"

"No, sir."

"Then what are our choices?"

"Somebody got in with him, killed him, and then got out before the run down the mountain or somebody caught up with him somewhere in the course of the ride, killed him, and then moved on."

"That's right."

"I still don't see how whoever did this was able to do it so fast and then disappear."

"That's easy, Jeff."

"How so, Lieutenant?"

"Because from what I can see here, one thing is pretty obvious."

"What's that, Lieutenant?"

"We're dealing with the first team here, son."

Jeff stood silent. Finally he spoke. "We've got the people who were riding with him."

"I see that," Calder said, "and I appreciate it, but the victim was in the back of the log. If they were all wedged in tight and had no inkling of what was going on behind them, I'm afraid they're not going to have too much to tell us. Maybe they'll remember whether or not the victim was riding alone, but you load front to rear, I bet."

"Yes, sir, we do."

"Then unless they were paying a lot of attention they probably didn't notice who was in the back of the log. Still, we'll give it a try. What we really need to do is find the people who were riding behind in the next log. They're the ones who might have seen something."

"We've got their picture too," Jeff said proudly.

"Did you detain them, Jeff?" Hadley asked.

"No, but we've got their picture. We can find them."

"How many are in the park today, son?" Calder asked.

"I don't know, Lieutenant . . . maybe twenty-five or thirty thousand."

Calder's expression didn't change as Jeff's chin dropped an inch or two.

Jeff went off to get the picture of the riders in the log behind the victim's; it took him nearly ten minutes to do it.

"This is it," he said. "The negatives are all numbered. I made sure I had the right one."

"Let's take a look," Calder said.

He studied it for a minute and then handed it to Hadley. "Not much help there, Curtis."

There were six people in the log, two young Hispanic kids, one with a Raiders hat, the other with a Dodgers hat, both shading their eyes. Behind them were a young couple. Her eyes were closed and most of his face was masked by her hair. The final pair were Asians, each around twelve or thirteen years old.

"I was wishing for something obvious or prominent," Calder said, "even if it was unrealistic to hope. It's not going to be easy to locate these people."

"No," Hadley said, "but we can get a lot of names through our records. People pay by credit card to get into the park; they use teller machines, cash checks at our bank, rent strollers. Most of them buy something on the way out from one of the shops on Main Street and a lot of them use credit cards and personal checks. The odds are pretty good that we can get the name of at least one of the six people in that log."

"We'll set up people at the exit turnstiles and at the monorail station that carries people over to the hotel," Calder said, "try to catch one or more of them before they leave today. Going through all those credit card chits will take forever."

"That's a fact," Hadley said, "but we'll be happy to help in any way that we can."

"I appreciate that," Calder said. "Maybe you can free up some of your people to help us now. I'll call in as many of ours as the captain can spare. Then I'll chat with our friends over there who survived the ride with the victim."

Calder asked Jeff to have as many copies of the picture made as the shop could turn out. Then he went to phone his station. As he walked by the two couples on the bench, the vocal young man stood up and asked him whether or not they were going to be questioned.

"You certainly will be," he said. "Meanwhile, take a load off. This is the safest place you can be right now."

"So you think we're in danger too."

"I most certainly do," Calder said. "Aren't you comfortable sitting there in the shade?"

"I guess we're a lot more comfortable than the guy in the back of the log."

"Just hold that thought, son," Calder said.

THIRTY

"Here's the secret," Jack said. "You always start with a large bowl—large enough for the pasta to move around in without falling over the sides. First you hold the bowl over the pasta pot for a second. The steam makes the bowl moist and helps the cheese cling to the sides. You don't want a lump of cheese in the bottom; you want a nice coating all around. Then you grate the cheese into the bowl. Some people use Romano, some use a blend of Romano and Parmesan, but I always go with pure Parmesan. You cover the inside of the bowl with a dusting of the cheese. Fresh-grated; none of that shit in the green tubes with the sliding tin tops. Then you dump in the drained pasta and toss it around. What happens is, the damp pasta picks up a thin coating of little flecks of cheese. Then you ladle on the sauce and toss the pasta a second time. Watch . . ."

"That smells great," Frank said. "That'll be a hell of a big lunch, though."

"You're a working man," Jack said. "You need your sustenance. You want to know another trick?"

"What's that?"

"You don't scarf down a basket full of bread before you eat your pasta. I know it tastes good, especially the really fresh, crusty stuff, but it bloats you. You're here for pasta and salad and wine, not for bread. If you want bread, just eat that, but don't fill your stomach with it so that you can't enjoy the rest of your meal. You've got to let the pasta do its thing. Then you've got to eat the salad. If you don't gorge yourself on bread you'll always have room for some cannoli and a cappuccino."

"I love Italian desserts, especially with cheese," Frank said.

"You mean the mascarpone cheese."

"Yes. That stuff is great."

"This is the ideal meal for you, Frank. You know why?"

"Why?" Frank asked.

"Because women love the smell of Italian food on a man."

"You mean the smell of *garlic*?" Frank asked, incredulously.

"*Especially* the garlic, but not a lot of it—just a hint."

"What is the garlic supposed to do, change the pheromones or something?"

"No," Jack said. "Nothing like that. Women don't care about specific smells. They care about the things they *associate* with certain smells. With Italian food, what they like is the fact that *you're* cooking. They love men who cook. They love men who'll cook for *them*. It's sexy, Frank. It's something warm. It's something shared. You're giving them life and energy. Most important of all, you're not expecting them to do it."

"Where did you read that?"

"It's common knowledge," Jack said.

"Where, in *Woman's Day* magazine? You've been to the dentist, haven't you? You were stuck in that waiting room with nothing to read but *Woman's Day*. That's it, isn't it?"

"Trust me," Jack said.

"But you're doing the cooking; I'm just doing the eating."

"How will they know who did the cooking? It only matters that they *think* you did the cooking. Come here, lean over this pot a little, get some of the steam from my sauce on your cheeks and behind your ears."

"What makes you think I need tomato sauce steam to attract women?"

"When are you going to trust me, Frank?" Jack said.

"With regard to women?"

"Yes."

"Probably never."

"Then don't complain to me when you see women's eyes glaze over while they're talking about my cooking."

"You think I'm going to see that?"

"I know you are. Here, sit down. Try some of this."

Jack put two large ladles of mostacciolis on a red china plate and put the plate in front of Frank. Then he put together a small salad of bib lettuce, spinach, carrots, black and green olives, and artichoke hearts, and doused it with a light oil and vinegar dressing. "Here," he said. "After the pasta."

A few minutes later he sat down at the table with Frank.

"This is really good," Frank said. "Is the pasta homemade?"

"It's bought homemade. If you were a woman I'd get a pasta maker and go through the whole ritual, but I'm not trying to make *your* eyes glaze over."

"That's reassuring. I wouldn't want people to talk."

"Here, try a splash of this."

Jack poured two half glasses of red wine.

"I'm on duty, remember," Frank said.

"I know. I'll give you more, don't worry."

Frank tasted it. "I know you didn't make this."

"It's good, isn't it?"

"It's terrific. What is it?"

"Frank, you sound like the commercial. 'Why, it's Gallo Sauvignon Blanc.' 'Son-of-a-big-shaggy-bitch, so it is, you cheap bastard.'"

"I know it's not Gallo. I was thinking maybe . . . Italian Swiss Colony."

"That's Gallo too, I think."

"Surprise me."

"It's Australian; it's a Shiraz."

"It's damned good."

"Isn't it?" Jack refilled Frank's glass. "What have you got on for the rest of the afternoon?"

"We're setting up a stakeout on a warehouse off of Huntington Drive."

"The good end or the bad end?"

"The bad end. We've had a lot of recent activity in that area, most of it involving burglary and all of it involving violence. Whoever's responsible doesn't like witnesses. They take out the guards, passing motorists, innocent people on the street, anybody who might have seen them. We've been baiting this one building for three days now—bringing in boxes of high-ticket items in small boxes, things that are easily fenced. If they take the bait we'll take them down. What have *you* got on for this afternoon?"

"Not all that much, really. I was over in Burbank this morning, picking up a case file from Valley. They want me to keep an eye on a car dealer in Duarte. He's had a few too many thefts and Cliff thinks the guy may be light-fingering his own goods, ripping off Valley, and then reselling the stuff later. I'll check his security system, see how plausible his stories are—that kind of thing."

"How will you do that while the salesmen are fluttering around, trying to sell you something?"

"That's easy. I'll tell them I have to get a *very* good trade-in deal to buy anything new. Then I'll tell them my current car is in the shop. I'll tell them it's a Simca, with only 97,000 miles on it. They'll scatter."

Frank's beeper went off.

"Hold the cannoli a minute," he said. "I'll be right back."

Frank was on the phone for ten minutes. "What happened?" Jack asked. "Did somebody lose the key to City Hall?"

"Second victim," Frank said.

"Like the one in England?"

"Yes, it looks too similar to be a coincidence. That was Ray Calder in Anaheim. The second guy was hit at Disneyland."

"Cute," Jack said. "How?"

"They're not sure yet. They think he was poisoned. They found him at the end of the Splash Mountain ride, sitting in the back of his log, with clear plastic tape over his mouth and two steel rods driven through his hands, pinning him to his seat."

"Almost like a crucifixion."

"Yes. From Ray's description the rods sound like miniature versions of the thing that was used on Michael Crimmins in the London underground station. This time it looks as if the killer put some poison in the grooves and channels that are carved into the shafts. It might have been something else, but that's the best bet at this point."

"Do they know the victim's identity?"

"Yes. Mr. Seven Percent: William Devens."

"The real estate guy," Jack said.

"Yes, very successful," Frank said. "Not exactly a captain of industry, but somebody who had relieved a lot of people of a lot of money."

"Any obvious connection with Crimmins?"

"Not yet. They're just starting to check. There were some particularly interesting details on this one."

"Like?"

"Along with a couple grand in cash, Devens was also carrying a loaded revolver, a gravity knife, and an antique straight razor."

"It doesn't sound like any of them did him a hell of a lot of good," Jack said.

"No, but it looks as if he knew somebody was coming for him."

"Or he thought he was going after somebody," Jack said.

"Yes. Maybe a little bit of both. There were also two PI's there, apparently functioning as bodyguards."

"They didn't do him much good either."

"No."

"Do you know their names?" Jack asked.

"Carmichael and Mallin. Sound familiar?"

"Yes. Lou Carmichael and Dan Mallin. Carmichael played semi-pro football. Mallin's an ex-cop; retired early—by the citizens. He's from out of state, I think Nevada. A couple of bottom-feeders."

"Wait a minute. Didn't you get a call on your answering machine from some guy looking for a bodyguard?"

"Yes. A guy named Bill."

"I wonder if it's the same one," Frank said.

"I don't know. I recorded over that section of the tape already."

"No matter."

"What happened to Carmichael and Mallin?"

"They were zapped with a mixture of CS and Mace."

"Dandy," Jack said. "So their eyes were running and burning while they were busy trying to puke all over themselves."

"Something like that."

"Hard to guard bodies when you can't see them or walk a straight line. Whoever did this, Frank—he's *damned* good."

"Or he's got a lot of help."

"Either way. Look at the product. It's good work. Any physical evidence?"

"Nothing yet."

"There won't be any," Jack said. "Count on it."

"So, are you glad you didn't take the job?"

"Yes, but it's an interesting case. I'll tell you what. You drive to Anaheim, meet with the locals, and go over their reports. I'll see what I can find out about Devens and Crimmins. I'll try to save you some time. You don't have very much of it left."

"What do you mean?"

"What I mean is that that asshole from Justice will be back here in five and a half hours and then you'll have to deal with him at the same time that you're trying to solve the damned case."

"You're right."

"You want me to call the inspector in London—let her know what's happened, give her the name and see if it rings any bells?"

"I'd appreciate it. Here . . ."

Frank took out her card and jotted down her number on a paper napkin.

"Go," Jack said. "Detect."

"Thanks for lunch, I appreciate it."

"Forget it. We'll eat the rest later."

"Where will you be?"

"I'll start at the Pasadena library—run the *Times* index and see if anything jumps out."

"Call Jerry if you have any trouble getting through to me."

"Will do. If you need me, put a message on the answering machine. I'll call in and play it back every half hour or so."

"Fine. If the asshole from Justice arrives when I'm in Orange County . . ."

"Yes?"

"Be so kind as to give the gentleman a message from me."

"And what is that?"

"Tell him to go fuck himself."

"Anything else?"

"Yes. Tell the careerist son-of-a-bitch not to touch my cannoli."

THIRTY-ONE

Frank was on the Santa Ana, passing through La Mirada and coming up on Buena Park, when the call from Jack was patched through.

"I talked to Detective Inspector Harding. She misses you."

"What did she say?" Frank asked.

"She asked when you're going to start cooking her pasta and telling her stories about your exploits as a Lieutenant of detectives."

"Right. What else did she say?"

She said that the name Devens didn't ring a bell, but that she'd make some calls and do some checking."

"It's pretty late there now."

"Almost 11:30, but crimestoppers never rest."

"Right," Frank said. "Thanks, Jack."

"You're welcome. Do you think I should say *Roger, out*, now?"

"A simple *Ta-Ta* should be enough."

"I'll talk to you later. Remember to keep an eye on the rear-view mirror."

"It *was* a poison," Calder said. "It worked on the central nervous system. Like nerve gas or roach spray. He was alive long enough to feel the spikes in his hands but not much longer. His lungs shut down and the rest of him followed."

"What do you know about this guy, Ray?" Frank asked.

"Not a lot. Late-forties. A big house on the west side. Long Lincoln Town Car. White. They always like them white—makes them look bigger. A nice bank account. Delusions of grandeur..."

"Why do you say that?"

"Because he came armed, thinking he'd have a chance with this guy. Obviously, he didn't. Neither did his bodyguards. When the killer was through with the two of them they were in the Disneyland infirmary for the better part of an hour and a half."

"Could I see the spikes you took from his hands?"

"The lab techs have them, but I can show you some pictures. Here..."

Calder opened the folder on his desk and handed Frank a set of polaroids and a magnifying glass. He studied them for a full minute and a half.

"Identical," he said. "Carbon copies, except for the fact that they're smaller."

"Just like the one they pulled out of the guy in England, huh?"

"Yes."

"But he took it up the ass and bled to death, didn't he?"

"That's right."

"I wonder why the change with this one."

"I don't know. One thing's for sure—the two are connected. The weapon in London was described very vaguely in the tabloid press, but no one saw a picture of it except for the people at Scotland Yard. Whoever took out Devens used a smaller-scale version of the exact same weapon. It can't be a copy-cat murder, Ray; the killer couldn't have known what it was that he should have been copying."

"The whole thing is like a graph, isn't it?" Calder said. "You got your two axes and your two lines. Find out where they cross and why, and you're only a step or two away from finding out who did it."

"Both victims were from Los Angeles," Frank said. "Either they did something together that gave somebody a reason to kill them or they each happened to have the bad luck of pissing off the same person—somebody who likes to go around sticking sharpened steel into other peoples' bodies."

"Either way, it should be easy to solve."

"Why do you say that?" Frank asked.

"First, we've got a connection with the common murder weapon. Second, the first killing occurred outside the country, which narrows down the number of people with opportunity. As soon as we find out the nature of the connection between the victims we can start ticking off suspects and talking about motive. And let's face it, Frank, this is not exactly a common M.O. We're not gonna run it through the computer and get a long printout. The whole damned thing is just too cute. People who go to this kind of trouble to knock other people off are usually easy to find. The tough cases are the acts of random or professional violence—the alley fights or the drug-turf drive-bys. This looks more like something personal. It's got a signature as big as a billboard on the Sunset Strip."

"Maybe."

"You're shaking your head. What's the problem?"

"I agree with everything you said, except for one thing."

"What's that?" Calder asked.

"Whoever did this was a *pro*, Ray. Maybe not a professional killer in the usual sense, but a pro."

"So?"

"So, what have you got in the way of physical evidence?"

"Besides the weapon?"

"Yes."

"Truth?"

"Of course."

"We don't have jackshit."

"That's what I thought," Frank said. "And you know what?"

"What's that?"

"You've got as much as you're going to get."

"What are you saying?"

"What I'm saying is that motive and opportunity may not be enough. London and L.A. are big towns; Crimmins and Devens were both pricks—or at least they could be. You toss out the motive and opportunity nets and they'll both fill up fast. The one thing you've got is a unique M.O., but that may not help you at all. You don't want something unique, Ray. You want something you can recognize, something familiar. The rarer it is the less helpful it is."

"I don't agree with that, Frank. If the M.O. is unique it will help us narrow the field."

"But without physical evidence or a credible witness you don't have squat. A lot of people like swords and arrows and read up on antique weapons. Mace and CS? That's standard issue shit, Ray. We're not talking about some rare juice from Pago Pago. You know what's rare about this case?"

"What's that?"

"The skill in the execution."

"True. Maybe we'll get lucky."

"Maybe I'll be captured by some wealthy female bikers from northern California and turned into a rich love slave."

As they stared at one another a uniformed officer came to the door. "Lieutenant . . ." he said.

"What have you got, Leo?"

"We got the couple that was in the log behind the victim."

"Where?"

"In the interrogation room. Jimmy Lorenzo spotted the woman on their way out of the park."

"I'll be right there, Leo. Tell Jimmy good work."

Calder turned to Frank, as if to say, "You see—*progress*."

———

"Lieutenant, this is Carol Baudry and her friend, Kevin Graham."

"Hello, Carol. Hi, Kevin. My name is Calder. I'm investigating the Disneyland murder. This gentleman is Lieutenant Frank White from the LAPD. We appreciate your coming in to talk to us."

"No problem," Kevin said. He was wearing a T-shirt with a faded yellow Maui emblem on the front. His girlfriend was wearing a sleeveless white sweater and snug black slacks.

"You were riding in the log behind that of the murder victim, is that correct?" Calder asked.

"That's what they tell us," Kevin said. "We didn't really see anything though. Carol and I talked about it when we were riding over here and neither of us could really remember much of anything, except for the ride itself and all of the excitement at the end."

"Did you get a good look at the people in the log in front of you?"

"I guess we must have, but I don't remember," Kevin said. "There were a lot of people in the park today and we didn't really pay all that much attention. We saw them, I guess, but we didn't really *see* them, if you know what I mean."

"Carol?"

"No, I wasn't really thinking about anything then but the ride. It's a really good one and it was our first time to ride it. The line wasn't too long and we were able to get right on. Kevin and I were excited. We don't usually look all that much at the other people, unless there's something special about them. I did see this guy with a big hat that had a coke can on top and two plastic straws coming down to his mouth. You know—we notice people like that, but not normal people."

"Did you see the man with the coke hat on the Splash Mountain ride, Carol?"

"No, actually I think it was on Mr. Toad's Wild Ride."

"Yeah, that's right," Kevin said. "There or on Peter Pan."

"OK. Can either of you say how many people were in the log in front of you?"

"Not me, not really," Kevin said.

"No, me either," Carol added.

"Let me ask you this," Calder said, "as you were on the ride, going around the track, did you see anybody walking or running?"

"What do you mean?" Kevin asked.

"Somebody who was on foot, not in one of the logs."

"Just the Disneyland employee," Carol said.

"Not on the starting platform. On the ride itself."

"Yes," Carol said. "The person who tells you to stay in your seat and not try to stand up. Just at the bottom of the mountain, before you make the climb."

"Standing on the ground," Calder said.

"Sure. Right there at the bottom of the hill. On the back side. Not on the briar patch side after you come down."

"Hold on a second, I'll be right back," Calder said.

Frank stayed with the couple. Calder was back in less than a minute.

"What did the man look like?" he asked.

"Hmmmm," Carol said. "I don't think it was a man. I think it was a girl."

"A girl?" Calder said.

"Yes."

"Kevin, do you remember?"

"Not really. If Carol says it was a girl then it was a girl."

"Are you absolutely sure, Carol?" Frank asked.

"No, I think it was, though."

"Listen, I want to thank you again for your help," Calder said. "Lieutenant White and I have to talk to somebody else for a second. We'll excuse ourselves and you can try to remember anything else that might be important."

"Sure," Kevin said.

———

Frank and Ray Calder went out in the hallway.

"There *are* no employees stationed at the base of the mountain, are there?" Frank asked.

"No."

"What she did was wear an employee's shirt underneath whatever she had on top. She killed Devens, whipped off the shirt or jacket, and jumped out of the log. When the next log came by she acted like she was an employee. Then she took off. Jesus, what a piece of timing. Do you have a map of the park?"

"Yes, right here." Calder opened the folder and handed the map to Frank.

"Look," Frank said. "The Splash Mountain ride is scrunched back in a corner of the park, surrounded by foliage. Once she got a few feet away from the ride she could slip her shirt or jacket back on, make her way back into the crowd, and head straight for either the parking lot or the monorail. She was gone before Devens' body was cold. Hell, she was gone before Devens' bodyguards had even stopped puking."

"You keep saying *she*," Calder said. "You think Carol Baudry is right?"

"Why not?"

"It seems like a lot for a woman to do."

"That depends on the woman," Frank said.

THIRTY-TWO

Frank took Calder into an empty interrogation room and picked up the phone. "I'd like to bring Jerry Dailey in on this, Ray. You remember Jerry—my lab man. He's good with wounds and weapons. I'd like to have his reaction."

Calder nodded his approval.

Frank reached Jerry in Boyle Heights. The three of them met at the park fifty minutes later.

"I love the way that siren parts the traffic," Jerry said. "It really works—one of the few things that does." He was eating a late lunch from a rectangular tin.

"You remember Ray Calder, don't you, Jerry?"

"Sure. Hi, Ray. Sardine?"

"No, thanks."

"You sure?"

"Yes, I'm sure."

"Frank?"

"No thanks, Jerry."

"They're the kind with the oil and mustard sauce."

"I'll pass," Frank said. "We want you to look at the crime scene and give us your impressions."

"Be happy to. Last chance on the sardines . . ."

"We better go to work, Jerry."

He pulled out the last two and dropped them into his mouth, smiling. "I'm ready, lieutenants. Lead the way."

By the time they got there the crowd had been dispersed and replaced with several miles of yellow and black Police Line tape. Jeff was waiting for them when they arrived and he reopened the Splash Mountain ride, sending through several logs at their usual pace. The park superintendent was standing in the background, watching and listening. Frank checked times with a stopwatch and made notations on a blank sheet in the back of his notebook. Calder paced off distances while Jerry walked in circles, looked occasionally in several different directions, and rooted around in his pockets for dessert. He finally found a Rolo candy in his inside jacket pocket. Sliding off two pieces at a time and chewing on them slowly, he stopped every few seconds, looked at his watch, and checked the five-story mountain from different angles.

He reached in his pocket, took out a ballpoint, and tried to find his notebook. When he couldn't, he took the cap off the pen and made several marks on the back of his left hand. Frank saw him nod to himself two or three times and then make some more marks, this time on the back of his wrist.

Frank walked over and stood beside him. "What do you think, Jerry?"

"Give me another minute or so, Frank. Rolo?"

"No thanks, Jerry."

The three of them reassembled four minutes later. "Anybody want to ride the ride?" Calder asked. "It might help us see things a little more clearly."

"Maybe after we're done," Jerry said. "I think I've seen enough now."

"Frank?"

"No, not now. Let's see what we have first. Talk to me about exit routes, Ray."

"Clearer than the yellow brick road, Frank. Straight out the back, past the third turn, and into the trees. Six or seven seconds, max. Getting out was easy. The problem was making sure that the killer wasn't seen at the moment that Devens was actually being killed and in the few seconds right after, when the killer was taking off his jacket and climbing out of the log."

"*Her* jacket," Frank said.

"OK, her's."

"I figure she had eight or nine seconds until the log behind them came through the tunnel and turned toward the base of the mountain," Frank said. "That's not a hell of a lot of time to work with. One slip or one snag and the whole thing would have fallen apart. Jerry?"

"I agree. Eight . . . maybe nine at the outside. Nothing more than that."

"So how did she do it, Jerry?"

"I'll tell you this much," he said, "she was strong."

"No question about that," Frank said.

"I think she still would have needed some kind of help though," Jerry said.

"What do you mean, help?" Calder asked. "No one else could have fit in the log behind them and the other two couples in the log were wedged in in front of them. *They* couldn't have been involved. At least I don't see how."

"I don't mean another person," Jerry said. "I mean some kind of boost. She couldn't just staple him to the seat. With his adrenalin pumping and with the motion of the log he would have been too hard to control, at least too hard to control that precisely. Maybe she gave him a shot or something."

"A shot?" Calder said.

"Not with a gun, with a needle. Were there any marks on the body?" Jerry asked.

"They haven't done the autopsy yet, but there were no obvious marks other than the puncture wounds through the back of the hands. That's why they figured he was poisoned."

"Nothing at all?" Jerry asked.

"I think they said something about a red mark on the small of the back, but there was no blood and no tear or puncture in the flesh. They figured it was just a scuff of some kind—possibly from bouncing around in the log, but more likely from the gun that he had in the back of his pants. He had some red marks on the sides of his knees too."

"It could have been a taser gun or a prod of some kind. Probably a prod. Tasers are strong medicine. Things could get messy."

"To soften him up, you mean," Frank said.

Jerry nodded. "Exactly. She didn't have time to wrestle with him. And she sure as hell wasn't going to try to *persuade* him to cooperate. She had to distract him in some way, some way that was quick and efficient. Then, when he was disoriented, she could pin his hands to the seat. She probably just gave him a quick, short jolt. She didn't want to really fry him and have him piss on the couple in front of him or anything like that."

"That's a good point, Jerry."

"You know, Frank, I have to say—this was really a nice piece of work. Precision, you know what I mean? Not like the sloppy street shit you and I usually see."

"How did she do it, Jerry?"

"It had to be quick and sure. I figure she had something rigged on each of her arms. Spring-powered, probably. What she did was reach around, grab his wrists, drive his hands against the seat, and then somehow trigger the mechanism. The darts were on the outside of her forearms. In order to release them she had to clench her hands or flex her forearms in some way. When she did it—whatever it was—that released the darts straight into the back of Devens' hands. Now think about that for a second, Frank. Think about designing it. Think about testing it—without tearing the shit out of your own hands in the process. Then think about putting on the matching contraptions and having some kind of clothing that would cover each arm without setting off the mechanisms. Think about the angles she needed. And think about the force tests. She didn't want to just scratch him and she didn't want the darts to go straight through. She needed him pinned in place. *Precisely*. Jesus, what nice work."

"Serious planning, Jerry. Serious."

"And perfect execution, Frank. There was no room for error. None. Not if you wanted this result. I have to say, I am impressed."

"You're impressed by the way one human being kills another human being?" Calder asked.

"Well, it's not like he was a really *human* human being," Jerry said, smiling. "What I mean is, you've got to admire the workmanship. I see stabbings and bludgeonings and all of that kind of shit every day. This is a once-in-a-lifetime one. You've got to have a little respect."

"Jesus," Calder said, turning away.

"What's with him?" Jerry said to Frank.

"Too much conscience and not enough curiosity."

"Pity," Jerry said. "You've got to learn to appreciate the finer things."

THIRTY-THREE

JACK SLIPPED ON A light jacket and picked up his car keys as the sheets of gray cloud began to move toward the base of the San Gabriels. He saw the first drops of rain hit the sidewalk and puddle on the dusty roofs of the cars parked on the street below. Then the skies opened. The weathermen had predicted it two days earlier, rescinded their prediction a day later, predicted it again, and rescinded it again. The storm system had first formed some thirty or forty miles behind the channel islands; then it began to change its mind and drift southwest, back off to sea. Finally it reversed itself, formed again, and came back with all the conviction of a religious convert. The weathermen had studied it the way a three-year-old studies a carefully wrapped Christmas present: shaking it and turning it, guessing hard, and then shaking it again—looking, guessing, seeking confirmation, and then waiting for that special moment that would fix the attention and stir the imagination.

Jack turned on the radio on his kitchen counter and started looking for his umbrella. The local announcers were preparing for the feeding frenzy: sig-alerts across the basin, jams and backups, floods, mudslides, and assorted human-interest pap—enough to carry them through the evening news, the late news, and at least three days of *Today* show and *Good Morning America* breaks.

There were problems already on the 405 and half of the west Valley exit ramps of the 134 were beginning to flood. A retaining wall in Topanga Canyon had given way and the people in Coldwater Canyon were starting to think seriously about the cement pierings that anchored the steel stilts that supported their two-mil homes. The storm was moving east at thirty miles an hour. The heaviest stuff was due to arrive just at the moment when Jack would be trying to make it from his parking place to the Pasadena public library.

He gave up on finding an umbrella and walked out to the hall closet to look for a raincoat. He checked his watch, settled for his old Army field jacket, made sure he had his keys, and walked down to his car. He had removed the subdued insignia from the jacket but left on the name.

Jack pulled out of his reserved space, drove around the southeast corner of his building, and was surprised to see that the security gate was closed. Usually the manager left it open between nine and five. Jack fished around in his coin purse, found the small aluminum key that opened the gate, and let himself out.

———

Both the library and the protected areas of the entry square in front of it were crowded with street people, all of them hanging near the inside door and the entry arch, waiting for the rain to subside. The pair of outside phones protected by the roof overhang was three deep with business types trying to call taxis or friends. Inside, dozens of people paced, fidgeted, fussed with bags and briefcases, and stared out the windows. A few flipped through magazines or books on the Best Seller display. The librarians were visibly bothered.

Jack walked past the reference librarians on the right, turned left, and walked downstairs to the fiche and film section. He told the librarian there that he needed the *Times*' films and access to a reader. She looked up and smiled. "Certainly, sir," she said. "I'll be happy to help you. Not everyone in the library today is here for serious purposes."

"Thanks, I appreciate it," he said, figuring that the search for the killer of two citizens—even a talking head like Crimmins and a thief like Devens—qualified as serious.

The library had purchased new cabinets for their newspaper collections two years earlier. The cabinets were beige steel. Each drawer held a year and a half of the *Times*: seventy-five rolls of microfilm each. Each cabinet contained ten years of papers. When the new cabinets (and new film readers) were installed, the *Star-News* had covered the story; Pasadena invented the slow-news day.

"These should all be on CD-ROMs," the librarian said. "As usual, we're a generation behind."

Jack smiled. The woman's name was Hendrix. No relation to Jimi.

"The most important thing in the community and always the last to be funded," Jack said.

"Exactly," Mrs. Hendrix said. "Could I get you a cup of coffee while you're working?"

"That would be very nice," Jack said, sliding his field jacket over the back of the oak chair at one of the cleaner film reader tables. She went to the employees' lounge and brought back a ceramic cup with steaming black coffee.

"Now I know why this is my favorite place in Pasadena," Jack said. "Thank you very much."

"You just go about your work," Mrs. Hendrix said. "If you want a second cup, don't hesitate to ask."

After another brief exchange of pleasantries, Jack settled in to work. He had to feed the film through the lens housing and into the receiving spool twice to get the feel of the machine. He looked at his watch and at the wall of cabinets behind him. He didn't have time to diddle with a recalcitrant film reader; there was too much work to do. As the image came up on the green screen and the lens auto-focused, he settled into his seat and took out his notepad.

He had begun with the index reel for each year. There were constant stories about Crimmins, most of them innocuous pieces placed by publicists and policy flacks. The *Times* had much less to say about Devens, though he was featured from time to time in the Real Estate sections—usually wearing a reassuring grin and grasping an investor like a hungry boa doing his best to be patient until dinner.

It took him forty-five minutes to make his way through four years of the *Times*. As he worked he continued to replace the reels neatly and make brief notes on his yellow legal pad. Mrs. Hendrix approached and asked him if he was ready for a second cup of coffee.

"I hate to see you go to that trouble," he said.

"Nonsense," she answered. "Coffee tastes good on a rainy day."

———

At 6:00 Mrs. Hendrix ended her shift and was replaced by Mrs. Borodin. She smiled at Jack once and then turned to the pile of paper on her desk. Jack was working in the file for 1980. There was nothing about Devens, but there were a few, brief pieces on Crimmins. One was an account of a talk he had given to some defense-industry types in Orange County; the second was a Johnson administration reunion story with a picture of Crimmins standing five rows behind Bundy and McNamara. All of them were smiling, probably because the Johnson administration was history and the public attention span was short.

He moved more quickly through the 1970s as the stories began to thin out. The farther he moved down the stack of file drawers the more skeptical he became that he would find anything worth the time and attention he had already invested.

He decided to stretch his legs, visit the men's room upstairs, and get a drink of water. When he walked up the oak stairs and looked around he realized that the windows were dark and the interlopers had all left. The rain had stopped, though the windows were still streaked and, except for a dozen or so regulars and the thinning members of the library staff, the periodical room had cleared. He flexed his legs. The right leg was still stiff, even after the recent, successful operation on it. He stretched his arms, took a sip from the drinking fountain, and then went into the men's room. He splashed cold water in his face, combed his hair, and washed his hands.

When he returned to the film reader Mrs. Borodin was standing at his table. She was younger than Mrs. Hendrix, cool, professional, and a little rough around the edges. "I thought you might be finished," she said. "I was going to straighten up."

"I'm still going strong," Jack said. "Don't worry; when I'm finished I'll put everything away neatly."

"I'd appreciate that," she said, forcing her lips into a narrow smile. "These materials get a good deal of use and I want to keep them in order."

At 9:15 he opened the drawer containing the files for the late-1960s, his optimism all but gone. Mrs. Borodin was starting to look at the clock and shuffle her feet. She noticed that he was looking at her and she smiled politely.

He started to work more deliberately, fearing that if he didn't he might miss something. He knew that he was chasing a long shot. His leg was cramping and his eyes were starting to burn. The notes on his yellow pad had begun to trail off. He turned the page to a fresh sheet, put the file for 1968 back in its place, and pulled out 1967.

Forty minutes later there was no one else left in the library but the remaining members of the staff, and an old man at a reading table, his head across his forearm, sleeping soundly.

Jack depressed the *forward* button, advancing the film and scanning the index pages. Working through the C's he found a series of references to Crimmins and made a note of them on his yellow pad. Then he checked the D's and found a similar set of references to Devens. He checked his pad. The dates and page numbers were exactly the same. He rewound the index reel, rechecked the first reference date, and located that reel in the drawer. He slipped it over the mounting post, fed the film through the reader and onto the takeup spool, and hit the *forward* button, searching for the first page of the story.

When he found it he read it straight through without making any notes. Then he pulled the reel for the second reference, read it straight through, and pulled the third. Then the fourth. And the fifth and the sixth. There were eight references in all. Thirty minutes later he pushed back his chair and let his hands fall into his lap. His head fell back and he ran his hands through his hair.

"Are you all right?" Mrs. Borodin asked.

He didn't hear her.

"Are you all right?" she said again, her voice much more insistent.

He turned toward her. "I beg your pardon . . ."

"I said, 'Are you all right?'"

"Yes," he said.

"Is there anything that you need?"

"No. I just found what I needed. Thanks."

"Well, it's nice that you located what you were looking for."

"There's nothing nice about it," he said. Then, realizing how that must have sounded, he apologized.

"That's quite all right," she said. "If you're looking for pain and suffering there's no better source than the *Los Angeles Times*."

"I found them," he said.

"What is it you found, if you don't mind my asking?"

"Something that would make the angels weep."

PART THREE

The Mountain

THIRTY-FOUR

It was 11:05 when Jack reached Frank. They decided to meet at Crown City, a combination brewery, bar, and restaurant at Del Mar and Raymond, south of the old Pasadena railroad station.

"That was quick," Frank said. "I didn't expect you to find anything this soon."

"I didn't either," Jack said. "There was nothing in the recent past, at least nothing that made it into the *Times*. I kept going back further and further. Finally I found something."

"Something promising?"

"I think so."

"Grounds for murder?"

"*I* would have killed them."

"Run it down for me," Frank said, lifting his pint mug and taking a deep drink.

"Mid-60s," Jack said. "A young first lieutenant stationed in a forward area in Vietnam. His name is Daniel Wilken. His wife, Susan, is living in Los Angeles and needs to reach him because of a family emergency. Lieutenant Wilken is involved in operations that are described as 'highly classified.' The pentagon won't budge, so Susan goes to a local person who might be able to help her . . ."

"Michael Crimmins."

"Right. Crimmins is a local celebrity; his name's been splattered all over the *Times*. He's on the fast track at Defense, one of McNamara's best and brightest. Susan Wilken contacts her congressman, who in turn contacts Crimmins. Crimmins agrees to meet with her. He's back in L.A. for the weekend and he invites her to come over and talk to him. He's having a get-together for a couple of friends and tells her he'll make time to see her."

"And does he?"

"Oh yes, he sees her all right. She comes over and he introduces her to his friends and offers her a drink. She declines. He insists. She finally agrees, but presses him to try to do something about her husband. He changes the subject and tells her not to worry. Everybody has some more drinks, one thing leads to another, and Crimmins starts hitting on her. She tells him she's not interested, that all she wants is help in contacting her husband. Crimmins starts calling her names and eventually forces her into his bedroom. His friends join him and together they help him rape Susan Wilken."

"That son-of-a-bitch."

"It gets worse," Jack said. "It turns out that the family emergency has to do with Susan's health. She's pregnant. Things aren't going well and she needs her husband's help. Instead of getting help she gets raped. After the rape she miscarries. She tries to reach her husband through other channels, but Crimmins makes sure that her husband is kept incommunicado. He's stuck somewhere near the DMZ. And, thus, his wife is forced to take on her attackers alone."

"Didn't she have them arrested?"

"She tried to, but she didn't act immediately after the rape. She had miscarried on the way home and with all of the pain and shame she couldn't face her attackers again without some time to compose herself. Instead she washed and she waited."

"So that when she finally pressed charges there was no physical evidence."

"That's right," Jack said. "Plus, Crimmins' friends all marched in and testified on his behalf. They said Susan Wilken was a power groupie, that she had come on to Crimmins hoping he'd do some improper favors for her. When he refused to use his office in that way, she retaliated by crying rape. They painted Crimmins as the gallant public servant, upholding his oath of office, and fending off a nympho influence seeker."

"What about the miscarriage?"

"They said she wasn't that far along, that she couldn't even have been sure that she was pregnant."

"That's bullshit."

"Of course it is, but they had half of the board-certified obstetricians in L.A. County on their witness list."

"So what did the police do?"

"They didn't do anything. Susan Wilken was forced to bring a civil action."

"And that didn't get her anywhere either."

"No. All it did was get her humiliated in open court. Crimmins hired the first team and they mauled her. Every fact, every detail was dragged out. They got four former boyfriends to testify. They even managed to get their hands on disciplinary records from her grammar school. They annihilated her."

"And the rapist walked."

"Yes."

"How many were there with him?" Frank asked.

"Two."

"Devens and who else?"

"The third person was Ernest Jeffers."

"Jesus," Frank said, "Ernie Jeffers."

Ernest Jeffers owned Mobile Intelligence Systems, a defense contractor that produced surveillance systems for fixed-wing military aircraft. When he wasn't selling to the Department of Defense, he was selling to each and every foreign government that the White House permitted him to approach. He was the third largest defense contractor in the state of California, a major political and financial supporter of the incumbent administration, and the principal officer of the Jeffers Foundation, which made gifts and grants to enough worthy recipients to insulate him from any possible public criticism. Prince John in Robin Hood's clothing.

"Ernie was just getting started then," Jack said, "but he was already starting to get tight with the defense establishment. He started out making pistol belts and jungle boots but soon graduated to manufacturing 4.2-inch mortars and M79 grenade launchers. Devens was the small timer in the group. He just came along for the drinks and the ride. Ernie gave him short shrift. He was much more interested in working Mikey and his newfound friends. Crimmins tolerated Devens because he was a voter who could eventually help him buy other voters. The three of them had gone to college together. They got together once or twice a year to get wasted and talk about old times. When Mikey got the job at Defense the three of them suddenly got a whole lot more chummy."

"I should call Jeffers and warn him," Frank said. "Of course, if he's got any brains he should be able to see how this is shaking out, especially if he was guilty. You know something—I never really liked that greedy, profiteering bastard."

"Neither did I," Jack said. "He's a smarmy, holier-than-thou asshole—always turning up at just the right events, smiling and dancing around in front of the camera in his goddamned tuxedo. Meanwhile the pig bastard is quietly selling military hardware and state-of-the-art technology to two-thirds of the tin gods and dictators in the third world. They never show you the blood on his hands, but there's a hell of a lot of it there."

"So this poor woman took on those three pieces of shit alone and lost," Frank said.

"Only the first round," Jack said. "This time she's batting a thousand. Two down and only one more to go."

"Why did she wait so long?"

"I don't know. That's a damned good question. I'm going to go to City Hall first thing in the morning and try to find out whatever I can. I want to know a whole lot more about the husband—see what his role is in this."

"I should arrest her, if only for her own good," Frank said.

"What do you mean?"

"Think about it, Jack. Ernie Jeffers isn't going to be as easy to get to as Crimmins and Devens. He may be crooked and he may be dirty, but he sure as hell isn't stupid. He'll be ready and he'll have a small army surrounding him. I'd hate to see her walk in and get blown away."

"How can you arrest her?" Jack asked. "You've got motive, but you don't have opportunity or physical evidence, at least not yet, and the motive is more than two decades out of date."

"That's true," Frank said. "You can also figure that if she was smart enough to whack Crimmins and Devens without leaving any evidence, she'll be smart enough to protect herself against prosecution. She was fucked over by the legal system the first time around; she's not going to let that happen again."

"Is McGann here yet? One thing you've got to remember, Frank—the government is going to be embarrassed by this. They'll do everything they can to minimize the damage. That means they'll protect

Crimmins and Devens and smear Susan Wilken. I don't want to see that happen."

Frank looked up at the clock on the south wall. "His plane should be touching down within the hour."

"I'll tell you what. You keep working the Disneyland witnesses and I'll see what I can find at City Hall. It'll take McGann a while to put all of the pieces together. If I can stay a few hours ahead of him we may be able to protect everyone. Jeffers will be on his guard anyway. You don't have to worry about him. I'm more concerned about the woman. I don't want to see McGann and his people march into her house and spray everything in sight with automatic weapons fire. That will be their first impulse and I think she deserves better."

"We owe her something," Frank said. "The world's already a better place without Crimmins and Devens."

"I agree."

"There's only one thing that bothers me," Frank said, pausing as he took a long sip of his beer.

"What's that?"

"You seem more worried about protecting her than protecting her next victim."

"I don't see any problem with that," Jack said.

"No? Why not?"

"She's a citizen too and she's in danger. She's also innocent until proven guilty. Your job is to prevent death, not inflict it. That includes protecting people from their own worst selves. You don't have to worry about Ernie Jeffers. He can take care of himself; he always has. What you have to do is protect Susan Wilken."

"I know all that. And I'm not for a minute excusing what those bastards did, assuming that the allegations are all accurate. What I'm saying is that you seem to be taking her side, regardless of the consequences."

"OK, I'm taking her side. Why not? I don't like pricks who beat up on women and I especially don't like pricks who beat up on defenseless women."

"What about pricks who beat up on defenseless women when their husbands are busy serving in the military?"

Jack didn't answer.

"Well?" Frank said.

Jack still didn't answer.

"You'd like to help shove in the next blade, wouldn't you?"

"Yes, and then twist the son-of-a-bitch hard."

"I don't think you would do that."

"No, I probably wouldn't," Jack said.

"You're sure?"

"Yes, but I'm also sure of something else."

"What's that?"

"If McGann gets to her before we do, she's going to die. People like him don't give a damn about justice. All they care about is how a case like this makes *them* look. If she's in their way they'll drive over her without giving it a second thought."

"So what are you going to do?"

"Everything I can, on this side of the law."

"Stay in touch with me on this, Jack."

"I will, Frank."

"And one other thing..."

"What's that?" Jack asked.

"Don't do anything that will end up hurting you."

"Why not?"

"Because she's not your responsibility."

"Whose responsibility is she? Her husband's? Last time out they kept him in southeast Asia, playing with his life there while they played with his wife and the life of his unborn child here. I'm not going to let them get by with that kind of shit again."

"Jack..."

"Look, Frank, she's entitled. Besides, unless her husband surfaces, there's nobody else. You sure as hell can't do it, not and continue to wear that lieutenant's badge."

"I'd feel better if you weren't in this alone."

"Then relax," Jack said. "After I called you, I called Charles."

"Why did you do that?"

"Because I wanted to bring him up to date on the case."

"And because you know how he feels about people who can't protect themselves."

"Charles is a very caring person."

"Yes, he's a caring person. If he comes in on this we'll have World War III in Los Angeles and the U.S. government will lose."

"That depends on who you think the government is," Jack said. "I don't want to believe that it's only people like Crimmins and McGann."

"Yes, well..."

"What does the press know now?"

"Only that Devens is dead. We've held back the information on the weapons."

"What did you tell them?"

"That he appears to have been poisoned."

"So they won't pick up on the Crimmins connection right away," Jack said.

"We thought we should give ourselves a little lead time."

"Good idea, but we don't have much of it. The *Times* will be combing through their morgues for Devens' obituary; it won't be long before they know what we know."

"You've got tomorrow and tomorrow evening," Frank said. "I wouldn't plan on any more than that. At least they won't leak anything to the networks in the meantime; they'll protect their exclusive story."

"I wish McGann didn't know either."

"We couldn't hold that back," Frank said.

"I know."

Frank looked at his watch. "He'll be landing in thirty-five minutes."

THIRTY-FIVE

McGann's flight had been delayed by an hour and he was fuming when he arrived. He called Frank to a 2:00 AM meeting in the Bonaventure Hotel and ordered him to extend every courtesy to the members of his staff and then to stay the hell out of their way. Then he called Ray Calder and told him to reassemble the witnesses for an 8:00 meeting.

"Do you need anything else from me?" Frank asked.

"No. Just get the hell out of here so I can sleep."

"Pleasant dreams," Frank said.

"Don't get cute with me, White," McGann said.

"And don't you get cute with me, either," Frank said. "This isn't Constitution Avenue. It's Bunker Hill. The people in this neighborhood won't kiss up to you and run for your coffee; they'll cut out your heart for a pocketful of loose change. Let me tell you something, McGann. I don't give a rat's ass about your authority and your cheap-shit techniques. You're in a foreign country here. If you want anybody to help you, you'd better check that fucking attitude at the door, because we don't care where you get your hair cut and your shirts monogrammed, or how big the goddamned nameplate is on your goddamned desk. We're not taking any of your shit and we're not going to run fucking errands for you. Treat us the way you want to be treated yourself."

"White..."

"What?"

"Shut up and get the fuck out of here so I can get some sleep."

"Chester..."

"What?"

"Say hi to your twin brother for me in the morning."

"What twin brother?"

"Mickey Mouse."

———

The custodians were doing their final cleanup before the onslaught of the lawyers in the Civic Center. Two of them—one named Marty and another named Fred—knew Jack and said good morning to him. He said hi to both of them and walked down the central hall to the vending machines near the assessor's office. He dropped fifty cents in the coffee machine, heard some nondescript clicking and gurgling, and watched the top sign light up: *Your Coffee is Now Being Freshly Brewed.*

"Yeah, right," he said, "they squeezed poor Juan Valdez's ass into the back of that machine and he's grinding the beans by hand while Mrs. Olsen is wedged in beside him, collecting quarters and saying, 'It's the *richest* kind.'"

Jack tasted it, shook his head, and walked toward the elevator. He opened his cardboard accordion folder, checked for pencils and pads, and then looked at his watch. McGann was in Los Angeles now. The

Civic Center offices would open in three minutes. After that there would be no more time for coffee.

There had been no phone numbers listed for Daniel or Susan Wilken in any of the local directories. As soon as the assessor's office opened, Jack checked the tax rolls; it took him ten minutes to find Daniel Wilken's name. Wilken owned a modest house just east of Santa Monica on Bundy; the mailing address for the tax bill was in Sunland. Jack wrote down both addresses and hurried back to his car. It all seemed too easy.

Driving against rush-hour traffic, the volume on the Santa Monica freeway west was moderate. Jack reached the Wilken house on Bundy Drive in twenty-seven minutes. He waited in his car for a second, collected his thoughts, and then walked toward the building—a tiny yellow cottage that sat no more than ten feet from the street. There were some scraggly boxwoods along the west lot line and a single, limp banana tree in front of the porch.

He knocked on the door but no one answered. He knocked again and heard a dog bark. By the third knock he could hear footsteps. The door opened but the woman inside kept all three of her chain locks in place.

"Yes?" she said.

She was Asian and at least sixty years old.

"Hello," Jack said. "I'm looking for Mr. and Mrs. Daniel Wilken."

"They don't live here," the woman said.

"Can you tell me where they are?" Jack said.

"No. We rent from them, but we never see them."

"If you don't mind my asking, where do you send the rent checks? This is very important, a matter of life and death."

"I send the check every month to a post office box in Los Angeles," the woman said. "Who are you?"

"I'm a private investigator," Jack said, showing the woman his license. "Is there any way that you could think of that I could reach the Wilkens?"

"No, there isn't."

"Who do you call when you have a problem with the house?"

"The owner has a maintenance contract," she said. "We call them: Investment Properties Management. I'll give you the number if you'd like me to."

"Thanks very much," Jack said.

He could see her walk out to the kitchen and take a card off of a board next to the refrigerator. Then she disappeared from sight. She was back at the door in a few seconds and handed Jack a piece of used envelope with a number written on the back. "That's who we call," she said. "We ask for Mr. Blanchard."

"Thanks very much," Jack said. "I appreciate your help. And your name, ma'am?"

"Mrs. Fan."

———

Jack drove to a Union station on Santa Monica Boulevard and called Blanchard.

"Sorry, Mr. Grant, I can't help you," he said.

"This is very important," Jack said. "Look, I'm not some outraged renter trying to make trouble for a landlord. I'm a private investigator working on a case. Would you like the number of my license?"

"That's not necessary," Blanchard said. "I don't have a name or address to give you. I work through a post office box in Los Angeles. Both the management fee and my reimbursements come by cashier's check. It's not uncommon, you know. A lot of landlords want to remain anonymous."

"Thanks for your help," Jack said, and hurried back to his car. He looked at his watch; it was 9:01. He turned east on the boulevard and headed for the 405. With rush hour traffic on the 134 it could take him an hour to get to Sunland.

There was still some flooding near the off ramps on the 134, but the traffic was moving steadily until the interchanges for the Hollywood and Golden State. He kept moving to the left-hand lanes, following the signs for Pasadena. As he passed through Glendale he started moving to the right side of the freeway. Finally catching the 210 he headed northwest, toward San Fernando. He looked at his watch; it was now 9:40. The 210 was a straight shot and he found his Sunland exit in twelve minutes.

Mountain View Drive paralleled the freeway. On the corner was an old Mobil station with a large red Pegasus against a white background. Jack drove northwest, catching glimpses of the freeway traffic behind the long row of frame and adobe cottages that lined the west side of the road. Three-quarters of a mile from the Mobil station the cement pavement narrowed to a lane-and-a-half wide, gravel road. Jack kept driving.

The address to which Daniel Wilken's tax bills were being sent was a tree and shrub nursery that backed against the freeway. In all, Jack estimated that there were at least five acres of ground surrounding the small, single-story, frame house in the center. The nursery itself was in disrepair. The plantings needed to be trimmed and some of those that had died had not been uprooted and replaced. The yellow paint on the house was flaking and the small porch in front showed signs of termite damage. There was a faded Dodge Dart parked beside it with exhaust stain on the rear bumper and a piece of heavy wire holding the trunk in place.

Jack walked up to the screen door, opened it, and knocked. An elderly Hispanic man opened the inside door but stayed behind the screen. "Yes?" he said. His face was lined from the sun and his eyes were sunken. He was wearing overalls and a pair of work boots.

"I'm looking for the Wilkens," Jack said.

"They don't live here," the man said. "I watch the nursery for them."

"Could you tell me where I could find them?"

"I don't know where they are. What is this about?"

Jack took out his PI license. "My name is Grant," he said, showing the man his license. "I'm a private investigator. It's very important that I reach Mr. and Mrs. Wilken."

"Mr. and Mrs.?" the man said. He seemed surprised.

"Yes," Jack answered. "Is there something wrong?"

"No. Give me your number. Sometimes they call me here. If they do I'll tell them you want to speak to them."

"I appreciate your help, but it's more urgent than that. I have to talk to them right away. It's a matter of life and death."

"Life and death?" the man said.

"Yes. Is there any chance that you could reach them?"

"Only if they call me," he said.

"Please," Jack said. "It's really important."

"I understand, but I don't have their number."

"Do you have an address for them?"

"No."

"Could you give me your number, in case I need to call you?"

The man stood there, thinking, for a minute. "I guess it would be OK. Just a second."

He closed the door behind him without locking it and returned a few moments later. "Here it is," he said, handing Jack a single sheet of paper with the number written in pencil.

"I appreciate it," Jack said. "And your name, sir?"

"My name is Cesar."

"Thanks again," Jack said. He hurried back to his car and drove straight to the Mobil station. Frank was still in Anaheim, but he got Jerry Dailey.

"Jerry, I need a favor."

"Name it, Jack," he said.

"I need a check on a phone in Sunland. I want to know if anyone has been calling that number regularly and, if so, what the location of the caller is."

"What's the number, Jack?"

"It's 790-2730."

"Where are you, Jack?"

"I'm in a Mobil station in Sunland."

"Give me about ten minutes," Jerry said.

"I'll tell you what, I'll call you," Jack said. "I don't want to stand next to the phone here; it's too noisy and I've got something else I need to do."

"I'll wait to hear from you."

"Thanks, Jerry," Jack said, and got back in his car. He drove back to the 210, turned onto the northbound on-ramp, and drove toward the back of the nursery. A few hundred feet before the last house on Mountain View Drive, he turned onto the shoulder lane and eased forward. There was no sign for the nursery along the freeway and no phone number or hours posted. Either the nursery was out of business or they dealt exclusively with retailers or contractors.

He drove to the next exit, found an old diner, and filled his thermos with coffee. The public phone was outside. Jerry had had twelve minutes to track the telephone traffic on the nursery's line. Jack put his thermos on the floor beneath the phone, took out a small notepad, and called Jerry.

"I've got the information," Jerry said. "There are two numbers that repeat. One is a residential address in East L.A.; the name is Colon."

Jack wrote down the address as Jerry dictated it. "First name?"

"Cesar."

"How about the second one, Jerry?"

"The second one calls about once a week."

"Where, Jerry?" Jack got his pencil ready.

"A public phone, Jack."

"Where is it, Jerry?"

"The L.A. County library."

"Damn," Jack said.

"Sorry," Jerry said. "That's all I got. Does the Colon number mean anything?"

"That's the name of the caretaker who looks after a place for the person I'm trying to find. That's probably just his wife and kids calling him. I'll check it out just to be sure. Thanks for your help, Jerry."

"Any time, Jack."

"Have you heard from Frank?"

"Not since he left for Anaheim. This guy's in town from Washington; his name's McGann . . ."

"Yes, I know who he is."

"He's a four-star asshole. He had the Attorney General call the Chief. The Chief called in Loram and ordered us to give the guy whatever he wants. Frank's with him now. McGann keeps making these king-shit noises about how he and his people are going to take down Crimmins and Devens' killer. He brought about a dozen of them with him. I think he's under some kind of deadline because he keeps looking at his watch and calling the people back in D.C. Frank told me to tell you about that. He said that McGann might move more quickly than he should and that he's got enough reinforcements with him to be dangerous."

"Tell Frank I appreciate the warning, Jerry."

"What's your involvement in this, Jack?"

"Damage control, Jerry."

THIRTY-SIX

As he figured, there was no one at the Colon address but the Colon family: Mrs. Colon, a daughter living at home, and three grandchildren. There was no real room in their small house for anyone else and no indication that anyone else was living there. Jack thanked them for seeing him, got back in his car, and drove back to the Civic Center.

He was prepared to work his way through every building, every office, and every file, but each time he looked at his watch he knew that whatever he found he would have to find, and use, quickly. McGann's group would be right behind him, hungry for information they could twist to their own purposes. Their employers hated many things, but humiliation was the deadliest of sins on their agency's list. The Crimmins rape case was suddenly alive again and this time it wouldn't be buried so easily. Its shadow was long and broad and it would be weeks before the broadcasters and writers were finished with it. If Ernie Jeffers was killed also, the weeks would stretch into months.

Dredging up the embarrassments of the past was bad enough; seeing the resulting murder cases cracked by local cops or a small-time PI would be far worse. This was McGann's show. Finding the killer first would give him the chance to suppress facts and manipulate spin. Seeing Jack Grant or Frank White get there before the suits from Justice would be unthinkable, and McGann's superiors would impose a host of immediate punishments for any collateral damage incurred.

Jack needed the Wilkens' address. He went to the Recorder's office to check the specific records on their property. It took him a few minutes to find the mortgage on the Bundy Drive property, but when he located it the mortgage had been cancelled. He checked the date. It had been cancelled in August, no more than five weeks before Crimmins' death.

He found the copy of the Mountain View property's mortgage; it had been cancelled in late July. He hurried back to the assessor's office and spoke to a woman named Margo Norman. Mrs. Norman informed him that it was not uncommon for the same name to appear on the tax rolls after the property had been deeded to a new party.

"It's all a matter of timing," she said. "The taxes for the period in question would be settled at the time of closing and then escrowed. We always get our money, Mr. Grant. You needn't worry about that. When the property is sold we put the new owner's name in our computer but we don't generate new tax rolls every time there's a transfer. We simply put in a handwritten notation."

"But there was no handwritten notation there," Jack said.

"Oh, we're always a few months behind in doing that," she said. "We're very short-handed here, in case you haven't noticed. But it's really not a problem. As I told you, we always get our money."

"Can you tell me who the new owners are of these two pieces of property?" Jack asked.

"I could get the information for you," she said, "but it would take a few minutes. If you're in a hurry you should really go back to the recorder's office and look at the deeds. They're copied within seventy-two hours of the time of their actual recording. They have a much larger staff than we do, you see. They can give you the information instantly. There's another reason why you should look at the deeds."

"What is that, Mrs. Norman?"

"If the property was subdivided it would take the engineers months to redraw the plat books. Your best source of information is always the deed. Don't bother with anything else, at least not for four or five months."

"Thank you very much," Jack said. "I appreciate your help."

"That's what we're here for, Mr. Grant," she said. "Have a nice day."

The Bundy property had been sold to a realty firm, Jackson Tanner, Inc., and the Mountain View nursery and land had been sold intact to one of the Wilkens' competitors: Crews Landscaping. The seller's name on each deed was Daniel Wilken; there was no mention of Susan. In each case the property had been leased back through the end of October. The Fans' sublease on the Bundy property would have to be honored by their new landlord. When it ran out they could attempt to sell the property, which they were doubtless buying on spec. Cesar

Colon might be out of a job when the people from Crews came in to put the nursery back into heavy production, but for all Jack knew Colon might actually be Crews' man.

Jack found the record of the marriage of Daniel and Susan Wilken as well as the Sheriff's docket notation on Susan's civil suit against Crimmins, Devens, and Jeffers. The decision for the defendants was there in black and white and there was no record of any appeals. The actual court documents would be voluminous; there was no time to go through them now. Perhaps he could do that later.

Jack was ready to check with Jackson Tanner and Crews to see if they could provide any information on the Wilkens' address, but he knew it would probably be futile. Any family that protective of its privacy would work through agents and middlemen and continue to use box numbers instead of street addresses.

Instead, Jack decided to run a quick check on the Wilkens' marriage. Susan's name should have been on the deeds. Joint ownership with a survivorship clause was standard. Somewhat reluctantly, he checked the Domestic Relations Court files, but there was no record of any divorce.

Relieved, but still confused, he checked the mortality records and discovered the reason why Susan Wilken's name had not appeared on the two deeds. Susan Wilken had been dead for over fifteen years. He ran his fingertip to the bottom of the entry. The cause of death was noted with cruel simplicity: *suicide.*

He jotted down the date, threw his notepad and pencil into his cardboard folder, and ran down the steps and through the central hallway, clutching his folder in his left hand and the keys to his car in his right.

THIRTY-SEVEN

THERE WAS A LIGHT on in the left front window of the nursery cottage. Jack skipped the steps, jumped up on the porch, and knocked. When there was no immediate response he knocked again, this time much louder. Cesar Colon opened the door.

"I have to talk to you," Jack said.

"Yes?"

"Can I come inside?"

Colon didn't answer the question, but instead came out on the porch and stood next to Jack. "What do you have to talk to me about?" Colon asked.

"Susan Wilken is dead," Jack said.

"Yes, of course," Colon said. "No one said that she was still alive. Mrs. Wilken died many years ago."

"But . . ."

"Is there anything else?" Colon asked.

"I have to see Daniel Wilken," Jack said.

"I'm afraid that is impossible," Colon said.

"Why? Is he dead also?"

"Mr. Wilken? Of course not."

"Then why can't I see him?"

"Mr. Wilken isn't well. He doesn't see visitors."

"I'm not a visitor, Mr. Colon. I'm an investigator. I *must* see him."

"I'm sorry."

"Can I be of some help?" The voice came from behind Jack. He turned and saw a woman in her late twenties or very early thirties. She was wearing a brown suit and cream-colored blouse, with a pearl necklace and earrings. She was carrying a leather folder and a small clutch purse. Her chestnut hair and green eyes were the most striking features of a near-perfect set.

"My name is Grant," Jack said. "I'm an investigator."

"Karen Crews," the woman said. "What are you investigating, Mr. Grant?"

Colon excused himself and went back into the house. There were two wooden chairs on the porch. The young woman wiped one off with a tissue and sat down. "Mr. Grant . . . ?"

Jack sat down next to her. He didn't bother to wipe off the seat.

"Your family has purchased this property," Jack said.

"Yes. Mr. Wilken is not in good health. He can no longer operate the business. We were happy to be able to acquire it."

"How long has Mr. Wilken been ill?"

"For quite some time," she said. "I believe I asked you what you were investigating, Mr. Grant."

Jack paused for a moment before answering. "I appreciate your willingness to help, Ms. Crews, but it's not something I'm at liberty to discuss."

"Is it about the killing of Crimmins and Devens?" she asked.

"As a matter of fact, it is."

"I'm quite familiar with that. All of Dan's friends are. How much do you know about the case?"

"I know that his wife was raped by Crimmins and his friends and that two of them are now dead."

"*Allegedly* raped, Mr. Grant. Most would have said that. Her claim was never proven."

"I assumed she was telling the truth," Jack said.

"Why?"

"Why would she lie, Ms. Crews? What would she have to gain? Even today women think long and hard before putting themselves through the circus of a rape trial. Susan Wilken's damage claim was modest. It seems obvious to me that what she really wanted was justice."

"And who are you representing, Mr. Grant?"

"Actually I'm not representing anyone," Jack said.

"Then how can you investigate the case?"

"I'm a friend of the LAPD lieutenant who is handling the case. I can do things that he can't do."

"Such as?"

"Inform the family that there are people here from the Justice Department who are prepared to resolve the case in the most expeditious manner possible, without regard to consequences."

"What you're saying is that they will shoot first and seek justice later."

"Exactly."

"Why should you want to do that for someone you don't know? Obstruction of justice is a felony, Mr. Grant."

"So is killing a suspect unnecessarily."

"And you came here to warn Dan?"

"Actually I came here to warn his wife. I just learned this morning that she died years ago."

"You thought she was the one who killed Crimmins and Devens?"

"There is no eyewitness on the Crimmins case. Devens appears to have been killed by a woman. Susan Wilken was the most likely suspect."

"Her suit for rape was over two decades ago. Why do you think someone would wait that long to take their revenge?"

"I don't know, Ms. Crews. Why do you think they would?"

"I don't know either, but I can guess. Dan Wilken was in Vietnam when his wife was attacked. She was expecting a child. They were looking forward to their future life together. They had made plans. As soon as his tour was over he intended to return to California so they could get on with their lives. Crimmins ended all of that. Susan lost her child. She lost . . . everything. Eventually she took her own life."

"But why would *whoever* killed them wait this long?"

"Perhaps because they were waiting for Crimmins and Devens' own lives to come together. The propitious moment, Mr. Grant. The more that they had to lose, the sweeter would be the revenge."

"And who would you suggest that I warn, Ms. Crews?" He was looking at her hands and her wrists, wondering how much strength was in them.

"The murderer, Mr. Grant?"

"Yes."

"I can think of many people who would like to see Crimmins and Devens dead."

"Including yourself, Ms. Crews?"

"Certainly."

He searched her eyes for something more. "Could you help me find Daniel Wilken, Ms. Crews?"

"Why would you want to talk to him?"

"To warn him and to tell him to warn anyone he thinks might be responsible."

"I'm sure he would appreciate your concern, Mr. Grant."

"It's more than just concern, Ms. Crews. Now that both Devens and Crimmins are dead it will only be a matter of hours before the feds discover the connection with the Wilkens and come after him. There's something else . . ."

"What, Mr. Grant?"

"There was a third person involved in the assault on Susan Wilken."

"Ernest Jeffers," she said.

"Yes," Jack said. "Jeffers will have his own men protecting him. He is much richer than Devens and far more powerful than Crimmins. Killing him will not be as easy as killing the first two. I can see why whoever killed the first two would want to complete the set, but taking on Jeffers, along with the Justice Department, would be very, very hazardous."

"And you want the person or persons who killed Crimmins and Devens to escape alive?"

"Let's just say that I feel I should warn Daniel Wilken of how much there is at stake."

"And you want to warn him out of a feeling of sympathy and, what, public spiritedness?"

"I was in Vietnam, Ms. Crews. My wife died while I was there. I don't understand exactly how he feels—no one could understand that—but I can come closer than most. At this point there isn't much that I can do for him, but I can at least do this."

"I'm sorry for you too," she said, "but you should be thinking about your own position here. You could be risking a lot."

"Let me tell you something, Ms. Crews . . ." He was looking at her hands and wrists again as he moved up to her eyes. "There is no physical evidence yet to connect anyone with the two murders. The motive is there for the Wilken family, but that's not sufficient to convict. At this point neither the government nor the LAPD have a case. The head of the Justice group is a man named McGann. The fact that he doesn't have a case will not deter him. His goal will be to bring this to a quick conclusion. I don't want to see anyone killed unnecessarily."

"Why not have the LAPD warn Dan?"

"McGann has had the Attorney General order the LAPD to cooperate with him fully in the investigation."

"Are you saying that the LAPD is no longer free to act independently?"

"In effect. But I'm a private citizen who just happens to be interested in the case. Like I said, I can do things that the LAPD can't do."

"Would you really like to meet Dan Wilken, Mr. Grant?"

"Yes, I would. Can you take me to him?"

"Of course."

"We can take my car," Jack said.

"That won't be necessary," she said. "He's right here."

She got up, walked over to the door, and turned the knob. Colon was standing there. When he saw it was Karen he stood back out of the way.

"Come in, Mr. Grant," she said. "He's right through that door." She was pointing toward the far side of the living room, in the back of the cottage. "Go ahead, just knock."

Jack walked past Colon, who was now sitting in a chair next to the front door, like a guard at a gate. He crossed the living room and knocked on the door but there was no response. He turned the knob and walked in.

He found himself standing in a room decorated with green nylon chairs and heavy chests and tables of blond oak with gold pulls. There were carved-cedar souvenirs sitting on some of the tables and wooden lamps with black plastic lacing around the tops and bottoms of their shades. Each of the pictures on the walls and in the small, table-top frames were from the days prior to Susan Wilken's death. On the wall closest to the door was a picture of his family: Dan Wilken in his lieutenant's uniform, his arm around Susan, whose eyes were fixed on him rather than on the camera lens. They were in the mountains, surrounded by broad white rocks and tall evergreens, all deep green in the filtered sunlight. Between them sat a small girl in a white dress with a full smile.

In the far corner was a lava lamp with red blobs bubbling and breaking into elongated orbs. Just to the right of the lamp was an overstuffed chair with cylindrical wooden legs ending in circular, brass feet.

The form in the chair was sitting in semi-darkness, the right side of his face partially illuminated by the single lamp. He was wearing one-style-fits-all GI glasses and the light from the lamp was reflecting in their lenses.

"Mr. Wilken?" Jack said.

"Yes?" The voice was thin and uncertain.

"Can I speak with you?"

"Of course," the voice said.

Jack approached the darkened corner and saw what was left of Daniel Wilken—a shrivelled stick figure of less than a hundred pounds, his body contorted, his hands gripping the arms of his chair, anchoring him to some twilight reality.

"My name is Jack Grant," Jack said. "I've been looking forward to meeting you."

"How do you do," Daniel Wilken said, releasing his grip on the arm of the chair for a moment and extending it into the light.

Jack took his hand. It felt like a broken bird, dry, warm, and bent into a small, twisted shape.

"Did you see Karen, Mr. Grant?"

"Yes, I did. She was very helpful."

"She's a wonderful girl, isn't she? I think she should be in school but, you know, she likes to stay home here with me."

"She's just outside," Jack said.

"Yes, I expect she wants to play with her friends. Her mother and I are so very proud of her."

"You should be," Jack said.

"What did you want to talk to me about, Mr. Grant?"

"Nothing specific, Mr. Wilken. I came to your nursery; Karen told me you were here, and I thought I'd just say hello. I was in Vietnam too. I thought we might have served there at the same time."

"It's possible," Wilken said. "I've only been back for a few years and I'm always surprised that I hear so little from the people in my unit."

"You were up near the DMZ, weren't you?"

"Yes. Where were you?"

"A little farther south. I think we may have met once or twice on R and R. Where did you go?"

"Honolulu."

"Me too," Jack lied. "I'm trying to think—did I meet your wife there?"

"Susan? Oh no, we couldn't afford for her to fly all that way. She still talks about those days. Women do. I've tried to forget them. Would you like something to drink, Mr. Grant? I like to drink orange juice. Karen thinks it's good for me. She says that it keeps me from catching cold."

He held up his empty glass in a silent toast.

"No thank you, Mr. Wilken. I really need to get back to work. It was a pleasure to meet you." Jack reached out to take his hand, but Wilken was reluctant to release his grip on the arm of the chair. Instead he just nodded and curled his lips into a sweet smile.

"Take care of yourself," Jack said.

"You do the same, Mr. Grant," Wilken said.

Jack walked back into the living room, closing the door behind him. Colon was still sitting next to the front door. He turned his face to the side as Jack walked out onto the porch. Karen was sitting in the sun, holding her leather folder, staring at Jack in silence.

"How long has he been that way?"

"Since he lost his wife," Karen said. "Initially he stopped eating. The business began to slide. Eventually, he locked himself in a darkened room. He lost eighty-five pounds. After eighteen months he began to speak again and eventually he was able to recognize voices. From time to time we had to take him to the hospital and have him fed intravenously. He's very good today. Did he speak to you?"

"Yes, he did."

"The sunshine seems to help. Last night, when it was raining, he stayed in the room. He wouldn't eat. This morning he was better."

"Who is going to take care of him if you get caught or killed?" Jack said.

"I don't know what you mean," she said.

"Yes, you do," Jack said.

She paused for a full minute before speaking again.

"Would you like to help me, Mr. Grant?"

"How?" His voice was edged with skepticism but he had already anticipated the question.

"It wouldn't be anything very complicated."

"You'll have to tell me what it is you want me to do."

"I'd like you to do two things. Today is Wednesday, Mr. Grant. I'd like you to come back here tomorrow evening."

"For what purpose?"

"I can't tell you that. I'd just like you to come back."

"At what time?"

"At eight o'clock."

"What else would you like me to do?"

"Something simple, something you'll have no trouble doing."

"What's that?"

"When you come and people ask you what you found I want you to tell them the truth."

"What *will* I find?"

"You'll have to wait and see. No one here intends you any harm, I can assure you of that."

"Miss Wilken . . ."

"Why are you calling me that?"

"Because I prefer the truth."

They sat staring at one another until Jack spoke again.

"Please don't do anything foolish. Please remember what I've already told you."

"I appreciate your concern for us, Mr. Grant. I truly do."

"Can I ask you a question?"

"What is it?" she answered.

"What are you trying to do, Karen?"

"That's very simple. I'm trying to free us of the past so that we can finally begin our lives."

"What if you sacrifice your life and your father's life in the process?"

"We're still here so far—you have to admit that, Mr. Grant. Besides, I want to see my mother's story told. I want to see it told to its conclusion. I want everyone to hear it. Everyone. My mother can no longer tell it, so someone else must."

Jack didn't answer her.

"I have no interest in dying, Mr. Grant, and I will not allow my father to suffer further. We simply must free ourselves of the past and begin to live our lives."

"You can do that now. All you have to do is walk away. But you refuse to do that."

She smiled softly. "There are some things that must be done first. Then we can leave."

Again he just stared at her.

"I know why you're bothered," she said.

"Why is that?" Jack answered.

"Because if you were in my place you would do exactly the same thing. You look at me and you see a reflection of yourself. I know you do," she said. Then, after a pause: "By the way, we're both *right*, you know."

"About what, Karen?"

"About the fact that we can't let them do these kinds of things to us. Not to individual people like Susan Wilken and not to the country. They *did* do it to the whole country, don't you think?"

"Yes, I believe that they did."

"I'm just telling our tiny part of the story."

"My advice stands," Jack said.

"I know," she said. "What about my request for help?"

"I'll be here at eight o'clock."

"I knew you would," she said, getting up from her chair and walking toward him. "If I never see you again, thank you," she said, kissing him on the cheek.

He got back in his car, turned around, and drove away toward the city. She sat back down in the chair, opened the folder and put the 9mm pistol back on semiautomatic. Then she hit the *stop* button on the miniature tape recorder strapped above it, as a single stream of tears welled up in her left eye and flowed slowly over her cheek.

THIRTY-EIGHT

Frank was sitting on the porch of Jack's second-floor apartment, looking up at the San Gabriels as the late afternoon blanketed Mount Wilson in pink and soft orange layers of light. Looking toward Del Mar, he saw his uncle's car signaling a turn toward Jack's building.

"There's Charles," Frank said. "He just turned the corner."

"I'll get the rest of dinner on," Jack said, as he put an oval teak platter on the metal table next to Frank. On it were a block of Vermont cheddar and a wedge of Danish blue cheese, with equal, parallel rows of mixed crackers.

"Very orderly," Frank said.

Jack brought a knife and stuck it in the portion of cheddar. "I know how you like to play with edged instruments," he said.

"Just like our suspect," Frank answered.

They both heard the knock at the door. Jack walked into the dining area, passed through the living room, and opened the door.

"Hi, Charles, how about some quiche?" Jack asked.

"Thanks, I'll pass," Charles said. "I *would* like a little Boston lettuce, though. Maybe with a light vinaigrette. Better yet, just spray on some lemon juice."

"Coming right up," Jack said. He went back into the kitchen, filled three old-fashioned glasses with ice, and covered the ice with Maker's Mark. The ice was exceptionally clear and the reflected light shimmered through the bourbon.

"I hope you each have a hearty appetite, gentlemen," he said.

"Excellent," Frank said, taking a sip.

"You must have found the killer," Charles said.

"Why do you say that?" Jack asked.

"Because of all this ceremony. You love this kind of thing, Jack. You love to make announcements and watch Frank's eyes widen. You broke the case; I know it. Now tell us about it."

"More salad?" Jack asked, topping off their glasses.

"What happened, Jack?" Frank asked.

"Where do you want me to start?"

"Give me the short version and then we can ask questions," Frank said.

"OK. To begin with, Susan Wilken is dead. She took her own life fifteen years ago. When she did, her husband joined the walking wounded. Physically, he looks like somebody who was finally allowed to sit down after finishing the Bataan death march. He holds onto the arms of his chair as if he's afraid he'll fall off the edge of the earth. When he lost his wife he died inside. Mentally, he's locked in the past. He won't acknowledge that his wife is dead and he won't acknowledge that his daughter is a grown woman.

"Which, by the way, she is. The mother's gone and the daughter's avenging her rape and death and her father's subsequent disintegration. After he came home from Vietnam they rented out their house in Santa Monica and bought a nursery in Sunland. Looking for a fresh start, I guess—growing trees rather than burning them—but after living through the rape and the miscarriage and the trial and then reliving all of it again and again in her nightmares, his wife was unable to put her life or herself back together. She finally gave it up and when she did her husband retired in silence to a dark corner of a caretaker's cottage. He's still there."

He let that sink in. After a few seconds, Charles spoke.

"Why do you think the daughter waited this long to kill her mother's attackers? We're talking about fifteen years; that's a hell of a long time."

"I'm not sure," Jack said. "From what she told me I think that she wanted them all to get successful and comfortable. She wanted them to have something to lose and the more they had to lose the better. She also had to grow up herself; she had to learn how to plan, and she had to learn how to kill. When Susan Wilken was attacked she was pregnant. She miscarried as a result of the rape and the trauma. I think the daughter thought the whole family was coming together through her mother's pregnancy and then, with the rape and miscarriage, it was all suddenly coming apart. These kinds of patterns run through her head. She sees that the lives of her mother's attackers have finally come together and that makes her want to take them apart."

"OK, but why kill Crimmins in England?" Frank asked. "I don't understand why she would want to complicate things unnecessarily and add so much risk to what she was trying to do. Why not just kill the son-of-a-bitch right here?"

"I've been thinking about that a lot," Jack said. "The Brits are hung up on that question and so are the suits from the Justice Department. It simply doesn't make any sense. Or at least it doesn't until you look at the facts of the rape case. The answer has been right there all along. Her mother was attacked on September 26, so she killed

Crimmins on September 26. It just so happened that he had planned to be in England on September 26, so she followed him there. She would have killed him *then*, regardless of where he was."

"Happy anniversary," Charles said, lifting his glass.

"Exactly."

Charles' lips narrowed. "Tell me, Jack. Do you think she's completely sane?"

"Yes, completely."

"Why the exotic methods?" There was more curiosity in Charles' voice than skepticism.

"Two reasons, I think. The first is the irony of it. Crimmins raped her mother, so he now finds out how it feels to be raped. Maybe Devens held her mother down while Crimmins raped her; I don't know. What I do know is that her daughter pinned Devens' hands down and let him struggle in pain; she did that for a reason. The sword design makes sense too. It was functional. Crimmins was to bleed to death and no one was supposed to be able to help him. The blades and barbs and channels worked perfectly. For Devens, it appears, she used the interspersed grooves to introduce the poison, since she wanted him dead, but she also wanted to impale him at points that would not be fatal."

"Claire and I met with this weapons expert in London," Frank said. "His name was Jaffee—a real piece of work. The sword blades were quadrangular, in the stiletto form. I'm sure she was trying to send some kind of symbolic message with that. This type of dagger or sword was said to inflict a wound that would never heal. She was telling us what those three dirtbags had done to her family and then, in turn, what she intended to do to them."

"That's a good point," Jack said. "And that's exactly how she would think about it. But there's one last question: why? *Why* do all of this in just those ways? Why go to such trouble and to such lengths? You *do* see where this is all going, don't you?"

They each paused and took a long sip of their bourbon.

Charles finally spoke. "Where is this going? I'll tell you exactly where it's going. She's adding a wing to media heaven. She's wrapping up a Christmas present for them that will carry them halfway through the next decade."

Jack refilled Charles' glass. "Think of the possibilities," he said.

Charles took another sip. "What are you trying to do, Jack, loosen up my imagination?"

"Something like that."

"OK. Possibilities . . . how about these: a couple of best sellers; two or three made-for-TV movies; front-page stories on every paper in the country; Congressional investigations; witch hunts; exposes; indictments . . . ? Tell me when to stop."

"It *won't* stop," Frank said, "not if she kills Ernie Jeffers and is then able to avoid arrest. As long as she's at large people will think about her and her mother and their family and what those three worthless assholes did to them."

"I can assure you," Jack said, "that she fully intends to avoid arrest."

Charles cut a piece of cheddar, skipping the cracker. He washed it down with half of his drink. "It's really the whole damned war all over again, isn't it?" he said.

"What do you mean?" Frank asked.

"A couple of suits get together behind a closed door and decide how much fun it would be to play with somebody else's life. Then when the screaming starts and people begin to suffer and die they lock arms, lie, and hide behind their mahogany desks. Three minor-league assholes like this or a whole cabinet full of them, only with bigger weapons, bigger budgets, and a bigger game board."

"That's a bit of a stretch," Frank said.

"No, it isn't," Jack said. "Not to Karen Wilken."

"I don't think it's that much of a stretch either," Charles said. "She felt it on both levels. Her father went off to war and now he's lost. Her mother stayed behind, here, and now she's dead. Meanwhile, the sleazoids who did it have never had it better. She wants to change that and she wants to tell her side of the story."

"Maybe she's also a little like you, Charles," Frank said. "Maybe she likes to clean out the riffraff."

"Possibly. She's been doing a damned good job of it so far. I'd hate to see them stop her before she's finished."

Jack refilled Charles' glass and his own. "I'll drink to that," he said.

"Wait a minute," Frank said. "Don't tell me you intend to help her."

"I don't intend to get in her way," Jack said.

"Do you know what you're saying?"

"Yes, Frank, I know what I'm saying. Have you seen her and her father?"

"No."

"If you had, you'd know why I was saying it."

"Hold it," Frank said. "Before we say any more, let's be clear about where this is going. What you're talking about is obstructing justice."

"I'm not talking about obstructing anything," Jack said.

"Of course you are. You've got evidence and you intend to withhold it."

"I don't have squat," Jack said. "I just met somebody and we talked. There were no confessions. There were no weapons or serious physical evidence lying around. Nothing. We talked in general terms and we danced around the subject of the murders. I learned some things, at least I think I did, but I didn't learn a damned thing that you could take to court. All that you had before was motive and motive is all that you have now."

"But *she* has something," Frank said.

"What's that?"

"Your ear and your sympathy."

"So?"

"She's got more than that," Charles said.

"What do you mean?" Frank asked.

"She's got my sympathy too. Three pieces of shit who the world considers respectable raped her mother and caused her to lose her baby. They turned her father's head into pea soup and they destroyed his family. I don't like that very much, Frank, and the fact that they did it while the woman's husband was fighting a war in a foreign country for a group of arrogant, goddamned, White House liars makes me like it a whole hell of a lot less."

"So what are you going to do, Charles?"

"Well, I'm not going to get in her way, Frank. Are you?"

Frank sliced a piece of the blue cheese, put it on a cracker, and said, "Gentlemen, this case is in the hands of our all-knowing colleagues from Washington. The Justice Department has flexed its collective muscles and ordered the LAPD in general and this young black lieutenant in particular to shut his damned mouth and to speak only when he is spoken to. I intend to follow the directives of my superiors."

Jack refilled Frank's glass and topped off his and Charles'. "Let's drink to following the orders of our superiors."

Charles took a drink and showed a little of the smile he usually reserved for shavetail second johns who told him that *they* knew the proper time to stick their heads out of a foxhole.

"Tell me, Jack, if you don't mind," Frank said, "what else have you agreed to do besides stay out of the young woman's way?"

"What do you mean?"

"You know what I mean."

"No, I don't."

"Jack, you're a good friend and a first-rate investigator, but you are one piss-poor poker player."

"I didn't agree to anything that would affect the case. She said she'd like me to come back again, that's all."

"And you think that doesn't have anything to do with the case?" Frank asked.

"I don't see how."

Charles picked up another piece of cheese and laughed.

"What's so funny?"

"Tell me, Jack," Charles said, "do you think this woman is organized or not?"

"She's organized."

"Does she plan or does she not?"

"She plans."

"Does she kick ass, take names, and leave a cold trail?"

"She kicks ass, takes names, and leaves a cold trail."

"You think she wants you to come back so that you can take a seat in her drawing room, have a cup of hot tea, and talk about old times?"

"Possibly not," Jack said.

Charles and Frank both smiled. "We'll visit you at Club Fed," Frank said.

"No we won't," Charles said. "If Jack links up with her, the two of them will disappear without a trace. She's got plans for him."

Frank smiled. "He's been looking for a way to upgrade his social life. Did you see the look in his eyes when he was talking about her?"

"So what the hell else do I have to do," Jack said, "sit around on a porch with you two, eating cheese and drinking whiskey?"

"It'd be a hell of a lot safer," Frank said.

"Like I said, you haven't seen her," Jack answered.

They both smiled.

"When is this supposed to happen?" Frank asked.

"I probably shouldn't say; if you knew they could torture it out of you."

"I'll make a deal with you," Frank said. "I'll tell you what I know if you tell me what you know."

"What do you know?" Jack asked.

"Ernie Jeffers got a call today."

THIRTY-NINE

"What was the call about?"

"I don't know. McGann won't tell me. He didn't even tell me that Jeffers got the call."

"How did you find out?"

"We used basic investigative techniques."

"I bet. What did you do?"

"One of McGann's people gave him a piece of paper with a written message on it. He asked to use a phone in an empty room, so Jerry took him into one of the interrogation rooms that's equipped with a speaker. Then he smiled politely, walked outside, and tuned him in."

"I like that," Jack said.

"Unfortunately, we didn't learn much. We heard him call Jeffers by name and we heard him ask when the person called. Then he said, 'Today? When?' We didn't find out when the call came in or what the person said, but it must have been important enough to make Ernie call his friends in Washington and be referred to Chester McGann."

"Then McGann must know about the Wilkens."

"I don't have any way of knowing, one way or the other," Frank said. "The conversation was too one-sided. McGann told Jeffers he'd call back later and then quickly hung up."

"Too bad you didn't have the phone tapped," Jack said.

"We do now," Frank said. "Jerry put a FAX machine and a bunch of shit in there for McGann to use. Now it's his home away from home."

"And Jerry probably tapped the FAX line too," Frank said.

"No, he had Bill Griffin do that for him. Jerry was busy down in the garage, putting the first beeper under McGann's bumper and making sure that we could track it. Those damned things can be temperamental sometimes. That's why we decided to put in a backup behind the catalytic converter."

"You should have shoved one up his ass too," Charles said. "If you couldn't see him wobbling you could always follow him on your screen."

"We wanted to, but we had too many volunteers for the job. We didn't know who to choose."

Jack smiled and said, "I know somebody in Sunland who could do a good job. She's experienced too."

"I wonder what he's doing now," Charles said. "Probably storming around his office, giving orders, barking into his phone, and saying what a terrible person my nephew is."

"Let's find out what he's doing," Frank said. He reached into his inside pocket, took out a miniature cellular phone, flipped it open, and punched in some numbers. "Jerry," he said, "Frank. Where is our subject now and what is he doing? . . . Un-huh . . . Yes . . . That's nice . . . Un-huh . . . Really? . . . Wonderful . . . He did? . . . I love it . . . What an asshole . . . Good . . . Really? . . . OK."

"It's good, isn't it?" Jack said.

"Nothing that far out of the ordinary, considering . . ." Frank said.

"What happened?" Charles asked.

"McGann and three of his dweebs just went out to dinner. I guess they were looking for something authentic, because they went to Musso and Frank."

Jack smiled. "Which waiter did they get?"

"Ralph."

"Wonderful," Jack said.

"That's what I just said."

"I know. I heard you. What did Ralphie do this time?"

"McGann must have mouthed off to him, because he put his salad down on the table so hard that half of the lettuce bounced off and into his lap. McGann started to get even more testy, so Ralphie asked him if he'd like some freshly ground pepper on it. McGann said that as a matter of fact he *would* like some freshly ground pepper on it, so Ralphie reaches across the table, picks up the pepper shaker, and slams it down in front of him, whereupon the other half of the lettuce bounces into his lap and all over the table. McGann says to Ralphie, 'That's enough of that shit, wiseass, I want to see the manager.' Ralphie says to him, 'You want to see the manager? You really want to see the manager?' McGann says, 'You're goddamned right I want to see the manager.' 'OK,' Ralphie says, reaching into his back pocket, 'here's a picture of the sonofabitch.' McGann rips it out of his hand and it's a picture of this old lady with her middle finger extended, saying 'Have a nice day, fuckface.'"

"I didn't know he still had that," Jack said.

"Oh yes. Anyway, McGann blows again, gets up to walk out, and Ralphie asks him if he'd like a wrap on the salad. By now you can practically see the smoke coming out of McGann's ass. He turns to Ralphie and whispers something that Jerry's guy can't hear..."

"What did Ralphie do?" Jack asked.

"He whispered something right back."

"And?"

"McGann was standing there steaming and Ralphie pulled out the manager's picture and showed it to him again."

"What did McGann do then?"

"He left," Jerry said. "He was so damned mad he could hardly operate the handle on the car door."

Jack took a drink of his bourbon and smiled, but Charles' expression was serious.

"What's the matter, Charles?" Frank asked.

"I don't like it," Charles said, "an asshole like that . . . arrogant, bad-tempered, a little stupid—that's a dangerous combination. He's wound too tight, Frank. You better watch him closely. If he acts like that with a waiter in a restaurant, what's he going to do when he's in a real situation, facing down somebody with a weapon and a motive for killing him?"

"I know what he'll do."

"What's that?" Charles asked.

"He'll spray everything and everybody in sight," Frank answered.

FORTY

"So you're not going to tell me when you're supposed to see Karen Wilken again," Frank said.

"Maybe later," Jack said. "In the meantime I want to give you *deniability*."

Frank smiled. "I have to make a phone call; I'll be back in a few minutes."

"Why didn't he just call from here?" Charles asked. "He's got his cellular phone in his pocket."

"Because he's calling London to talk to his friend of the female persuasion," Jack said. "It's about 8:30 in the morning there now. She's just ladling a little brown sugar into her coffee, waiting for her daily call from her brave comrade-in-arms across the sea."

"He calls her every day?"

"Well, he says he's just bringing her up to speed on the investigation, but I think he's making nice-nice too. My guess is that she's looking for a reason to justify coming over here and Frank's doing his best to help her find one. They don't even have a suspect in custody yet, and if they did it would really be a job for the diplomats and extradition lawyers, but they're still trying to find a loophole. I should warn you, Charles, these calls can take awhile. Would you like some coffee or another drink?"

"Let's wait till he gets finished. Maybe he'll want to go out and get a sandwich or something."

The phone rang in the kitchen. Jack turned to Charles and smiled. "At least he's using his cellular instead of one of mine. Excuse me a second..."

Jack walked into the kitchen, answered the phone, listened for a second, and then hurried back to the porch. "He's on the move, Charles; we've got to get out of here."

"Where?"

"I'll tell you on the way."

They collected Frank, who continued his call as they walked down the steps. "Something's breaking," he said. "I've got to run... I'll stay in touch... Yes, same time tomorrow... you too... right... bye for now." He closed up the phone and slipped it into his pocket. "What's happening?"

"McGann's on the move," Jack said. "Let's take my car. McGann hasn't seen it yet."

"Where?"

"He's heading east."

"East L.A. or *east* east?"

"Toward the desert," Jack said.

They waited for the security gate to open, then drove north, took Del Mar to Lake, and headed for the freeway. "That was Jerry calling. He couldn't get through to you on your cellular so he called me. After he left Musso and Frank, McGann went back to the Bonaventure and grabbed a sandwich in the coffee shop. He was there for about ten minutes when one of his people hurried in with a message. McGann said something to the guy, the guy left, and they all met downstairs in the garage and left in a hurry. It's got to be important, because McGann was still due a piece of pie at taxpayers' expense and he didn't even take a sip of his coffee."

"I wonder if he ever got his salad," Charles said.

Jack smiled.

"If she's ready to take out Jeffers it would be a serious change in her M.O.," Frank said. "She's usually a day person and it's now 11:45 p.m. We don't know about Crimmins but we know that she gave Devens enough advance warning to enable him to hire some bodyguards before he was to meet with her the next day. This is all too sudden."

"They're on the 60, heading due east," Jack said. "I'm going to take the high road and try to catch them. Try to raise Jerry. He's got somebody in an unmarked sedan staying with them."

The reception was poor, but Frank was able to get through. "They crossed the 605 and stayed on the 60. They just passed the Azusa exit."

"Good," Jack said.

"What are you going to do?" Charles asked.

"Take the 210 as it turns south, catch the Corona Freeway, and head toward the 60."

"The Corona isn't really a freeway."

"There's only a couple of lights," Jack said. "That won't hold us up. It's better than backtracking."

"That's true," Charles said.

Fifteen minutes later Frank raised Jerry again. "They just hit Diamond Bar," he said. "That makes them, what, fifteen minutes ahead of us?"

"No more than that," Jack said.

"They could be heading toward San Diego. It's a little out of the way, but it beats the hell out of the 405. They could pick up that little piece of the Riverside Freeway, then drive down the east ridge of the Santa Anas on 15, through Escondido."

"Or use that to cut over to one of the beach communities," Charles said.

"They're not that smart," Jack said. "Jerry said it's just McGann and three of the suits from Washington. They'd need a guide to pull off anything that fancy. I think they're headed for a rendezvous in the desert."

"Then we better hurry," Frank said. "There's a hell of a lot of it out there and I don't want to arrive two minutes after they've finished the body count."

Jack eased the accelerator down. He was driving 85 past the exits for San Dimas, but slowed to 65 for the Corona Freeway off-ramp. Fifteen minutes later he was just below Ontario on the 60. Frank got on the phone and was patched to Jerry.

"They just passed through Riverside," Frank said.

"Did they stay on the 60?" Charles asked.

"Yes."

Jack looked at Charles. "They're heading toward Palm Springs."

"It's nice this time of year," Charles said. "I can't imagine why you'd want to visit at 1:30 or 2:00 in the morning, but that may be when she set Mr. Jeffers' appointment to meet his creator."

"Do you know anybody in Palm Springs, Frank," Jack asked, "anybody you can trust?"

He had already started to punch in the numbers. There were two misses before he connected with a lieutenant named Piersall. They spoke in broken sentences for about five minutes, fighting static and a weak signal.

"Right, Kenny," they heard Frank say. "This is strictly between us. Don't worry, we'll stay in the background. Right. Right. I owe you one for this. I know, but I also know what you're risking. Thanks."

"Nice guy," Frank said, as he clicked off the phone. "We've done each other some favors in the past. Nothing quite like this though."

"What's up?" Jack asked.

"As best we can reconstruct it, Jeffers must have called the hotel around 11:20 and told McGann's people that something was coming down. They called Washington and had their patrons there call the Palm Springs PD. Same deal: complete cooperation, no bullshit, no questions asked. Kenny's captain is supposed to bring some shooters and meet McGann in Palm Springs."

"What do you mean, shooters?" Charles asked.

"Experts with rifles."

"Snipers," Charles said.

"More or less, yes."

"Where are they supposed to meet?" Jack asked.

"At the Aerial Tramway," Frank answered.

FORTY-ONE

Jack looked at the face of his watch. For the last hour and a half it had been Thursday. He was scheduled to meet with Karen Wilken in a little more than eighteen hours. That meant that any work she intended to accomplish in Palm Springs would have to be done in less than sixteen hours, unless she was flying back to Los Angeles. That was unlikely, since the Palm Springs airport could be shut down with a single phone call. If she tried to fly out of the Coachella Valley in a private plane or helicopter, she could be picked off like a sick bird fluttering over a skeet shooting range.

No, she would be driving out, if at all, and that meant that she had very few options: 111, then the freeway, unless she tried to drive southeast, through Rancho Mirage and Palm Desert and double back through the pines-to-palm highway and the San Bernardino Forest into Banning. That would take hours. Maybe that's what she had in mind. Maybe she was going to try to take out Ernie Jeffers at first light and then spend the rest of the day working her way back to Sunland.

"How high exactly *is* the mountain at the top of the tramway?" Charles asked.

"High," Jack said. "The mountain itself is over 10,000 feet. I think the tram hits it at a point about 8,000 feet above the valley floor. Have you ever been on it, Charles?"

"Once about eighteen years ago. I was working with some Navy people at China Lake. I remember it though. It's a hell of a piece of engineering."

"What it is," Frank said, "is the longest, single-span lift in the world. What's the exact length, Jack? I know it's well over a mile."

"About two miles. You go through four or five towers along the way. The ride itself takes over twenty minutes. You wait for your tram in a staging area. Each departure is timed; it's almost as complicated as riding the shuttle from L.A. to San Francisco. By the time you get to the top of the tramway you've gone through four or five different climatic zones. The temperature difference is about thirty degrees. They sell drinks at the bottom and at the top and they do a hell of a business. That particular section of Mount San Jacinto is the largest piece of open rock face in the world."

"And she's going to kill Ernie Jeffers *there*?" Frank said. "I've got to hand it to her. She's got a flair for these things."

"You ride in a huge gondola," Jack said. "There are two of them on parallel cables; each of them holds about eighty people."

"I remember now," Charles said. "When I rode on it there were no seats. You could stand right up against the windows. People wanted to do that, so they could see. They didn't think about what a perfect target they'd make."

"You still have to stand," Frank said. "Marie and I were on it a year or so ago. We were there in the summer. It was about 108 degrees on the valley floor and in the 70s on the top of the mountain. I didn't think it would be crowded, because a lot of Palm Springs closes down in the summer, but there were thirty or forty people on the gondola with us."

"It's a hell of a target," Jack said, "and the mountain is filled with trees and ridges, crevices, and boulders. She's got her choice of where she wants to hide."

"Assuming she wants to shoot him," Frank said. "She may have other plans."

"Right," Jack said. "That gondola moves right along, but it could never outrun a .50 calibre machine gun or a rocket launcher. Each time it approaches a tower it slows down; it feels as if you're riding over a hump, remember? Then there's a little bounce and it takes off again. Everybody in the gondola winces a little and then acts as if they're really enjoying themselves. She could have one of the towers mined with explosives or she could simply shut down the whole system and toy with him while he's swinging back and forth against the sky."

"When I was there you could hike around the summit," Charles said.

"You still can," Jack said.

"That means she could strike from the top and then disappear into the forest," Charles said. "It's a damned big forest. She could set up a nice escape route. All she'd need is a little planning and you know how good she is at that."

"The bottom would be much tougher," Jack said. "There's a single road in from the highway. What is it, Frank, two or three miles?"

"Yes, and that's all desert there. She couldn't hide a vehicle. She'd have to go out on foot, but she'd have miles to cover and they'd be ready for her. If McGann shut down all the traffic on the road her escape car would suddenly be very obvious. She'd be forced to either crash through his roadblock or drive off the road, but even if she drove off the road her car or motorcycle would be as obvious as a deer in an open field. It might take a few minutes to run her to ground, but it wouldn't be very difficult, even for somebody like McGann."

Jack pulled off of the freeway and onto 111. "We'll be there in approximately 10 minutes," he said. "See if you can raise Jerry."

Frank flipped open his phone and punched in the numbers. He had to change codes now that they were so far beyond L.A.

"Hi, Frank," Jerry said, through the static. "Where are you?"

"We just pulled off onto 111."

"Welcome to Palm Springs."

"Are McGann and his suits at the tram?"

"Yes. They're at the lodge at the bottom of the mountain. We followed them without lights as far as we could and then parked in a lot a few hundred yards down the road. I parked over in a corner and tied a red handkerchief around the door handle to make it look as if my car was disabled."

"Good idea, Jerry."

"Yeah, I never thought that thing would come in handy. We're on the ground now, keeping our distance. I've got one guy moving in a little closer, but the rest of us are hanging back."

"Stay back, Jerry. I don't want you to end up on any shit lists unnecessarily."

"Right," Jerry said.

"What are they doing now?"

"Not a whole hell of a lot—mostly walking around and trying to see up a 10,000-foot mountain with a burglar's flashlight and a hand-held searchlight. There's a civilian talking to them. He's wearing old clothes, as if he just got out of bed. There's a single black-and-white from the Palm Springs PD and then McGann's car. I figure they woke up the poor bastard who runs the tram and hustled his ass down to give them a briefing. They called out whoever they could find from the Palm Springs PD. Now they're just checking things out. I figure that whatever's going to happen is going to happen later. They're just trying to scope out what they're up against so they can figure out how many people and how many weapons they're going to need."

"That makes sense, Jerry," Frank said.

"Yeah. They know they're up against somebody who plans these things out. They got the call from Jeffers and they got the hell out here as fast as they could to start getting ready."

"But there's no heavy artillery or reinforcements yet," Frank said.

"No. This is the night crew, Frank. They're just starting to run through scenarios and get some ideas from the locals. I'll tell you what, there's a motel down the road a little way past the entrance to the tram on 111. It'll be on your right as you head toward Palm Springs. I'll place a couple guys here and meet you there in about forty-five minutes. Check into a room. If anything breaks in the meantime I'll let you know immediately, but you should get off the highway. There aren't a hell of a lot of people driving around here at 2:00 in the morning and you don't want to attract any unnecessary attention."

"Sounds good, Jerry. We'll rent the room in your name. That way you won't have any trouble remembering it."

"I saw the motel, Frank. I don't think they've ever had anybody sign in whose name wasn't Smith or Jones."

"We'll wait to hear from you, Jerry."

Frank turned off his phone. "I think we've got some time yet," he said. "It may even be a matter of days."

Jack looked at his watch, but didn't say anything.

FORTY-TWO

Mobile Intelligence Systems' corporate headquarters was comfortably housed in a twenty-floor postmodern palace across from the Gateway Building at Santa Monica and Sepulveda. Ernie Jeffers had replaced a vacant lot containing a mobile hot dog wagon with $180 million worth of mini-skyscraper designed to prop up Jeffers' ego as well as house the core of his operation. The MIS diaspora spread from Orange County to the Central Coast with outcroppings in Seattle and Colorado Springs, but for the company's owner and chief executive officer the headquarters property was home.

His own office occupied half of the nineteenth floor, with views of Malibu, the coastal highway, the Wilshire corridor, and the Hollywood hills to the north, and mile upon mile of the San Diego Freeway to the south, its silent ribbons of red and white light marking its undulating course to Westchester, LAX, and beyond. To the west was the Pacific, and on clear, cloudless days, Catalina. Twenty stories of steel, masonry, plastic, and double-paned, insulated glass that turned the basin and city below into a vast, moving canvas, a silent toy to be turned and felt and enjoyed by corporate hands.

"Thank you for coming, gentlemen," Jeffers said. He had practiced his speech for an hour and a half, rehearsing each word and intonation, checking his profile time and again in the mirror, and adjusting each pause and breath. It echoed through the acoustically pure, twentieth-floor boardroom. He had set aside his dual-breast brown Armani with the soft lapels and the tie with subdued blue geometricals. Instead he was in his dark-gray worsted with red regimental tie and heavy black wingtips, the points of his pocket square aligned like the sharpened teeth on a northwoods saw. Thirty men sat around a walnut table, with ample room to spare, their legs spread over burgundy and gray carpeting as they sat in oversized chairs with soft deco patterns in Italian fabric. Each of the men was fit and each of them was armed: the senior security directors of each of MISs local installations, recruited from military and paramilitary organizations from around the globe.

"I would like to explain the nature of this assignment," Jeffers said. "Many years ago I was falsely accused of assault by a woman seeking to exploit the political position and influence of a close friend. Since that time my friend has been murdered and a second individual—also named in the woman's complaint—has been murdered as well.

"You may have seen reports of this in the local newspapers. Congressman Michael Crimmins was both my friend and a friend of this community. William Devens was a business leader whom I and many others remember fondly. Both were cruelly struck down by a murderer whose ferocity is matched only by his skill.

"The Justice Department has now taken charge of the investigation and has determined that the woman who filed the groundless complaint against us over twenty years ago has since taken her own life, doubtless because of recriminations over the false charges she brought against three innocent men. Her husband, however, remains alive, and it is he whom the Justice Department suspects of committing these most recent outrages.

"The man's name is Daniel Wilken. He was a combat soldier in Vietnam and he should be considered heavily armed and extremely dangerous. Last evening I was contacted by this man. He used a distortion device to mask his voice, but there can be little doubt as to his identity. He demanded that I meet with him this afternoon. It is perfectly clear that his intention is to murder me, just as he has murdered Congressman Crimmins and William Devens. I do not intend to let him do that. *That* is the purpose of our meeting.

"The Justice Department will seek to both protect me and apprehend the murderer, but I want you there as well. As your current contracts do not require you to perform this particular type of service, each of you will receive additional compensation of two thousand, five hundred dollars for today's work. If any of you are unwilling to accept this assignment, please excuse yourself at this time."

Each of them stayed in his seat, accepting Jeffers' job of work as if it were nothing more than a 7-Eleven run for milk and a morning paper.

"Good," he said. "I expected that. In addition to your normal sidearms you should draw protective vests and .30-.30 rifles with telescopic sights. Those materials are being assembled now. Lauren . . ."

Jeffers' secretary rose from her seat in the back of the room. None of the security people had heard or seen her enter. "Miss Carroll is distributing folders to each of you. When you receive them you may break the security band and examine the contents. Thank you, Lauren . . .

"As you can see, your folder contains maps and aerial photographs of the eastern face of Mount San Jacinto. In addition, there are also brochures describing and photographs depicting the tramway that carries passengers from the base of the mountain to a point approximately 8,000 feet above the valley floor. Mr. Wilken has asked that I ascend the mountain via the tram at precisely 2:00 P.M. this afternoon. He will then speak with me in the lodge at the upper terminus of the tram.

"Needless to say, this is a transparent ruse. Once I am aboard the gondola I would be an easy target for anyone wishing to blow me out of the sky. Wilken has no intention of allowing me to complete the ascent to the top, for he realizes that the lodge could be easily sealed and he would be immediately surrounded by law enforcement and security officials. He is not a stupid man. Thus, we expect the attempt on my life to occur somewhere between the base of the mountain and the summit, after I have boarded the gondola and have begun the ascent—exposed to rifle or other fire from any one of a hundred possible angles and locations.

"With your help he will not have an opportunity to do this. On the contrary, with your help he will be apprehended and promptly brought to justice. In the case of the murder of Congressman Crimmins he acted with the advantage of surprise. With William Devens there was some advance warning, but his intention was not altogether clear and the kill zone which he selected was one that was difficult to defend without risking the lives of countless innocent people.

"Now he has overstepped his bounds. In his twisted desire to harm me and his pathetic need for public attention, he has chosen a site where we can exert far greater control over the terms of the situation and constrain his opportunities for success and escape. We shall deny him the opportunity to harm me and we shall seal his escape routes, so that no matter what he might attempt, this crime will either result in his own immediate death or it will carry him to the California gas chamber, where the people of California will execute the sentence against him.

"I should point out, gentlemen, that it is immaterial to me *and* to the Department of Justice whether he meets that fate today or needlessly depletes the resources of the citizens of California in endless legal maneuvers and appeals as he attempts to avoid what will surely prove to be inevitable. America will not tolerate the ruthless murder of her elected representatives and her private citizens.

"Each of you will have a particular role to play in this action and those roles will be explained to you when we arrive in Palm Springs. Each of you should now change into leisure attire and return here in precisely one hour. At that time we will proceed by corporate rotary-wing aircraft to helipads at adjacent medical centers in Palm Desert. We will then proceed to the aerial tramway in Palm Springs by unmarked sedans, which will be ready for us upon arrival. Please wear loose clothing so that your protective gear is not immediately apparent. Since there is a drop of some thirty degrees between the temperature on the valley floor and that on the summit, it will not occasion surprise if you wear light jackets or windbreakers. Such apparel would also serve to hide your sidearms. Gentlemen, are there any questions?"

A hand went up in the far corner of the room.

"Yes?"

"Sir, Robert Fancher, Simi Valley Division. Do we have a photograph of the suspect?"

"Not at this time. We are securing one from Washington. It will not be current but it may still be of some use. Those pictures should be available when we reach Palm Desert. Any further questions?"

A hand went up from the opposite, distant corner. Jeffers called upon him; his patience was thinning.

"Sir, James Carlow, San Marcos Division. Is it the view of the Department of Justice that the murderer has been acting alone?"

"Yes it is. If he has had an accomplice or accomplices they do not appear to have been directly involved in the killings."

"Thank you, sir," Carlow said.

"Now, are there any other questions?"

No one raised his hand.

"Good," Jeffers said, relieved. He checked his watch and looked up disapprovingly. "Your hour has now been reduced to fifty-eight minutes. I will expect you all back here then. Dismissed."

FORTY-THREE

THE ROOM CLEARED AND Jeffers returned to his office. He quickly filled one of his crystal glasses with ice, splashed three fingers of scotch over it, turned it in his hand against the light from his desk lamp, thought for a moment, and drank down half of it. He was thinking about the events of the previous night. "First you hear the ping," the distorted voice had said, "and in the next instant all that's left of you is a smear of blood and a patch of ground flesh."

He was driving through the flats of Beverly Hills when his car phone first rang. "First you hear the ping . . ." He had no idea what that meant, but he called McGann to let him know that the killer had made contact. Then he heard something strike his car. He heard it to his left, low and behind the front wheel. It was evening and he was driving to Chinois. Then he heard the second ping—a few blocks before he turned into his driveway. He pulled into his garage, closed the automatic door, and flipped on every available light. There were tiny craters in both the right and the left front rocker panels of his new, green Range Rover. He could see them clearly. He could put his fingertips in them. Then came the second call; the distorted voice explained them: "The ping is the tracer round when it strikes the side of an armored vehicle. Then comes the rocket or the 105 shell. The tracer warns you that you're sitting in the center of your enemy's sights, but once you hear it, it's too late to defend yourself. The serious round is already on the way, the last round you hear, Ernie. I'm your enemy, Ernie, and I know where you are. I've hit you with a .22 on each side of your car—in different places, at different times, and in the middle of heavy traffic. It's as easy as dropping a ball and hitting the earth. Now I'm going to tell you what I expect, Ernie, and if you fail to follow any one of my instructions you'll hear that ping again. Then, for a fraction of a second, you'll hear the side of your Range Rover shredding and shattering as it explodes in your face and eyes. When they find you they'll lose whatever's on their stomachs in the nearest gutter. They'll peel what's left of you from the pieces of steel and plastic and upholstery fabric that tear and fragment and scatter across the highway.

"Your choice is an easy one, Ernie: you can talk to me on my terms or you can wait for me to grind your heart and lungs and spleen and splatter them over the landscape. Look at your car, Ernie. Look at the panels behind the right and left front tires. See the holes. Touch them. Remember the sound of the ping. Nothing much in itself. Just a tiny warning before the end. Think about waiting for the sound of the next one, Ernie. It won't be a warning shot. It could be minutes or hours or days, months, or even years. I have all the time in the world, but the police don't and you don't, Ernie. We both know that no one can protect you that long."

Jeffers had cursed under his breath as the voice continued.

"And what should I use, Ernie? So many weapons; so little time. I could use a high explosive round—always a nice, conventional choice; it's quick and sure and the flash brightens the sky for a single, magnificent instant. Or I could use a huge, inert slug that would punch through the side of your vehicle, cut you in half, and keep on moving. A quick thud and a big hole. Nice collateral damage to catch the attention of any bystanders. Or how about something a little more exotic? Have you ever seen white phosphorus, Ernie? Have you ever seen what it does? It lodges in your flesh and then it burns down to the bone, like a fiery, steel splinter, sizzling and smoking. And you can't extinguish it, Ernie; it even burns under water. Once you're struck by white phosphorus there's nothing you can really do but wait to die, or pick out the fragments from your flesh with the point of a knife. I hope you don't have shaky hands, Ernie.

"Actually, I'm leaning toward a fourth option. What do you know about flechettes, Ernie? Hundreds of tiny little darts in a single round, all of them slightly off balance, tumbling through space as they hurtle toward your flesh. Then striking and ripping, taking chunks and gobbets of skin as they tear and sear and expose your shattered, bloodied skeleton.

"Remember each ping, Ernie. I hit you twice today. I can hit you anyplace and anytime I choose. Think about those flechettes too."

"What do you want?" Now, hours later, he could hear his voice again, remember it echoing in his head, remember his terror and his sudden desperation.

"Meet me at the lodge above the aerial tramway in Palm Springs. Meet me tomorrow afternoon. Take the 2:00 tram. If you disobey me in any way I'll be back for you later. Here are my rules, Ernie. They're simple enough. Don't forget them. First, come alone; I don't want to see police and I don't want to see bodyguards. I just want to see you, Ernie. Second, I don't want you to clear the tram of civilians. Let the people have their fun, Ernie. Mix with them. Enjoy your ride. When you finally get to the summit I'll be there to meet you."

"How will I know what you look like?"

"Don't worry about that, Ernie. I know what *you* look like. Drive to the springs. Take your ride. Relax and wait. I'll approach you when I'm ready. Then we can talk, Ernie."

"It's obviously a trap. You want to kill me."

"Why didn't I kill you tonight? You know that I could have. I could have killed you twice."

"Why do you need to talk to me there?"

"Because that's where I *choose* to talk to you. Where we talk is none of your concern."

"I'll be there," he said, holding his tone and holding his breath. What other choice was there—taking his chance that his tormenter could be trapped on the mountain or giving him a free hand to find him later, alone and unprotected, vulnerable? The mountain was his chance. He would be exposed, but so would the man who sought to kill him. He would never survive the dark streets and long nights that lay before him—too many kill zones, too many death traps.

To refuse was to die. To agree was to seize a chance, an opportunity. He would ascend the mountain, but he would not ascend it alone. He called McGann to tell him of the threats and of the rules.

"No one will harm you," McGann said. "This time we'll be ready. Whoever it is that is trying to harm you will either surrender to me or come off that mountain on a stretcher or a gurney."

The scotch was almost gone. He poured a second, another double. He knew he had a chance. Crimmins was helpless and Devens was stupid. This time the feds would be there, along with his own people.

He slipped out of his suit and put on more comfortable clothes: cotton slacks, a wine-colored polo shirt, and a black windbreaker. He put on rubber-soled shoes, light in weight but thick enough to protect his feet from rocks or exposed tree roots. He reached up to the shelf above the clothes bar in his closet and took down a wooden box. Inside was a utility knife, a circle of thin, steel cable, and a dirty little surprise: a functioning two-shot pepperbox with a brass-knuckle guard over the handle. He slipped it into his ankle holster. He could shoot if he had to, but if he had the time and opportunity he would beat in his tormenter's face until his smile was broken into a dozen pieces of crushed bone. Then he would go for the windpipe. Take away that voice, that voice that he couldn't drive from his memory.

FORTY-FOUR

TAKING A HARD LOOK at the day-old danish before venturing a second bite, Frank gestured to Jerry Dailey to hand him his cup of coffee. Jerry said "Cream?" and Frank shook his head no. Kenny Piersall had freed himself from McGann just long enough to return Frank's call.

"Certifiable. That's what this son-of-a-bitch is," Piersall said. "He paces and stomps and gives orders to anybody within earshot. Then he reaches in his pants, plays a couple of rounds of pocket pool, stomps some more, and picks at his ear with a pencil point. Then he yells at somebody, calls Washington and kisses as many asses as he can get his lips on, and asks what in the hell happened to his coffee and why hasn't somebody given him a fresh cup. He drove one of our best secretaries off in tears but those who remained told him they weren't going to take any more of his shit. 'I'm a county employee,' one of them said, 'and I don't get coffee for people who don't ask nicely.'"

"He made some wiseass comment to her, hoping to intimidate her, and one of the others suggested she cut off his dick with her scissors so he could use *it* to pick around in his goddamned ear. 'I'm sure it's small enough that it would fit,' she said."

"Got them all on edge, huh?"

"I thought I'd seen arrogance before, but this bastard really sets the pace. He keeps saying shit like 'I'll have your job' and 'I'll be your worse nightmare.' He must go to the movies a lot or watch all that old shit on television. If he wasn't so full of himself he might be able to give us some real help, but all he does is look in the mirror, straighten his tie, and call his boss in Washington to tell him that the situation is under control. Under control. Can you believe that? He doesn't even know what the damned situation *is*. The only thing he's got under control is the frigging telephone. He won't let anybody else get near the goddamned thing."

"Watch him, Kenny. He may be stupid and he may like to play King Shit, but he's also dangerous."

"That's what we figured. One of my detectives said he seemed like the type who would get rid of mice by bombing the building rather than by setting traps."

"I think your detective is right. I'm going to be on the mountain with a couple of my men, Kenny. I'll stay out of your way, but I want to make sure that this doesn't turn any uglier than it has to. He's going to be ordering you and your men around because he's in your jurisdiction, but we're all here on our own time and we can do things that you can't. Do you have any problems with that?"

"No, Frank, none. The chief and the captain might, but they're at some damned conference in Florida. I'm still trying to reach them. They're learning something about Total Quality Management, but the people running the meeting changed the room on their session and no one seems to know where in the hell they are. How's that for total quality?"

Frank laughed. "You know where we are, Kenny. There are only a few of us, but we'll try to do some good for you if we can. Do you have any idea yet when this is supposed to go down?"

"No, I don't, but I know that McGann does. He just keeps telling us to be ready to go at any time. He likes his little secrets. What we'll do is keep a close eye on him. The more he picks at his ear and plays with his dick the closer we'll be to getting started. I'll try to give you a warning. I've already asked one of the secretaries to call you the second we leave."

"Which one, the one that was ready to go after McGann with the scissors?"

"Yes. Lorna. She may still have a try at him yet. He told her to do something for him before and I noticed she had her hand in her desk drawer, running her fingers over the handle and blades."

"Good for her."

"Wait a minute," Piersall said. "I've got to go . . ."

He hung up the phone without completing the sentence.

The helicopters came in from the southeast, swinging over Temecula, past the southern edge of the San Bernardino National Forest, skirting La Quinta, and flying low into Palm Desert.

The cars were ready when Jeffers and his men stepped out onto the helipads. They got in them in silence and when the last door shut they pulled out immediately, driving onto 111 and heading for the southern edge of Rancho Mirage. They crossed Frank Sinatra Drive and headed toward Palm Springs. Ten minutes later, looking toward the west, they saw Bob Hope's home sitting on a high slope, its smooth roof like the skin of a faded, flying saucer. They stared right through it, their thoughts on the tramway and what awaited them there.

———

Jerry Dailey took the noon tram to the mountain station and went directly to the cafeteria. He bought a barbecued beef sandwich, french fries, a Diet Dr. Pepper, a wedge of apple pie with a side scoop of cinnamon-vanilla ice cream, a one-ounce bag of Ranch-flavor Doritos, a dark-chocolate Bounty Bar, and a large cup of chili. The Bounty Bar went in his pocket, for later.

The larger tables on the patio overlooking the full expanse of the Coachella Valley basin were crowded, but Jerry found a single table near the railing that was still open. When he approached it he realized why it had been abandoned and avoided. Somebody had spilled catsup all over the table and then played in it with salt, pepper, sugar, and artificial sweetener. There was a sliver of dried pickle resting on the edge of the red pool like a disabled green kayak as well as some crusty red splatter on each of the remaining chairs. Jerry wiped off one of the chairs, put down his tray over the red, white, and gray mess, and tried the chili. Then he put a french fry in his mouth and called Frank on the cellular.

"I'm in place," he said. "What's happening down there?"

"Nothing yet," Frank said. "The bar is starting to fill up. The next tram leaves in fifteen minutes and the riders are fortifying themselves with the sacraments. How was the ride?"

"Fun," Jerry said. "A little too much bouncy-bounce for some people's taste. One woman kept her eyes closed the whole way and left permanent fingerprints on the bracing bar. She said she's not going back down the same way. I don't know what they're going to do with her. There were also a couple of teenagers who were grab-assing, trying to scare the tourists, but all in all it was OK. I'll tell you this—it's one high son-of-a-bitch and each time you pass over one of the support towers your stomach falls a floor or two."

"Is it crowded up there?"

"It's not too bad," Jerry said. "Most of the seats are taken, what with lunch and all, but there aren't too many people up on the hill behind me and the lodge itself is pretty much empty. I guess they use it for dinners at night and they have a bandstand and all, but as soon as people get their drinks and food they come outside."

"Where's Charles?"

"Beats the hell out of me," Jerry said. "As soon as we got here he took off for the woods behind the lodge. He's checking the cliffs and trails for escape routes and he's looking for places that will give him the best views of what's going on. Do you want me to call him?"

"No, not just yet," Frank said. He could hear Jerry's mouth and teeth. "What are you eating?"

"Chili now."

"How is it?"

"I'll be able to hold it down, but it's not going to rate an entry in my personal diary."

"I'll get back to you later," Frank said. "Right now all we can do is sit tight and watch."

———

Jack asked the bartender whether or not he was selling much of the Crystal Pepsi.

"Yeah, some," the guy said. "It tastes sort of weird. It's not really awful, but then it's not really good either. The thing is—you can drink it, but you don't want to drink it very fast. People seem to like that—a glass lasts a long time. You want one?"

"No thanks, give me some coffee," Jack said.

"What do you want in it?"

"Nothing, black is fine."

"You been up to the top yet?" the bartender asked.

"No. I'll go up a little later."

"I understand. You want to sit here and think about it a little first."

"Maybe."

"I sell a lot of gin," the bartender said, "but not a hell of a lot of vermouth." Jack leaned forward so he could read his name tag: *Leon*.

"I bet it's a gold mine."

"You got that right," Leon said. "You know what I tell them?"

"What's that?"

"I tell them if they want something that will work fast they should drink champagne."

"Why is that?" Jack asked, his eyes scanning the room and the entrance to the lodge, just below the bar.

"Because the bubbles somehow keep the stomach valve open. The alcohol goes straight into the bloodstream. That's why it always makes you lightheaded. Champagne gives you an instant buzz. Plus, the markup on it is sweet. I got all kinds; each of them has Prince in the title: Prince Andre, Prince Michel . . . Ernest and Julio make most of the stuff. It's not really that bad, either."

"Somehow it doesn't seem like the champagne crowd here."

"No, it's not," Leon said. "We get a lot of 'bago drivers and we get more than our share of the biker and 4x4 crowd, but before any of them reach for a Blue Ribbon or a Black Label they have to slow down for a second and think through what it is they're about to do. You see, your authentic beer drinker will always look around for a men's room before he places his order. He doesn't want to leave *terra firma* and get into a gondola with eighty people and no porcelain. It's about a twenty-minute ride to the top—as you'll see—and that won't be so long that it will bother your gin and champagne drinker, but believe me, that's a long twenty minutes if your bladder is trying to expand down into your legs and up into your throat."

Jack noticed a young woman entering the bar, her body backlit by the sun. At first he thought it might be Karen Wilken, but as she got closer he could see that this woman was taller and older. "So that's why you tell them to go for the champagne," Jack said.

"That's right, but they usually take the gin instead."

"Gin works fast too," Jack said.

"Yes it does," Leon said, as he rinsed glasses and put them on the sink rack. He turned to say something, but Jack was suddenly gone.

FORTY-FIVE

McGann and his retinue entered the lodge with all of the subtlety of a Rottweiler in heat. Their clear-plastic earpieces were as obvious as their shoulder holsters and pocket radios. McGann leaned over and whispered a lot, rare behavior among adult men in a relatively quiet, public place. After they entered together and exchanged a few private words, they suddenly dispersed, hurrying off in a half-dozen different directions, like inexperienced actors, late for a costume change.

Jack was standing just outside the men's room, at the side of the souvenir counter, looking over the top of a current edition of *Newsweek*. He could see the base of the tram line in one direction and the lodge parking lot in the other. He paced slowly across the northern side of the room and caught a glimpse of two of McGann's men, positioning themselves around the perimeter of the building. Then he walked to the other side of the room, turning the pages of the magazine in rapt attention and absentmindedly bumping against a chair. Righting himself, he continued to walk as he read. When he reached the opposite window he could see McGann, standing behind the starting platform for the parallel gondolas. He was leaning against the wall, trying his best to appear inconspicuous. His best wasn't very good. When he leaned down to say something into his armpit—presumably figuring that that would deceive anyone with regard to his possession of a two-way radio—Jack wondered what he might be capable of doing if someone began firing a weapon.

Frank was in the parking area a few hundred feet below the lodge, sitting in the back seat of Jerry Dailey's sedan, scanning radio frequencies. It took him forty-five seconds to tie into McGann's net. As his men checked in to be sure that their signals were crisp and clear, McGann verified their positions and told them to stay in touch with him whenever they noticed anything. No matter *how* minor. He was calling himself Blue Leader One.

"Jesus Christ," Frank said. "This asshole is going to get us all killed." He picked up the cellular and called Jerry. "There are probably some of McGann's people coming your way," he said. "They entered the lodge a little over twenty minutes ago."

"They just got off the tram," Jerry said. "Two of them, and not exactly undercover experts. They could have worn *Hi, I'm a G-Man* T-shirts and they wouldn't have been much more obvious than they were."

"Where are they now, Jerry?"

"One of them's in the mountain station bar; the other's out on the deck where I was eating my lunch. He's got a pair of binoculars and he's scanning the area like he just lost his girlfriend in an avalanche. Just a second . . . the other one just ordered some bottled water. He's nursing it as if he has to stretch the damned thing across the next week and a half. He should be wearing something that says *Hi. I'm on a stakeout. What's your sign?*"

"Your government in action," Frank said.

Jerry sighed, broke out the Bounty Bar, and bit off a third of it. "Any sign of Ernie Jeffers yet?"

"Wait a second," Frank said. "I think this may be him."

The column of cars was led by a Palm Springs PD sedan. It was unmarked, but Frank knew that the factory didn't equip Ford Tauruses with shotgun mounts, computers, and portable roof lights. "It's him," Frank said. "He's in . . . just a second . . . the fourth car. God, they've got a whole convoy of them. Jeffers must have brought along every strongarm type in his organization."

"They'll be tripping over McGann's people," Jerry said.

"Call Charles, Jerry. Tell him the curtain's about to go up."

"I will. What about Jack?"

"Jack's in the lodge, in the middle of the tourists. Listen, tell Charles that Jeffers has about thirty men with him. They're dressed in slacks and blousy poplin jackets."

"All armed, I'm sure," Jerry said.

"Yes. And easy to spot: pure whitebread all the way. They each look like their name should be Gunther or Friedrich. Very serious and very physical. They just got on the wheeled tram to drive them from the parking lot up to the lodge. Show time, Jerry."

"Listen up, people." It was McGann, opening up his net. "The subject is here and we're ready to go to work. I don't want any mistakes and I don't want any excuses. We're coming down off of this rock with a very dead or very sorry suspect. Acknowledge."

Each of his people reported in order as the gondola for the 2:00 tram approached the platform.

Four cars away from Frank a figure sat in the back of a Plymouth van, her equipment housed in a single attache case. When McGann's people acknowledged him, in turn, she turned off her tape recorder and plugged in her microphone.

FORTY-SIX

Jeffers was surrounded by his security force as he stepped off of the wheeled tram and entered the lodge. McGann nodded toward him through the window as he approached the ticket counter. The group went through the parallel turnstiles and walked into the waiting area adjoining the starting platform. McGann was on his radio, alerting his people that Jeffers was ready to board the tram. Jack turned the page of his magazine and scanned the room. Still no sign of Karen Wilken.

"It's two o'clock, gentlemen," Jeffers said to his men. "Let's do this right."

They mingled with a few dozen tourists who wondered who they were and what they were doing there. One elderly couple looked them up and down and decided to pass on the 2:00 and return to the souvenir stand. A family with a child in a stroller was taken aside quietly by one of McGann's men and told to wait for the next tram. That left a mix of men and women who were either anxious to get to the top, anxious to get the ride over with, or ready to go along with Jeffers and his security force out of curiosity.

The driver opened the gate on the tram and motioned them forward. They entered the tram quickly, Jeffers and his men gravitating toward the center, away from the windows. Two minutes later, without any fanfair, they left the ground and began their climb. As if on signal Jeffers and his men reached inside their jackets and took out matched caps and sunglasses. They put them on and then began changing position, always weaving and always staying toward the center of the tram, with their eyes looking inward, away from the windows. There was no way that a sniper could identify Jeffers with any certainty and no way that a shot could be fired without endangering the lives of a half dozen innocent people.

As they approached the first tower they could see the Palm Springs PD officers at the base, dressed as workmen, but guarding the tower and keeping it from being mined. The Tramway officials and the Palm Springs PD bomb squad had swept the structure and inspected the cables before first light and each guard had been in place since the check. One of the tourists noticed a sudden gleam in a distant crevice at four thousand feet. Probably the sun hitting a white rock at just the right angle. No thought that it could have been the sight of a high-powered rifle.

As awkward and obvious as McGann's people had been, Piersall's officers had been efficient and inconspicuous. There were forty-five of them, including the twelve on loan from Palm Desert and the eight from Rancho Mirage. The recent storms had blanketed the upper reaches of the mountain in fresh snow and Piersall's men had made the most of it and the surrounding rocks for cover and concealment. The mountain station was guarded; the entry lodge was guarded; the towers were each protected, and the face of the mountain was dotted with armed officers, ready to take out a sniper or prevent his entry or escape. Including the tramway's own security personnel, there were ninety-four people prepared to protect the life of Ernest Jeffers.

The tram ride was smooth and the bright sun was warming the air inside the gondola, even though the temperature outside had dropped by ten degrees. They passed the second tower and the jerk felt as if they were in a light car briskly passing over a high speed bump. There were some gulps and then sudden smiles of accomplishment.

"I didn't think we'd feel it that much," one of the tourists said. "I'd just as soon not pass through too many of those towers."

"You ain't got any choice," her husband said, "unless, of course, you want to just hang out here in space and not go on to the top. That wouldn't scare you *too* much, would it?" He was smiling, waiting for her response.

"Is Earl always such an asshole?" her girlfriend asked.

"Only when he's at home or out in public," his wife, Melba, answered.

They all smiled.

"It ain't no big thing," Earl said. "You better get used to it. You've got three more here and then all five again when we come back down."

"Thanks," she said. "I needed that."

"Well, I'm just tellin' you . . ."

———

As they approached the third tower a voice came over the speaker on the tram. The box was next to the door, above the main controls. It was garbled, like the voice of a foreign dispatcher over a Manhattan taxi net.

"What is it?" the driver said.

"Stop the tram at the next tower," the voice said. "I'll be back in touch then." This time everyone could hear the voice plainly.

"What's the problem?" Earl asked.

"I don't know," the driver said. "Don't worry, this happens sometimes."

"Don't *worry*?" Earl said. "What the hell is that supposed to mean. We're hanging over a face of sheer rock at five or six thousand goddamned feet and you tell us you're going to stop and that we shouldn't *worry*. What in the *hell* is going on here?"

"I don't know, sir. Look, the tram is fine. Just stay calm."

"*Calm*? Jesus Christ. Why should we be calm? You're going to stop the goddamned tram."

"Shut up, Earl," his wife said. "Let the man do his job."

"His job is to get us the hell up to the top of the mountain. I want to know why he isn't doing that."

"So all of a sudden you're the one who's scared," Melba said.

"I'm not scared, goddamn it. I just want to know what's happening. If we stay up here all day, swingin' in space, attached to that little goddamn wire, I know who's gonna be scared," he said.

One of Jeffers' men leaned over and said, "Sir, why don't you just stay calm and stop getting everybody so upset."

"Who in the hell are you?" Earl said. "Why don't you mind your own fucking business."

"I don't want you bothering other people on the tram," he said. "If you don't keep your mouth shut I *will* give you something to be upset about."

"Don't talk to my husband like that," Melba said.

Jeffers' man stood back, pulled down the zipper on his poplin jacket, and exposed the handle of his automatic.

"You a cop?" Earl asked.

"Tram security," the man said. "Now put a lid on it."

Earl and his wife looked at one another, shrugged, and moved closer to the control panel so that they could hear the next message when it came through. Melba reached out and held on to the bracing bar.

When the driver killed the power at the third tower the tram began to rock back and forth. The tourists put death grips on the chrome bracing bars and the security force tightened around Jeffers. Four of them moved to the sides of the tram and looked out the windows, but there was no one in sight who appeared in any way suspicious. Piersall's men were still visible—standing at the base of the towers, looking, talking, trying to figure out why the tram had suddenly stopped.

After a full minute and a half the voice came back on the speaker. "Gerry?"

"Yes, I'm here."

"Stay where you are. We've got a little problem we're trying to work out."

"What is it?" the driver asked. There were beads of perspiration forming at the top of his lip and above his eyebrows.

"Someone just called the director's office and told us to stop the tram."

"Why?"

"There was a threat, Gerry."

"What kind of a threat?"

"It's probably a hoax, Gerry. I don't want to upset the people on the tram."

"Tell him we want to know," Earl said. "Tell him not to give us any bullshit."

"I'll be back in touch, Gerry," the supervisor said.

"Wait a minute," Jeffers said, his men gathered around him. "Ask him about the *nature* of the threat. Do it."

The driver could see the hands reaching inside the poplin jackets. He flipped the radio switch.

"Mr. Slater. Please tell us the truth," Gerry said.

"I can't do that."

"Please. You have to."

"Goddamn it, Gerry, I can't."

"You have to," Gerry said, his voice quivering.

"It was a man's voice. It was distorted. The voice said that the water tank contains an explosive device and that it would be detonated if we didn't stop the tram."

"What kind of device?"

"He didn't say; all that he would tell us was that it was a big one."

"What does he want us to do?"

"He didn't say. He just said to first stop the tram."

Jeffers said to the driver, "Where in the hell is this water tank?"

"Right above you," he answered.

"What the hell do you mean, right above me?"

"Each tram carries 400 gallons of water in a hollow space just above the passenger compartment—in case we get stuck."

Jeffers turned to one of his assistants. "That son-of-a-bitch. He put a bomb in the water so the dogs wouldn't be able to smell it."

The assistant nodded.

"And he can throw the switch anytime he wants to and smear us all over the front of the mountain, like bugs on a goddamn windshield."

The assistant nodded again.

"So how in the hell do we get down from here?"

"You can't," the assistant said. "If you try to climb down the tower you'll be right out in the open, in the middle of his crosshairs. He could pick you off from a distance and be gone before anyone could get to him."

"That's exactly what he wants," Jeffers said. "That's why he stopped the tram. He's opening the door and telling me to go right ahead and walk through it. Then he's going to blow my head apart. I'm right, aren't I? You know I'm right. So what in the hell do we do? We can't stay here and wait to be blown up. What do we do? Come on, what in the *hell* am I paying you for? Well?"

"I don't know what we can do, Mr. Jeffers."

FORTY-SEVEN

"We could put something over each of our faces," one of Jeffers' men said. "That way he wouldn't know who he was shooting at."

"Cute. What if he decides to kill us one by one? Who's going to climb down the goddamn tower after he blows the head off of the first person out?"

"We could get as many people on the tower as possible, force him to kill everybody to get to you."

"Wonderful. Maybe then he'd just throw the switch and blow all of us into red vapor. Why shouldn't he? He's killed twice already and they can only put him in the gas chamber once."

"Well . . ." the first man said, reaching.

"Look," Jeffers said. "This is what we're going to do. I'm going down in the middle of the civilians. If he wants to kill me he's going to have to kill some of them too. Get the driver over here. Keep him busy. I don't want him interfering. A couple of the security people can go down with two or three of those tourists, then I'll follow with the next set."

One of Jeffers' people, a man named Sievers, approached one of the couples. "Come on, we're going down," he said.

"Down? What the hell are you talking about?" the husband answered. "You think we're going to climb down that damned tower? That's ridiculous."

"Do you want to stay here and be blown up?"

"Hell no, but I don't want my wife to fall off of that tower either. She could never make it. I say we try to hold out for a while longer, give the security people a chance to find the nut who's responsible for this. It's probably a damn hoax anyway, just like the guy on the radio said."

"Look, it's no hoax," Sievers said.

"How the hell do you know?"

"Trust me on this. If we don't take control of the situation we're all going to die here."

"You call *that* taking control of the situation—climbing down an icy tower in a high wind? I call that suicide."

The supervisor came back on the radio: "Gerry, can you hear me?"

"Yes, what's happening?" the driver asked.

"We got another message."

"Yes?"

"He wants the security people out of the gondola. He wants them to climb down the tower."

"What do you mean?" Gerry asked.

"There's a guy on the tram named Jeffers. He brought his security people with him. They've got to get out of there."

"Why, Mr. Slater?"

"How in the hell would I know, Gerry? All I know is that we've got to save as many people as we can, and I'm not going to debate with this guy when he's got his finger on the button."

"It's all right," Jeffers said. "Tell him it's all right."

"Are you Jeffers?" Gerry said.

"No, I'm Alberto Tomba. I came here to go skiing down the fucking side of Mt. San Jacinto. Of course I'm Jeffers, you asshole. Tell your supervisor my people are coming out."

Sievers came forward, ready to try to dissuade him.

"Save your breath," Jeffers said. "What else can we do? At least I'll be here with the driver and the civilians. I don't think he'll blow us all up."

"Well, he's not going to let *you* go. That much is certain."

"He won't *want* to let me go, but don't you see—this will help us buy some time. Pass the word to the others to climb down as slowly as they can. When you get to the bottom, I want all of you to try to help the cops find this cocksucker."

"Are you sure, Mr. Jeffers?"

"What do you want—a chart and a set of goddamned directions?"

"No, sir. I don't need that."

"Then get the fuck out that window and climb down that tower. And remember: *slowly.*"

"Don't worry," Sievers said.

The wind stirred the powder on the face of the mountain and filled the gondola with a sudden shot of icy air. Sievers had a piece of rope that he was tying around the central bracing bar. Then he lowered himself over the top of the open window in the southeast corner of the gondola and swung himself toward the tower. The gridwork spacing did not make his task any easier. He climbed from strut to strut, but had to slide between sections, clutching the supports with his legs, like a kid working his way down a heavy rope. He felt the cold steel through his cotton slacks; after ten minutes his forearms and shoulders were cramping and his hands and fingers were raw. He looked above at those who were following him, but kept his eyes off the canyon floor below. The tourists had been right. They never would have made it. Sievers wondered how many of Jeffers' security force would.

When Sievers dropped the final ten feet to the ground, he slipped and fell at the feet of two of Piersall's men. He looked up and the reflected light from the snow on the mountain face dazzled his eyes. He could see the dark outlines of dozens of men, following him down the tower, their hands gripping the structure, their feet slipping as they reached out for the next strut or support. Their bodies were all in different positions. They looked as if their nearly lifeless bodies had been washed there by some great flood and they were clinging to a giant steel tree, their hair blowing wildly against the sky.

The last man out was halfway down the tower when Slater's voice came over the intercom: "Gerry, can you hear me?"

"Yes, Mr. Slater. I can hear you."

"Turn the power back on and bring the tram back to the platform. Do it immediately."

He reversed direction and began the descent. "What's happening, Mr. Slater?" he asked.

"I don't know. One of the government people here told me to bring you down."

"Did they catch the bomber?"

"What did I just say, Gerry? I don't know. Just get down here."

"Yes, sir."

Jeffers smiled and looked toward the tourists for approval, but they were huddled together, clutching the bars, their backs turned against him.

"Report your position, Blue Leader Three," McGann said.

"I'm approximately one hundred and fifty yards due east of my initial position, in fast pursuit."

"Do you see him?" McGann said.

"I did, just a second ago. He was headed toward a cluster of pines. He just slipped behind a set of rocks."

"Don't get too close," McGann said. "We'll be right there."

McGann was the third person out of the lodge. He sent two of his younger men ahead, running in the direction of the fourth man, the one who had sighted the suspect. The others he left at the lodge to protect Jeffers. The first group spaced out as they got farther away from the lodge, the two younger men giving chase, McGann watching from a distance, protecting the rear.

Three minutes later McGann's voice came over the net. "We've got him surrounded and we're ready to open fire. Get Jeffers out of there now. I'll call Piersall's driver and give the order to pick him up right in front of the lodge. You join us here. I don't want this son-of-a-bitch to escape and get anywhere near Jeffers."

"You got it," McGann's man answered. He put his radio back on his belt and told the men with him to go ahead. Then he turned and went back into the lodge. Jeffers was standing among the tourists, trying to stay behind anyone he could, but also trying to look out of the windows in both directions.

"Jeffers," the man said, "there's a driver coming for you. Right in front. Get in and get the hell out of here. We've got the suspect surrounded. Move."

Jeffers wanted to stay, wanted to get a little taste of revenge. They finally had the cocksucker trapped. He had gotten Crimmins and he had gotten Devens, but this time the son-of-a-bitch had reached for more than he could grasp. Maybe he'd try to escape. Jeffers hoped he would—and then get shot to hell by McGann's people so that they'd have to put him together with steel pins and rubber bands before they wheeled his ass into the gas chamber. That piece of shit, that hairball cocksucker—putting him through that ordeal. Fucking explosives—just above your head on a fucking aerial tram, thousands of feet above a desert floor with fucking cold winds and snow and ice. Security people climbing like a bunch of fucking monkeys. He himself stuck up there like some kind of asshole with a bunch of white-sock tourists and a tram operator with the brains of a piece of limp cauliflower. That *son*-of-a-*bitch*. Getting his fucking jollies by humiliating somebody as important and powerful as Ernie Jeffers. A few minutes of fame. Playing King Shit for the crowds at Ernie Jeffers' expense. Trying to make it to the tease for the six o'clock news. No fucking way. Not this time.

If I could only see him, only see him squirm and piss in his pants, watch his body jerk back and forth with the automatic-weapons fire. Watch McGann gloat when the stretcher came through.

He heard the horn honk. The unmarked sedan was at the bottom of the steps, where the wheeled tram dropped off the tourists. He saw the roof light turning. Jesus, I wish I could stay, he thought.

FORTY-EIGHT

Jack was running from the lodge as fast as he could, the pain shooting up his right leg as he tried to keep his balance in the sand and gravel. Frank was a few hundred feet ahead of him. Charles and Jerry were on the mountain station platform, waiting to board the tram and join them.

Jack and Frank each knew what the other was thinking. Would they be able to get there in time? Could they keep McGann from opening fire before Karen had had a chance to surrender. *Would* she surrender, or would she try to shoot her way through them?

Two minutes later Jack caught up with Frank, who was working his way up the side of a small hill, doing his best to retain some cover as he tried to get a better view of the surrounding area.

"What's happening?" Jack asked.

"Look," Frank said, "straight ahead."

There were a half-dozen men, sweeping the area, duck-walking behind rocks or high-crawling across open areas.

"Where's McGann?" Jack asked.

"I don't know."

"I haven't heard any shots," Jack said.

"There haven't been any," Frank answered. "Look . . ."

McGann's men were all standing now, walking back toward the lodge. "Stay here," Frank said. "Let's see where they're going."

They waited for them to pass and then followed them at a distance. A few hundred feet from the lodge they fanned out and began to search the area. Jack looked at Frank, but he didn't say anything.

Four minutes later one of them called out. "Over here . . . hurry." The rest of them ran in the direction of his voice. They stopped and then fell to their knees.

"Come on," Frank said.

The two of them ran over and found McGann's men in a circle, leaning over the ground. They got closer and saw a man's body lying in the dirt, his blue suit covered with dust and desert grit.

"What the hell are you doing here?" one of the men said to Frank.

"Trying to enjoy my day off," Frank said. "What are you doing?"

"Get the hell out of here," the man said.

"Is he dead?" Frank asked.

"What did I just tell you, Lieutenant?"

"Who is it?"

"Don't worry about it," the man said.

"One of yours?"

"If you want to help you could call for an ambulance."

Frank walked toward them. "They'll want to know what's wrong so they know what to bring."

"I don't know what's wrong. Tell them one of our people is unconscious."

"Any contusions or open wounds?"

"No."

"How's the breathing?"

"Stable, but a little labored."

"I'll call an ambulance," Frank said. "Where's your boss? Didn't he come with you?"

The man just stared at him. Frank turned toward Jack, nodded, and the two of them walked a few feet away. "They don't know *where* he is," Jack said.

"I know," Frank answered. "Sweet, isn't it?"

Frank took out his cellular and made the call for the ambulance.

"I've got an idea," Jack said. "Follow me."

"Where are you going?"

"Over to the other side of that hill."

"Why?"

"Because she wouldn't leave the two of them together. She's trying to buy time."

They walked three or four hundred yards. "Look," Jack said, pointing, "they were looking for their guy over there, due east of the lodge. Instead he turns up over *there*, south of the line from the lodge to the point where they expected him to be. Let's try north of that line, over there in that gully."

It took them a full minute to get there. "What did I tell you?" Jack said, pointing east. "He's right there . . ."

They hurried over and found the body, lying face down. Jack rolled him over. "Hello, Chester," he said. "Taking some time out for a little nap?"

"See anything?" Frank asked.

"Nothing obvious," Jack said. "He's breathing all right. Except for the slobber on his chin and the dirt on his forehead, he looks pretty normal."

Jack was going over the body inch by inch.

"The stupid look on his face is still there," Frank said.

"Wait a minute," Jack said. "OK, yes, here it is."

"Here is what?"

"In his neck—a little pinhole and some dried blood. Probably a dart or a needle. It must have been quick: Hiya Chester, night-night, Chester. They were all on their way to find Karen and their lead guy. They didn't know that she had already taken him out. McGann was a few hundred feet behind them. Suddenly he dropped out. Nobody heard anything and nobody saw anything. Meanwhile the search party is wandering around in the desert, not able to find the guy who cried wolf and not aware that their boss has just gone down. They still don't know what in the hell happened."

"Nice work."

"The best," Jack said.

"How did she do it?"

"Good question," Jack answered.

"I've got a better one," Frank said. "Where is Ernie Jeffers?"

"Ernie Jeffers? Ernie's on the road to nowhere."

FORTY-NINE

THE DRIVER WAS COMING down from the base of the mountain at fifty miles an hour, chasing the heat waves rippling from the pavement and bouncing over the ridges and dips as the police sedan got closer and closer to the valley floor. It was still a mile and a half to the main highway and as the road began to level the driver depressed the accelerator. They passed the backs of the signs, advising drivers to cut back their air conditioners to prevent their vehicles from overheating and finally came in sight of the intersection at route 111.

Jeffers kept turning, looking behind him for some sign that the killer had been caught. He started to roll down a window to listen for gunfire, but the window wouldn't move. Like the doorlocks, it was controlled by the driver. Standard police issue. The metal grillwork between him and the front seat was reinforced by a piece of hard plastic, set in a runner on the driver's side. It was designed to protect the police from the noise, the smell, and the spit from the back seat.

The driver hadn't even spoken. Concentrating on the task at hand: getting Ernie Jeffers out of there. Making sure Ernie Jeffers was safe. Making sure that if something went wrong back on the mountain Ernie Jeffers would be miles away. Driving off in an unmarked sedan. Not attracting attention. No convoys this time, just a single escape vehicle. Smart. For a hick cop Piersall wasn't bad. Not that he had helped all that much back on the mountain. Thank God, Ernie was smart enough to take charge and extricate himself.

"Where are we headed?" he said to the driver.

"Safe house. Just this side of Banning."

"How long will it take us to get there?"

"Not long."

The late afternoon sun fell across his legs, warming the inside of the car. Ernie leaned back and finally began to relax. He watched the shadows in the mountain canyons, looked for dune buggy tracks, and even started to count the rows of old black tires that were strung together to break the movement of the drifting sand. Checking his watch too. Wondering what had happened to the killer. Hoping it had been ugly. And decisive. He looked at his hands. There was still some dried blood on the cut across his knuckles. He had jumped from the gondola, slipped, and raked the back of his hand across the gate on the starting platform. The hand hurt. It even trembled a little as he held it out in front of him, looking at the pores and creases in the bright sun. Pain did that to you sometimes.

At least the bastard lost. He went through all of that bullshit and Ernie Jeffers was still alive. Probably the security he had. Scared the shit out of the little prick. Let him know there was no way out this time. He had made a big mistake—going up against the first team. Hopefully it was his last.

The only remaining problem was the media. Fucking scavengers. They'd dig out the details of the Wilken case and start asking him a lot of embarrassing questions. Try to fuck up his business. Grab some headlines at his expense. Cocksuckers. He'd put his PR people on it as soon as he could get to a phone and call them.

Get the initial spin. Turn Ernie Jeffers into a victim, a patriotic citizen stalked by a lunatic who had already killed a congressman and a prominent businessman. Fucking nuts these days. They're all around us and we're helpless. Sometimes we get lucky and the good guys win. Good guys like Ernie Jeffers. But nobody is safe, not in a world of schizos and crazies, all trying to build up their own pathetic selves by tearing down somebody else. Somebody *prominent*. Somebody *decent*. He could bring up some spades and beaners from the loading dock; get his picture taken in the middle of them: somebody *fair*.

It would probably play. If it didn't he could try something else. Maybe the lawyers could seal the court records—invasion of privacy and all that shit. He could threaten to sue the papers and the networks. That was a bitch to make stick, but he might have to try it. Who knows? The whole thing could turn out to be a yawner. A youthful indiscretion. Some people get together; they have some drinks; somebody misunderstands the signals and suddenly some girl is crying rape. Shit, this is the nineties. A boink here or there, or a little stretch of the truth—who really gives a shit? Teddy Kennedy keeps getting reelected and Willie Smith is off playing doctor. Bob McNamara is still giving speeches and pulling down heavy lecture fees. Nixon keeps coming back like a fucking vampire with his newest best seller, Mac Bundy became a goddamn college professor, Clarence Thomas is sitting on the high bench, and Ollie Stone's making millions of dollars claiming that St. Jack was killed by his own government. What in the fuck difference would it make if Ernie Jeffers and a couple of his buddies just happened to have a little fun one night with a woman with a high school education and a nice ass? Over twenty years ago.

———

"We should be getting pretty close, don't you think?" Jeffers said.

"We're almost there," the driver answered.

"What's it like," he said, "being a lady cop?"

"It has its moments," she answered.

FIFTY

She passed the gas station with the giant dinosaurs and then the adjoining outlet mall. It was crowded. Cars were circling, looking for parking places with some shade. People out on a hot, desert afternoon, trying to find a bargain, save some money.

She drove another mile and turned off of the highway.

"This looks pretty damned deserted," he said, craning his neck, trying to see through the dust on the side of the window.

"We're almost there," she said. The two-lane asphalt road turned to gravel a mile and a half from the highway. She drove a few hundred yards to an abandoned shed. Just behind it there was a car with California plates. She turned around in a makeshift driveway and aimed the police cruiser back toward the gravel road.

"This is your idea of a safe house?" he said. "It's a goddamned abandoned shack."

"You're right," she said, turning around. "And I'm afraid it's not very safe either."

"What the hell are you talking about?"

"I'm talking about you, Ernie," she said. "You're not safe here, not as long as any of the Wilkens are still alive. You're not safe at all."

"What the hell is this, some kind of sick, fucking joke?"

"It's not a joke, Ernie."

"Well, what the fuck is it then?"

She reached over for the velvet bag on the passenger seat and pulled out a miniature crossbow. He couldn't see that she was wearing gloves with metallic grips. She put the pointed bolt in place, cocked the weapon, brought it up quickly, and inserted the bolt through the grillwork, and aimed it at a spot equidistant between his eyes.

"Why don't we call it a history lesson, Ernie?"

He lurched to the side and instinctively grabbed at the edge of the bolt, which barely protruded through the grillwork. The sharpened steel cut his hand like a straight razor and he screamed in pain.

"Maybe a lesson in sharpened objects also," she said.

He was squeezing his right palm with the fingers of his left hand, trying to reduce the pain. The blood soaked between his fingers, filling in the ridges above his knuckles. He thought about the pepperbox in his ankle holster, thought about his chances of reaching it before she could shoot him with the crossbow.

"One other thing," she said. "It wouldn't be a good idea to try to duck or flail around like that. This bolt weighs a pound and six ounces and if I released it into your back it would shatter your spine like a stick."

"What the fuck do you want?" Jeffers said, choking out the words as the drops of blood from his hand soaked into his trousers.

"I want to talk to you, Ernie. I want to talk to you about a night many years ago, a night when you and your friends had a little fun at another person's expense—a person who had come to you for help."

"That was all a misunderstanding. She wanted it. Believe me, I was there, and she *wanted* it."

"Oh, did she now?"

"Yes, she *did*."

"You're a liar, Ernie. You're also a war profiteer, an influence peddler, a thief, and a soulless bag of shit. You bleed our treasury and then you turn out crap—crap our soldiers are supposed to defend themselves with; then you have lunch with your friends on the Hill, and you bleed it some more. People die and you buy municipal bonds. More people die and you buy mutual funds. Still more die and you shelter your take in Orange County real estate. You greedy little prick—you're as hollow as an empty can of cheap dog food. You go to black-tie dinners, give speeches, and throw back one-tenth of one percent of your profits to the adoring multitudes. Then you go and make more. You're a lot of things, you miserable little arrogant piece of shit, but most of all you're a pig and a liar."

"Fuck you," Jeffers said with contempt.

"Fuck *me*? I don't think so, Ernie." She triggered the crossbow and the bolt shot into his right shoulder, penetrating the upholstery, and pinning him to the frame of the car.

He cried out in pain, his eyes flashing. Reaching for the shaft with his free, left hand he flayed the skin from his palm and fingertips and cried out again.

"Sharpened, Ernie, remember?"

She reloaded the crossbow as his body was trembling in pain. Without seeming to take aim she released the second bolt, which penetrated his left shoulder, pinning him again. This time all he could move were his head and hands and legs. His legs and torso were shaking violently, his black hair was wet with perspiration, and the smell of urine was beginning to fill the car.

"Now where were we?" she said, "something about fucking me?"

His eyes were rolling and his breathing was heavy. His arms were soaked with blood and his body was shivering with terror and pain.

"I know what happened, Ernie," she said. "I know exactly what happened. It took three of you to rape her. Devens held her down. He did, didn't he, Ernie? He pinned her with his hands so she couldn't move. Isn't that true?"

Jeffers didn't answer. He was turning his head away from her, trying to catch his breath as the mucus poured from his flared nostrils and ran over his lips and into his mouth as his eyes filled with tears.

"And then Crimmins said he thought he'd fuck her. He'd *fuck* her. Brave words, Ernie. Big man. With one of his pals holding her down he'd show her what a man he was. Only she wasn't interested. She fought. So it took the three of you to handle her. Devens had her hands and you had her feet, so Crimmins could take off her clothes, which he did. Except that he had to rip off her underwear, because she was still kicking and his buddy Ernie wasn't strong enough to restrain her.

"So you all had a laugh and Crimmins was finally ready to *fuck* her. That's what he said. But he couldn't, could he?"

Jeffers didn't answer.

"That was where you came in, Ernie. You tried to stick your finger in her and you found out she was still dry. She was fighting you in the only way she could. You even commented on the fact, didn't you? 'She's still dry,' you said. 'I know how to cure that.' That's exactly what you said, isn't it?"

"No," he gurgled.

"Liar," she said. "Then what did you do, Ernie? Do *you* want to say it or do you want me to say it?"

He twisted his head from side to side, trying to avoid the sound of her voice and the point of the third crossbow bolt.

"You started to lick her, didn't you, Ernie? You let Crimmins take over holding her feet and you told him to spread her legs. Then you started to lick her. You said *you'd* make her wet. Big man Ernie. Always so helpful, aren't you—helping your Washington pals rape the country or helping your local pals rape defenseless women. Good old Ernie. Ernie the tongue, always ready to make the women wet.

"And finally Crimmins raped her. You held her down, you stuck your filthy tongue into her body, and then you watched as Mikey raped her. Was that an average night for you three boys or was that something special? Was raping helpless women your long suit or just a sideline? What did you do after she left? Have a drink and a laugh? Talk about how good she felt? Talk about how good she tasted? What did you say, Ernie? Did you brag about how you could always make your women wet?"

His eyes were flashing now and his legs were convulsing. The seat was covered with blood and his chest was heaving. He jerked his head to the left and hit the bolt protruding from his left shoulder. The pain shot to the center of his back and down his left arm.

"So what do you think, Ernie? How does it feel? You're pinned down, you're frightened, and you're helpless. You don't know whether you're going to survive or not. You don't know why this has to be happening. You thought I was going to help you. You came to me for help, but I'm not helping you at all, am I? Instead I pinned you down and caused you pain. I humiliated you. How does it feel, Ernie? You know what? I also made you wet. Very wet. Of course, it happens to be a mixture of blood and piss, but then, we do what we can. It's not very pleasant, is it? Of course, it wasn't very pleasant for her either, but that wasn't something that really concerned you, was it? *Was it*?"

She aimed the bolt at his forehead. "Think about it, Ernie," she said. "Think about all of it. After your night of fun she lost the baby she was carrying. It was a little boy, by the way. She was going to give him his father's name. His father was off at war. It was going to be a surprise. You didn't know that, did you? Then, years later, when she couldn't stand it any longer, she killed herself. Her husband fell apart. His mind became frozen in time. He couldn't accept the pointless loss of a woman he loved so much. He *wouldn't* accept it, Ernie, and as a result he sits in a chair in a dark corner of his house, hoping it isn't so. You helped kill a family, Ernie. And why not? You and your friends had all but killed our country. What was another family, here or there? Especially when it could give you pleasure. Make you feel important. Make you feel like a man. You know what I see when I look at you? I see something dead in an expensive suit. I see a bloated title on the door and a lot of grainy pictures in the *Style* section of the *Washington Post*. I see Ernie Jeffers—the man who makes money from death, the man who holds women down and sticks his tongue in their bodies, and thinks the world should consider him important. The honorable Ernest Jeffers. Friend of the world's leaders. Giant of industry. Liar and rapist. I wouldn't trade a thousand of the scum like you for a single dead infantryman, trying to do what he was raised to believe was right, even though the strings were being pulled by a bunch of lying, cynical ticket-punchers and pocket-liners. Good-bye, Ernie. I don't know where you're going, but you better pray that you don't meet any people there who know what you really are."

His eyes were fixed on her. He tried not to blink as the point of the bolt made tiny circles in the center of his forehead. Then it dropped suddenly and he heard the click and felt the point plunge through his tongue, into the back of his throat, and through his neck. His head was locked in place, his eyes still open, as the final chokes and gurgles ended in a single, sustained gasp.

She listened until it stopped; then she was out of the cruiser, loading her crossbow in the trunk of the escape car. She changed her clothes in the shed, put the police uniform into the trunk, put her sunglasses back on, and drove out to the highway. The traffic was light in both directions and the road extended before her. The sun was warm on the side of her neck, like the first day of the world.

FIFTY-ONE

"I DID NOT GIVE any orders to have Jeffers driven away," McGann said. His tie was loose, his collar dirty with fingermarks, and his head wet from the vomiting and the nausea.

"We heard your voice, chief," one of his men said.

"It wasn't my voice, asshole," he said. "How many times do I have to say it? Wilken was impersonating me."

"It sounded exactly like you," the man said again.

"I don't give a rat's ass who it sounded like; it wasn't me."

"It was a woman who drove him away," Piersall said. "Two witnesses saw her. She had to be a ringer; I didn't have any female officers out here."

"Jesus Christ," McGann said. "You sound like that NOW pussy from Anaheim—what's his name, Calder? He kept trying to tell me that it was a woman. Take the shit out of your ears and listen: this was *not* a woman. Do you really think a woman could have taken out a guy the size of Devens? Do you really think a woman could have taken out Michael Crimmins and then escaped so easily? What do you think we're dealing with, fucking Wonder Woman? Listen. We got

Daniel Wilken's military file. He had both airborne and ranger training. They used him to lead long-range patrols. He's an expert on silent weapons. He's five-eight, 150 pounds. He's a fucking commando wearing a wig and a skirt. I don't want to hear any more shit about a woman doing this.

"And another thing, where is that fucking White? I want to talk to him. I want to know just what in the hell he was doing here today."

"He already left," Piersall said.

"Who told him he could go?"

"What do you mean?"

"Who in the *fuck* told him he could go?"

"Where's your authority for keeping him here? What do you think this is—martial law? It was his day off. He decided to come to the desert. You can't keep him from coming and going."

"Fuck you, Piersall. You think you two locals have got me fooled? I know how you assholes stick together. When this is over I'm going to have your balls on my office wall as a fucking trophy. Jesus, I'm dying of thirst in this shithole. Somebody get me something to drink..."

Two of McGann's men got up. The first told the second to stay and then went off to the bar. The director's office was crowded and the smell from McGann and the other man who had been taken out with the hypo were crowding out the scent from the director's air freshener.

"Give me a ginger ale with a lot of ice," the man said to the bartender.

"Did they catch the woman yet?" the bartender asked.

"It wasn't a woman. It was a man dressed up like a woman."

"Yeah? Are you sure?"

"What did I just say? Of course I'm sure."

He put down the ginger ale. "I was just thinking—maybe those Washington pussies are too embarrassed to admit that they got beaten by a woman."

"*I'm* from Washington," McGann's man said.

"Oh yeah? That'll be $1.85 for the ginger ale."

"A buck eighty-five for a goddamned ginger ale?"

"Have a nice day," the bartender said, "and a nice flight back to Washington."

———

"See if you can get that air conditioner to put out a little more cool air, Jerry," Frank said.

Jerry turned up the knob on the wall unit.

Jack and Charles came into the motel room with two six-packs of Labatt's. Frank took one, popped off the cap, took a drink, and said, "So what do you think, Jack?"

Jack took a drink of his. "This is good, isn't it?"

"Yes," Frank said.

Jerry pulled the half-empty bag of Doritos from his jacket pocket, offered them around, and then took a drink of beer.

"I think it was brilliant," Jack said. "It was just so . . . simple."

"It's like that magician—David Copperfield," Charles said. "He makes the Statue of Liberty disappear and your mouth falls open. You believe it because you've got your eyes on the Statue of Liberty all the time. You want to catch him in the act. You're looking for the trick. Only the trouble is you think he's actually going to do something with the damned Statue of Liberty. So that's what you're looking at. You're staring up at the lady with the torch and the pointy hat and he's busy picking your pocket. And the smarter you are, the more you believe, because you want to catch him. You think you're smarter.

Only you're not smarter; you're an out-of-town sucker, ripe for the picking."

"Exactly," Jack said. "Mark your calendar, Frank. It was a classic. She was sitting outside all along, playing with her microphone and voice filters. All she had to do was tap into McGann's net and record a couple of voices. Then she programmed the magic box to take her voice and make it sound like McGann's and his dweeb's. First she took out the dweeb and cried wolf with his voice. Everybody came running. Then she took out McGann and used his voice to put out the order to remove Jeffers. The suits believed every word. So did Ernie Jeffers. She pulled up and he dutifully got into her car. He sat back and relaxed. She locked him in and then she took him for a ride. His last."

"Meanwhile," Charles said, "there are about ninety cops and rent-a-cops swarming all over the mountain and climbing down the tower, thinking they're about to save the damned world. They're playing with their guns and jabbering back and forth with all of their 'ten-four' bullshit. They're checking the tram, running around in the snow, looking for snipers, and sniffing for bombs. Then they're back on their radios again. 'Ten-four.' 'Ten-four.' Meanwhile, Ernie Jeffers is heading into the sunset. What it was was *inspired*."

"Like you say," Jerry added, "it was so simple. Hell, one of my kids dragged me to a concert at Universal back in the early eighties. Some woman with spiked hair named Laurie Anderson, dancing around and playing all of this electronic shit. I guess she's big in New York or something. Anyway, she was using those voice filters then. Halfway through the show she was singing with this mask on and I thought she was a man. Then she took off the mask and there were those dimples and that hair—all slick and pointy. 'Holy shit,' I said to my kid, 'I could *use* one of those things.' That was *years* ago. We're talking seventies' technology. She took it and wiped up their ass with it."

"It was a moment worth years," Frank said. "Seeing that pathetic asshole McGann. She faked him so far out of his jock that he's been running bare-assed around the Valley for half of the afternoon."

A steady hum came up over the side of the building. "Choppers," Jerry said.

"They're going to look for Ernie Jeffers," Frank said. "I hope she's heading in the opposite direction. She won't be able to outrun a helicopter."

"She knows that," Jack said. "Ernie's already in the dust with the other desert vermin."

"How do you know?" Frank said.

"Because she wants to be chased."

"Why?" Frank asked.

"I don't know why, but I know how she plans. She drove up to the base of the mountain in a car or van, but by now she could be in a dune buggy, on a dirt bike, or God knows what else. She knows that the only way they could follow her is to use a chopper. That must be what she wants."

"You've got a lot of confidence in her," Frank said.

"Look at the product," Charles said.

FIFTY-TWO

McGann could hear the voice on Piersall's police radio: "We found the cruiser, Lieutenant."

"Occupied?"

"Yes, sir."

"Do we need the paramedics?"

"No sir, we don't."

It took them twenty minutes to get there. She had left one of the windows open; the flies were at Jeffers' face, tasting the blood around his mouth and flying in and out of his ears and eyes. The blood flow from his shoulder wounds had covered the back seat. By now it was turning black around the edges. The chopper blades were churning up the dust and hot air, but the flies continued to go about their business.

"Number three," Piersall said. "A clean sweep."

"What the hell do you mean, a clean sweep?" McGann said. "You think we're going to let this asshole win? You think it's over? It's *not*."

"It's over for them," Piersall said.

"Cocky bastard. He's going to pay big time."

"You think so?" Piersall said.

"Whose side are you on?" McGann said.

"I'm on the side of justice," Piersall said.

"You think Jeffers got justice? Look at that body. What in the hell do you think happened here? An unarmed man was tortured to death. This happened in your jurisdiction, Piersall. They're going to hang your ass out to dry. Have you thought about that at all? Do you have any idea what the *L. A. Times* is going to do with this? Your ass is going to be all over the front page. You know that?"

Piersall didn't answer.

"This is murder, pure and simple. Don't talk to me about justice. Justice belongs to the people and I'm going to make damned sure that the people get it. The fucking reporters and TV talking heads can laugh at you and these fucking hicks you call police, but we're going to catch the asshole who did this and make him pay."

"Why not just skip the trial altogether and save time?"

"Don't wise off with me, Piersall. You want a trial? You want a jury. You want to waste the taxpayers' time? Sure you do. That's what keeps you going—the taxpayers' hard-earned money. You drive around out in the desert, playing with yourself, while murderers escape. And you talk about justice. Fuck you, Piersall. Drive yourself home. We're taking the chopper."

There were five seats in the helicopter, one next to the pilot's and three in the rear. One of Piersall's men was sitting next to the pilot. McGann walked over to the passenger side, flashed his badge at the pilot, and said, "You—get the fuck out of there. Ride home with your jerk-off lieutenant."

The man got out of the helicopter.

"Take us to L.A.," McGann said.

"Where in L.A.?" the pilot said.

"As close to the Bonaventure as you can get."

"Get in," he said.

As soon as they were airborne McGann got on the radio and called his man back at the hotel.

"Hanley? We're on our way."

"I've been trying to reach you, chief."

"Why?"

"I called the Palm Springs PD; they told me what happened."

"So?"

"I talked to them about five minutes ago. As soon as I hung up I got a call."

"From who?"

"I got it on tape. I think you should hear it yourself."

"Don't play games with me. Who the hell called? What's going on?"

"Where are you, chief?"

He turned to the pilot, who told him.

"We just flew over Riverside."

"We've got enough time," Hanley said. "I'll be waiting for you here. I'll brief you as soon as you arrive."

One of McGann's men leaned forward. "It's better, chief. You never know who could be listening."

"Don't remind me," McGann said. He turned toward the pilot and said, "Will this piece of shit fly any faster?"

"A little."

"Then what the fuck are we waiting for?"

FIFTY-THREE

Jack looked at his watch. It was 5:23. "I've got to get going," he said to Frank.

"Why?" Frank said.

"I've got something I have to do."

"You're going to meet her, aren't you?"

"I'm not sure. I really don't know what I'm walking into, Frank."

"Charles and I are going with you."

"I don't think that's a good idea."

"You're probably right, but we're going anyway."

It was 7:50 when they pulled into the grounds of Wilken's nursery. The glow of the moon illuminated the outline of the San Gabriels against the evening sky. Jack held the face of his watch under the dashboard light. "I've got ten more minutes," he said.

"We'll be outside, watching and listening," Frank answered. "If you need us, feel free to let us know."

"I'll scream uncontrollably," Jack said.

"Don't joke about it. That's exactly what you could be doing."

Jack waited until 7:58 and then walked toward the house. He could see a pale glow at the rear window, the window of the room in which Karen Wilken's father spent his lonely days. He climbed the few steps in front of the porch, pulled back the loose, torn screen door, and knocked. There was no answer. Over the years the cottage had settled and the floor of the entryway was slightly tilted. The house leaned awkwardly. Into the fun house. Jack opened the front door and let it swing closed behind him.

Charles heard them first, no more than a minute and a half later—a group of six cars, running without headlights. They entered Wilken's property and passed Jack's car, which was parked behind a toolshed, forty yards from the gravel driveway. They didn't stop to check it. Charles took Frank by the arm, gestured toward a stand of poplars and overgrown shrubs at the rear of Wilken's property, and guided him there in the dark.

"We can do more from behind them than we can in front of them," Charles whispered.

"Stay here. I'm going to circle around and warn Jack," Frank said.

"Just a second," Charles said. "Let's see who it is, first."

McGann got out of the lead car and directed his group of men and the available locals he could scavenge to take up positions in a half-circle around the building. As they positioned themselves on the ground, behind tree stumps and boulders, Charles and Frank could see that they were armed with automatic pistols and shotguns: all up-to-date pieces—Tec-9's and Streetsweepers. McGann was holding a bullhorn, but he was carrying it at his side, waiting.

Frank wanted to go again but Charles held him by the arm. "Only if he's in danger," Charles said. "They're just waiting now."

Jack went through each room of the cottage but each was deserted. When he got to the back room he saw a small desk lamp, with a 25-watt bulb, barely enough to attract insects. Beneath it was a sheet of paper and a single yellow rose. On the paper were two lettered words: *Thank You*. As he picked up the rose and the note he heard McGann's voice, echoing through the trees: "Come out of there, Grant. Come out at once."

Jack put the note in his pocket and the rose inside his jacket and walked back through the cottage, opened the door, and walked out onto the porch. He was immediately silhouetted in bright light. "Get over here, Grant," McGann said.

Jack walked toward him nonchalantly. "What the hell were you doing in there?" McGann asked.

Jack paused, remembered what Karen had told him, and said straight out, "I was hoping to meet with Wilken's daughter."

"What daughter?"

"*The* daughter. What do you mean? Didn't you know he had a daughter?"

"Why were you meeting with her?"

"I didn't meet with her. I told you I was hoping to meet with her."

"Why?"

"I thought I might learn something from her. She said I could meet with her tonight at 8:00."

"What did she tell you?"

"She didn't tell me anything," Jack said. "Didn't you hear what I said? She wasn't in there."

"Who *was* in there?"

"No one. The place is deserted."

"Bullshit," McGann said.

"Look, I was just in there. If you don't believe me, go in and look for yourself," Jack said.

"Get the hell out of my way," McGann said. He pulled the bullhorn up to his lips as Jack walked behind him. "OK, Wilken, this is McGann of the Justice Department. You have fifteen seconds to come out of there. Don't fuck with me."

Jack shook his head and kept walking.

McGann was watching the sweep-second hand. At sixteen seconds he said, "Give him the CS. Let's see how the son-of-a-bitch likes puking *his* brains out."

The canister crashed through the front window and flashed. The smoke was visible from the window and around the door in a matter of seconds. "Toss a couple in the back too," McGann said.

Two of his men high-crawled around the sides of the cottage and lobbed in the vomiting agent. The second canister filled Wilken's room with smoke; the third canister ignited some paper in the kitchen and the flames lit up the east side of the cottage. Suddenly a shot rang out. "Look out," McGann said. "Stay down."

The flames spread to the front of the cottage and suddenly there was a succession of shots. Jack was on the ground, behind the circle of Justice suits. McGann was laying on his side behind a dead poplar. He put the bullhorn to his lips. "Fire at will," he said. "Level that son-of-a-bitch."

His men arched up into the prone position. The sound of the handguns and streetsweepers filled the night air, as chunks and shreds of wood splintered on impact. McGann's men were spraying the building from side to side and top to bottom, even though they continued to hear the return fire. After five minutes of constant bombardment the joists and studs began to shatter and the building leaned forward on its concrete-slab foundation and started to collapse. Still there were the sounds of shots coming from the direction of the building, but no one was hit. There had also been no ricochets.

Jack stood up and backed away from the ring of McGann's men. In the light from the flames he saw Charles and Frank. He signaled them to stay where they were.

After eight minutes the cottage was completely destroyed. Collapsed, and engulfed in flames, it smoldered and flashed, but except for the movement of insects in the glow and smoke there was no sign of life, human or animal. The shots had stopped a few minutes before.

McGann and his men advanced with their searchlights and picked through the riddled walls and timbers, but they found nothing. Jack was standing 150 feet away. McGann saw him and walked toward him. Jack met him halfway. "What the hell were you doing here," Jack asked, "looking for Patty Hearst?"

"What the hell do you mean?" McGann asked.

"It seems like a simple enough question. Do you want me to get you a translator?"

"Look, you called *us*, asshole."

"I didn't call you," Jack said. "What the hell are you talking about?"

"We have a tape of the call; I'll play it at your goddamned trial. You said you were coming here at 8:00 and that we should meet you here a few minutes later."

Jack smiled.

"What's so fucking funny?"

Jack didn't answer.

"Don't fuck around with me, Grant. What is so goddamned funny?"

"Everything."

"What the hell are you talking about?" McGann said.

"You were tricked."

"No, we weren't *tricked*. You decoyed us, you son-of-a-bitch. You helped Wilken escape."

"Why in the hell would I do that?"

"I don't know, but you did it."

"Check your tape again, McGann. Do a voice print on it. I'll tell you what you're going to find: it's a goddamned ringer. This was all done with electronic mirrors."

"What the hell are you saying?"

"You're not real quick, are you, McGann?"

"Listen to me, fuckhead. You're in deep shit. I hope you know that."

"No, I'm not. There's no law against coming to a person's house. Especially not to a house that turns out to be deserted. I'll tell you who's in deep shit, McGann. You fell for the same trick three times in the same day. That's got to be some sort of a record. What's more, you destroyed a perfectly good building for no reason. I'll tell you what to expect. Your bosses in Washington are going to look in the *Guinness Book of World Records* under 'Biggest Asshole in the World' and they're going to see your face."

"Didn't you hear the shots, you dumb shit?"

"I'm sorry," Jack said. "Let me correct what I said before. You fell for the same trick three times in one day and then you fell for a similar trick that night. What does that equal—three and a half or a full four? This is Hollywood, you shithead. Those were all blanks. The house was rigged with dummy rounds. The heat set them off. You know what that means, don't you?"

"What?" McGann said, the disdain seeping through his teeth.

"You got the phony message and you raced back to L.A. like an angry six-year-old, hungry for revenge. You spent the next couple of hours choosing your toys and getting your ammunition. Then you got your bullhorn and your battle plan and you set up your convoy. You drove out here, hoping to play the death-dealing G-man. I got a flash for you, McGann. While you were doing all that, your suspect was four martinis and two thousand miles into his escape plan. By now he's sitting on a beach in the moonlight, drinking a toast to the gods, and hoping that all of his adversaries will always be as dumb as you. What do you think?"

"You think you're pretty fucking smart, don't you, Grant? You're going to find out just how smart you are."

"No, I don't think I'm smart. I just think you're too fucking stupid for words. And we're both going to find out just how stupid when your reviews come in. Take my advice. Cancel your subscription to the *Post* and don't turn on your television for a month or two."

"This isn't over, Grant."

"Yes it is," Jack said. "That's your problem. It *is* over. And you lost big."

"I'm sure he'll like his new job," Frank said, directing Jack through the back streets of Altadena.

"Washington is very forgiving," Charles said, "especially after they've been hung out to dry in the press. They'll have some nice position ready for him when he returns—maybe make him Permanent Latrine Orderly, responsible for replacing the urinal cakes in the Hoover Building men's rooms."

Frank laughed.

"They could also put him in charge of taking care of Edgar's dresses until the Smithsonian is ready for them. Dry-clean and iron those puppies, make sure the moths don't get at them."

Frank laughed again, harder this time. "They could make a statue of Edgar, put him up there with the first ladies in their inaugural gowns," he said. "McGann could plan the ceremony."

Charles was laughing too.

"That's all fine, except for one thing," Jack said.

"What's that?" Charles answered.

"He'll want to take me down with him."

EPILOGUE

Upon his return to Washington McGann immediately attempted to clear himself by focusing all of the agency's attention on Jack and his alleged culpability, but that dog refused to hunt. In fact, each time McGann tried to release it from its kennel the Attorney General made it disappear faster than David Copperfield's Statue of Liberty. The private response to the Crimmins-Devens-Jeffers case was that it should be instantly buried and erased from the organization's corporate memory. Daniel Wilken—it was learned—had been a helpless invalid for many years and the only other remaining member of Susan Wilken's family was a daughter, Karen, who, far from being a three-time killer, was a Girl Scout leader and hospital candy striper. The murderer was clearly a sometime acquaintance of the family, part of a circle of individuals that encompassed, literally, thousands of people. The official response was that the search would definitely continue, along with—the *Post* editorialized—the search for Jimmy Hoffa, the abominable snowman, and the killer rabbit that nearly took out Jimmy Carter.

Charles was right: red faces don't go well with gray suits, at least not in the Justice Department. Chester McGann was given the opportunity to take an abrupt and early retirement with the additional proviso that any public comments on the aforementioned case would be punished instantly and summarily. For his final weeks in the Department McGann was relocated to a field office in Balko, Oklahoma, a small town in the panhandle, his fourth choice after the AG turned down his requests for Gaffney, South Carolina; Dimock, South Dakota; and Arkadelphia, Arkansas.

In a feat of bureaucratic legerdemain, Claire Harding convinced Deputy Commissioner McCarren to permit her to travel to Los Angeles in order to secure the precise facts of the Crimmins case, lest the London afternoon papers pick up the story, twist its facts, and replace Camilla, Charles, and the third-page, topless lovely with the embarrassed visages of the principals at the Yard, the latter possibility brought dangerously close to reality by a succession of torpid news days that began when the Princess of Wales became publicly ill during a bout with influenza at the much-heralded Men at Work Wembley reunion, segued into a sighting of Charles napping noticeably at an architectural conference in Saffron Walden, and finished with a peremptorily interrupted romance between one of Her Majesty's favorite Welsh Corgis and an exceptionally forward fox terrier with an iron determination and a total disregard for the presence of no less than twenty-seven classic Leicas, each equipped with 1/2000th of a second shutter speeds, and each capable of utilizing high-resolution film and recording the most precise of physiological details on that bright, cloudless winter afternoon when the scent of spring was beginning the first of its many attempts to break through the crisp, cold air.

Frank greeted Claire at LAX, holding a sign with the words: Claire Harding/Los Angeleez Limousines. They promptly drove to a place that Frank promised would be particularly suitable for uninterrupted briefing sessions of the sort required by the complex dimensions of the case: the Ritz-Carlton, Laguna Niguel. Actually at Dana Point, as he was quick to explain. He promised an additional day-trip to Palm Springs and Rancho Mirage and a number of evenings driving north to Newport Beach as orange, coastal twilight played on blue water, their Newport Beach mission being the systematic sampling of representative local selections of lobster, crab, and estimable white burgundies, as they numbered the dock and harbor lights shimmering in the water below.

Charles made his annual trip to Washington, to take a turn at the tables near the Wall. He left his uniform and ribbons at home, declined a speaking invitation from a political group in Northwest, and passed on a trio of photo ops with, respectively, the Secretary of the Army, the junior senator from California, and the Vice President of the United States. As always, the news people attempted to interview him at the Wall, and, as always, they quickly dispersed when he told them in terms they could not mistake that he would prefer not to speak with them.

―――

Jack continued his work for Valley Mutual, helping Frank with the occasional case, his thoughts turning from time to time to the Wilkens and the 8:00 meeting with them that had never taken place. His notoriety spiked with a morning-after, page-three story in the *Times*, outlining the charges that McGann lodged and then withdrew a little less than three hours later.

He kept some of the clippings, read them from time to time, wondering always where Karen and her father might have gone on that October evening.

As the days lengthened into months he returned to the case whenever he could, finding scraps and pieces in the hope of some day completing the picture: discovering Karen's engineering studies at UCLA, the time purchased dearly in the days when she was caring for her father as well as supervising his nursery business. The common opinion was that she could have graduated first in her class if she hadn't spent so many hours tutoring the young and the poor, helping them get past the freshman-filter courses and survive as erstwhile engineers.

She graduated third, behind two grinds who disappeared into a Caltech luminary's lab and were never heard from again. Karen stayed on her own, taking care of Dan Wilken and surfacing from time to time in the company of patent attorneys and industrial heavies with silk suits and wide grins.

The income was saved. She lived simply—thinking, learning, and planning. She waited patiently for vengeance and justice, working in society's midst, counting the days and months until the precise moment, refining her skills, strengthening her body, developing her plans. From the moment her resolve was set, her mother's attackers were dead men, their fate as certain as the tick of a clock or the changing of the seasons.

Jack sifted through the records and the memories, following her silently, sensing her pain, seeing her determination, watching her destiny take shape, her plans emerge. Her life was a crusade; her mission was to restore the truth; her talisman was her father's love and mother's memory.

When her task was complete, the media rewarded her generously, telling her mother's story in all of its dimensions and recounting the symbolic outlines of the deaths of her attackers in full detail. They favored the vengeance over the justice, but that was to be expected; they still managed to cover both. It probably wasn't enough for Karen. It would never be enough for her, but it was more than enough for the memory of her mother and the reputations of her mother's attackers. One tiny fragment of history was set right.

Months later, precisely a year to the day after, a delivery van pulled into half of a parking space in front of his apartment. Blocking a portion of the building's driveway, the driver ran up to Jack's apartment, handed him a blue box with a white ribbon, and hurried back to the truck without waiting for any more of a tip than the loose change that Jack was carrying in his pants pocket.

Jack took the box to his dining room table, opened the lid, took out the single yellow rose and the note and read it aloud:

> *Thank you again. He speaks of you often.*
> *He remembers more and more each day and appears to*
> *understand just how much you did. Think of us,*
> *as we often think of you. Good work. Your friend. Always.*

ABOUT THE AUTHOR

Richard B. Schwartz is the author of *Nice and Noir: Contemporary American Crime Fiction*, four novels in the Jack Grant series, and numerous other books. He is Professor of English and Dean of the College of Arts and Science at the University of Missouri-Columbia. Visit his website at www.richardbschwartz.com.

If you enjoyed this book, you'll want to read our next *Jack Grant Mystery,* coming in March 2007. The following excerpt is from the forthcoming

AFTER THE FALL

by
Richard B. Schwartz

ONE

However it ends, it always starts with tears.

I had been looking for her for four and a half weeks. Usually they're found much sooner than that or never found at all. Her body had come to rest twenty yards from the shoreline of a small gray lake that's not even named on small-scale maps, a single rough-edged dot beside route 18 in the San Bernardino forest. Midway between Crestline and Lake Arrowhead, it sits on a sloping, dusty ledge, just south of the highway. You park in the burn or you belly your car on the underbrush and partially exposed rocks at the edge of the treeline, then walk a few hundred yards through the wild grass and pine scrub. A local group still stocks it with bluegills, crappies, and any panfish the federal government is anxious to give away. Most people prefer to fish Silverwood, Gregory, or Arrowhead. Bigger fish; better parking.

Back in the late fifties the American Legion and the V.F.W. used to hold functions there: a quiet lake, a few hours of adventure for the city kids and an afternoon outing for their parents—all bathed in warm, shadowy sun, steady wind off the mountains, and the smell of smoky grills and thoughts of deep steel tubs of cold beer in icy longnecks. Back then they parked above, along the main highway. It was still safe; they didn't have to dodge the teenagers in their trucks and the drunks in their 4x4s, taking the mountain turns at straightaway speeds and scaring the hell out of wayward tourists lured to Lake Arrowhead by come-on ads in L.A. hotel magazines.

A local eccentric named William Clyde Brattle had had a wooden gazebo built at the east end of the lake, complete with a brass gift plaque bolted above the center arch. The recipients of his philanthropy liked to call it The Bandstand, though there was barely enough room on it for five people to stand side by side without hitting their heads on an arch or nicking their elbows on a splintery section of frame. The top and sides are covered now with brown and yellow lichen and the flooring has been lost to rot, earth, and undergrowth.

The poor started coming here when there was no one left to bother them. They come up for the day and try to catch their dinner in the lake, first turning over the ground for redworms and nightcrawlers as the kids run off and throw pebbles or pine cones. Just before sunset they picnic in the trees below the shore. Grandma and grandpa sit in foldup chairs in the shade and watch the rest—aunts, uncles, cousins, neighbors, friends, whoever could be squeezed into the back seats of their old sedans.

After the Fall

When they found it there were piercing, hysterical screams. A finger at first, just above the rust-brown bed of dried pine needles—the right, index finger, pointing up through the trees and toward the sky. Then the hand and arm and what was left of the head and torso and legs. Each time Oscar or Carlo or Frederico Montalvez cleared another handful of dirt someone yelled "que horror!" or "malisimo!" Nice people, the Montalvezes. Conscientious. Trying to do their part to serve the cause and clean up their tiny portion of the world. Just there for the day from Covina with another family from East L.A. A day away from the lube pits, the griddles and grease traps, the machine shops, the crack vials, the sprayed walls, and the desperate eyes.

Frederico never expected to have his two-year-old daughter, Teresita, stumble upon the finger of a dead woman's body in a shallow grave, then try to shake hands with it.

No one had thought the drought in the mountains would end as quickly as it did, especially not the woman's killer. The sudden spring rains had brought up the lake level, spilling into the trees, and loosening the dry earth. Then the desert winds dried up the standing water, exposing what remained of the shrivelled finger of the right hand of Cynthia Bladen. There was even a trace of dried grass from the shoreline—the broad, sharp-edged kind we used to tear in strips and lay between our thumbs to make whistles. When they found her it was wrapped around her finger like a wedding band. Married to the earth now, lost forever in its first deadly embrace.

EXCERPT

Bladen, Cynthia A., 37. Beloved daughter of Rachel R. Simonds and the late James W. Simonds of Chestnut Hill, Massachusetts. Devoted wife of Donald N. Bladen of Los Angeles. Dear mother of Charles Bladen, 5, and Amy Bladen, 3. Mrs. Bladen was a graduate of Columbia College and Law School, a partner in the law firm of Briggs and Billings, and a member of the First Episcopal Church of Westwood. She was active in professional, church, and community affairs. A memorial service will be held next Saturday evening at 8:00 p.m. in the garden of the family residence. There will be no visitation.

And no open casket.

―――――

A few other things too. Five feet, seven inches. Most of what could have been a model's body still evident. Short brown hair, green eyes, and thin brows. Character. Brains. Class. Excellent health. No conceivable reason for her life to end so quickly in an act of grotesque violence.

And one other thing. Cynthia Simonds and I had dated seriously before her seven-year marriage to Donald Bladen. I don't know why, but my name was still there in her Rolodex. Luck or fate, maybe the remains of something more. When her husband called and left a message on my machine to call him back, he was angry and upset. He told me she was missing and that it was urgent he talk to me, that if I was listening I should turn off the goddamned machine and pick up the receiver. When I returned to my apartment and played back the message I felt surprise and a lot of other things, some of which I hadn't felt in a long time. I thought about it for nearly an hour before I called back. When I finally did, he told me Cynthia had been missing for over a week. He said he wanted to see me right away; he wanted to talk to me; he wanted me to forget everything else I might be doing and find her.

He and I had never met or talked before her disappearance. By the time Donald Bladen had begun seeing Cynthia, I was already out of the picture, living thirty miles away and dating a surgeon named Laura Weeks. And yet, the moment he saw me his gray eyes were searching mine with that special form of loathing that comes to those who need the help of someone with whom they have shared the feelings of the same woman. He grasped my hand in his and it felt stiff and dead. He never mentioned how he knew about us and I didn't ask.

He ushered me into his house, closed the door, and demanded to know why I had taken so long to return his call. Before I could answer he started to list his other demands. At that point I would normally say something that rich people weren't used to hearing in their living rooms, but I let him talk. I knew how he felt because I knew how much he stood to lose and I don't usually curse a man—even a man I dislike—when I see that his hands are shaking. I also knew the odds of his wife's being found alive and happy; I didn't tell him how bad they were.

After fifteen or twenty minutes he was apologizing, calling me Mr. Grant, and sobbing into a succession of watery drinks that he kept clutching tighter and tighter with each sentence. I turned away, looking at a black and white picture of Cynthia in a silver frame on their ebony piano, waiting nervously for the glass to shatter in his hand.

As we talked and I began to pursue realistic possibilities with him I continued to wonder how he knew about me and his wife. By then he had collected himself, made a fresh drink, and sat back down in the yellow silk couch behind his glass coffee table. The table was still covered with condensation rings but he put the glass square in the middle of what looked like a soggy Venn diagram. He didn't seem to notice the stack of cocktail napkins on the end table next to the couch. Instead he paused, looked at me hopefully, and asked if I would do whatever I could to find his wife. He kept referring to her specifically in that way: as his wife. I promised I would help.

A month later Frank White called me with the news of Cynthia's death. I drove to Donald Bladen's home and told him that his wife's body had been found. He told me he didn't want to hear any of the details. He said he didn't want to identify the body and he didn't want to talk to me further. He said it was obvious that I hadn't done enough and that he wanted me to leave. This time the gray eyes were streaked with red. He was staring blankly at the floor, clutching his hands together to keep them from shaking.